# Also by R.F. Ryan

FINNEGAN GILHOOLEY

*Between Greed and Manhood*

*Of a Different Stamp*

*Scorn to be Guilty*

*As the Crucible Closed*

# Trample Over the Dead

# Trample Over the Dead

## Finnegan Gilhooley
## Book 5

R.F. Ryan

**Trample Over the Dead**
Paperback Edition


Wolfpack Publishing
1707 E. Diana Street
Tampa, Florida 33610

www.wolfpackpublishing.com



Paperback ISBN 979-8-89567-588-5
eBook ISBN 979-8-89567-587-8

*I have no more to say. What you do here is at the risk of many lives. Before you enter those mills, you will trample over the dead bodies of three thousand honest working men.*

—Hugh O'Donnell, July 6, 1892

*To expect that one dependent upon his daily wage for the necessities of life will stand peaceably and see a new man employed in his stead is to expect much. There is an unwritten law amongst the best workmen: Thou shalt not take thy neighbor's job.*

—Andrew Carnegie
*Forum Magazine*, 1886

*As the vast majority of our employees are Non-Union, the firm has decided that the minority must give place to the majority. These works therefore will be necessarily Non-Union after the expiration of the present agreement.*

—Henry Clay Frick, April 4, 1892

# Trample Over the Dead

# Chapter 1

## *HELENA, MONTANA*

### May 10th, 1892

"I know it is no less than the grace of God Almighty that you have been delivered into my hands, Pinkerton man!" The freighter slid rounds into the loading gate of his Winchester rifle. The small, dirty man grinned while he did it and then set the rifle across the bed of the wagon he had been loading only moments earlier. He pointed the muzzle of the weapon toward the telegraph office where Finnegan Gilhooley and his luggage had been lingering.

Finnegan, for his part, was not overly distressed by the events that had facilitated his retreat to the rear of the telegraph counter. He had been in the process of dictating a message to his wife when the end had been nipped off his cigar and the telegraph key had been removed from the top of the clerk's station. Without pausing to consider recent developments, Finnegan had leapt the counter with his bags still in his hands. He could hear the occasional rifle round thud into the railroad ties the building was constructed from and make out his assailant yelling something or other from the opposite side of the muddy rut the locals referred to as a street.

Sitting across from Finnegan in the small space that comprised the telegraph agent's office, the agent gripped the hand that had been too close to the sending key when a bullet had deconstructed it. The man wore a purely shocked visage. It appeared as though he was rarely fired upon during the course of his duties.

Finnegan moved his head to one side when a bullet knocked a collection of telegraph forms down from the countertop. "Sir, do you, by any chance, know the fellow across the street?"

The telegraph clerk nodded slowly. The movement made his well-waxed mustache bounce. "He is a freighter, Michael Malone by name."

"To your knowledge, he has no reason to hold a grudge against you, currently?" Finnegan watched as the agent shook his head. "Very well, then -- I will assume he is firing at me, rather than you."

The agent nodded. "I believe that to be a safe assumption. Do you know the man?"

"I do not." Finnegan popped his head up over the counter and surveyed the scene for an instant before a fresh fusillade caused his retreat. "Bloody damn inconvenience." He pulled a wooden case from the straps of his valise and craned his head a bit to better yell over the telegraph counter. "Sir, I would not claim to understand what has fomented this disagreement, but I know to a certainty there is no need for this. I am in no way acquainted with you. All this is likely no more than you having mistaken me for another fellow, and I am more than willing to let bygones be bygone if you will only depart and cease this foolishness." Finnegan opened the case and removed two highly polished pieces of steel from within.

The voice of the freighter came across the street. "You killed my own good brother, Caleb. Shot him down for nothing more than asserting his God-given rights, Pinkerton scum!" The declaration was followed by several more bullets.

Finnegan sighed and snapped the two pieces of fine English steel together. That done, he affixed the forearm to the Purdey rifle. He looked to the agent. "The unfortunate truth of the matter is that neither that fellow over by that Conestoga nor myself can say with any degree of certainty whether or not I did, in fact, shoot his brother. As I freely take responsibility for my past actions, I can also admit a great deal of the fault for this predicament lies with myself." The agent only stared blankly while Finnegan placed two long fifty caliber rounds in the twin chambers of the rifle. "Even so, I can assure you that his brother's infraction, if I was in fact the man to bring him to task for it, was no mere trifle. Due to some motivation I cannot fathom, antagonists of this freighter's ilk always attempt to make out as though I shot some member of their clan or club for sport or some such. It becomes a terrible bore after a time." He craned his neck once more. "Sir, if you can only bring yourself to see the sense in disengaging from this fight, I will offer you complete assurance that I will pursue the matter no further."

"Damn you to hell, sir!"

Finnegan drew in a deep breath. "It is a true shame when a man is unwilling to accept reason." He turned away from the agent and got into a crouch behind the counter. Three more shots in quick succession hit the wood on the other side, and Finnegan peeked just above to see the muzzle of the man's rifle was pointed skyward. He took this as an indication that the freighter was reloading once again. In one quick movement, he sprang up, took a rest on the telegraph counter, and fired off two shots at the wagon just above where the freighter's legs could be seen through the wheel spokes. A dark form fell to the ground on the far side of the wagon and Finnegan ducked back down. Methodically, he removed the two spent pieces of brass from the express rifle and replaced them with two loaded ones. The agent had a far off look in his eyes. "I believe those rounds found their mark, sir. This rifle is more than capable of penetrating both sides of the wagon and finding the freighter behind. It is likely this discomfiture has come to an end."

The agent grunted and cleared his throat. Beads of sweat hung on his face and mustache. "My apologies, sir. This has been my first conflagration involving firearms."

"Truly?"

"I had so far managed to live a quiet and somewhat unremarkable life."

"Yes, well, I can appreciate how an incident such as this might cause some consternation for a fellow such as yourself." The agent nodded and moved to stand. Finnegan put out one hand and held him down. "I would recommend against any hasty action, my friend. As a man with considerable experience in such matters, I would advise we wait here for some moments before exposing ourselves. Best to allow the fellow across the street to completely settle."

"Settle?"

"Exsanguinate."

"I do not understand."

Finnegan picked up his cigar from where it had fallen on the telegraph office floor. "We would be well served by waiting a few moments to allow the man's blood and spirit to depart."

The agent appeared shocked. "You would suspect the man would fire upon us while he lay dying?"

"Many a fellow practicing my occupation has been killed by dead men over the years, or rather men who appeared to have perished." He lit the cigar and let out a puff. "Of course, we find ourselves in a republic where the common man is free to do as he pleases. If you wish to be on your way this very instant, I will not be the one to detain you."

The agent sat back against the wall. "Perhaps I will wait here a bit longer, given your wealth of knowledge in the matter."

# Chapter 2

## *HELENA, MONTANA*

### May 12th, 1892

Only about eight years had passed since Finnegan had last spoken with the two men he had come to Helena to meet with, but both of them appeared to have aged considerably. When Finnegan had first come to Montana, both Samuel Hauser and Granville Stuart had rather obviously been men in the later half of life, but both seemed spry and invigorated by the prospects offered by the burgeoning cattle industry. Now, the grey had crept from the temples of both men to cover their beards and what hair remained on their heads. Stuart had lost the sharp edge the life of a ranch manager imbues to a man, and Hauser had surely spent far too much time behind a desk. Both evinced an attitude toward Finnegan which was both nervous and angry. The Pinkerton did not care for the general atmosphere of the room.

Finnegan sipped the coffee Hauser's secretary had offered. It was not a bad brew. The gunman cleared his throat. "I was sorry to hear of the passing of your eldest daughter, Granville."

The pioneer's features softened. "Yes, well, thank you, Finnegan. I should say I am more than a little surprised to hear you were aware of her demise."

Finnegan nodded grimly. "The schoolteacher you hired some years ago, Miss Meagher, is now Mrs. Gilhooley. She rather consistently kept in correspondence with your daughter and was made aware of her passing by your second eldest."

"I see." The pioneer folded his hands and thought back on the last few years. "Her passing not long after my first wife departed...well, it was both a tragedy and an extremely untimely inconvenience, as you may well imagine."

Finnegan nodded. "As I recall, you had a somewhat impressive number of children. It must have been difficult to see to their caretaking after your losses."

Stuart smoothed his long beard. "I found myself with no alternative to leaving them in the keeping of the sisters at St. Ignatius." He grimaced and stared out a nearby window. "Perhaps it will be for the best in the long term. A certain stigma always followed them among whites. The other Indian children at the mission will undoubtedly be more accepting. Many of them are half breeds, as well." He turned back to Finnegan. "I have since remarried. You may find it humorous to contemplate that I am now wed to Miss Meagher's replacement."

Finnegan chuckled. "In my experience, the marrying of schoolmarms is a fine vocation."

Hauser let out a long sigh. "If it would be all right with you gentleman, might you catch up on old times and offer formalities to each other after we have concluded our business here? I am terribly busy most days, and today is no exception."

Finnegan looked at the banker and arched an eyebrow.

"Mr. Hauser, I can appreciate how a man such as yourself might be harried by any number of men wishing for an audience, but I did not notice them in the outer office on my way here." He sipped his coffee again. "Could it be that you are merely in a hurry to have me leave the premises, so as to minimize the chance we will be known to be associating?"

Hauser rubbed one temple. "Any number of conclusions could be drawn from your presence here, Mr. Gilhooley. Suffice it to say, I would prefer to not be personally linked to a man of your reputation."

Stuart grunted. "Ah, hell, Sam. Finnegan rode with me and the boys and came in damn handy once or twice. You freely associate with me whenever the mood strikes; what's the difference with this Irishman? Last time I heard, they still called our committee Stuart's Stranglers, not Gilhooley's."

Hauser licked his lips. "The difference, Granville, is that you did not shoot down a local freighter two days past. A local freighter, I might add, who was both well-liked, a customer of this bank, and somewhat active, formerly, in labor relations. The man was once a miner and attempted, on several well-documented occasions, to unionize several of the mines in Butte. Now that Mr. Gilhooley has seen fit to spread the man's guts all over the boardwalk opposite the railroad depot, any number of foul rumors may be circulating."

Stuart shrugged. "He is hardly the first man to meet his end down in the vicinity of the depot."

Hauser rubbed his eyes. "I have no doubt many an incident of violence has occurred in the general area. What I would declare, unequivocally, is that those men who previously perished there were not nearly so sluggish in expiring and did not spend their last hours cursing the name of a man formerly employed by the Stockgrower's Association."

Finnegan raised his hand to get the banker's attention. "The fellow ranted a great deal before he died?"

Hauser offered a slow nod. "Your rounds avoided the vital organs, and our town is currently occupied by a Jew with no small talent at surgery. From what I have been told, given more prompt delivery, the freighter might have lived -- quite crippled, of course. Our last doctor was little better than a butcher. This fellow appears to have received superior training in Boston."

"Did the freighter, by any chance, explain his reasons for firing on me?"

Hauser blinked a few times and licked his lips. "Mr. Gilhooley, are you attempting to be jovial?"

"No." He sipped his coffee yet again. "I am genuinely interested as to the root of the man's angst toward me. I believe he yelled something regarding a brother, but it is difficult to understand a fellow under those circumstances."

Hauser sighed. "Honest and truly, you cannot readily discern what past acts might have aggravated the fellow?"

Stuart chuckled. "Finnegan has been at his labors a long time, Sam."

Hauser shook his head. "The surgeon informed me that the freighter made mention of you murdering his brother during a labor dispute at the McCormick Works in Chicago."

"Ah, I see." Finnegan set his coffee cup down and shook a finger at the banker. "This is the very sort of thing that causes such grievous vexation on a regular basis. I would certainly never claim to have passed through life without earning my share of opprobrium, but I am surely not responsible for every foul act ever committed on this poor earth." He sighed. "The original Mr. Pinkerton saw fit to somewhat publicize my activities when they properly fit his future intentions. As a result of that, I often find the sins of every Pinkerton man laid at my feet. I was not among the Pinkerton men at the McCormick Works, and have never participated in the suppression of a strike. I functioned in the capacity of a detective, not a preventative."

The banker hung his head for a short moment. "Mr. Gilhooley, I do not much care whether you murdered the man's brother, mother, or dear old aunt. All that concerns me is that you surely killed the freighter and are now loitering in my office giving the world the notion we are somehow connected. Clark and Daly near constantly stand accused of hiring Pinkerton men for nefarious schemes. I have enough accusations already hung about my neck; I hardly require an additional one."

Finnegan withdrew a cigar from his pocket and rolled it between his fingers. "Let it never be said that I did not take every opportunity to preserve the reputation of a friend. As you find yourself embarrassed at the moment, I will make haste in explaining my visit." He found a match. "In the year of our Lord eighteen hundred and eighty-four, your Stock-grower's Association employed me to sort out an issue involving horse theft. Now, as I am sure Mr. Stuart will attest, the matter was seen to in keeping with the prearranged contract. That contract entitled me to a percentage of the profits or the increase in herd size from the various ranches in the Association. In short, gentlemen, I have come to collect my due and proper."

Hauser let his gaze stray over to Stuart for a moment. Finding the pioneer's face rather blank, he turned back to Finnegan. "Mr. Gilhooley, I am not certain you are fully familiar with the changes that have occurred in the cattle industry since the winter of '86. That year, and the blizzards that came with it, formed something of a watershed for cattlemen. The herds were decimated, fortunes were lost, and the financial landscape was thrown into upheaval. Most of the Association membership from the era you were employed in are no longer involved in the industry." Hauser chuckled and threw his hands in the air. "The DHS Ranch is no longer in our possession. Mr. Davis no longer lives. You can hardly expect us to recompense you under the somewhat spurious terms of a contract pertaining to a business venture we are no longer involved in, with dead men for partners and past association members cast to the four winds."

Finnegan sparked his match on the edge of the banker's desk and lit his cigar. "Yes, well, I can appreciate the difficulties faced in such an endeavor. It has been quite some time since you gentlemen contracted with me, and I fully understand how time and distance can cause matters to become distorted." He let out a plume of smoke and smiled. "That is why I have taken the liberty of settling on terms I am willing to accept." He puffed the cigar, appearing quite satisfied with himself. "As I recall, you gentlemen were all extremely optimistic as to the future profits obtainable from the cattle industry in this territory. If the herds had increased in size as you once predicted, I might have garnered no less than ten thousand per man in the association."

Hauser brought up one wizened hand. "There is little purpose in discussing what might have occurred without the disaster of '86. I assure you, Mr. Gilhooley, every man who formerly owned a cow in this territory has already discussed the matter at great length."

Finnegan knocked ash down to the floor. "Yes, I suppose they have. Being as the matter has already been thoroughly debated, I will simply say that I have come to the conclusion that two thousand dollars should suffice for compensation."

Hauser let out a guffaw. "You honestly expect the former

members of an association to pool together two thousand dollars based on nothing more than your request?"

"Surely not, Mr. Hauser." Finnegan grinned and shook his head. "I would ask nothing of the sort from any man who was not present when our deal was struck, or had not empowered you or your associates to conduct business for him." He took a small drag from his cigar. "And I did not mean to insinuate that two thousand dollars in total would be sufficient. I speak of two thousand dollars per member, naturally." He glanced between Hauser and Stuart. "Now that I am a married man, I cannot be as carefree involving matters of finance as I once was. In past days, I have often forgotten past debts. Now that I am a family man, I cannot continue the practice. I am sure you gentlemen can understand."

"Preposterous!" Hauser flopped back in his desk chair. "A more ludicrous suggestion has never been uttered to me."

Stuart cleared his throat and looked to the Pinkerton. "Uh, Finnegan, I know a bit better than to go around calling you such as ludicrous or preposterous, so I'll just come right out and tell you plain: I ain't got two thousand dollars to give you. I'd be damned hard pressed to offer twenty." He searched the Pinkerton's face for sympathy. "I got me a new wife, too."

"I can surely appreciate your difficulties, Granville." Finnegan smiled at the fellow by way of commiseration. "I would never ask you to hand over your last nickel, my friend. I would only point out that in your present position as the state land agent you could easily exchange two thousand dollars' worth of ground with me and we can call the whole matter settled."

The pioneer appeared quite shocked by the suggestion. "Finnegan, my position as state land agent does not allow me to simply hand out land grants to pay off personal debts as it pleases me."

"So then, you have transferred no land over to the esteemed Mr. Hauser here?" Finnegan let his smile broaden. "I would assume you have, and that you are still in his debt from the financial debacle resulting from the loss of the DHS herd. Perhaps your position as land agent is not quite so sacrosanct as you might suggest?"

The pioneer grimaced. "Yes, well, Sam has come to somewhat of an understanding with the legislators, and..."

"Ah, I see." Finnegan grinned. "One does so detest the idea of betraying the public trust without first gaining permission from their elected officials." He tapped more ash to the floor. "Since you are so comfortable transferring land to the possession of Mr. Hauser, I would suggest you merely transfer a bit more to him and he can compensate me in the form of cash money." Finnegan turned to the banker. "It seems an elegant solution to me."

Hauser sat forward and set his elbows on the desk. "Mr. Gilhooley, you honestly expected to waltz in here and leave with four thousand dollars this day?"

"I expect to leave here with six thousand dollars, sir. As I said, I have settled on the amount of two thousand dollars from each man who previously employed me. That includes Mr. Davis."

Hauser's eyes narrowed. "Davis is dead."

"And you are the executor of his estate, Mr. Hauser." Finnegan puffed his cigar. "Quite obviously there is a debt you failed to settle."

"Mr. Gilhooley, it is clear that you have little experience in civilized financial matters." The banker shook his head. "You cannot burst in upon men, announce your terms, and expect funds to be issued. This is not how business is executed."

Finnegan nodded. "Of course, I am more than willing to defer to your vast knowledge and experience in these matters, Mr. Hauser. Certainly, there is no man in the state more well-versed in such things. If it pleases you, we can extend this negotiation for as long as you would prefer. I can easily extend my stay at the hotel and may even decide to become something of a regular resident in this place." He puffed his cigar and let the smoke roll from his lips. "Sadly, any number of freighters, miners, sheepherders, and grocery store clerks may feel the need to enter into conflict with me while I am lingering in town. It would be a pity if the blame for that violence was to be associated with you, sir."

The banker sneered. "What if I were to tell you that there is no need for you to linger, Mr. Gilhooley? What if I were to tell you that there is no chance of convincing me that you are owed money, and that I will never, under any circumstances, pay you what you are demanding?"

"Oh, well, it is difficult to say what a man may do when he is faced with an intractable situation. I might do something as subtle as making myself available to the local press so that they might be fully informed as to the past adventures I enjoyed with Mr. Stuart, or..." He rolled the cigar in his fingers and contemplated it for a moment. "Granville, would you care to venture a guess as to what my reaction to Mr. Hauser evincing unremitting stubbornness in this matter might be?"

Stuart swallowed with an audible click and smoothed his beard. "Sam, a fellow such as Finnegan can be reasonable under most circumstances, but that's only so long as folks are reasonable with him."

Hauser sighed. "What precisely are you getting at, Granville?"

"Sam, I am attempting to explain that if you don't show some sense here, it's likely old Finnegan will kill you." The pioneer shrugged and folded his hands neatly in his lap. "You hired him all those years ago to kill horse thieves. There ain't a nag in this whole country worth six thousand dollars. As he likely views it, you're a far greater scoundrel than any horse thieve that ever lived, so he won't lose no sleep over laying you low."

The banker appeared dumbfounded. "Kill me?" He turned from Stuart to Finnegan. "Is that...factual?"

Finnegan waved his cigar around a bit. "Oh, his words, not mine, Mr. Hauser. Although, I would point out that, in my experience, if you do wish to kill a man, it is best to allow the fellow to go on believing he is in no danger whatsoever up until the time is fitting for him to meet his end. A labor-saving device, you might call it."

Stuart hung his head and smiled. "He would be the one to know such a thing, Sam. I have seen the man work." The pioneer rubbed the back of his neck. "In my opinion, six thousand dollars is a fair price to not see the man work again."

Hauser let the astonishment wash over his face. "Mr. Gilhooley, you are a rare man, indeed. It is not every day you meet a fellow who can be so readily paid to not labor."

The gunman shrugged. "Some of life's matters are complicated, some are very simple."

"Given the situation, I find your terms acceptable." Hauser sucked on his bottom lip. "I will open an account for you and place six thousand in it."

"Very good." Finnegan puffed his cigar. "When the funds have been transferred from that account to the First National Bank of Minnesota, and I have received word of their having been transferred, I will be on my way, and you may be assured I will darken your door no longer."

Hauser scowled. "You wish for the funds to be transferred to another institution?"

"If I was of a mind to leave the funds in your possession, Mr. Hauser, I would not have bothered to journey here." The gunman raised up out of his chair. "Well, I suppose I shall let you gentlemen get back to your business." He set his hat on his head and tipped the brim to Stuart. "Always a pleasure, Granville."

The pioneer shook his head and grinned. "I cannot say as I would necessarily classify it as a pleasure, Finnegan, but our visits are quite consistent. We discuss money and murder and little else."

Finnegan stubbed out his cigar in the ashtray on Hauser's desk. "The world is concerned with little else, Granville. As minor actors on the larger stage we can hardly be held accountable for such a sad state of affairs."

# Chapter 3

## *CHICAGO, ILLINOIS*

### June 2nd, 1892

William Pinkerton, eldest son and heir to the Pinkerton Detective Agency, set a glass of warm milk by his bedside and drew back the covers. He had eaten dinner, seen his few servants out, and then retired to his study to read for a while before changing into his bedclothes. He was a man with much on his mind, and the warmed milk seemed to still some of the chaos that continually whirled in his busy brain.

In some ways, attention to detail, in particular, William was not unlike his father. In other ways, they differed greatly. Allan Pinkerton had thrived on the whirlwind. As the world grew more and more mad around him, the family progenitor had grown more calm and more focused. William had always marveled at his father's ability to manage a multitude of projects with only a few hours of sleep to draw from. The original detective's font of energy had always appeared boundless, very nearly until the day he died. In that respect, William never could match him. William emitted a low groan and turned to slip under his bedcovers. He desperately wished for rest. Events in the eastern states were unfolding that he knew to be the harbinger of yet another storm in his business affairs. Only time would tell if the agency would survive and prosper, or plummet into ruin. Allan Pinkerton would have entered the fray grinning, a glint in his eye as he considered the possible enterprises of the future. William only felt exhaustion, and the battle had not yet begun.

"I do not know if I have ever seen a silk nightshirt before, William." At the sound of Finnegan's voice, the man of the house tore open a drawer in his bedtable and withdrew a small revolver. "I have already unloaded that pipsqueak, William. As you well know, it is not safe to leave charged weaponry lying about unattended. No need to thank me; I am certain you would have noticed the oversight presently."

William Pinkerton set the small Smith and Wesson down on the nightstand and ran a hand over his face as he sat down on the edge of his bed. "Good God, Finnegan. Did my brother send you here to give me an apoplexy so that he may assume complete control of the business?"

"I have been spending some time visiting with former associates, collecting debts, settling accounts." Finnegan left the door of the bedroom and strolled to one post of the four-poster bed. "Finding myself in the grand city of Chicago once again, it quite naturally occurred to me to stop and visit with my old friend, William."

Pinkerton licked his lips. "As you well know, I am available at my office during normal business hours."

"Ah, but as I said, we are old friends. We have known each other since boyhood. I did not think you would mind an informal visit."

"Sneaking into my home as a burglar might and unloading my pistol is quite informal." The businessman hung his head. "I suppose it was arrogant of me. There are only so many loose ends a man can hold in his fingers. I might have known it would be you come to kill me. Perhaps it is best to let things end much as they began."

Finnegan cocked his head to one side. "Now, dear William, what, pray tell, do you imagine I might wish you dead for?"

Pinkerton slowly raised his head. "I...I do not know as I can say, precisely. Perhaps you have become angry over some old slight. Perhaps someone had merely given money in excess of the stipend we pay you for hunting railroad bounties. I have never known you to need much reason to kill a man; why should I be any different?"

"As it happens, William, I have not visited with the intention of killing you. Although, I must congratulate you for accepting the notion so stoically. Bravo, truly -- I have seen hardened soldiers face the reaper with less grace."

Pinkerton cleared his throat. "Um, I thank you for the compliment." He glanced about. "If you have not come here to murder me, why slink into my house?"

"Would you have admitted me to your office for a conversation?"

"I might have put you off, given our history."

"So then, it seemed prudent to, as you put it, slink into your house. I notice your wife and children are absent and your servants have left for the evening." Finnegan smiled. "By the by, one of them is slowly spiriting your silver out the door. Your butler, I believe. Tall fellow, silver hair."

"Clarkson, the blackguard."

"Yes, well, at any rate, it simply will not do for a man who owns a detective agency to be robbed by his servants. What would your father say?"

"He might have considered the whole thing quite the jolly game."

Finnegan nodded. "He might of, at that." Finnegan

lowered himself into a chair. "Which is not to say that my methods were not designed to remind you that no man is an island in this world, and the only way any of us can hope to live in peace is by showing kindness and friendship to our fellow man. With that in mind, I have come to discuss the matter of my pension."

Pinkerton raised his eyebrows. "Pension! Sir, I will be damned. You had better murder me and be done with it."

"Oh, come now, William. No need for hysterics. Many a hard laboring fellow is compensated in his dotage by the company he slaved for. Of course, it is even more warranted in my case, since I will continue to provide a service to the agency in my retirement."

"Service? What damned service?"

"I will labor every day to remind myself that speaking to the gentlemen of the press regarding your father's company would be disloyal to the memory of a great man. If that is not benefit enough to please you, I will happily add discretion to the deal. I see no reason for a pensioner to discuss the matter of Major Townsend Duran with your brother Robert."

Pinkerton sneered. "I have no inkling of who Major Duran might be, and I could not care less if you discussed the fellow with my brother."

"Really, William, I have already explained that it is not my intention to murder you this evening. Is not subterfuge a bit beneath us? I imagine you came across the details of the Duran incident at some point, and when you began to consider me something of an encumbrance, you passed the information on to the dead colonel's son. The scamp proved rather vexing to deal with. He had more flare for clandestine activities than his father."

"I cannot be held responsible for every bit of paper that is somehow or other smuggled out of the file room. You are not without enemies, Finnegan. Nearly any man you have ever met might conjure a reason for such a prank."

Finnegan nodded. "And you were not without your reasons for perpetrating it, William. I can readily understand how a man such as yourself might wish to be rid of... well, shall we say, an antiquated bit of machinery. That understanding is why we are chatting instead of the less pleasant alternative you mentioned earlier. I am all through with grudges and foolishness in that vein, William. I am a family man, now, and I am only interested in a quiet life. Possibly a farm."

"A farm?" Pinkerton said the words as though Finnegan had suggested running for Congress. "You intend to farm?"

"Not to any great extent, hence the need for supplemental funds." Finnegan removed his slouch hat and contemplated it for a moment before setting it on his knee. "You need not fret about my driving you into poverty, William. I would consider the sum of one hundred and fifty dollars a month more than sufficient. I do not wish to live in splendor, only comfort."

"One hundred and fifty. It would cost me less if you simply came to rob me every month on the new moon. This sort of extortion may be effective with others, but I am only too well acquainted with your reputation, or the version of it my father presented to the public, to be swayed by..." Pinkerton trailed off, staring at the gunman in his bedroom. "I can only assume your other attempts at retrieving the monies owed to you have been successful?"

Finnegan shrugged. "So far, former associates have been quite cooperative and generous of spirit."

"Yes, well, I suppose they might be." Pinkerton's eyes narrowed, an indication that he smelled the possibility of profit. "I would also assume that, so far, you have simply requested the funds and payment has been prompt? You have not been forced to resort to any of the more unsavory methods sometimes required?"

"As I said, so far I have encountered only generosity."

"You may well encounter a bit more this night." Pinkerton stood and took up his glass of milk. "Might we move this discussion to the kitchen?" He rubbed his chin. "If you do not wish to murder me, but do not wish to leave, I suppose we might as well make ourselves more comfortable."

"I would not object to a cup of coffee. Not that I would ever wish to impose."

"It is no imposition, Finnegan. When a man breaks into your house in the middle of the night, it is only Christian to offer him a cup of coffee." Pinkerton put his bare feet into a set of slippers and hopped, wrestling one over his heel. "Let us go down and see if that damned butler has made off with all the pie in addition to the silver."

The two men descended the stairs, with Pinkerton holding a lamp and Finnegan following. When they entered the kitchen, Pinkerton stood by while Finnegan lit the lamp above the table. The heir glanced around and took up the coffee urn that sat on one countertop. "Do you know how this is made to function?"

Finnegan rubbed one eye and selected the coffeepot from a nearby cupboard. "The process is begun with this piece of machinery, William. I would think you would know the fundamentals of brewing coffee. How is it you never learned, being dragged about by your father?"

"We generally had staff about." Pinkerton took a seat at the table and watched as Finnegan located a sack of coffee.

"I have a particular love for this beverage. I never once tasted it before coming to this country, and now find I crave it nearly as much as cigars or money." He searched a cupboard and found a grinder. "If forced, I believe I could manage a method to brew coffee in an old boot with once-used water."

"It is always of interest to discover what you hold sacred, Finnegan." Pinkerton rubbed his face. "Who is it you are in the process of collecting debts from?"

"Not having been born to the occupation, I cannot say for certain, but I have been told that it is poor form for one to discuss the business of others with those who are not financially involved, William."

"Yes, I suppose that is correct." He took to rubbing his chin. "It must be a fine thing, indeed, to be able to receive funds owed through little more than a fearsome smile and a veiled threat. I am frequently forced to employ attorneys for that sort of work."

"A man such as yourself must behave in a more civilized manner, William."

"Even so, I would much rather face your pistol in the dark once a month than issue another check to one of them. Vile creatures. Any man who studies the law should be promptly hung when he is declared competent, in my opinion."

"Yes, well, being attorneys, I believe that constraint would only cause them to remain just slightly less than competent. It is their natural way, William." Finnegan worked the pump handle to spill water into the coffeepot.

"What do you know of the steel industry, Finnegan?"

"Steel is the substance used to form my guns. Beyond that, I know little."

"And a lucky man you are. Have you heard of Andrew Carnegie?"

Finnegan chuckled. "I recall reading a few lines about him in the Post, recently. They claimed that he would enjoy being named King of Scotland by Vic, and that he has purchased a castle on the off chance the old bat is not intractable on the matter." He lit the stove and set the coffeepot on top. "The article suggested he is already, more or less, the king of Pennsylvania."

"And several states adjoining it." Pinkerton cracked his knuckles. "What about Henry Clay Frick?"

"That gentleman, I am unfamiliar with."

"If Carnegie is the king, Frick could be considered his prime minister. While Carnegie is off entertaining harlots and queens at his castle, Frick has been left in charge of the empire. Under normal circumstances, there could be no better choice. Frick built the Pennsylvania coke industry. The man knows every trick, and invented many of them. He is not the sort of man to let his humors act on business decisions, but the chink in his armor may be revealed presently."

Finnegan took a seat opposite Pinkerton while the coffee slowly began to boil behind him. "I suppose every man has his weakness."

"Frick shows a damnable inflexibility when it comes to labor. The man hates unions. I believe he would pay a man twice as much, so long as he never joined a union. It has been his ardent wish for as long as I have known the fellow to drive all the union men out of the steel mills. He has accomplished that very thing in a few of them. Soon, he will set to trying at the Homestead Mill. Homestead is the largest mill ever built, with more union men than any other operation in the entire country. A strike at Homestead will cripple the steel industry. The union knows this, and Frick does, as well. The union holds this knowledge as a card they dare not play, and the knowledge of it preys on Frick's mind day and night."

"It is a common condition that a man with many millions finds himself fixated on some point that another man might never even pause to ponder." The gunman took out a cigar and set it on the table. "If I ever find myself in possession of several million, I will likely gift the majority of it to widows and orphans to avoid such an insufferable embarrassment."

"Yes, that would undoubtedly be for the best." Pinkerton folded his fingers and set his elbows on the table. "Frick is rather unique in his view of the unions. Even men like Rockefeller occasionally waver in labor disputes. Carnegie himself is particularly fond of gladhanding his workers. Frick could not care less. Any man who gives him trouble can be forced out by armed guards and readily replaced by a bohunk."

"As you are the man who supplies the armed guards, I imagine you are quite fond of Mr. Frick."

"Fond does not enter into it." Pinkerton waggled one thick finger at the gunman. "If Frick has his way, Homestead will be an open mill. If Frick gets his way, every industrialist in the country will at least attempt to follow suit. The contract for the majority of the skilled workers at Homestead is expiring soon. When the contract expires, Frick intends to cease negotiations with the union and hire men individually on a pay scale. The next few months will determine if a man's property is truly his own in this nation, or if the capitalists such as Carnegie intend to knuckle under to the communists, socialists, anarchists, and other foreign riffraff that continue to invade our shores."

Finnegan stood and retrieved the coffeepot and two cups. He set one in front of Pinkerton. "Careful, William. For a moment you sounded not unlike your father. He was the crusader; you are a businessman. I am certain what you meant to say was that the next few months will determine the long-term profits afforded to the firm. If the men at Homestead are not offered a new contract, and Frick holds out against them, you and your preventives will have more work than you know what to do with for years to come, as every mill in the country itches to do away with the unions."

"You have a keen understanding of such matters for an assassin, Finnegan."

"Your agency is the source of my pension. Naturally, I take a keen interest in its wellbeing."

"Yes, well..." Pinkerton sipped the coffee Finnegan had poured him. "With that in mind, what would be your inclination toward assisting the agency's financial wellbeing and profiting...say, an additional five thousand dollars? In addition to your pension, of course."

Finnegan resumed his seat at the table. "What would be involved, William? I certainly have no interest in clouting men on a picket line, and I know you can find cheaper men for such labor."

Pinkerton waved one hand. "Any barroom drunkard can hold back a union picket. I would make use of you in a more specialized capacity. Andrew Carnegie is a man of odd inclinations. He is fairly obsessed with maintaining his image as a friend of the working man. For that reason, he has placed Frick in the role of a villain during any and all labor disputes. Frick somewhat relishes the role, of course, but eventually, I fear it will be the death of him."

"That may be a bit overly dramatic, William."

"It is not the union men I worry over. Presently, there is hardly a crown head in Europe who does not lay awake at night awaiting an anarchist bomb. Frick will rapidly become the figurehead of this strike. He will require protection, and I can think of no better man for the job. Your reputation, alone, will deter most aspirants."

Finnegan rubbed his face and took up his unlit cigar. "What sort of chap is Frick?"

"I have never met a man with less imagination or a more

boring demeanor. His only interest seems to lie in collecting art, and even that is of a mundane nature. In short, he is the perfect capitalist." Pinkerton grinned. "He should not annoy you overly much. I have never known him to indulge in chitchat."

"And how long would I be looking out for his safety?"

"You need only keep him alive until the strike is ended. That is all I would ask."

"Ended, regardless of the outcome? I should not care to be held accountable for the final result."

"Frick's continuing heartbeat is all you shall be held accountable for."

Finnegan nodded and sparked a match to light his cigar. He let out a puff of smoke. "Five thousand dollars will buy a fellow a great deal of protection, William. Ten thousand will buy near twice as much."

Pinkerton slowly nodded with a thin smile on his lips. "I suppose this is no time to appear the skinflint." He extended his hand across the table. "Ten thousand, if he lives to the end of the strike."

Finnegan took his employer's hand and shook it. "Hmm, once again I cannot help but wonder if I could not have asked for more."

"Do not rush too quickly to become a businessman, Finnegan. I assure you, the simplicity of your current occupation will be missed."

The gunman poured himself a cup of coffee and took a small sip. "Have no fear on that score, William. I am more than willing to leave the world of capitalism to men such as you and Frick. All I would ask is a small portion of the profits, so that I might enjoy a few moments of solitude with my darling wife from time to time."

Pinkerton sipped his coffee. "Yes, I had received word

that you married." He chuckled. "Of all the news I have ever received regarding you, I must say, that is the only bit of it that ever came as a shock. Telegrams describing killings and mayhem had become commonplace. Matrimony took me off guard." He sipped his coffee again. "If you do not mind my inquiring, what sort of woman is she?"

Finnegan thought on it for a moment. "Mrs. Gilhooley is a woman who can appreciate the division between what a man would wish to do and what he must do, on occasion."

Pinkerton took another slow sip of coffee. "Then she is likely an excellent match for you, Finnegan."

# Chapter 4

## *WASHINGTON, D.C.*

### June 20th, 1892

FINNEGAN HAD NEVER HAD CAUSE TO ENTER THE Capitol Building during all his visits to Washington. Viewing the inside of the massive structure, he found himself rather impressed by how far the bespectacled young man he had met several years earlier had climbed amongst the marble and granite. To have an office in such an edifice, a fellow must truly be a potentate of the young nation.

The gunman was gawking at the moldings around the ceiling above the rather uncomfortable wooden bench he sat on when a young lady came out from the oversized oak door that guarded the bureaucrat within. "The Commissioner will see you know, Mr. Gilhooley."

He stood and straightened his coat so his guns would not show. "Thank you, ma'am." Finnegan followed her through the door and was directed through another door, where a fit and frenetic man stood behind a desk. A brass nameplate identified him as Theodore Roosevelt, Commissioner of the U.S. Civil Service.

A jack-o'-lantern-like grin was spread over the Commissioner's face. "Finnegan Gilhooley! I must say, it is a joy to see you once again, but never in all my born days did I imagine you might come marching through my office door."

Finnegan reached out and took his hand. "I cannot say as I expected to find you in such circumstances, either, Mr. Roosevelt. Have they gone and made you President? I cannot imagine what else might warrant such lodgings."

"I assure you, the challenge I face here promises to be more grueling than any task ever assigned to a President. I am currently charged to bring the Civil Service into line with our great nation's ideals of democracy and egalitarianism."

Finnegan nodded. "That should make for quite a chore, sir."

"It very well may. Of course, the somewhat corrupt nature of the Civil Service is nothing unique to America. Favoritism, cronyism, nepotism: these are the hobgoblins that wreak havoc wherever honest men attempt government. One has grown to expect such behavior in the monarchies of Europe or the opium-ridden courts of China, but such business is in direct contravention to American ideals. I am honored to be the man chosen to root it out for all time." Roosevelt pulled his glasses from his face and gave them a vigorous wiping.

"A noble goal, Mr. Roosevelt."

"Please, call me Theodore. We are men of a similar mindset; no reason to stand on formality."

"Ah, very good." The gunman smiled. "Please call me Finnegan. Now then, Theodore, might I inquire as to what exactly this Civil Service is?"

"Oh, yes, my apologies. I forget that the nomenclature of this building is often obscure to those who are of foreign birth, or even those not directly affiliated with government." He motioned to a chair for Finnegan and resumed his seat behind his desk. "The Civil Service is comprised of all those who labor under the banner of the federal government. Ah, with the exception of the military and the politicians, of course." Roosevelt could see that the concept was still not clear. "Those who handle the mail, census takers, the men in Indian Affairs, and so on."

"I see." Finnegan rubbed his chin. "These men are corrupt?"

"Well, to be sure not all of them are, at least not in their day-to-day habits. A great many of them are even apt to deliver substantial contributions to the public good. What I have been tasked with is changing the methods utilized to choose those who are employed by the Civil Service. Up until recently, the ability to gain any of the more lucrative positions has hinged not on the merits of the candidate, but rather on the candidate's relation or who may owe the man a favor. Crude backroom deals will not serve to produce the sort of men required to allow this country to step onto the world stage with the other great powers."

"Certainly." Finnegan shifted in his chair. "How do you intend to go about locating superior men? Do you have a culling process in mind for applicants?"

"I do, indeed. I am in the process of developing an exam, partially in written form to assess the applicant's skills in terms of literacy, followed by a regimented interview before a board of experienced personnel who will assess the applicant's ability to serve the public and to determine what position, if any, the applicant is best suited to. If applied properly, I believe this system should eventually produce a bureaucracy more efficient, effective, and trustworthy than any other in the world. Just imagine what might be possible with such a well-oiled machine serving the will of the people."

"I can foresee the dawning of a new age, Theodore."

The Commissioner laughed and slapped his hands together. "Yes, bully, quite. Of course, it remains to be seen if even a single one of my revelatory suggestions will be implemented." He sighed. "The wheels of government turn very slowly. I sometimes wonder if any man who finds himself working the handle can live long enough to see improvements come to fruition." He shrugged. "It is very decent of you to allow for a fool to so thoroughly elaborate on his folly, Finnegan. There is nothing I enjoy more than discussing my labors, which most of humanity regards as the dullest of drudgery. Even I cannot go on all day, though. Perhaps it would be best for us to move on to the business that has brought you here. You are, after all, the party who is taking the time for this chat."

Finnegan folded his hands in front of him. "I cannot simply stop in when I learn an old acquaintance is nearby?"

"I suppose you may, as any man might. Although, I cannot help but doubt it in this instance. I received a telegram from old Sam Hauser recently. I would assume he sent such a missive to all former members of the Stockgrowers Association." Roosevelt's face grew serious. "Hauser made the ridiculous claim that you were traveling about extorting money by threat of murder."

The gunman fought back a laugh and cleared his throat. "If I were to issue such a threat, Theodore, what might your response be?"

"Ah, yes." The bureaucrat held up one declarative finger. "While my position with the government does not permit me to condone such behavior, my manhood would demand that I meet you on the field of honor. If for no other reason than to serve as an object lesson to those who would lower themselves to the use of violence to gain their ends. This is a civilized nation, but there is no recourse when confronted by uncivilized circumstance. I gained that wisdom in the Dakotas, and it rings no less true here in Washington."

"Very well put." The gunman set one boot on the other knee, looking very relaxed. "I have been made privy to a rumor that your old associate, the Marquis de Mores, made an attempt at forcing you into just such an action."

"Antione?" Roosevelt shook his head. "That incident was more the result of rabblerousing on the part of some other settlers and cattlemen who were annoyed with Antoine's liberal use of funds. They could not outmaneuver him on the range, so they endeavored to create a rift between his better friends. In that instance, they were very nearly successful. I dare say, only my steady nature saved us from a dire situation."

"How did you manage to remedy matters?"

"Antoine let it be known that he felt slighted and, as they say out west, called me out for it." Roosevelt chuckled. "I responded with a letter wherein I explained that, while I considered Antoine to be a dear acquaintance and a man of unimpeachable honor, whose friendship I would never wish to compromise, I was more than willing to meet him at a place and time of his choosing. My only caveat was to insist on the use of rifles as opposed to the usual choice of pistols." Roosevelt slyly leaned forward over his desk. "Antoine never possessed much skill with a rifle, while I am somewhat known for luck with that instrument." He leaned back. "Surely, my prevailing on him to recall our long and loyal association dispelled any ill feeling he might have harbored. Certainly, a man that brave would not have considered the choice of weapons a factor."

"Most certainly."

"Yes, well, such tawdry recollections are best saved for cocktail chatter. We had best get to the business at hand. What brings you to my door, Finnegan?"

"A small matter in the grand scheme of things. As you may have already guessed, I have no interest in dueling you out in the street and would consider anything less an affront to the dignity of us both. I have come to receive payment for my labors in the service of the Stockgrowers Association. As one of the members of that cadre, you will surely recall that I was to be paid for my services from the coffers of the membership -- upon completion, of course."

"I see." Roosevelt stared down at his desk blotter. "In totality, the events described in many a periodical regarding yourself and Mr. Stuart surely should constitute completion." He tapped one finger on the desk. "You have received payment from Hauser?"

"I have."

Roosevelt sneered. "I can well imagine he took some convincing. Sam Hauser is always loath to part with a nickel, even if the nickel belongs to another man who has been previously bilked out of it."

"Some men require convincing; eventually they come to honor their commitments. Speaking of which, I had hoped that you might be able to point me in the direction of your old friend, the Marquis. On my way here, I discovered that he has departed the Dakotas."

"Ha, yes. I should say he has. I have only mixed reports to offer you as to his location. Some say he is attempting to build a damn railroad in French Indochina, if you can believe such tales. Another fellow I spoke with some time ago told me the Marquis is fighting rebels in Algeria. I could not say which is the more credible theory. At any rate, for your purposes the whole matter is academic. After the winter of '86 I was forced to, in essence, dissolve my ranching interests. Antoine was kind enough to buy me out so that I could at least hold my head up and claim I had not been a complete fool. For that I will always be grateful to the man. As I owed the fellow a favor, he asked that I see to any and all of his debts and look to a few minor business concerns when he went abroad. He has left funds on deposit for occasions just such as this." Roosevelt opened a desk drawer, dug in it for a moment, and produced a large check book. "Will this serve, or do you require coin of the realm?"

"Knowing you to be a man of impeachable character, I will gladly accept a good faith paper."

"What do you consider to be proper payment for your services, Finnegan?"

"Three thousand per member of the association. In this instance, six thousand, if you so please."

"That sounds quite reasonable." He flopped open the folio checkbook and selected a pen from a nearby holder.

"Just that quickly, Theodore?"

"The duty you were charged with was no common task, and one I have, thankfully, never found myself burdened with. Who am I to dicker with a man of your experience?"

"And you do not believe the Marquis will be discomforted by this use of his funds?"

"The money was left in my keeping to settle any outstanding debts the man might have. This surely falls into that category. I have no doubt that, upon his return to this country, the Marquis will consider the disbursement of six thousand dollars to be a minor expense. I am sure he would prefer to have Finnegan Gilhooley as a friend and given to a friendly disposition. Antoine somewhat prides himself on the collection of enemies, but in this case, I believe even he would admit it is a needless risk and a careless absurdity." Roosevelt looked up from the checkbook. "All his bluster aside, the most deadly Marquis has only managed to shoot a number of men you might consider a good start to a long week of labor."

"There is no shame in the pursuit of excellence in one's profession."

"Certainly not." Roosevelt tore the check free from the book. "I truly would have met you on the field, sir. That being known, I am more than gladdened that it will not be required." He grinned.

Finnegan reached out and accepted the check. "If you will agree to keep the knowledge in the strictest confidence, Theodore, I will admit to feeling great relief that you conjured a more civilized solution, as well. A man who stands solely on principle is often very difficult to knock down."

"What, other than principle, could possibly be worth fighting for?"

"A great many men choose women, vanity, or money, but it has been my experience that they are not nearly as satisfying in hindsight."

"On the subject of women, I am told you are now a married man."

Finnegan folded the check and placed it in his pocket. "You are correct. Some two years now."

"I have never truly cared for the bachelor's life. I indulged in it during my time in the Dakotas, but as appealing as riding and hunting and the free life of the open range is for a man without attachments...well, all that becomes so banal if you do not have someone waiting to be bored by the retelling of the adventure."

Finnegan nodded. "I find that to be true, Theodore."

"Now that you have collected the brunt of your outstanding debts, what do you plan to do with yourself?"

"I have a minor matter to see to here in the east. William Pinkerton has brought me back into the fold, so to speak, for a short engagement. When that is ended, my wife and I are considering setting up housekeeping, possibly in the environs of Idaho. It is lovely country, from what I am told. With any luck, my affairs will be seen to at approximately the same time hers come to conclusion."

"What occupies your wife?"

"She is acting as an intermediary of sorts between the Lakota Sioux and the government. Surely you are aware of the incident that occurred involving that tribe at a place called Wounded Knee Creek."

Roosevelt shook his head. "Most unfortunate. I had truly believed such times were past us. I wish her luck in remedying any remaining grievances. The sooner the tribes resign themselves to entering general society, the better off the entire nation will be. How did your wife come to occupy her position?"

"That is a long tale and impossible to relate before you would have to resume your labors."

Roosevelt gave the gunman a curious look. "Might you have time to inform me as to the errand Mr. Pinkerton has dispatched you on? I have always harbored an interest in the daring-do of fellows such as yourself."

Finnegan moved about in his chair and rubbed his chin. "I suppose there is little harm in the telling of it. My charge involves nothing beyond what is common knowledge, or will be, very soon. I travel from here to the village of Pittsburg to watch over one Henry Clay Frick. The man intends to join the fray of labor agitation and disarray. It is rumored that someone amongst the unions, anarchists, communists, socialists, or even the milkmaids may attempt an assassination."

Roosevelt pursed his lips and sank lower into his chair. "Have you made Frick's acquaintance?"

"I have not."

"He is an interesting specimen. I first heard his name in connection to coke. Coal is placed in furnaces to form coke. Coke is needed to produce steel. Frick began buying up coke producers some years past, and eventually came to control the majority of them. His transition to the steel industry and his current position as Carnegie's Mephistopheles is a quite natural progression." Roosevelt sighed. "Change is the only constant in this world, my friend. This country, a republic born of revolution, is entering a new era. As wealth becomes concentrated, those unable to obtain it, or those who feel they are disallowed from obtaining it under fair practices, will inevitably strive to improve their lot. What form that may take, I cannot say. They may make their stand at the polls by electing...I suppose the term populist could be considered an apt term. At worst, they will choose the sword, as so many of the downtrodden previously have. I can only pray that men such as Frick and Carnegie will do all in their power to avoid exacerbating the situation in the meantime."

Finnegan groaned. "What Mr. Frick chooses to do is his own affair. Captains of industry rarely seek my counsel, at any rate. I am charged with keeping the silly bugger alive until he reaches some truce with his working men. If accomplished, I will be recompensed well enough to secure my future comfort." He shook his head and stood. "Men such as I are not meant to consider the greater world. It is best if I only consider what is before me and what must be done. I will leave the steering of the great ship of state to men like yourself." He extended his hand across the desk.

Roosevelt stood and took Finnegan's hand. "I doubt I will rise above my current station, but I appreciate your confidence in my prospects."

"You are an honorable man, Theodore. Do not hesitate to call on me if you require assistance. There are few enough men who take their obligations seriously."

"I dare say that offer is well worth the Marquis's money."

# Chapter 5

## *ST. CLAIR, PENNSYLVANIA*

### June 24th, 1892

Finnegan stared down at the tombstones. Dead leaves from the previous fall still laid about on the ground around them, wet and glistening. Small sprigs of green grass could be seen rising beneath. The gunman sighed and flicked a few leaves from the top of the most recently installed stone. Hearing footsteps behind him, he turned to see a stooped old man with a rake in one hand. Finnegan nodded to the fellow as he approached.

"If either of them two are your kin, I ought to say that I am only one man and them leaves never cease to accumulate inside this fence."

"You will not receive complaints from me regarding the grounds, sir. I know well enough these souls are past concerning themselves with such matters." Finnegan motioned to the tombstones. "Were you acquainted with either of these ladies?"

The groundskeeper came forward and gazed down at the markers. "I would dare say every man, woman, and child in St. Clair had cause to know Mrs. Wallace. She was a fine lady. Very kind to those who suffered ill luck." He looked to the other marker. "The other young lady, all I can say regarding her is that she was the wife of the Methodist minister, but lies here to be near Mrs. Wallace."

Finnegan nodded. "Annabel came to live with Mrs. Wallace in...I believe it was '77. It was very decent of Mrs. Wallace to take her in, as she was already missing a husband and burdened with several boys. It is right she should lie with the only mother she ever truly knew." He looked to the town. "Is her husband still about?"

"If you wish to find him, he may surely be found at the Methodist church on the north end."

Finnegan looked at the all-too-recent date on the stone. He had inquired of the telegraph clerk as to where Annabel Hardy might be found. The clerk had sadly related the location of the cemetery. "The fellow who dispatched me here did not know how the girl died, precisely. Do you, sir?"

"Giving birth to her third child, sir." The old man shook his head. "The child still lingers, but the sisters caring for it do not hold out much hope." He rubbed his white beard. "I did not know she was kin of a sort to Mrs. Wallace. Although, I have only been here a handful of years. Came down from Erie."

Finnegan held out a silver dollar to the man. "For their continued care, my friend."

The old man took the dollar. "Did you not just claim they was past caring?"

"They are, but many still among us still do." He nodded and walked off in the direction of the Methodist church.

Minister Hardy sat at his desk, considering what the subject of his sermon ought to be upon the resumption of his duties. For the remainder of the month, Minister Walden from Cleveland would handle the congregation and see to the needs of the village poor. This was common practice when the wife of a minister passed on. Matters temporal sometimes took precedence over matters spiritual, although the minister knew that he must someday reascend the pulpit. When that day came, he wished to be prepared, but so far words failed him. As a man of the cloth, he should remain ever optimistic in view of his flock. He set his pen to one side of the blank paper before him. Perhaps it would simply be best if he remained out of view for the foreseeable future.

Looking up from his desk, he saw a tall, thin man standing in the doorway. A frock coat hung about the fellow and a few bulges showed beneath the garment. Hardy stared at the man for a long moment before speaking. "If you seek the minister, I will have to refer you to Mr. Walden, sir."

"I seek Mr. Hardy." The man came forward to the desk. "I was formerly acquainted with your late wife, sir." He put out his hand. "Finnegan Gilhooley."

The minister slowly extended his hand. "Gilhooley? Truly?"

"Yes, sir."

The minister sat back in his chair, staring unbelievably. "Mr. Gilhooley, I must confess that one of my more shameful indulgences is the reading of wretched pulp such as the *Police Gazette*. That periodical has commented on your endeavors frequently over the years. When my wife initially claimed to have known you, I did not necessarily credit it, but..." He smiled and rubbed his face. "As she told the tale, she was of some assistance to you around the time of that horrid Molly Maguire business."

"It was around that time, but she assisted me in a separate matter." Finnegan looked sullen, thinking back on his short association with Annabel. "I only knew your wife a short time, but it was long enough to know she was a fine lass. If any soul truly belongs in heaven, I would place my wager upon that young lady being admitted." Finnegan cleared his throat. "I found myself traveling in the area and had hoped to have a visit with Annabel while I am Pennsylvania." He frowned. "Now I find that will not be possible."

"Yes." The minister wiped his eyes. "It is most unfortunate."

"Yes, well." Finnegan produced a wad of bills from his pocket. "During our association, I came to consider myself somewhat responsible for the wellbeing of Miss Annabel. Now that she is passed, I would appreciate the opportunity to offer some small gift to you and her children." He set the bills on the desk. "I am aware any decent man must balk at receiving cash money, but I must insist. Your wife...the young lady did me a great service. There has been but one instance in my entire career when I appeared the proper detective, and it was solely the product of your wife's intervention. For that, I will always be grateful to her, and surely owe her heirs something." He nodded to the Minister and turned to go. "Good day, sir."

"Mr. Gilhooley." The gunman stopped and turned. "It is a comfort to know that I am not the only man to mourn Annabel's passing."

"She was a fine lass." Finnegan set his hat on his head. "I think of her often."

# Chapter 6

## *PITTSBURG, PENNSYLVANIA*

### June 26th, 1892

FINNEGAN WAS NOT THE ONLY MAN WHO WANTED A moment of Mr. Frick's time at his offices on 5th Avenue. It appeared as though there were several fellows of various stripe and inclination waiting to visit with the industrialist at any given moment. Almost a dozen men were currently seated on benches or leaning against the wall just outside the great man's office door. Instead of a secretary, Frick made use of a broad, and rather imposing, negro in a butler's uniform he referred to as an attendant. This butler asked a visitor's business and transported the information to Frick. At that point, Frick presumably made a decision as to whether the visitor would have to wait, could be seen immediately, or needed to be thrown out into the street. So far, Finnegan had only witnessed one fellow, an obvious huckster, being thrown out on his ear by the attendant. The chap had managed the chore without so much as rumpling his well-pressed jacket, and showed great facility at the execution of the thing.

After he'd remained on the bench for the better part of an

hour, the butler finally strode in front of Finnegan. "You may go in now, sir."

The gunman slowly stood to discover the butler was at least a full four inches taller. "It has been said that a well-trained butler is hard to find, but I cannot imagine how anyone might lose track of you, sir."

"If I am not here, I am looking to Mr. Frick's dinner." He motioned to the door.

"Yes, well, thank you." Finnegan moved to the office door and let himself in, as he had seen several men do already. While waiting on anyone grated on Finnegan's nerves, he could at least say that Frick appeared quick with his various interviews. As he entered and closed the door, the two men within looked up from folios. The gunman stood in front of the closed door. "Finnegan Xavier Gilhooley, at your service, gentlemen."

The man behind the desk had a very stiff look on his bearded, somewhat sallow face. He seemed fit for a fellow who spent all day poring over ledgers, and had a glint in his eye that made him appear energetic. The man across the desk from him had grown a beard to ape his employer, but did not look nearly as inspired. The desk owner nodded. "I am Frick..." He pointed with one sharp finger. "This is Leishman." He leaned forward. "Are you the harbinger of my army?"

Finnegan licked his lips. "Army, sir?"

The industrialist sighed. "Leishman, can you conceive of a reason why these Pinkerton men constantly attempt obfuscation?" The minion shook his head. "Neither can I. When I attend the theatre, no one among the troop attempts to convince me they do not wish to do *Hamlet* for me. When I go to my haberdasher, the man does not attempt to convince me he does not sell clothes. For some reason I cannot comprehend, the Pinkerton Agency, a company whose sole business is providing armed men in times of disturbance, will not give me a straight answer as to when my men will be provided, or as to what form or quantity those men will be presented in."

Finnegan rubbed his chin. "It may be that the fault lies with your approach, sir. You may have incorrectly appealed to William Pinkerton's better nature when you ought to have begun with the offer of money. In my experience, matters of a monetary nature always take precedence with dear William."

Frick chuckled. His minion was too indecisive to offer a response. "That has always been my assessment of William Pinkerton, as well. I have been discussing the matter with his brother, Robert, at any rate."

"Ah, that may well explain the root of the problem. I can assure you that Robert Pinkerton will never present you with an army. Robert is so very particular regarding such terms. You may well contract with him for a number of men that might equal a battalion, but they will never be referred to as such. They will be a mere handful, with no mention made of the colossus that possessed the hand. How many men do you hope to have provided, sir?"

"Two hundred might do. Double that number would be preferable."

Finnegan shrugged. "I have always believed myself to be the equal of a hundred men. As for the rest, I can offer no predictions."

Frick laughed. "Very well, then. Aside from offering entertainment, what is your purpose here?"

Finnegan smiled. "I have been dispatched here by the previously mentioned William Pinkerton to ensure your safety in the coming days, sir. Mr. Pinkerton feels you may be in danger from various parties and individuals."

"That is absurd." Frick shook his head.

"Sir, I may, on occasion, jest regarding certain qualities of William Pinkerton, but it cannot be denied that he is very well informed and extremely capable in these matters. If he is concerned for your safety, you ought to be concerned, as well."

"My safety, what an absurd notion. There is nary a union man on this continent who would raise his hand against me. Such an act would only substantiate the necessity of hiring Pinkertons, closing mills, and bringing in unorganized Slavs to do the work at half the cost. A workingman would have to be quite mad to shoot me down." Frick squinted. "What name did you give?"

"Finnegan Gilhooley."

Frick tapped one finger on his desk. "Leishman, why is that name familiar to me?"

The minion cleared his throat and glanced between the two men. "He is...well, the gentleman is a well-known assassin, sir. The original Mr. Pinkerton made much of his exploits, and the newspapermen frequently..." Leishman appeared a bit regretful at the declaration.

"Oh, have out with it, James," Frick chuckled. "I imagine the fellow will not murder you here in the office. A professional shootist would certainly wait until you are on your way home." The industrialist grinned.

The minion cleared his throat once again. "Mr. Gilhooley frequently provides subject matter for both newspapers and pulp books." Leishman shrugged, almost apologetically. "I recall one tome that included both the pursuit of the Haymarket bomber and a gunfight with Geronimo, the Indian chief."

Frick's grin only broadened. "I suppose only the constrictions of profitability kept them from relating your retrieval of the holy grail."

Finnegan shook his head. "Likely a commitment to faithfully relate the facts. I crusade for the grail when my work here is done. I am certain a scribe such as the one who penned that volume would never stoop to fiction."

Frick chuckled again. "Yes, well, you are an entertaining fellow, Mr. Gilhooley, but what is your purpose here, truly?"

"As I said, Mr. Pinkerton has dispatched me here to watch over you and see to your safety for the duration of... well, shall we call it the coming unpleasantness?"

Frick's eyes grew a bit wider. "I am afraid I do not follow, sir. Do you intend to stand in this office and act as a nanny? I assure you, I have occupied this office and this position for quite some time and have, so far, not suffered so much as a foul word being passed my way on the street. I am not the Russian Tsar." He smiled slyly. "I have more resources at my disposal and am worth a good deal more alive than dead, at least to any who might wish to do battle with me."

Finnegan slipped his hands into the pockets of his coat. "I did not conceive of the notion, Mr. Frick. If you are not partial to my presence here in your offices, perhaps I can be of use to you in another capacity. As you are not apprehensive, I see no reason for me to linger about constantly. Might I suggest a compromise?"

Frick shrugged. "You have the floor, sir."

"Mr. Pinkerton has sent me here to look to your safety and placed me at your disposal. If I remain in the general area for the duration of your current labor dispute, I am certain I can be of some use to you and placate Mr. Pinkerton's concerns simultaneously."

Frick folded his hands and sat back in his chair. "A very reasonable suggestion, Mr. Gilhooley." One side of his mouth moved up into a smile. "And one that will surely allow you to continue drawing your pay from Mr. Pinkerton. But I must confess, I am having difficulty theorizing as to what service you might provide me with. I have never employed an assassin, and am rarely bothered by either bombers or Indian chiefs."

The gunman smiled. "I am being well compensated for my time here, Mr. Frick. In truth, I do not much care if I spend my time watching over you or assisting that large butler in the preparation of your meals."

"I doubt my attendant would appreciate the interference, but..." Frick scratched his bearded cheek. "Were you involved in the war between the states?"

"Yes."

"What do you know of fortifications?"

"As much as any mother's son who ever cowered behind one."

Frick rubbed his chin. "Yes, well put. If you insist on loitering about the area, Mr. Gilhooley, and you are not the advance guard of my army, then I will send you on another errand."

Finnegan nodded. "As I said: at your service, sir."

"You will make haste to the Homestead works and inspect the fortifications that have been placed there. See to it that they are substantial enough to resist any conceivable force and that they are placed correctly for their intended purpose."

Finnegan leaned a bit forward. "Mr. Frick, what purpose do the Homestead works serve?"

"It is a steel mill, Mr. Gilhooley. At this time, possibly the largest in the world."

"I see. And what purpose are the fortifications you spoke of to serve?"

Frick scowled. "Leishman, please explain the additions that have been made to the works."

The minion brightened, glad to have a topic to discuss that he was familiar with. "Ah, yes, well, in effect we have constructed a fence about the place, all around the works; our property. The fence has been explained away as a guard against vandals, but... well, we intend that it be used to keep the workmen out if it should become necessary to close the works for an extended period."

Finnegan cocked his head to one side. "Keep them out?"

"Yes." Leishman began glancing back and forth again. "We cannot have them wandering about willy-nilly as it damn well pleases them. The works are our property."

Frick shook his head. "Mr. Gilhooley, does Mr. Pinkerton plan to compensate you based on the degree to which you are useful?"

"Not precisely, no."

"Then be off to Homestead and we can discuss the details of the damn fence when you return."

"That would seem a reasonable compromise, sir." Finnegan nodded and turned toward the door. He stopped with his hand on the knob and looked back. "Mr. Frick, I would assume the skilled men currently employed at the Homestead works labor under a contract?"

Frick nodded. "Of course."

"And when does that contract expire, sir?"

"The 30th of this month."

"Ah, well, I should be about my business quickly then."

Frick laughed. "I dare say you should, sir."

# Chapter 7

## *HOMESTEAD, PENNSYLVANIA*

### June 27th, 1892

The town itself seemed oddly subdued. Finnegan had walked the streets of many a company town, and they were rarely sedate. Mines and mills always operated with multiple shifts of men. When released from their labors, those men sought liquor and distraction at all hours of the day. None of that behavior could be seen around the village of Homestead. What should have been a town in turmoil was quiet, except for the chirping of birds and the flap of wash being hung.

The gunman found the calm nature of the place somewhat unsettling. Frick had been doing all within his considerable power to agitate the skilled workers in the town for the better part of three months and, to a lesser extent, the previous three years. Despite the roiling from above, the town in no way appeared on the verge of an uprising. All things considered, Finnegan might have preferred an angry mob. While unpleasant, the actions of a mob could at least be predicted.

The Pinkerton left the train depot and strolled through

the town and down to the millworks. The town was neat and clean and the freshly whitewashed plank board fence surrounding the millworks appeared just as tidy and well cared for. Finnegan paused before passing through one of the gates that stood wide open. Every ten feet or so, a small square, perhaps measuring six by six inches, had been cut out of the face of the plankboards. These tiny windows were at about shoulder height and had been covered with small doors on the inside, then painted to match the rest of the fence. Whoever had gone through all this trouble had surely wished the small additions would go unnoticed, but any fool could see the openings were engineered to serve as firing ports. Finnegan sighed, and continued on.

A handful of yards from the gate, Finnegan found the large brick edifice that served as the general office building for the Homestead works. He presented himself to a lady who occupied a small counter on the ground level. "I would appreciate a few moments of the general manager's time, ma'am."

"I believe he is available and in his office, presently." She motioned toward a flight of marble stairs. "Mr. Potter is the first door on the right. Please knock before entering."

Finnegan nodded to the lady and ascended the stairs. As suggested, the first door on the right bore the name of Potter. Finnegan knocked with one knuckle. Several seconds passed before a shaky voice on the other side could be heard to utter an invitation. The gunman slipped through the door and stood in front of the seated Potter. "Sir, my name is Finnegan Gilhooley; I come by way of Mr. Frick."

Potter was a thin man with an equally thin covering of black hair perched on his sweaty head. His lip quivered as he gazed at Finnegan. "You...Frick sent you?"

"Yes, sir."

"Ah, God preserve me, what fresh hell is this, then?"

Finnegan chuckled and hooked his thumbs into his belt. "Mr. Potter, I am known for neither cheerfulness nor optimism, but I must say: you appear needlessly sullen for such a fine spring day."

Potter let out a long gasp. "By God, sir, I can only wish it was the deepest winter. Men cannot so easily lay on a siege when it is below freezing." Potter first withdrew a handkerchief from his pocket to wipe his brow, then retrieved a small bottle of brown liquid from his desk drawer. "Damn that Frick. Damn him and all like him." The man took a long pull from the bottle and smacked his lips. "Do not presume to threaten me with informing Mr. Frick as to my utterance, sir. It is all very well for that...administrator to sit in Pittsburg and issue proclamations. He is not the man who will face the cannonade." Potter sneered and drank from the bottle again. "As a matter of fact, I invite you to inform Mr. Frick as to my opinion and inclination. The information may well win you my position. You shall rapidly discover what a joy it is to possess."

Finnegan could not help but grin at the fellow. "I assure you, Mr. Potter, I have no intention, whatsoever, to usurp your position here. I have merely been dispatched to inspect the...the most recent additions to the mill to determine whether or not they will be of use should any unpleasantness arise."

"Ah, so now our emperor is concerned with the condition of Fort Frick? Well, that is quite a comfort. Surely you are well versed in such matters. Tell me, how many inches of pine would you consider sufficient to repel a horde of many thousands of men? You should take into account that the horde is quite well paid by this company and overly fond of purchasing firearms with their disposable income."

Finnegan nodded. "I can see you have given this matter a great deal of contemplation, sir."

"As I said, one tends to show greater concern when one is present and on the chopping block, as it were." Potter closed his eyes and took a deep breath. "How is it you were chosen for the auspicious duty of inspecting our fence?"

"I am a Pinkerton man."

Potter gaped at his visitor. "You are a Pinkerton man! Truly, I do not know as I have ever met a braver fellow. That simple announcement will quickly earn you no less than a rope for a collar and a fine placement amongst the trees in the town. If I were you, sir, I would inspect that damned fence and then flee this place with all due haste. I would also cease uttering the name of your employer until I had exited the great state of Pennsylvania."

"A fine offering of advice, sir." Finnegan turned his hat in his hands. "I take it you do not agree with all of Mr. Frick's conduct, thus far."

"Our beloved Mr. Frick plays a dangerous game, sir." Potter drained his bottle. "He began with dickering, offered terms that would surely not be agreed to, then moved to dictating terms seemingly designed to enrage these men." He pulled open a drawer and cast the empty bottle inside. "Meanwhile, these dolts sit and wait for old man Carnegie to deliver them as though he were Holy Moses. They do not keen how Frick and Carnegie can more than afford to wait out the winter while they will starve. I would go so far as to say Frick does not keen it, either. If you are a Pinkerton, where are your brethren? If Frick wishes the mill closed, close the damn place. If he wishes to run it with freshly bamboozled bohunks, then let us be about our business. This...damned dissembling and obfuscation will not do, and will only serve to anger the workmen until...well, much more of this, and the smoke will roll from the buildings instead of the stacks. Do you understand me, sir?"

Finnegan licked his lips. "I can certainly sympathize with your discomfiture, Mr. Potter. Sadly, I can only offer sympathy. Such matters as you have described are outside the scope of my commission here. I have been sent to inspect the fence, and the fence alone." He shrugged. "Although, if you truly have cause to fear arson, I can only suggest you drill whatever fire brigade you possess and trust in their abilities, as you would any other day."

Potter laughed. "The fire brigade, ah, yes. I dare say these works employ the finest and best trained fire brigade to be found anywhere in the civilized world. Every one of them a most solid union man and damned proud of it."

Finnegan shrugged again. "I can readily understand how you may face difficulties in the coming days, sir." He motioned outside the office window. "Might there be someone about who could show me around the fence and its general area?"

Potter lolled in his chair for a brief moment. "Certainly, I am of the opinion that every fellow in the state, and, of course, all the school children, should have a proper tour of Fort Frick. Best to see it now before it is gone." He pointed to the window. "Do you see that large shed out there, just inside the second gate?"

"I do."

"Thereabouts you should find Amsted Kemp. He is a negro and very well thought of in this town." Potter grinned. "He has been retained by request of Mr. Frick to whitewash the fence, towers, and other components of the battlements. Mr. Frick, ever the plotter, felt that between his dark complexion and his position in the community, no union man would dare shoot him down while he labored."

Finnegan rubbed his chin. "When I look for him in the shed, I suppose I will discover if Mr. Frick was correct."

FINNEGAN WALKED over the rolling hills the recently installed fence traced around the Homestead works. His guide walked with an easy stride that belied his years. The only certain sigh of Amsted Kemp's age was the white beard that occupied his rutted face. The whitewasher paused at the crest of one small hill. "Was you in one of them engineering brigades in the war?"

Finnegan shook his head and leaned against the inside of the fence. "No, I found myself in the service of Mr. Pinkerton early on."

Kemp nodded. "I was just pondering on why Mr. Frick would have sent you here to check up on this fence. I seen to it being built, I seen to it being painted, I was in one of them engineering brigades. We put most of the bridges back into condition after the Rebs tore them up coming north."

Finnegan withdrew two cigars from his pocket and held one out to Kemp. The whitewasher took it with a smile. "In truth, sir, I believe my presence here is more the result of Mr. Frick wishing for me to absent myself from his offices. I know no more regarding emplacements than any other soldier." He passed a match to Kemp.

Motioning up and down the fence with the match before lighting his cigar, Kemp seemed pleased with the offering. "If you know as much as any soldier, then you know this fence ain't nothing but a silly burr placed under the heel of them wishing to negotiate their contract. Plankboards and nails wouldn't keep the local washer women out of this mill for more than an hour, let alone them big strapping steel men. A couple of pinch bars and some sweat will bring this jest down to the ground." He puffed his cigar. "'Course, that being the case if there ain't nobody in here to defend the line. If there was a man with a Winchester at every one of them cutouts, well, this fence might prove quite sturdy."

"That is true." Finnegan lit his cigar. "What of the dock and the river down there? Why has the fence not been expanded to cover the waterfront?"

Kemp laughed. "Ah, noticed that, did you. I imagine many a skilled union man has, as well. Almost seems like Mr. Frick is expecting visitors and did not wish to appear impolite by leaving the door latched."

"It is somewhat obvious, I suppose." Finnegan puffed his cigar and looked over the works. "You are not fond of the men who have organized into a union?"

Kemp thought on it for a moment. "I suppose fondness don't enter into it. The day them they call skilled workers let a negro into their union will be the day old Abe Lincoln comes back and leads us to the promised land." Kemp laughed and knocked the ash from his cigar. "My view of the matter more or less comes down to the fact that they ain't got no use for me, so I ain't got no use for them."

Finnegan nodded. "Not all men in the mills are union men, but you do not work in the mills?"

Kemp arched one snow white eyebrow. "Can't help but notice you ain't working in there, either."

Finnegan chuckled. "Yes, indeed. Although, I do not make my home here in Homestead."

Kemp motioned off toward the town. "A place like this, them that are in the mills are too good to do much else. I work for the town fixing their buildings. I work for the union, keeping up their hall. I build fences and even dig a ditch if the pay is right. The only work a negro can get in them mills is shoveling, anyhow. Leastways, I get to shovel on my own time and I ain't licking up coal dust while I do it. Negros go into them mills whole and come out missing most of their fingers and coughing up blood."

"Mr. Potter made mention of the fact that you were selected to see to this fence partially because you are not likely to suffer reprisals. Perhaps your lack of association with the mills can be to your advantage, on occasion."

"I suppose that depends on what you consider an advantage to be. None of them men around here are apt to beat me or lynch me for the sole reason it would make 'em look like Rebs, and the only thing a member of the glorious Army of the Republic would never do is get caught acting like a damn dirty Reb."

"It is an intriguing position you find yourself in, Mr. Kemp."

"I suppose it ain't no stranger than some of what you Irish got." Kemp grinned. "Time was, plenty of these mills wouldn't even let *you* shovel." Kemp eyed his visitor. "That ain't the way it is nowadays, though."

Finnegan grinned back. "Ah, yes, matters have improved greatly. Although, I dare say my people have made use of a strategy your people have never attempted. We have gained a foothold in this land by simply overrunning the place. A great frontal assault, as you engineers might call it."

Kemp nodded, ruminating on the statement. "Your numbers have increased a great deal. I often wonder, how many men were there in Ireland before you all elected to travel here?"

Finnegan shrugged. "I have only a dim remembrance of such matters, but I must say, it did not seem nearly so crowded as to produce the throngs that currently occupy both New York and Boston, much less seemingly all of Pennsylvania. I can only assume my kind discovered a curiously quick method for breeding after my departure."

"I am told there are many millions of negros still wandering the jungles of Africa; perhaps my folk should conjure some method to bring them here as you have. I have seen maps that show Africa to be much larger than Ireland. I imagine we could surmount your position in a very short time."

"If you wish to occupy my position here, Mr. Kemp, you are more than welcome to it. All I would ask is that you arrange for my transportation to Africa. I am told there are wonderous opportunities there for hunting."

Kemp shook his head and puffed on the final portion of his cigar. "I have never met a Pinkerton man who thought of much other than shooting or drinking."

"Sadly, I do not drink. That leaves me with little other than shooting to contemplate."

WITH LITTLE ELSE TO occupy his time, Finnegan had taken up a position on one of the long wooden benches that adorned the railway platform. The sun was shining, the birds were chirping, only pleasant white clouds dotted the sky. Enjoying the sunshine, Finnegan had found the book Roosevelt had gifted him in Washington and was some twenty pages into *Hunting Trips of a Ranchman & The Wilderness Hunter* before footsteps on the platform stole his attention.

The gunman looked up to see two solidly built men in working clothes standing on the other end of the planks. Neither appeared interested in scanning the horizon for the train; rather, they were focused on the platform's sole occupant. Finnegan frowned, disappointed to leave Theodore's Dakotas for the far more mundane reality of Pennsylvania. He snapped the book shut and placed it inside the valise at his feet.

Seeing they had Finnegan's attention, the two men slowly crossed the platform and stood before the gunman. The younger of the two, possibly in his thirties and without grey in his beard, offered a smile. "Hello, sir, how does this lovely day find you?"

Finnegan looked over the town and mills spread out below him. "Very well. It is a rarity, but now and then a man is allowed a brief idyllic moment such as I have been enjoying."

A bit of surprise passed over the men's faces. "Yes, well..." the younger man continued. "My name is Hugh O'Donnell, and this..." He motioned to the man next to him. "Is John McLuckie. He is Burgess here."

Finnegan nodded to them. "A pleasure to make your acquaintance, gentlemen." He smiled at the older man. "I have met several mayors in my time, but I believe you are the first burgess I have run across."

The potentate let a scowl show beneath his beard. "It is my sworn duty to watch over the families and best interests of this town, sir. Following that commission, I frequently ask visitors their business. I would also mention that when men introduce themselves to you, it is customary to offer an introduction in return."

"Ah, and so it is." Finnegan stood from the bench, making sure his coat opened enough to reveal his guns on the way. Standing, he gave a small bow to his new friends. "Finnegan Xavier Gilhooley, at your service, gentlemen." The expressions of both men turned from anger and swagger to unconcealed shock.

McLuckie swallowed and took a half step backwards. "You are a Pinkerton man."

"Since my innocent youth, yes, sir. Allan Pinkerton himself brought me into the fold before I required my first razor. Now, I am proud to say, I have made myself of such ample use that his son and heir finds labors for me on occasion."

McLuckie stammered. "Sir, we will not have Pinkerton men sneaking into this town, especially Pinkerton men known to be..."

Finnegan shook one finger at the Burgess. "Mr. McLuckie, I would take umbrage with that statement. I did not sneak anywhere. I purchased a ticket and rode behind a great billowing locomotive as any other man might do. Now, what was it you meant to say I am so known for?"

O'Donnell took a step forward and placed himself between the two men. "Gentlemen, there is no need for tempers to flare here. Mr. Gilhooley, I am certain the Burgess only meant to suggest that your reputation precedes you, as it should." He cleared his throat. "Most of us Homestead men follow professions that require many years of toil and experience to master. As such, we readily recognize and respect another man devoted to his occupation and skilled in its practice."

Finnegan looked to McLuckie. "You have cause for anxiety, sir. Mr. O'Donnell seems quite the skilled politician. He may seek to replace you, if you are not careful."

O'Donnell shook his head and turned a bit red. "I must first finish occupying my current position before considering another. It remains to be seen how badly I may bungle things from the start."

"It is always wise to be cautious." Finnegan somewhat

enjoyed the diversion. "What position do you currently hold, sir?"

"I am proud to say I have been elected chairman of the workers' strike committee."

"An auspicious office, to be sure." Finnegan shrugged. "I must say, it has been thrilling to chat with two such esteemed members of the citizenry, but I am at something of a loss as to what matter you could possibly wish to discuss. If you have approached me in error, believing me to be another fellow, I will take no offense if you beg your leave."

McLuckie arched an eyebrow. "You cannot imagine what matters we might wish to discuss? You are a Pinkerton man, as you have boldly admitted."

Finnegan nodded. "Yes, but hardly the species of Pinkerton man that currently occupies your mind. As you said, you are in a state of agitation regarding Pinkertons sneaking and slithering into your quaint town. As you can easily see, I rarely sneak and I never slither. You have asked my name, and I have given it. You have inquired after my employer, and I have explained. For your part, you have told me you are a burgess and the chairman of a strike committee. I do not reside in this town, so I cannot conceive of any business I might have with the local burgess. As for strikes, I can assure you both, I do not involve myself with such affairs, either professionally or personally. Now, then..." He glanced between the two men. "Taking all that into account, do you now understand how I might not imagine what matters you would have to discuss with me?"

O'Donnell chuckled. "Mr. Gilhooley, I have heard your name many times over the years and have read of your exploits many times. I can honestly say, you are not quite what I would have expected you to be." He slipped his hands into his pockets. "Please do not misunderstand our approaching you. Mr. McLuckie bears you no ill will and would only appreciate the opportunity to buy you a beer at the local tavern so that we may explain a few local developments to you in the hope that the information may be passed on and appreciated by those who have contracted your services."

"I see." Finnegan looked about. There did not appear to be an angry mob concealed anywhere. "I am sorry to report that I do not partake of alcohol, gentlemen."

"Perhaps a cup of coffee at that nearest café." O'Donnell pointed toward a small building just north of the depot.

"I can see no harm in that. For a free cup of coffee, I would sit down with the devil himself." Finnegan turned to pick up his valise.

"You may leave your bag unattended, sir." O'Donnell motioned around. "There are no thieves in this town, only honest working men."

"Intriguing." Finnegan began slowly walking toward the café. "Perhaps I ought to consider changing careers and becoming the one and only thief in this fine town. It is, after all, so very enjoyable to find oneself the sole practitioner of a given trade in a given place."

The three men walked to the café and took up one of the three tables in the place. A squat woman of about fifty brought them three cups of coffee and left the carafe on the table. Finnegan sipped the brew and found it pleasing, while the other two men merely stared at their cups.

McLuckie, not surprisingly, was the first to speak. "We were aware of your presence on the train more than three stations back. You were watched as you approached the mills, and we know all you did while you were within the fence. You were watched with Kemp, and you will be watched when you depart."

Finnegan nodded. "I can only pray you are paying such close attention to my valise."

O'Donnell chuckled again. "What Mr. McLuckie is simply attempting to explain is how vigilant the strike committee has become. We have men posted on the rails and rivers. We have men set to report on any...large number of fellows who may approach, and we are more than prepared to send those fellows back in the direction from whence they came."

"Got to send at least one back to tell the tale." McLuckie finally took a sip of his coffee.

"I was informed that your committee always spared one man." Finnegan grinned. "That is why I traveled here alone."

McLuckie scowled again. "Sir, I do not believe you appreciate the grave nature of the situation here."

Finnegan sampled his coffee once more. "And I do not believe you fully appreciate how little of an interest I take in your situation." He set his coffee cup on the table and withdrew a cigar from his vest. "Gentlemen, you have been so kind as to be completely forthright with me regarding all the activities of your strike committee, so allow me to be forthright in kind regarding what I know of Pinkerton activities, of late." His audience appeared rather surprised. "I recently met with William Pinkerton to negotiate the matter of my pension. We settled on a sum and then dear William asked if I would come to the city of Pittsburg to guard the wellbeing of one Henry Clay Frick. As Mr. Pinkerton offered me a great deal of money for this labor, I was only too pleased to accept. When I arrived at Mr. Frick's offices, he scoffed at the notion of being guarded and boldly announced that he was in no danger from anyone, most certainly not from union men."

O'Donnell nodded vigorously. "He is correct. We wish

only to negotiate a fair pay scale and avoid all violence of any sort."

"His sense of the situation, precisely." Finnegan produced a match and lit his cigar. "Now, then, the following portion of the story is not particularly crediting to my character, but as working men I am sure you can be sympathetic to my plight." Finnegan shook out the match. "Mr. Frick did not feel my presence was required, but if I were to depart completely, I would not receive my rather generous compensation from Mr. Pinkerton. Mercifully, Mr. Frick and I were able to arrive at a compromise wherein I would inspect his newly constructed fence, though I know precious little regarding fences. This compromise occupies my time, keeps Mr. Frick happy, and provides Mr. Pinkerton with a modicum of satisfaction, as well." Finnegan sat back in his chair. "Now, then, you know all I know regarding the grave situation here, gentlemen. Is there any other matter you would care to discuss?"

"That damn fence is irrelevant," McLuckie hissed out the words.

Finnegan shrugged. "As fences go, it seems a fine specimen. As far as what purpose it might serve, I could not tell you. As I have said, I know little regarding fences."

O'Donnell leaned across the table. "Mr. Gilhooley, what the Burgess is attempting to convey to you is that we will not allow Pinkerton guards or blacklegs into these mills. We have already told you that watchmen have been posted. Our men have been organized on a truly military basis. Any attempt by the Pinkertons to act as a vanguard for strikebreaker scabs will be met with staunch opposition."

Finnegan groaned and took another sip of coffee. "Gentlemen, I assure you, I have no interest whatsoever in your labor dispute. I might also assure you that neither Mr. Frick nor Mr. Pinkerton is likely to seek my counsel regarding this labor dispute. There is little purpose to this conversation, but since my coffee is not yet diminished and I have only recently lit this cigar, I suppose there can be no harm in continuing. In truth, I must confess, I have followed the progress of several labor disputes over the years and have always been somewhat puzzled by the behavior of you union men."

O'Donnell finally took up his coffee cup. "There is something puzzling in the way a man wishes to improve his lot in life through hard work and fair pay?"

"I understand your motives well enough, it is your methods that confuse." Finnegan waved smoke from his face. "I expect you men intend to walk out of the mills when Mr. Frick refuses to negotiate with your union? It is my understanding that he has posted notices stating the company will only negotiate with individual men from now on." The union bosses nodded. "Once the mills are silent, why would Mr. Frick be forced into any action as brash as importing armed guards and bohemian blacklegs? Would it not behoove the fellow to simply let the mills sit idle through the winter? I do not know Mr. Frick well, but after casual acquaintance it would appear the man has ample resources. I would surely wager you men will starve before he does."

O'Donnell smiled knowingly and held up a hand. "That notion does not acknowledge the way in which even men such as Mr. Frick can find themselves discomforted. The Navy means to refit their ships so that our fleet will be the match of any in the world. To accomplish that feat, the ships must be built of steel." O'Donnell smiled at McLuckie. "Frick has contracted with the government for plate armor. No plate mill other than Homestead's can produce plates large enough for the new line of battleships." O'Donnell held up his hands. "Mr. Frick has little choice but to come to terms with us. Even a company as large as Amalgamated cannot afford the loss of so large a government contract. If we close the mills, he must negotiate before summer's end, or he will default on delivery. Winter will not enter into it."

Finnegan puffed his cigar. "Mr. O'Donnell, that is a lovely tale, but I have heard its like expounded many times before. You claim that Mr. Frick must see his mills in operation before summer's end. Your opponent appears to be possessed of no small amount of determination. The mills are his legal property. If he wishes to populate them with Pinkerton guards and bohunks, that is his prerogative."

McLuckie pounded one hand on the table. "We will not allow that."

Finnegan sighed. "It is not your choice, sir. If Mr. Frick contracts to bring Pinkerton preventatives here..." Finnegan shrugged again. "I have seen their work many times. You may join in conflict with them, but they will not hesitate to respond. It has been my experience that a fair number of them take up the call solely because they enjoy responding. They are horrid brutes and any one you send home to the Lord would surely be a man we can do without here on earth, but that sentiment will not change the outcome."

O'Donnell appeared intrigued by the debate. "Sir, I would freely admit that the Pinkerton organization has broken the back of many a strike, but those men were not so well set as we are. Mr. Frick's fence will work against him. There are but a few points where the Pinkertons can enter, and we will be in control of all passage. The unskilled men are as ardently with us as those in the union. We will be many thousands against whatever paltry force your agency can offer. We will hold, sir, and cast back the invader."

Finnegan chuckled and knocked ash to the floor. "I applaud the thoroughness of your planning, Mr. O'Donnell, but to what end? If you do manage to repel even a hundred Pinkertons with Winchesters, it will only prove to be your undoing. The repelling of those men will constitute an illegal act. The mercenaries with Winchesters will readily be replaced by soldiers of the state militia with Springfields. Do you intend to make war with them? Is this village to become a sovereign state?"

McLuckie pounded the table once more. "If the militia is dispatched here, they will surely stand with us over some gang of hired Pinkerton thugs."

Finnegan nearly spit out a bit of coffee. "My apologies, sir. What's this now regarding the militia?"

McLuckie appeared incredulous. "The men of the militia are working men of Pennsylvania, born and bred. They would never have any truck with you interloper swine."

Finnegan let out a laugh. "Ah, yes, it has been some time since I have heard the word interloper. One forgets how easily it rolls off the tongue. Tell me, sir, was not your father or grandfather one of those unclean vagabonds?" Finnegan waved one hand at the man to calm him. "Oh, no cause for that, now. We may have a duel later on when we have finished our coffee. For the moment, I would rather discuss this strange notion you have concerning the brave men of the Pennsylvania Militia. You have considered the matter of their involvement and come to the conclusion that if they do present themselves here, it will be to assist you in keeping Mr. Frick from doing as he pleases with his own property?"

O'Donnell shook his head. "Mr. Gilhooley, it is not so much a question of who they may support as it is very unlikely they will be dispatched at all. The governor of this state cannot use troops against the citizens of his state if he wishes to be elected once again."

Finnegan groaned again. "That is a quaint notion. Mr.

O'Donnell. I do not frequent Pennsylvania, but I must say, from what I have seen transpire in this place, it is naïve to speak so. During my last visit here, the president of a mining company and railroad placed himself in the position to serve as prosecutor for the men accused of perpetrating terrorist acts against the man's own mines and railroad. I see no reason to believe matters have improved substantially since that time." Finnegan knocked more ash to the floor. "Now then, I am not aware as to the identity of your governor, but if this state does in fact possess one, I can unequivocally guarantee you Mr. Carnegie and Mr. Frick played a substantial role in his occupying his office. Making use of the militia to suppress your strike may make it difficult for that man to be reelected but, surely, losing the support of Mr. Carnegie and Mr. Frick would make reelection impossible. If Mr. Frick desires the militia dispatched, they will be dispatched, and their aim will not be to aid you gentlemen." He drained his coffee cup. "If, by some strange miracle, this state's militia were not dispatched or they did somehow or other come to offer you aid, I dare say that action would constitute a state of insurrection here in lovely Homestead. I am not certain either of you are of an age to have participated in the quelling of the last insurrection -- since I *was* a participant, let me assure you it is a very messy affair executed by professional federal troops who only owe allegiance to the fool named paymaster." Finnegan refilled his cup. "This road you travel cannot end well, gentlemen. I would advise you pick another."

McLuckie pulled his teeth back over his lips. "Just what the hell do you suggest by that, sir?"

"I suggest you attempt to discover methods that will avoid the burning of this town. Mr. Frick has offered to negotiate with you men individually." Finnegan glanced between them.

"Mr. Gilhooley, we are union men, and always will be." O'Donnell held his head up.

"Beware pride and stubbornness, Mr. O'Donnell. I have seen them place many a decent man in an early grave." The gunman sipped his coffee. "On the other hand, if you hold your pride in union membership so dearly, cede that these mills will no longer be the province of the union and move on."

O'Donnell leaned closer. "Move on! That is preposterous. You would have us uproot our lives and children? You would have us simply shrug and walk away from the mills we have built?"

Finnegan held up one finger and smiled. "The mills you were paid to build, sir. If Mr. Frick at any time offered you partial ownership, I have not heard of it." The gunman shook his head. "Yes, gentlemen, I would suggest you uproot yourselves and move on. Why is it that you Americans are so often so very loath to pack your luggage? Your fathers showed the initiative to cross an ocean and tame a wilderness, but their offspring would have a riot rather than board a train to the next mill town. Why is that so?"

O'Donnell coldly stared across the table. "Our fathers fled famine and oppression so that their sons might have better lives than they. Now, men such as Henry Frick would take that better life from us. What would you have us do, sir?"

Finnegan stared back as though the answer should be obvious. "I would have you show the same good sense as your fathers. When the king or that whore Vic elected to starve the sons of Ireland, your fathers did not travel east to die fighting the British Army. They ran west to find succor where the harlot had no hold on them. I would advise the same discretion. This is a war you cannot win, my friends. I saw many thousands of southern rebels die for a cause of pure principle. As they lay dying, they often appeared to regret the choice. I would offer you an advanced warning and pray you heed it." Finnegan stubbed out his cigar on his coffee saucer and produced his watch. "If one is to believe the fiction of railroad timetables, I theorize my train should be arriving shortly so that I may journey back to Pittsburg. I am quite willing to inform Mr. Frick as to all that has passed between us, though I doubt he will take much interest in the matter." Finnegan looked to McLuckie. "Unless, of course, you wish to pursue your due and proper in recompense for any offense I might have given. Recently, no less a personage than the Commissioner of the Civil Service in Washington suggested a duel to settle our disagreement. I had come to believe the practice had fallen out of favor, but perhaps it still lingers in these eastern states."

McLuckie stared with disdain. "Another time, perhaps."

"At your pleasure, sir." Finnegan stood and smoothed his coat. Well, then, I am off to see if my bag still remains unmolested on the platform. Good day, gentlemen."

# Chapter 8

## *PITTSBURG, PENNSYLVANIA*

### June 28th, 1892

Seeing no reason to present himself at Frick's offices too early, Finnegan took his time leaving his hotel room and then took more time to linger over his breakfast at the hotel restaurant. With little else to occupy his day, he perused a newspaper and sipped his coffee. Just after the waiter had been kind enough to refill his cup, Finnegan noticed the hotel concierge approaching. The man held letters and telegrams in his hand.

"Your correspondence, Mr. Gilhooley."

"Ah, many thanks, Mr. Buford." Finnegan took the small pile of envelopes. "Sir, while I have you, might you know of a book dealer in this city who trades in imports? I wish to procure a recent translation of a chap named Voltaire."

Buford grinned. "Ah, yes. I have read the fellow. Very humorous. Are you previously acquainted with his work?"

Finnegan scowled. "My dear wife finds the man endlessly entertaining. I am afraid I seldom understand what he mocks, which disallows much enjoyment."

"Perhaps a fresh translation will remedy the matter." The

concierge pointed down the street to the north. "For books only recently arrived from abroad, I do not believe you could do better than Stein & Company. I am often astounded at their selection. Perhaps three blocks up and no more than four down Lancaster."

Finnegan nodded and folded his newspaper around his telegrams. "Very fine, thank you."

Due to the effluence of its many industries, Pittsburgh was not a picturesque town, but Finnegan was discovering the place held at least as many niceties as Chicago. After coming from the west, the place appeared a veritable Babylon, with trains every ten minutes and an endless stream of workers coming and going to their labors. Finnegan followed the concierge's direction, imagining the town likely resembled New York City of fifty years past.

The gunman had no trouble locating the book dealer, and had even less trouble negotiating the sale of the very book he sought as a gift for his Molly. He placed the volume in his rapidly expanding pile of paper and exited the store, feeling he had already accomplished a great deal without yet truly beginning his work. In the street, just outside the shop, an old woman stood eyeing a large basket of what appeared to be potatoes. The grey-haired old crone bent and attempted to pick up the basket, but was only able to lift it a few inches before abandoning the attempt. Finnegan watched as the woman drew in a deep breath and gave her best. The new exertion levitated the basket a handful of inches higher, but ended with the basket descending and the top layer of potatoes falling to the cobblestones.

"Here, now, madam, this simply will not do." Finnegan walked to the woman and used one hand to pick a stray potato from the street. He placed the potato on top and beheld the basket. "I will assist you, madam."

"Ah, God bless you, sir. I only require to place it in the wagon there." She motioned to the opposite side of the street.

"Yes, madam, think nothing of it." Finnegan surveyed the two handles on the basket. He moved his collection of papers from one hand to the other and back again before electing to force the whole pile inside the left side of his vest, where the tension of the fabric kept everything in place. He hefted up the basket and slowly crossed the street behind the crone. At the wagon, the quite matronly damsel in distress clapped her hands together, watching as her precious cargo was lowered in.

"Oh, I cannot thank you enough, sir."

"As I said, it was no trouble, madam." Finnegan turned and only saw a flash of a white shirt before he was pushed rearward and stumbled back into the wagon. Not perfectly understanding what had occurred, he first looked to the young man who stood in front of him, then recognized the fellow as the waiter who had brought him his coffee not an hour earlier. "What's this now? What do you mean by this?"

"You go to hell, Gilhooley! In the name of the Haymarket Martyrs." The waiter's thin, pale face spit out the words.

Finnegan glanced down to see a dagger with an ivory handle protruding from his chest. A glimmer of pain came to him. "I will be damned." He drew his Remington and shot the waiter twice in the chest. The boy staggered back into the street and slumped against the far curb. Seeing that his attacker appeared done for, Finnegan holstered his gun and reached to the dagger. Touching the handle resulted in a bolt of pain. He groaned and turned to the potato hawker. "Madam, might I ask a moment's assistance?"

The crone stepped to him on shaking legs. "Yes, sir?"

"If you would be so kind as to pull this implement from me?" He pointed to the dagger. "This here, madam. Please do me the favor of pulling straight back." He grimaced as she wrapped her leathery hands about the dagger and gave a hardy jerk. She nearly tripped as Finnegans papers and his newly acquired Voltaire fell to the stones. "Oh, bloody hell." He withdrew a kerchief and dabbed at the small wound behind his vest. "If that book proves to be ruined I will...well, since the young man has already departed from the living, I am not certain what I ought to threaten." He placed one hand over the chest wound and knelt to collect his book. "Madam, might you know where I could locate a physician?"

THE SURGEON WAS a small man with exceedingly thick spectacles. For the sort of fine work Finnegan required, in the form of having his wound stitched, the man might not have been his first choice. The great lenses perched on the fellow's nose did not bespeak of the talents of a seamstress. Vision notwithstanding, the doctor kept an office on the first floor of the same building Frick occupied, so he was at least readily available. A small amount of probing showed the wound to be somewhat superficial, and, despite his appearance, the physician proved quite capable with a needle and thread.

Finnegan did his best to appear stoic while the work was performed. "Were you a surgeon in the war?"

The doctor nodded and placed his bespectacled face near the stitches. "I was, indeed." The words had a distinct southern drawl to them.

"But not for the Union?"

The doctor smiled and shook his head. "A man is apt to find his position change. Partway through the War of Northern Aggression I found myself enjoying the hospitality of the Federals at Sandusky, the camp at Lake Erie."

Finnegan scowled as the man added an additional stitch. "I have been told the Union camps were unpleasant."

"I would not say it was an ideal existence." The Doctor seemed to be satisfied with his work and leaned back from his patient. "I suppose there is much to be said for finding oneself imprisoned by the victors. We never suffered from privation, only the usual maladies to be expected when too many are crowded too tightly." He picked up what looked to be a bottle of whiskey, took a small sip, and splashed a fair dose onto Finnegan's chest.

Finnegan gripped the sides of the chair he occupied and fought back the urge to strike the man. "By God, sir, there had better be good reason for that."

"I assure you there is, although I doubt a man such as you could comprehend it." The healer took another draught. "Many of the officers at the camp were men who had been wounded and served out the remainder in the capacity of guards. Many originally came from Ohio and I came to somewhat appreciate certain aspects of the northern states." He pushed a cork into the bottle and set it off to one side. "That particular treatment was endorsed by a Union surgeon and shunned by the Confederates. If they had been more liberal with their whiskey, perhaps they would have fared better."

Finnegan began to slowly button his shirt. His chest was beginning to stiffen from the wound. "It is strange you should mention that observation. I always attributed a good part of the southern defeat to an excessive liberality with whiskey."

"Both theories may be correct." The doctor turned away from Finnegan at the sound of his door opening. Through the crack in the door came the bearded head of Mr. Frick. The physician smiled. "Ah, Henry, come to consult?"

The industrialist swung the door open and leaned against

one side of the jamb. "I would never attempt to second guess your opinion, Abel. I am merely here out of morbid interest. I heard that a great killer very nearly met his end at the hands of a hotel waiter and could not resist the entertainment." He folded his arms, looking quite content with himself. "Are you to live, Mr. Gilhooley, or are you about to offer your benediction?"

Finnegan did up the final button on his shirt. "You are both busy men; I would not think to bother you with last words or any other such tripe." He moved his Colt and shoulder holster from on top of his vest.

Frick arched one eyebrow. "Mr. Gilhooley, did you, by any chance, make your way to Homestead, as requested?"

"I did, and made a fine inspection of your fence while I was about the place."

"So, then, it would appear that you may easily travel to a town rent by divisiveness, where every grown man would gladly mount your head on a pike, but are undone when you attempt to get your breakfast?"

Finnegan tried to shrug, then thought better of it. "One never knows what may prove difficult."

The doctor retreated to a chair and began cleaning his hands with a well-used scrap of rag. "I have seen a number of odd stab wounds in my time, Henry, but this is the first fellow I have known to find shelter behind overwrought French prattle." The doctor reached over to his table and held up the bloody and pierced copy of Voltaire. "I could not recommend such an item for intellectual improvement, but it does appear to be a passable implement for survival."

Frick chuckled. "Stabbed in the book, no less. I cannot say as I have yet found a legitimate use for you, Mr. Gilhooley, but you do provide the most interesting distraction. You may recall my attendant, Ridgeway?"

Finnegan began to don his vest. "Your rather large butler?"

"Yes. He was out on an errand and witnessed your unfortunate incident. He recognized your assailant and overheard an exclamation regarding the Haymarket."

Finnegan began buttoning his vest with his better hand. "If it would not be too much trouble, perhaps you could request the fellow offer up a forewarning when he happens to see I am about to be stabbed? He seems capable of impressive observation; it is only a matter of finding purpose for it, now."

Frick shrugged and grinned. "Ridgeway is paid to fetch my newspapers. He is in no way compensated to offer warning to endangered Pinkertons."

Finnegan finished with the vest. "In that case, inform Mr. Ridgeway that I would be happy to give him a dollar for his time when next I am assaulted. It would undoubtedly be more economical than paying the doctor."

"Ah, yes." The physician cast his rag aside and took up a receipt book. "Speaking of just such a dreary matter, will you be paying for the stitches, Mr. Gilhooley, or shall I include the sum in your next bill, Henry?"

"I would be more than pleased to pay." Frick chuckled again. "As I see it, in a roundabout way, Mr. Gilhooley has finally managed to provide me with a service." The industrialist switched to the other side of the doorjamb. "You suggested the presence of anarchists hereabout and, lo and behold, one emerged. As luck would have it, the dolt attacked you, instead of me. William may have shown some wisdom in sending you here. Could it be that you are truly more detested by these malcontents than I am?"

"Do not diminish your reputation, sir." Finnegan picked up his Colt and holster. "Given the opportunity, I am certain the chap would have preferred to murder you. The whole incident was only a matter of convenience."

Frick nodded vigorously. "Yes, truly, that is precisely how I would term it. The anarchist is dead, you are bleeding, and I am allowed to go about my day, taking only a small departure from normal routine. The whole matter is very convenient to me."

"The Pinkerton Agency serves our clients to the best of our ability." Finnegan attempted to sling the shoulder holster around himself and stopped halfway through. "Ah, yes, well, that will have to wait until tomorrow." He set the Colt on the table and picked up his Remington and holster. Putting the belt around his waist, he cinched it tight. One deft hand withdrew the pistol and opened the loading gate.

The industrialist watched as Finnegan ejected two spent casings and replaced them with loaded rounds. "You killed the waiter?" Finnegan nodded and replaced the pistol in its holster. "You shot him twice?" Finnegan nodded again and picked up his coat. "Just like that? Only a small matter, nothing to fuss over?"

Finnegan slowly put on his coat. "Truly, it is a shame that a man in the bloom of youth should die, but I did not choose his path. The fellow was more than aged enough to take responsibility for his action. If he did not wish to be shot, he should have abstained from stabbing pedestrians."

The doctor took a small nip from his disinfectant bottle. "Greater aptitude with his chosen weapon would also have been of use. I dare say any fool can murder a book."

Frick rubbed his chin. "He surely would have been better served attacking me. I do not travel nearly so well armed as Mr. Gilhooley."

Finnegan gave a somber nod. "Yes, well, now that the

existence of anarchists has been established, perhaps you find yourself more amenable to my being posted in your offices?"

Frick emitted a sharp laugh. "Oh, goodness no. I would no more have you around than a rattlesnake. You, sir, appear to be a magnet for the very sort of hooligan that attacked you today. You rather remind me of one of those..." Frick looked to the doctor. "What are those contraptions placed on barns to divert the destructive nature of lightning?"

"A lightning rod?"

"A rod? That is all?" Frick glanced between his fellows. "Terribly drab term for such an implement. At any rate, that is the capacity I wish for you to serve in, Mr. Gilhooley. You may act as my lightning rod. So long as you are prowling about, I have no doubt you will continue to draw such villains as that waiter to you and, by default, away from me. Certainly, the more of them you shoot, the better my situation will be in general." He shrugged. "Along with the overall betterment of the Commonwealth of Pennsylvania, of course."

Finnegan gave the man a skeptical smile. "Naturally."

The doctor began chuckling. Frick eyed the former Confederate. "And what, pray tell, is so amusing, Abel?"

"I only find it humorous that you believe any of this may benefit the Commonwealth. If this fellow sets about shooting every man hereabouts who detests you, Henry, very soon he will be out of ammunition and there will be damn few citizens of Pennsylvania left."

"You exaggerate, Abel." Frick appeared to do a bit of figuring in his head. "I should think the shooting of a mere handful will readily dissuade the rest from any attempt." He looked to Finnegan. What would your thoughts be on the matter?"

"I have found the shooting of a handful of men to be an

excellent deterrent under some circumstances." He picked up his Colt and holster. "Although, on occasion, it only serves to aggravate the situation. I suppose time will tell. What do you have in mind, sir?"

Frick waved one hand about. "Oh, only that you should stay in the general environs of Pennsylvania and...well, make yourself seen and noticed hereabout. Surely any man you encounter with ill intentions will prove to be one less fellow to trouble me. If you are amenable to the labor, I am certain I can conceive of a few errands for you to see to, while Mr. Pinkerton can spare you, of course."

Finnegan wrapped the straps of his shoulder holster around the Colt. "As I said, Mr. Frick, I am at your disposal."

# Chapter 9

## *JOHNSTOWN, PENNSYLVANIA*

### June 29th, 1892

Stepping off the train, the first aspect of the town Finnegan took note of was the abundance of newly constructed buildings. Pitch still leaked from any and all wood that was not freshly whitewashed. It appeared as though the whole place had been thrown up in the last few weeks. An entire town sprouted from the earth along the banks of a fairly unremarkable little stream.

After looking over the small village and receiving several less than laudatory glances from the citizenry, Finnegan took a small note from his vest pocket and reviewed its contents. Frick had scribbled out the short missive so that he might find his way to the meeting he had come to town for. Seeing no need for enhanced transportation, Finnegan strolled up a dirt path that led toward what appeared to be a small declivity outside town. The day was pleasant, and he enjoyed the walk through country that was both warm and green. He had been too long out west and had forgotten how verdant the east could be.

Upon reaching the declivity, he saw that it contained the

diggings of an old quarry with a few scattered shacks to hold equipment. As per the instructions in the note, he walked to the center of the quarry and stood, surveying the stone walls all around him. He withdrew a cigar and lit it. After the first puff, a voice drifted over to him through the smoke.

"A rifle is aimed at you, sir. Leave the envelope and be on your way." The voice had a strange Teutonic accent to it.

Finnegan tapped ash down to the moist earth. "A rifle?" He looked all around him. "And where is your marksman perched, my friend?"

"He is...he is where you cannot see him, but I assure you, he is well within range, sir." The voice had lost some of its accent.

Finnegan looked around again, then turned toward the shed he believed the voice was cowering behind. "If I cannot see him, how can he see me to shoot me down? I only ask, as I know something of these matters. Perhaps you have employed a man who does not."

"I do not wish to see you harmed, sir. Leave Mr. Frick's filthy money and be on your damn way!" The voice now contained a rather obvious Irish lilt.

"Oh, come now, my friend. The least that can be demanded of you is that you earn your pay." Finnegan drew his Remington and fired a round off into the shed. "Step out from there."

A small shuffling sound could be heard. "In truth, I would rather not."

Finnegan fired another round into the boards. "I have brought ample ammunition to do this until nightfall, my friend. How long do you believe your luck will hold?"

"Bloody hell." The indecisive shuffle could be heard again. "Very well, damn it. Do not fire. I am not armed, sir."

Finnegan kept the pistol trained on the shed. "That is a

damn unfortunate practice when one is about extortion, my friend." As the man stepped out from behind the shed, Finnegan saw a familiar face over the front sight of his revolver. "Well, now, though I ought to be in wonderment, I can only say I half expected you. Can you imagine no more inspired endeavor to occupy your time, Sam Rooney?"

The man let his hands drop. "Finnegan, as I live and breathe. How on earth did you come to be here?"

The gunman sighed and holstered his pistol. "How did I come to be here? I followed the instructions you provided in the ransom note, Sam."

Rooney smiled and shrugged. "Yes, well, I suppose I rather brought this on myself, then." He slowly walked over to his oldest surviving friend. "Might I buy you a bite to eat by way of an apology?"

"You surely ought to do something to compensate me. Any other man I could easily leave in this pit as a corpse and feel I had provided quite a decent service to my current commission." He shook his head. "I often find it difficult to remain loyal to our friendship, Sam."

"And yet, you always manage." Rooney clapped him on the shoulder. "The woman who operates the local café here fries a chicken as few others can. I am certain it will sooth your disposition."

Finnegan rubbed his chin. "In all the time I have known you, I do not recollect you ever standing payment for a meal."

"Many things change as the years pass, Finnegan. Since we were last associated, I have come to appreciate the blessings the good Lord sees fit to visit upon me, and that attitude has made me a great deal more generous." He shrugged again. "Sadly, my newfound generosity often leaves me in want of funds. I may have to dip into that envelope you brought."

"That surprises even less than your initial appearance."

Sitting in the café, picking over the bones of the fine plate of chicken the old woman had delivered, both men appeared quite jovial. Rooney waved one chicken leg about, gesticulating his way through a tale. "You see, in spite of your ardent advice, I returned to the great city of Chicago after our last parting. As you know, I intended to reprise my role as the villainous Professor Mezzeroff, scourge of the aristocracy."

"You are still the only man I have ever met who insists on creating fictional characters that endanger your life."

"Oh, piffle. You always were far too cautious."

"The unfortunate product of my wish to live. How did your former associates in Chicago greet you, Sam?"

Rooney took a large bite out of the chicken leg and wiped his mouth with the other hand. "As most men are apt to do, when their firmly held philosophical beliefs have been challenged, they made many declarations regarding their intentions for reprisals, and more than a few unflattering remarks were made pertaining to my character. Admittedly, the future appeared bleak for a short time. After a great deal of cajoling and a small amount of scampering from gunfire, I was able to convince O'Donovan Rossa that our only hope for both profit and survival lay in our continued association. Obviously, my former employment with the Pinkerton firm would mark me for reprisals but, by the same token, his recruitment of me would stain his reputation and endanger him at the same time. We agreed to continue on in something of a mutual aid society for the good of the cause."

Finnegan nodded. "When you speak of your sacred cause, are you referring to a free Ireland, or the avoidance of honest labor?"

"Can a man not pursue both at once?" Rooney tore a

hunk from the carcass's breast. "Reunited in purpose, that fine gentleman and myself left Chicago and made a tour of sorts through both New York and Boston. As you well know, I am often prone to accepting credit for any and all clever schemes but, in that instance, I must admit it was purely O' Donovan Rossa's genius at work. Have you ever heard the fables regarding the disappearance of the Confederate treasury, Finnegan?"

The gunman nodded and nibbled. "Oh, yes, old Jefferson Davis scampering off into the night with many millions and such. Never mind they barely had a nickel at the beginning, let alone at the end."

"Agreed, pure bunkum." Rooney grinned. "I only mention the incident because it illustrates a simple fact: who can say what becomes of funds that have been donated to a rebellious cause? It is not as though the insurrectionists must file a report for the stockholders. Whether the rebels are victorious or not, no one ever questions what became of their money. Once given, every dollar becomes ethereal."

"You are a man of low practices, Sam."

"To be adjudged so by an assassin is truly disheartening." Rooney took up the last chicken leg. "So then, O'Donovan Rossa and I begat to fundraising for the revolution. We were to collect funds, raise an army, and finally drive the bloody British into the sea where they belong. Naturally, to be successful, such an undertaking would take more than a few brigades, and no small amount of training and expense. Many a loyal and honorable Hibernian contributed, to be sure."

"What does a revolution cost? I have often wondered."

"I cannot say what it might cost to complete one. I can say that O'Donovan and I felt the sum of thirty thousand dollars made for a logical point at which to pause and assess matters. We came to the conclusion that we should see to scampering, not unlike Jefferson Davis before us."

Finnegan waggled one finger. "Now, there is the innovation for which you are so well known, Sam. I imagine it never once occurred to Davis to depart before the war had begun. He likely would have been a more content man for it."

"Most assuredly. At any rate, we packaged our ill-gotten gains into three violin cases and booked a state room on a fine steamer headed up the Hudson."

Finnegan chuckled. "Up the Hudson? A wrong turn at the docks, perhaps? I believe Ireland lies across the ocean, Sam."

"Indeed, it does. We felt traveling in the opposite direction would somewhat conceal our trail. Besides, the world is round, Finnegan. Regardless of which way a fellow travels, he will eventually arrive at Ireland."

"An excellent point."

Rooney assumed a gloomy look. "Sadly, even the best laid plans sometimes go astray."

Finnegan smiled, knowingly. "Allow me to venture: O'Donovan Rossa surely intended to betray you, so you quite reasonably felt it would be best to precede him in treachery."

"Who could possibly predict betrayal better than I?"

"Your talents would shame Judas himself."

"Precisely." Rooney cast down the devoured leg bone. "In celebration, I saw to it that O'Donovan Rossa, fine patriot that he was, imbibed a bit too much whiskey and became truly pickled by the early evening. That seen to, I selected the bare essentials and, of course, the three violin cases for luggage. I loaded all my necessaries into one of the streamer's launches and departed the boat."

Finnegan sat back and withdrew a cigar from his vest. "As I did not find you in a mansion this morning, I can only assume your plan went astray at this juncture. Even you could not have drunk up thirty thousand dollars' worth of whiskey in so short a time."

"Oh, if only I had." The fraudulent revolutionary frowned. "While I hesitate to assign blame to another, I must say, the captain of that steamer had grossly neglected his duties regarding the inspection of his launches. In no time, I found myself bailing water as though I was attempting to sail in a sieve. As the boat descended, I was once again forced to pick and choose amongst my luggage."

"Surely the violin cases took priority."

"My choice precisely. Have you ever found yourself in a position to swim while clinging to three violin cases?"

"It must have been an awkward situation, to say the least."

Rooney groaned. "Tragically, it proved impossible. The first case was quickly lost to the current and never seen again. After that, I continued to paddle and struggle as best I could. For a scant few minutes, the cases actually offered some buoyancy, but it did not last. In what seemed to be no time at all, they began to come undone from soaking and then came apart completely. A fortune sank to the bottom of that damn river that night, or became floating material for some damn bird's nest. Either way, when I made it to the far shore, I crawled from the briny depths with no more than two coins in my pocket, neither of which were dollars."

"You speak correctly, Sam. That is a tragic tale."

"Yes, it is truly a tale of great woe. In many ways, it reminds me of the story of Daedalus. A man has far to fall when he reaches for the sun." Rooney grabbed a last bite of chicken.

"So, how is it you found your way here, attempting to

rend money from such an exceptionally tightfisted fellow as Henry Clay Frick?"

"Pure happenstance, I can claim nothing more." Rooney held up his hands. "With little else to occupy my hands, I took to reading newspapers. Several articles regarding the flood mentioned Mr. Frick's association with the dam. I was in the vicinity at the time, so I thought I might take a chance and pen a letter. If it led to nothing, I would be out no more than the price of postage."

Finnegan rolled his cigar in his fingers. "You have lost me, Sam. You speak of a flood?"

Rooney sat back in his chair. "Three years ago...the Johnstown Flood...you are not familiar?"

"I cannot say I am."

"Your current employer, along with several other disreputable millionaires, once owned a hunting and fishing lodge upstream of this place. There was a dam to facilitate a rather large fishpond. During a time of very heavy rains, along with a few unfortunate accidents, the dam gave way and washed this entire town away in the dead of the night."

"Ah, that would explain why the place appears so newly minted."

"Indeed, the village has proved quite resilient."

Finnegan laughed. "But what does that have to do with you or Mr. Frick?"

Rooney sipped his coffee. "I penned a brief note to Mr. Frick stating that I had come into possession of papers pertaining to his personal involvement in the failing of the dam, lack of maintenance and such. The sum of five hundred dollars was requested to purchase silence. In truth, I never thought anyone would appear at the requested time. You could have knocked me over with a feather when an enormous negro walked into the quarry with a bulging envelope."

"His name is Ridgeway."

"Intriguing."

"Yes, a fine chap, though a bit less helpful than I might prefer. How is it you came to have Frick's papers?"

"What's that now?"

"Your proof of Frick's underhanded dealings, the basis for your foul blackmail scheme."

"Oh, Finnegan, how is it you have killed so many men but still remain so very innocent?" The gunman only stared at Rooney. "The underlying foundation of my dastardly deed is spun from whole cloth."

"I do not understand."

"It is a fabrication, Finnegan. Nothing more than an educated gamble. I read of the flood, I read of the dam. Frick and Carnegie were noted as owning an interest in the hunting lodge and, well...I drew a few cynical conclusions based on their reputations and decided to place my bet accordingly."

Finnegan gawked wide-eyed. "You possess no proof whatsoever?"

"Nary a jot."

"Sam, do you mean to say that you have taken to blackmailing one of the richest and most ruthless men in the nation, with nothing more for protection that a clever ruse and a great deal of guile?"

The blackmailer shrugged. "After one has watched a fortune disappear under the waves, he develops a different perspective in matters of risk."

"I would expect so." Finnegan lit his cigar. "Did it never occur to you that there could be dire repercussions for such an act?"

"What can Frick possibly do to a man who has already lost everything?"

"By way of an example, I would cite his sending me here to kill you." Finnegan passed a cigar across the table.

Rooney took the cigar. "I was quite tentative in the first encounter. That large negro seemed an affable enough errand boy. He was equally amenable during the second encounter. Perhaps I overplayed my hand by increasing the requested funds."

"You very well may have." Finnegan patted his vest pocket. "Two thousand dollars, Sam. I have charged a similar amount for ridding an entire territory of horse thieves. It is a bold sum to request for merely remaining silent."

"I began with five hundred, and then doubled the sum with no inconvenience. Doubling the sum once again only seemed logical."

"I can understand how a man such as yourself would come to that conclusion. Unfortunately, Mr. Frick took notice of the steady increase and likely came to the conclusion that placing you in the cemetery would be more economical than continuing involvement."

"And a damn fine assassin he chose." Rooney gave Finnegan a small salute and produced a match. "The voice commanding me to step out from behind that shed sounded rather familiar, but I never imagined it would be you." He lit the cigar. "Rumor had it that you had left the employ of Mr. Pinkerton's sons and gone to a fetid swamp in Arkansas to shoot Indians for a dollar a head, or some such."

"I did reside in Arkansas for a time. My endeavors there were not quite so simplistic as you have heard. I chased a few rambunctious outlaws for Judge Parker and found I had some aptitude for the labor."

"I am certain you did." Rooney grinned. "What, pray tell, prompted you to abandon that land of milk and honey? I have been told the Indian territories practically overflow with wanted men and bounties to collect. It must have seemed like heaven on earth to a man with your inclinations."

"Every era must come to pass. The time of lawlessness in the territories is rapidly coming to an end. At any rate, I was forced to depart when I received word that the lady formerly known as Molly Meagher required assistance in the Sierras."

Rooney raised one eyebrow. "Formerly known?"

"I am proud to say that she is currently Mrs. Gilhooley."

"Ah, Finnegan, I did not believe I would live to see the day you would finally become permanently entangled. I suppose you are quite pleased, especially after such a lengthy courtship."

"The matter did somewhat drag on, but during the brief period I paused to enjoy it, I found domestic life very agreeable. When I am finished with my current endeavors, I look forward to returning west and perhaps..." Rooney stared expectantly. "Well, I have not precisely decided, just as yet. Perhaps a small ranching operation, with ample men employed to manage the stock, of course."

Rooney nodded. "I do not recall you expressing much affinity for cattle or sheep."

"I do not." Finnegan shrugged. "When I am finished collecting on my outstanding debts and seeing to a few small matters with Mr. Frick, I am certain the correct venture will present itself." He shrugged again. "If it does not, there are a great many books I have never had the opportunity to pursue, or perhaps I will take up drinking."

"I have never much cared for literature, but drunkenness is a fine hobby." Rooney puffed his gifted cigar. "Does Mr. Frick truly possess enough enemies to require your services on a daily basis?"

"Mr. Frick has many talents; the creation of enemies is

one of them. Even so, he will not require my supervision for an extended period."

"What, precisely, will demarcate the end of your service to Mr. Frick?"

Finnegan chuckled. "So that you may return to blackmailing him and he may go about locating a gunman who is not a personal acquaintance of yours?"

"Hmm" Rooney rubbed his chin. "When you phrase it in that manner, further dealings with Mr. Frick become less attractive."

"I should certainly hope so." Finnegan shook his head, continually amazed by his old friend. "It occurs to me, dear Sam, you may best look to your own interests by entering into my service. I will only be in the area until Mr. Frick's impending labor debacle comes to an end."

"Ah, yes," Rooney nodded. "I have heard that the mills at Homestead are to be shut down today or tomorrow, at the latest. Working men do blather on so, especially when they are in their cups. I have been told that there is a bit of a race in the offing, the men attempting to walk out before Frick throws them out. There is something of a waiting game in motion, of course. The men wish to maximize their finally payday, naturally."

"Yes, well, when one side of the matter comes to a firm conclusion, Mr. Frick will be importing a rather large group. All brave, strong men of impeccable character in the employ of our old friend, William Pinkerton. Undoubtedly, they will number at least one hundred men, and will be the finest example of cannon fodder either of us has ever seen."

"Undoubtedly." Rooney smiled. "Certainly, you are not suggesting we join them in any capacity?"

"Oh, goodness no." Finnegan chuckled again. "I would hope one, or both of us, gained some wisdom regarding idiotic ventures and enraged multitudes during the war. I am of the opinion that no man ought to ever engage in marksmanship when partnered with more than two other fellows. Past that point, some of the gunmen may begin to consider themselves a military unit of some sort, and that way lies perdition, by way of regret."

"You may have forgotten, Finnegan, but I prefer to avoid gunplay at any rate or association."

"A wise policy." Finnegan tapped his vest. "Having been with you on more than one occasion when shooting was required and finding you wanting in talent, I would never think to employ you in that capacity. I suppose the only aspect still in question is what capacity you are willing to serve, to gain some of the money in what was formerly Mr. Frick's envelope."

Rooney pointed to the vest. "Finnegan, you know, as well as I, that every dollar of those funds rightfully belongs to me. Was it not I who schemed to have those bills placed in the envelope? Was it not I who dared and ran the hazard to receive the funds?"

"Was it not you, who, if not for mere luck, should be bleeding behind a shed now instead of dining in a café?"

"Yes, well, no plan can account for every variance." Rooney sat back in his chair and seemed to resign himself to earning his money. "Damn the luck, what would you have me do?"

"Simply continue on in your current capacity, more or less. You have proven yourself quite creative in the past. That is all I would ask. You are unknown to either Frick or his associates. I will keep an eye on Frick, and you will watch over me."

"What man would not be honored to serve as Finnegan Gilhooley's guardian angel?"

"It is good you appreciate the duty."

Rooney licked his lips. "Finnegan, I would never suggest either of us might be succumbing to the ravages of time, but what on earth might you require a guardian angel for?"

"Ah, an excellent question. You see, just the other day, I was very nearly murdered by a hotel restaurant waiter. Now, then, I have always understood that I will someday die, just as any mortal man is apt to do. What vexes me regarding the previously mentioned incident is largely the station and character of the would-be assassin. If I am killed by a damn waiter, I will be forced to enter heaven under protest. It will not do."

Rooney nodded. "Surely, you deserve to be killed by a grocery clerk, at the least. Preferably, you should be allowed the opportunity to irritate your new bride until she murders you in bed like a proper gentleman."

"I have missed your company, Sam."

"Then it is a very fine thing that I took it upon myself to blackmail Mr. Frick."

# Chapter 10

## *PITTSBURG, PENNSYLVANIA*

### June 30th, 1892

Finnegan stood in front of Frick's desk, waiting while the industrialist saw to the signing of several documents. After affixing his signature, Frick raised his head, showing a wide smile. "Mr. Gilhooley, you have successfully made it all the way to the office without a fresh wound. Did you see fit to shoot anyone on the way here? Perhaps it is best for a man such as you to take the initiative."

Finnegan smiled back. "No violence was necessary. I might even go so far as to say the incident with the waiter will be to my profit. The proprietor of the hotel has offered the remainder of my stay gratis. It would seem he is rather embarrassed by the actions of his former employee."

Frick scowled and shook his head. "I am more than a little surprised to hear that. I would think the proprietor's reaction would be to become aggravated. He is out a waiter; it is nearly impossible to find fit men for that position, currently. We are barely capable of having dinners at the club. The killing of a decent waiter is an almost unforgivable sin by the measure of a hotel owner."

"The gentleman may be under the impression that I was only assaulted, and the waiter met his end by another's hand."

"Perhaps you are more...sophisticated than you let on, sir." Frick sat back in his desk chair. "How did matters come to pass in Johnstown?"

"The...situation has been seen to and should no longer be of trouble to you."

Frick nodded. "I take it the funds are still in your possession, then?"

"They are."

Frick's smile widened to a grin. "Well, you certainly earned your...bonus pay. Well done, sir."

"The Pinkerton firm makes every effort to please its clients, Mr. Frick."

"I should say you do." Frick sat forward and put his elbows on the desk. "Speaking of such matters, I would assume you are well acquainted with Robert Pinkerton?"

"I have known the man since boyhood."

"He is just down the river putting the finishing touches on my army, or so he claims. I would like you to...well, shall we say, I would appreciate your visiting with your old friend so that you might form an unbiased assessment of Robert's work and report the assessment back to me."

Finnegan chuckled. "I could likely offer you an assessment of the army Robert is building you without ever laying eyes on it, sir."

Frick gave the gunman a quizzical look. "Of course, I would be quite interested to hear your opinion."

"Robert is sweeping together the scum of the earth, Mr. Frick. Oh, naturally, he will have a few men of useful expertise who have seen their fair share of desperate conditions. A fellow by the name of Fredrick Heinde comes to mind. I expect Captain Heinde will be front and center for a duty such as this. The bulk of the men, I am sorry to say, will not be of his quality, certainly not in terms of nerve. Most of the men who are to be trusted with guarding your property will inevitably be former convicts, drunkards, card sharps, and any other man who would rather be handed a Winchester than spend another night sleeping on the streets."

Frick raised one eyebrow. "So, then, in your opinion, these men will not be able to hold my property against a horde of striking iron workers?"

Finnegan shook his head. "I would almost certainly guarantee they will be able to...take possession of the works, or fight their way inside. It is what happens afterward that is generally any man's guess in these situations. You cannot trust such a man to show discretion or distinction, which is a damned poor quality for a fellow with a loaded Winchester. Place your fortune in the hands of such men, sir, and you run the hazard of having more than one angry rabble about your works."

Frick gave the matter a very brief consideration. "Well, a fellow cannot control every facet of a situation." He shrugged. "If you would not mind, I would still appreciate an inspection."

"As you wish, sir."

"Speak with Ridgeway on your way out. He will explain where your friend is concealing his army."

"Knowing Robert, he is likely the only man who believes them to be concealed. Will there be anything else?"

"Stop in and see Abel on your way out, as well. The good doctor would like to inspect your wound. For the product of such an abominable society, he is an extremely competent physician."

"He does appear quite capable." Finnegan nodded. "I will see the fellow." Finnegan turned on one heel and walked to the outer office. Ridgeway stood by the door, as stiff as a board. "I am told you are to direct me to my friend, Robert?" The butler held up a neatly folded sheet of notepaper in one crisp, gloved hand. "Many thanks." Finnegan took the note and began descending the stairs to the doctor's office. As luck would have it, the physician was without a patient when the gunman arrived. Finnegan gave the doorjamb a short knock to pull the doctor's attention away from a newspaper. "I am told you wish to see me."

The doctor closed his newspaper and set it to one side of his examination table. "So long as Henry wishes to pay for your care, your health is of grave concern to me."

"I have often found that a purely mercenary incentive produces the best results." Finnegan stepped inside the doorway. "You wish to inspect my wound, Doctor...What is your proper name? I do not believe you ever mentioned it."

"Hastings." The good doctor stood and stretched out his back. "I suppose Henry and I have become more informal than a doctor ought to with a...well, it is due to the fact that he is not my patient." The doctor paused and sneered. "That man would be a damned nuisance as a patient. There is no animal more difficult to assist than a man who is certain of all his inclinations. I imagine it is a trait quite useful in the execution of business, but one that is also likely to land a fellow in an early grave."

Finnegan removed his coat and hung it on a nearby hook. "You are not Frick's doctor?"

"I doubt the man has ever been examined by a member of my profession. No, sadly, his son is my patient, though there is little that I can do for the boy, aside from joining his parents in prayer."

Finnegan removed his vest and took his shirt down a few buttons. "What troubles the lad?"

"The poor thing swallowed a tack. Young children are so very fond of putting objects in their mouths, and this poor thing simply discovered the wrong item."

Finnegan grimaced and sat on the exam table. "A pity more cannot be done in such a case." He thought back to some of the surgeries he had been unfortunate enough to witness during the war. "I assume you have explained the gross hazards of attempting to locate the tack."

"I have." Hastings pulled back Finnegan's shirt and stuck his face close to the small wound. "We have been keeping a close eye on the boy since he swallowed the damn thing. His governess saw him eat the tack, but the child did not take heed. We have been keeping the boy in bed so as to...well, I have no way of knowing whether it will be of assistance in moving the tack along, or not. We have been hoping that it would make its journey without incident, but the boy has taken a turn for the worse recently and I have no reason to believe it is not related to the object within him." Hastings sniffed the wound and pulled away. "Nothing appears amiss with you, Gilhooley." He offered a somber smile. "You should live many years and shoot many more men in the service of your bankers and railroad barons."

Finnegan buttoned his shirt. "You are not fond of Pinkerton men?"

"I have cause to be aloof to a man famous for shooting my fellow Confederates, wouldn't you say?"

Finnegan hopped off the table and plucked his vest from the hook. "I assume you refer to the late Mr. James?"

"I do." Hasting grinned and resumed his seat.

"In that case, it may please you to know that I have also shot several Union officers, a Yankee Police Captain, and one of those awful railroad barons you mentioned. You may also take interest in the fact that, while I would not term it a friendship, I have recently formed something of an association with the elder of the James brothers, Alexander, or Frank, as he is commonly called."

The doctor leaned back in his chair. "You mean to say that you have, somehow or other, become chums with Frank James?"

"As fate would have it."

The doctor rubbed his chin as Finnegan put his coat on. "You are aware, sir, that your truest claim to fame, as they say, lies in your pursuit of Frank James?"

"I am."

"And somehow or other, the two of you were able to move past that small matter and form a friendship?"

"It would be more accurate to say we were able to disregard former grudges so that we might both survive and avoid killing each other." Finnegan shrugged. "I ought to have some time on my hands while I linger here playing guard dog to Mr. Frick. Perhaps we can discuss the matter over dinner some night. You may find the tale humorous, given your background."

Hastings nodded. "That is a tale I would enjoy hearing." A thought flashed across his face. "We had best dine at your hotel. I would not think there could be more than one waiter in any given restaurant bent on killing you, and if there is news of what became of the last poor sot, it has undoubtedly reached him by now."

"Yes, well, we can only hope the remaining waitstaff is not as dedicated to the cause as the other man was."

FINNEGAN TOOK a seat in the hotel lobby and picked up a nearby newspaper without giving so much as a glance to Rooney, who sat on the lounge opposite him. The two were far enough from the other lobby denizens that no one might hear them talking, and to all outward appearances they had nothing whatsoever to do with one another.

"This is a rather nice hotel for a slum such as Pittsburgh." Rooney flipped his newspaper.

Finnegan continued to pretend reading. "I would wager it is preferable to wherever you were taking shelter in Johnstown."

"It is rather difficult to find lodgings in a town that has only recently been rebuilt after a disaster. The citizens always look to their own well-being first. Quite a selfish practice, really." He adjusted himself on the couch. "I had my breakfast brought to my room and it was prepared precisely as requested. I have not been privy to such lavishness since I was a professor."

"My one true wish is to return you to the ranks of the upper crust, Sam." Finnegan flipped his paper. "When I leave here, I am off to visit with our dear friend Robert Pinkerton."

"Ah, Robert is in town? How lovely. You two always were so very close."

"As I recall, Robert took something of a dislike to you at some point, Sam."

"Purely the result of a misunderstanding."

"Oh, certainly. Even so, it will be best if you keep out of sight. You have a great talent for remaining inconspicuous but, I dare say, Robert surely would know you by sight."

"Yes, he surely would."

"What, precisely, was it that caused you two to fall out? I do not believe I was ever privy to the details of the case."

"As I said, merely a misunderstanding. There would be little purpose in rehashing the details of such a tired subject."

"Precious little, between the two of us. I only broached the subject so that you may begin to contemplate a proper explanation in the event the younger of the Pinkerton brothers lays eyes upon you while he has more than a hundred bloodthirsty fools at his disposal."

Rooney shrugged. "On occasion, you do offer the most singular advice, Finnegan." He folded his newspaper and set it on the lounge beside him. "In this rare instance, I may even take it into consideration."

About half a mile down from the town of Bellevue, Finnegan found the ramshackle warehouse Ridgeway had directed him to. Under most circumstances, the place would not have befitted a man of Robert Pinkerton's stature, but all men are apt to find themselves in strange circumstances when a great deal of money is in the offing. Finnegan walked to the small side door of the large wooden building and smiled to the man who stood there attempting to appear inconspicuous by smoking a cigar and closely examining passing clouds.

When the gunman approached, the fellow stood a bit straighter and offered an ugly grimace. He was more than large enough to fulfill his role, and had a smell about him that would deter most men from getting too close. "This here is private property. Be on your way."

Finnegan produced the captain's badge of a Pinkerton. "I have business here, sir."

The fellow eyed the badge. "I suppose having one of them means you do, indeed."

"Either that or I took the time to murder a Pinkerton on the way here."

"Just so you earned it, one way or other." The man winked and swung the door open.

Inside the warehouse, Finnegan found a series of lamps burning that somewhat led him toward the back of the place, past bales of cotton and bunks of lumber. Behind the various trade goods, he found four men gathered around a makeshift table. The man facing forward looked up as Finnegan approached. "Ah, we may all rest easy, gentlemen. Fearless Finnegan Gilhooley is here to save the day and, assumedly, Mr. Carnegie's empire."

Finnegan grinned. "Hello, Robert. I would not have thought you would ever be forced out of the office and into true labor again. Is the rapture at hand? If so, I would very much appreciate advanced warning."

An older man with a grey beard and wide shoulders turned from the table. "I have never known you to take much stock of anyone else's judgement, Finnegan. Why should the Good Lord be any different?"

Finnegan took the man's outstretched hand. "Hello, Fredrick. I predicted that the Pinkerton agency would trust no one but the esteemed Captain Heinde with such a ludicrous undertaking as this."

"Oh, balderdash, Finnegan." The captain chuckled through his beard. "Always the doubter. How a man with so little confidence has managed to live so long eludes me."

Finnegan grinned. "It is almost as if one may be related to the other, eh, Fredrick? At any rate, I certainly find myself enjoying better quarters. Clean sheets and dining in the hotel restaurant tend to make a man confident he has made correct decisions. I might inquire, if you are so brilliant, how is it you come to squat in this fishmonger's hovel?"

Heinde motioned around them. "Hovel? I must say you have become an intolerable snob, Finnegan. I knew a time when you would trade your very soul for a roof so fine as this above. Besides, I believe this dank hole is mostly made use of for freight. If fishermen lingered here, I might at least get a decent meal from time to time. Soup from buckets begins to wear on a man."

"I am not the only one growing soft in his dotage. I recall a time when you happily made do with half-cooked horse meat and chicory."

The captain shook his head. "I do not care what those damned Rebs claim -- that is not coffee and bears no resemblance."

"You surely did not add enough whiskey to the mix." A younger man, clean shaven, turned from the table and extended his hand to Finnegan. "Charles Nordrum. Well, I suppose it is now Captain Charles Nordrum, since Robert was kind enough to promote me for this minor endeavor."

Finnegan shook the man's hand and turned to Pinkerton. "Why is it you never produce any majors or colonels, Robert? How is one meant to know who is to blame for what is about to occur without a proper chain of command being established?"

Pinkerton smiled. "I believe you have more or less answered your own question there, Finnegan."

"I suppose I have." He turned back to Nordrum. "A pleasure to meet you, sir."

"And I am pleased to finally make your acquaintance, as well. A legion of tales regarding you circulates among these hoodlums."

"All drunken falsehoods and fanciful lies, I assure you," Finnegan shrugged.

"Some of which were not even conjured by my father."

Pinkerton pointed to the last remaining man, who wore a yellow duster and appeared to be half starved from his jaunt features. "This is J.W. Cooper, Finnegan. He is yet another freshly minted captain and, I am told, a rifle shot to rival you."

Finnegan shook the final man's hand. "I am certain you are my superior with the rifle, sir. As Robert has already mentioned, my marksmanship is mostly the result of the elder Mr. Pinkerton's penmanship."

Cooper let out a laugh. "Hell's bells, any man who will admit such a thing is bound to be worthwhile to know. I can only assume you were promoted to captain long ago." He grinned at Pinkerton. "I can conceive of no reason you should not sally forth with the brave men engaged in this daring endeavor."

Finnegan nodded. "Ah, well, thankfully, I can conceive of several excellent reasons I cannot participate." He faked a frown. "I will undoubtedly hold my manhood cheap forever more in the knowledge that I was unable to march into battle with you Spartans due to nothing more than a prior commitment. Damn the fates." He pulled a cigar from his vest pocket. "Blame your brother, Robert. He is the man who saw fit to place me elsewhere."

Robert Pinkerton took a seat on a nearby crate. "Yes, about that, Finnegan? How is it that you are here when I quite clearly recall William informing me that you were to safeguard Mr. Frick's person?"

The gunman shrugged and lit his cigar. "Mr. Frick and I have discussed the matter at some length, and he feels that my talents can be of more use in other capacities. Currently, I have been assigned the duty of drawing all available anarchist assassins away from him. Which is why I find myself so far from Mr. Frick and so close to you, Robert. Who better to face a horde of miscreant murderers than the son of the world's greatest detective?"

"I have always held that it was dangerous to be in the same carriage as you, Finnegan. It would seem Mr. Frick has come to a similar conclusion." Pinkerton chuckled. "In all earnestness, what is your purpose here? I know to a certainty you do not have the least interest in assisting the preventatives."

Finnegan let out a puff of blue smoke. "In that, you are quite correct, dear Robert. Do not misunderstand me, gentlemen: it is not that I do not care for your company, it is the company of the men you go to meet that I would prefer to avoid." He stuck his cigar in one side of his mouth. "I have been dispatched here by our illustrious client, Mr. Frick, so that I might be informed as to how your plans are progressing and what strategy you intend to employ to gain control of the works at Homestead. The man has developed a rather singular obsession with the subject. Why a man should show so much worry over something so paltry as a steel mill, I cannot explain, but he does."

"Ah, so, Henry has sent you here to oversee our plans and report back." Pinkerton rubbed his eyes. "The King of Coke must have taken a genuine liking to you, Finnegan."

"I offer rare entertainment." Finnegan found a seat on a crate of his own. "So, if you would not terribly mind assisting me in my commission, please inform me as to how you intend to occupy a position that is, as of now, firmly held and wholly surrounded by the enemy." Finnegan smiled. "An enemy force, I might add, that numbers somewhere around three thousand men." Finnegan made a show of counting. "If I am not mistaken, there are only four of you, Myrmidons though you may be."

Heinde raised his eyebrows. "I am truly insulted,

Finnegan. As you well know, I would never require the assistance of these other three to defeat so paltry a force as three thousand measly steel workers. I can easily bowl over a thousand men with the swat of a hand."

"Leaving only a thousand for the kick of one boot. Impressive, Fredrick."

The captain unrolled a map that sat on the rigged table and held the corners down with a few wood blocks. "As you can plainly see, Finnegan, the works at Homestead are hardly surrounded."

"Fredrick." Finnegan motioned to the map. "The works are surrounded by a rather imposing fence, which is surrounded by the town. The town is filled with men opposed to you entering the works, and thus guaranteeing the safe passage of blacklegs to replace the current workers. Any fool can see that placing a few hundred men about the fence gates should easily deny you entry, and the men in charge of this strike are not fools, per se."

Heinde nodded. "Yes, it is true; the gates can be easily defended, and we would be forced to pass through the town to get to them, at any rate. No, those three sides of the field are not within our abilities, but the fourth side should pose no problem."

"Oh, Fredrick." Finnegan hung his head. "Please say you are only crouching in this damp place by coincidence and do not intend to use that river out there for any particular purpose."

"The whole of the riverfront facing the works is built specifically for the docking of barges. We have already made arrangements for a tug to haul two barges up the river from here. We will dock inside the fence you so precipitously mentioned and never once be exposed to whatever rocks and eggs those misanthropic rollers and pourers might choose to hurl at us." Heinde appeared quite confident.

"Fredrick, they will surely hurl more than rocks."

Cooper patted one of the crates next to him. "We have more than three hundred revolvers, two hundred and fifty Winchesters, and ample ammunition for all. We are well prepared to answer any action by the rabble." The rifleman patted the crate once more. "At all events, once we are within the fence, we can make use of the sallyports and fire from concealment. Any man who shows the poor sense to come within a hundred yards of the fence will be little more than a duck frozen to the pond."

"You may well find yourselves to be a species of duck." Finnegan looked to Captain Heinde. "Fredrick, how is it you, of all men, could arrive at a plan such as this?"

The captain guffawed. "This is the same method Grant employed to take Vicksburg, in the broad strokes."

"Yes, and it proved effective. Albeit after many, many attempts, many thousands dead, and the passage of a year. Fredrick, this is not the sort of maneuver to be attempted with slow moving barges and a few hundred ruffians. You would do well to remember that these fellows you intend to bring along with you are not soldiers beguiled by a cause. Your men serve for wages and nothing more. I would also add that your approach will be well noted long before you reach the docks."

Nordum arched an eyebrow. "Certainly, you would not give credence to the fables regarding the posting of spies and watchmen? We face mill workers, not Jeb Stuart, Mr. Gilhooley."

Finnegan tapped ash to the warehouse floor. "Those mill workers have placed a man by the name of O'Donnell in command, and make no mistake: he is treating the position as a command. Frick has received several reports from foremen and the like that the workers are being broken up into regiments after a fashion. Some are charged with keeping order in the town, others guard the mills, while still others have observation for a vocation." Finnegan chuckled. One superintendent has even reported that a large mass of Slavs who do not speak five words of English between them has been set off to act as a reserve to thwart your impending approach. They have found two or three of them who speak both applicable tongues to act as officers. Oh, yes..." Finnegan pulled a yellow sheet of paper from his coat pocket. "You may find this of interest, as well. I inquired of the Ohio River Steamship Company -- I would assume they are providing you with your armada?" The various captains and Pinkerton nodded. "It would seem that they do business with a wide variety of gentlemen. They have leased the steamboat Edna to an organization with the rather astonishing moniker of The Amalgamated Association of Lodges of the Homestead Works." Finnegan chuckled again. "The boat is to be used to patrol the river in search of you fellows. I must say, it would make for no small bit of amusement if this endeavor resulted in the Pinkerton firm's first naval action."

Robert Pinkerton sighed. "Finnegan, for a man who does not wish to participate, you have performed a great deal of labor regarding this venture."

"Mr. Frick is not overly fond of having a guardian present. As a result, I find myself with time on my hands. Have any of you men recently visited the town of Homestead?"

Heinde laughed. "I have been told we are not welcome."

Finnegan puffed his cigar. "You may wish to obtain a case of hairbrushes and offer them to the local washerwomen.

Truly, Fredrick, you had best look the place over and determine an alternative course of action to this foolishness."

Now it was Pinkerton's turn to laugh. When his mirth subsided, he gazed at the gunman. "Finnegan, by God, you are always surprising. On any given day you are apt to rush into any fray that presents itself with nothing more to your credit than audacity, and now here you stand, labeling these fellows carefully laid plans as foolishness."

Finnegan shrugged. "If a strategy is doomed to fail, I suppose the amount of planning devoted to it does not much matter."

Heinde shook his head. "Very well, then, Finnegan. What would you suggest? If you know of a method to transport three hundred men into the Homestead mills that is preferable to the river, I would surely appreciate knowing of it. Perhaps we could tie each of them to a balloon and pray they drift correctly?"

Finnegan smiled. "From what I have seen of preventatives in the past, allowing them to drift off in their entirety would not represent a great loss." The gunman could see his audience was not amused. "Robert, in the past you have had no trouble insinuating men into these mills to act as spies and informers; why not continue in that manner? Pass five of these fools off as carpenters and get them into the mill. Follow that by five more pretending to be installing pipes for one of the gas furnaces. Smuggle firearms inside tool cases."

Cooper shook his head. "That would take nearly forever, and we would be bound to be discovered. At some point, they would surely notice that carpenters enter but never leave."

"Surely." Finnegan shrugged again. "However, if you could even manage to spirit twenty men inside the fence, you would at least have some measure of security when you approached with the boats. Twenty men can lay down a great deal of fire, if only for a short time."

Pinkerton shook his head. "Mr. Frick insists that the preventatives enter the works collectively."

"Collectively?" Finnegan could not hide his shock. "Now, Robert, if Mr. Frick is so very well versed in the assaulting of mills works, why on earth did he feel compelled to contract with the likes of you?"

Pinkerton sighed again. "As the man footing the bill, Mr. Frick is entitled to some measure of control. I must also say that, in this instance, he and I are in agreement. Moving all the men into the works as a mass demonstrates that we are not to be trifled with, and that Mr. Frick intends to fully exercise his rights to the property. Any subterfuge or obfuscation would only convolute the matter."

Finnegan nodded slowly. "Fredrick, I am not sure if you have ever been hit by a ball. Sadly, I have had the experience and, as I recall, the circumstances varied greatly. Try as I might, though, I cannot recall ever being shot to avoid convolution. I cannot say as I would care to be, either."

"I do not intend to be shot at all, Finnegan." Heinde pulled the only chair in sight to him. "This is hardly our first engagement offering chin music to a rabble of mechanics. Why should this be any different?"

Finnegan rolled his eyes. "Perhaps it will not be. All I can say to you is that these men are exceptionally well organized; they have even gone so far as to close the town's saloons so that no man may make a rash decision. I do not believe men such as these have gone through so much trouble to simply turn tail and run at the sight of a few armed Pinkerton thugs."

Robert let out a laugh. "Finnegan, no amount of preparation can bring about the impossible. There is no way on heaven or earth that these workers can take possession of those mills for any length of time. It is absurd to even contemplate."

"I made an attempt at explaining that very thing to them, Robert." Finnegan tapped the ash from his dwindling cigar. "These workers would hardly be the first men to fight for a lost cause, or to fight in spite of the knowledge that their cause was impossible. Reason rarely enters into matters such as this. If you bring your preventives up this river behind a doddering old tugboat, they will be fired upon."

Cooper appeared incredulous. "And we will return their fire, and they will scatter like chaff in the wind. Mr. Gilhooley, your reputation in your profession is beyond reproach, but how many times have you found yourself on a picket line against factory johnnies? These poor fools are not the hard-bitten gunfighters you are so well acquainted with. A man who hammers out plowshares to make his living generally has the good sense to flee at the first whiff of powder smoke."

Finnegan dropped his cigar to the warehouse floor, hopped off his crate, and stepped on the cigar. "These men abandoned their good sense long ago, my friend." He tipped his hat to the assemblage. "Robert, Fredrick, lovely seeing you both again. Lovely to meet you gentlemen, as well. I suppose we must all see to our duty in this life, and now I must see to mine by reporting to the much-adored Mr. Frick that an aquatic campaign is in the offing."

Pinkerton grew serious. "I trust you will report that we have matters well in hand."

Finnegan grinned at the business-minded fellow. "Now, Robert, this is a poor time to begin considering the opinions of clients. You should not give a fig if Mr. Frick is content or not. It is not as though there is a spare mercenary army hereabouts. I would assume he is rather stuck with you."

FINNEGAN EXITED the warehouse and walked down the riverfront for a short distance to the stable he had left his rented horse in. He could have taken a coach out to the warehouse, but he detested being at the mercy of coach drivers. If a man wished to harbor any hope of seeing a driver again after departing the coach, no small amount of currency needed to change hands.

Finnegan entered the small stable and flipped a coin to the boy in charge of the place. "Many thanks." The boy took the coin and departed to the rear of the small lean-to. The gunman moved to check his cinch, when he paused at the sound of a footstep behind him. He glanced back to see Rooney. "By your presence here, I can see I was right to only advance you a small sum."

Rooney moved into the stable. "It is unfortunate the policy can only be credited to experience instead of intelligence. If you did not know me so well, I am certain I would have been able to bilk you out of the entirety of Frisk's funds, along with whatever you and Molly have set aside for your dotage."

"Swindling a few misguided bog trotters has given you far too much confidence, Sam." Finnegan handed his friend a cigar. "Did you happen to observe anything of interest?"

"Strangely enough, I did. For a man who so often ignorantly nears death, you are oddly skilled at predicting skullduggery." Rooney lit his cigar. "There are no less than four fellows watching that same warehouse you entered. They reside in the loft of the warehouse set back from the water. The large red one."

"Men cannot linger in a warehouse? The place must

serve some purpose. How can you be certain those within are monitoring the activities across the way?"

"I am not certain what purpose the opposite warehouse serves, but it would be odd if the gentlemen within had nothing better to occupy their time than taking turns at the window." Rooney smiled around his cigar. "Since you are so very brave, I have always felt that my abilities involving stealth should be refined so as to make us a fair pairing. I ventured inside the warehouse and had a look about. You are aware that I am always curious as to the doings of working men."

"That tendency has long allowed you to avoid joining their ilk. What sort of work are they about?"

Rooney pulled the cigar from his lips. "I was intrigued to observe that they are likely in an occupation similar to yours. Unless you can conjure some reason lumber freighters should be fussing about with guns."

"I know nothing of lumber freighting. For all I know, shooting may be quite key to the profession." Finnegan shook his head. "I can scarcely imagine how Pinkerton, his valiant captains, or the buffoon guarding the door have so far managed to avoid noticing the assassins next door."

"Old man Pinkerton frequently commented that his sons had no place in the field." Rooney blew smoke about the stable. "Knowing is one thing, action is quite another. What might you propose?"

"Four, you say?"

"Four that I saw. I cannot swear there might not be another fellow or two off napping somewhere, waiting to begin their shift."

Finnegan let out a low groan and rubbed his chin. "Yes, I might very well find myself sinking into a quagmire if I attempt to dispatch them myself."

"The great Finnegan Gilhooley blustered by a number so meager as four. I cannot credit it as truth." Rooney chuckled.

"You have come to believe too many fanciful newspaper reports, Sam." Finnegan snapped his fingers. "What would you think of this? You can make your way to the rear of the building, or wherever you managed to slither inside previously. Once there, you set the place ablaze, and I will shoot down the fools as they flee out the front of the warehouse."

Rooney stared at his only accomplice for a long moment. "You wish to know my opinion of that plan?"

"I do."

"In my opinion, that would amount to both arson and murder."

Finnegan scowled. "Now I am to be lectured on the law by Pennsylvania's most prolific blackmailer?"

Rooney held up his hands. "I only make mention of the matter in light of the fact that we are meant to make use of subtleties in the course of this assignment. I doubt shooting down four union men while a warehouse burns around them will serve to sooth the nerves of the men at Homestead."

Finnegan arched an eyebrow. "Robert shipping three hundred thugs up the river in barges a few days hence is bound to jangle a few men's nerves, as well, but neither that nor this is my decision." Finnegan opened the unassuming leather case on the side of his horse and drew out two sections of a pump action shotgun.

Rooney stared at the weapon as Finnegan locked the sections together. "That is a rather wicked bit of machinery; where did you obtain it?"

"I collected it from a man I killed in Arkansas. That ass stole it from a Utah gunmaker of no small genius. Note the interrupted threads that allow the two parts to fit so snugly together."

"I have rarely known you not to glean some small profit from a killing, and I find the threads miraculous." Rooney shook his head. "Does Robert truly mean to float an army up this river to Homestead?" Finnegan nodded while slipping rounds into his shotgun. "Even I know that is foolish. They will be observed the entire journey. The mass of men waiting for them at Homestead...well, with that much forewarning they would be better off to take the damn fools and employ them in simply building a new works elsewhere." Rooney motioned to the shotgun. "Are you honestly intent on shooting those rather unskilled spies?"

"They are obviously intent on shooting our employer. Well, my employer, your former employer."

"You cannot know that to a certainty." Rooney appeared quite judgmental.

"Sam, we have both admitted to a limited understanding of the lumber business, but I would say that if they brought their guns, they surely mean to shoot someone, the illustrious Robert Pinkerton being their likely preference."

"That is hardly a great sin. Surely you cannot claim to have never considered shooting one of Mr. Pinkerton's brats."

"I gave serious consideration to that very thing not a month ago, but that is beside the point." Finnegan put a handful of shotgun shells into his coat pocket and then concealed most of the shotgun within the same garment under one arm. "Now then, are you to assist me, or do you wish to be off so that you may locate new targets for hypothetical blackmail?"

Rooney scratched his head. "Why do you term it hypothetical? I have the man's money in my pocket. What could be more tangible than that?"

"I call it hypothetical in that you only wagered a guess as to the man's nefarious activities. After having witnessed

Frick's normal workday, I might very well wager that he truly has no recollection of whether he caused that dam to burst or not. He strikes me as a man who can likely not keep track of his own behavior, good or bad, for very long."

"An interesting observation." Rooney nodded, as though a great truth had been revealed to him. "So, you would suggest searching out the overly busy, as opposed to the overly corrupt?"

"I would suggest you open a saloon, where you can only be a danger to your own health. Now then, do you wish to assist me?"

"As always." The confidence man offered a shrug that lacked confidence. "You know I am of precious little use in a gunfight."

"I know it only too well." Finnegan drew his Colt Lightning from his shoulder holster and handed it to Rooney. "Take that and fire in the air to cause a distraction if needs be. Linger behind me. I am in agreement that it would be rather unsporting to ignite and execute those fellows without fair warning. Not that I am wholly above unsporting behavior. I will return to Robert's warehouse and warn him and the others. If they consider the matter pressing, let them see to it. You and I are currently about the business of seeing to Mr. Frick's concerns. I should think Robert Pinkerton and several hired assassins should be able to handily defeat one poor bunch of sods crouching in a warehouse."

Rooney smiled. "You may be approaching something akin to wisdom in your old age, Finnegan."

"I rather enjoy old age and wish to enjoy more of it." Finnegan patted his friend on the shoulder. "As I said, remain to the rear." Finnegan left the stable and began retracing his steps toward the warehouse his ostensive employer had taken up residency in. He walked at a pace that was meant to appear unconcerned. As he strolled, the small door on the side of the opposite warehouse opened and two men stepped out. Finnegan did his best to peek over at them without appearing to be interested in the least. He took notice that both men were walking in the same awkward manner Finnegan had assumed to keep his shotgun from coming unstowed. "Bloody hell." Finnegan quickened his pace, and the two men on the opposite side of the road quickened as well. He raised his hand that did not hold the shotgun to the door guard. "Make ready," you damned fool."

"What's the fuss about?" There was a dull thud when the bullet slapped into the doorman's chest. He fell back against the warehouse wall and slowly slid to the ground.

Not pausing to mourn, Finnegan turned, knelt, and fired off two rounds of buckshot toward his pursuers. One man spun, while the other threw himself down into the dirt. Finnegan worked the pump on the shotgun and got back to his feet. He fired again without truly aiming and stumbled backwards into the door of the warehouse. The door gave, and he tumbled inside. From the floor, he spun clear and kicked the door shut again. He pumped the action of the shotgun and tossed a spent hull out onto the wooden floor. Cooper stood several feet away, a Winchester in his hands. "By God, my thoughts exactly."

Cooper appeared completely confused. "Have you managed to get yourself in a fight with some freighters or boatmen? Can you not go anywhere without bloodshed?"

"Do not chide me too thoroughly before you are familiar with all the facts." Finnegan climbed to his feet and began shucking fresh shells into his shotgun. "You are currently under attack by some men who have been observing you for some time. I returned merely to warn you. Damn poor luck that I happen to be here at the moment they chose to make themselves known."

Cooper shook his head. "Who the hell are they?"

"I would assume they are some of those cowardly mill workers who lack all determination or aggression."

"Ah, Hell's bells." Cooper ran a hand over his face. "You were shooting. If you killed one, it will be the devil to pay."

"I thought it best in the moment directly after they killed your watchman."

"They killed Bartleby? That is a damn shame; the man could play the mouth harp like no one I ever met."

Finnegan shrugged as a few bullets could be heard smacking into the outer walls. "If St. Peter does not find him wanting, he will now play a different harp."

An angry voice could be heard yelling from outside. "You damn yellow capitalist swine! We know you are in there, Robert Pinkerton. Today you will pay for your sins. You die in the name of the Haymarket Martyrs. Come out and face your fate."

Finnegan rubbed the back of his neck. "For a rather misanthropic collection, those damn Haymarket anarchists certainly have assembled a large group of mourners. Odd how some men can only be well liked after they are dead."

Cooper slowly approached a window. "I like them well enough. If these are anarchists and not union men, I see no reason not to shoot them." The glass blew out of the window and showered onto him. "If permissible, of course."

Pinkerton, Heinde, and Nordrum came running up, all holding rifles. "Damn those devils." Pinkerton spat the words out. "I have been waiting for this. The scum are here to attempt an attentat."

All the men paused to stare at Pinkerton, but only Finnegan spoke. "What's this now?"

Pinkerton narrowed his eyes. "An attentat, it is the assassination of a prominent figure to further their cause. I believe they have borrowed the term from the Russians, or possibly the Teutons."

"Robert, we are currently in a fight. This is not the time to flout your vocabulary, certainly not the time for self-aggrandizement." Finnegan moved a bit closer to his old friend and grinned. "I might also mention that it is never wise to suggest the armed men at the door wish only to do you harm, in particular. It can sometimes lead to your compatriots flinging you outside to face the music."

The color drained from Pinkerton. He turned toward Heinde. The captain feigned shock. "Truly, Robert, the thought never crossed my mind."

"You always were rather dull, Fredrick." Finnegan shook his head. "We had best tend to the matter at hand." He grinned again. "Now then, the way this place is situated you should be able to get out the back without being seen from where our assailants are set. There cannot be overly many of these fools. Fredrick, take dear Robert out the back and down the dock; I see there is a boat moored there. We will offer these anarchists some fire. Once they see the object of their assault has been denied them, they may very well quit the field, if we have not killed them already." Finnegan stared at his associates for a long moment. "Well, we had best get to it."

Heinde shook his head as more bullets scattered glass and wood. "You should take Robert, Finnegan. I cannot swim and do not know a damn thing regarding boats."

The gunman sighed. "Your nautical campaign becomes a more sound option every minute." Finnegan gave Pinkerton a shove. "Come now, Robert. As you know, I swim like a fish, and I have never met a man better than you with oars."

Pinkerton looked confused. "I paddled a lass around a

duck pond once in my youth. Other than that, I have never touched oars."

"Then keep the lass in mind while we flee. It may well calm you." Finnegan continued to push his employer toward the warehouse's back door. Once there, Finnegan pulled the large barn-style door open just wide enough to stick his head out and glance around. It appeared as though all the action was occurring at the front of the building. "I would not normally consider making use of such a craft; it is barely more than a rowboat. Although, by your own admission, that sized vessel is the only kind you have experience with. Let us get to it, then."

Pinkerton took a deep breath. "Very well then, unto the breech." With that, the heir to the agency bolted and made for the rowboat at a dead run. It occurred so quickly that Finnegan had neither the time to chide him nor the ability to keep up. The younger of the Pinkerton brothers was some fifty yards down the dock when he came to a dead halt. A man stood before him and only the man's hat was visible above Pinkerton's head.

Finnegan watched as his employer stood stock still with the sound of rapid gunfire coming from the front of the warehouse. The rifle in his hand only hung at his side. Finnegan could not see enough of the assailant to shoot. "Damn it, Robert, shoot the bastard!" The hat moved slightly, and Pinkerton took a step back, but not enough to allow a shot. Finnegan was in the act of stepping to the side to attempt to gain a better angle, when the boom above the dock, previously swung to the side suspending a net full of some sort of the barrels, swung around and catapulted the assailant into the Ohio River. Finnegan ran forward with his shotgun trained where the anarchist had gone beneath the water. When a form bobbed up, he fired two rounds and the man sunk once again. "Robert, I daresay, if not for the grace of God and some damn fine luck, you would now be the late Mr. Pinkerton." Finnegan looked up to see Rooney standing on the scaffold of the boom. "The grace of God and the good will of Professor Mezzeroff."

Pinkerton looked up, as well. He pointed, astonished. "Finnegan, is that Sam Rooney?" The fire at the front of the building grew sporadic, and then ceased. "Finnegan, why is Sam Rooney lingering about behind this damned warehouse? His face grew grim, and he began to raise his rifle. "Ah, blazes, he is in cahoots with the anarchists."

Finnegan reached out and forced the rifle down. "He is not a coconspirator with the ne'er-do-well assassins currently laying siege to us. He is here by my request."

"Here with you?" Pinkerton could not have appeared more confused. "But he is...well, the man is blackguard, beneath even your association."

The gunman snorted. "That is a fine thing to say of the two men who so recently saved your life." He shook his head. "At any rate, I am certain there are preferable venues for this discussion. From the sound of things, your captains have won the day, but that does not mean this place is free of danger."

The three men sat in the very back of an especially dingy café that obviously catered to the local rivermen and traders. Pinkerton aimed one accusatory finger at Rooney. "Sir, the good turn you provided on the dock does not mean I have forgotten the gross misconduct you engaged in when last the agency saw fit to employ you. My father did not build and raise this organization from nothing so that its reputation could be sullied by men such as you."

Rooney was just opening his mouth to respond when Finnegan let out a deep laugh. He finished, and glanced between his tablemates. "My apologies, Robert. I am certain that whatever matter you wish to discuss is of grave moral import. It is only that I am having difficulty imagining precisely what behavior Sam could have indulged in that, to your mind, would sully the reputation of one of the most loathed and condemned organizations in this country. Have you forgotten your father's propensity for dispatching me to... well, *dispatch* any and all he felt were in need of retribution?"

Pinkerton pursed his lips. "My father oftentimes found it necessary to engage in actions that were distasteful, but always the action was taken in the pursuit of the greater good." Robert pointed to Rooney once again. "What this man did was...simply reprehensible, and can only be deemed wholly self-serving."

Rooney rubbed the side of his face. "Robert, I can only assume you are referring to the unfortunate incident that occurred involving Enders Voorhees. Allow me to assure you, that man's untimely end was in no way the result of my actions, regardless of what you may have heard."

"What I heard was an unquestionably accurate accounting of the matter." Pinkerton seemed quite intractable.

Finnegan held up a hand. "Robert, before we continue with recriminations, perhaps it would be best if you described precisely what sort of mischief Sam indulged in."

Pinkerton cleared his throat. "I would willingly relate the tale, so that you might know what sort of man you are associating with."

Finnegan smiled. "I am always pleased to hear tales where Sam is featured prominently."

Pinkerton pointed one more time. "This man, and

another of our agents, were assigned to guard the person of Enders Voorhees, a well-respected gentlemen involved in banking in Manhattan."

Rooney assumed a bit of a pained look. "Yes, he was primarily invested in railroad bonds, as I recall."

"You would be the man to know, sir." Robert set his hands on the table. "While Mr. Rooney was assigned to guard Mr. Voorhees, he took it upon himself to first seduce the man's wife, and then chose to abandon his post to abscond with the woman."

Finnegan shrugged. "I would never make light of such an action, but I have heard of men committing more brazen sins. Somehow, I doubt he dragged the lass off kicking and screaming."

Pinkerton sighed. "The lady accompanied Mr. Rooney of her own unwise volition. We were never able to determine whether or not she was aware Mr. Rooney had departed not only with the man's wife, but in possession of all Mr. Voorhees bonds."

Rooney slowly nodded. "Well, now, Robert, when viewed from that narrow vantage point, I can readily comprehend how you might draw a dim assessment of my character. That being admitted, I can tell you from experience, and I am certain Finnegan would agree with me on the matter, circumstances in the fray are often not as cut and dry as they appear from the comfort of one's office." He held up a hand to hold back Pinkerton's retort. "The facts of the case at hand are near wholly composed of material not fit for public consumption. Mr. Voorhees was an unconscionable monster as regards the treatment of his wife. The man was given to the most horrid abuse and unspeakable violations of that desperate creature. I found myself in the regrettable position of being the girl's only hope for salvation, and would not have been able to continue calling myself a man if I had refused to come to her rescue."

Finnegan licked his lips to fight off a smile. "And the bonds, dear Samuel?"

As usual, Rooney did not disappoint. "What was I to do? I am only a poor wage earner who has always been forced to scrape by. Was I to leave the poor woman without funds and nothing but the clothes on her back? Without something to sustain her, the wretched soul would have no recourse but to sacrifice her virtue, or worse. No, I could not in good conscience allow it."

Finnegan slowly turned to Pinkerton. "Robert, the man is a saint. How can you possibly take umbrage with his actions?"

"Before we begin to build a shrine to him, perhaps Mr. Rooney will inform you as to what became of Mr. Voorhees."

Rooney shook his head. "All I can speak to is what was related to me secondhand sometime after. As was already stated, I parted company with Mr. Voorhees when Mrs. Voorhees fled."

Pinkerton offered a sarcastic smile. "Yes, I would assume you were so hurried that you could not spare a moment to consider the disposition of the man you were commissioned to guard." Pinkerton turned to Finnegan. "When Mr. Rooney departed, in the company of Mrs. Voorhees, Mr. Voorhees rather predictably became despondent."

Finnegan nodded. "A broken home and an empty safe will bring about that reaction."

"Quite." Pinkerton sneered at Rooney. "Discovering the various discrepancies, Mr. Voorhees dispatched our other agent in an attempt to collect Mr. Rooney, his wife, and his bonds before the transport to the British possessions could be arranged."

Finnegan chuckled. "Rather foolhardy. I do not believe Mr. Rooney would allow himself to be interdicted by a fellow Pinkerton man, certainly not one he knew by sight."

"Yes, well, in point of fact, the other agent was not able to apprehend Mr. Rooney, Mrs. Voorhees, or retrieve the bonds. In totality, that matter proved to be of minor import."

Finnegan arched an eyebrow. "I am afraid I do not follow."

Pinkerton scowled. "When the second agent was seen to depart the Voorhees' residence, several former and rather disgruntled business associates of Mr. Voorhees took advantage of the situation. They demanded payment for a disputed debt. When Mr. Voorhees was unable to produce the previously mentioned bonds...they flung him from a third story window."

Rooney sighed and shook his head. "Robert, truly, who can say what might affect the inclinations of such men. In all likelihood, if I had not assisted the lady of the house, Mr. Voorhees would have only managed to enrich those scoundrels before they flung him."

Pinkerton seemed incredulous. "The maid was quite clear as to the details preceding Mr. Voorhees death."

Rooney shrugged. "Maids become hysterical at the smallest upset. Who can say what truly occurred?"

Finnegan waved one hand about. "All this is largely superfluous, gentlemen. Sam, while I hesitate to suggest you are completely free of guilt in what Robert has described..." Finnegan turned to Pinkerton. "While he is not without blame, he was not among the men who defenestrated the banker. I would also point out that Sam was no less than instrumental in preserving your very life today, Robert. Perhaps the time has come to bury the hatchet."

Pinkerton stared at the gunman. "Defenestrate?"

"To toss a man from a window." Finnegan looked back and forth between the other two. "Such knowledge is the common result of wedding a schoolteacher." He produced a cigar. "At any rate, Mr. Rooney is currently serving to support my efforts for Mr. Frick. If you were a generous man, Robert, you would issue him a stipend for his troubles along with some well-earned gratitude. I dare say, you very well could be moldering at the bottom of the river, were it not for Mr. Rooney."

It was quite obvious that Robert Pinkerton was not particularly amenable to the suggestion, but Finnegan's argument clearly had weight. "Mr. Rooney...I greatly appreciate your actions this day. Given our prior associations and what was said between us the last time we spoke...your actions give credit to your character. I may have leapt to conclusions without fully considering the circumstances."

Rooney appeared as solemn as a statue. "Even after a lifetime of good deeds, such genuine thanks warms the heart."

Finnegan let a laugh slip. "Apologies, gentlemen. Robert, what must be understood when dealing with Sam, is simply that he is under the impression that God frequently loses interest in the actions of us mere mortals. To counteract this, Sam feels the need to shock the Good Lord back to attention.

# Chapter 11

## *PITTSBURGH, PENNSYLVANIA*

### July 1st, 1892

In what had become his usual position in front of Frick's desk, Finnegan waited while the industrialist put the finishing touches on a seemingly endless stream of papers. With a flourish, Frick signed the last page of an impressive pile. He looked up and smoothed his beard. "What news of my army, Mr. Gilhooley? Does it rival a Roman Legion, or does it only measure up to a Swiss Guard?"

"Having never served in either, I could not tell you definitively, sir." Finnegan glanced to the antechamber and then took a step closer to the desk. "You will have roughly three hundred men. They are to be loaded on barges and tugged up the river to the docks at Homestead. Their intention is to disembark inside the fence and take possession of the works. Once inside, they will provide a secure footing from which you may import as many additional workers as might be required to maintain the operation of the mills."

Frick sat back in his chair and folded his hands over his chest. "A bold plan. Formed by none other than Robert Pinkerton and his man Heinde, I assume."

"Indeed."

"And what is your assessment of this plan, Finnegan? Is it so foolproof that you have now decided to board one of the barges so that you may share in the glory?" A smile played around Frick's lips.

Finnegan sighed. "Sir, it is one matter to find amusement in the ill-conceived ventures of other men -- Lord knows, I have indulged in it often in my time – but, in this instance, you may come to regret your indulgence. I am told you have insisted that the Pinkerton force be brought into the works in one large group?"

Frick shrugged. "Is that not commonsense? I have often read that it is always a mistake to split one's forces in enemy territory."

"I have read much the same myself, sir, but we are not presently fighting a war, and I can only hope that all parties concerned would wish to avoid the situation degenerating into one. You only require a small number of men within the works to facilitate bringing in a similar number to supplement. I could easily manage to spirit twenty men inside over a period of time. Once twenty are within, twenty more could rush the gates under cover. With forty within...well, you can easily understand the mathematics."

Frick waved one hand. "Mr. Gilhooley, I have no doubt that such a scheme would ultimately prove successful. Please bear in mind that I have no intention to offend when I say that it appears to be a solution arrived at by a man used to taking matters into his own hands and laboring at small matters. There are larger principles and concepts at play here, Mr. Gilhooley. We deal in matters that dwarf mere men such as ourselves, and only bold gestures and actions will measure up. Should I take you suggesting an alternative plan as a sign that you do not have confidence in Robert's plan?"

Finnegan rubbed one side of his face. "Mr. Frick, confidence is hardly the point. Confidence does not stop bullets. In all likelihood, the barges will be spotted from the moment the men step on them. They will likely find themselves under fire the entire trip up the river. When they reach the docks, they will be denied landfall."

Frick cocked his head to one side. "Do not forget that they will land inside the fence."

"The mob will tear your fence down, Mr. Frick. It is a paltry barrier to men who will undoubtedly be worked into a lather after witnessing the attempted invasion. Once you begin shooting at your fellow man, minor matters such as property destruction are of no import. In truth, I believe you will be lucky if one of the crazed sots does not light the whole works on fire."

Frick waved one hand around carelessly. "They will not burn the works. Without the works, they have no purpose for the strike. Why search for victory if there is nowhere to enjoy it?"

"You might ask the same of any man who has become mad enough to make war. It is in the same manner as the drunken fool who kills his wife simply because 'if he cannot have her, no one will'. If they see the cause is lost..." Finnegan shrugged.

Frick sighed. "This sort of debate is often stimulating, Mr. Gilhooley, but matters little. I suppose we may jab back and forth the live long day and never arrive at a firm conclusion." He rubbed his chin. "I would rather be informed of the details regarding the incident that occurred down by the Smithfield Street river docks."

Finnegan licked his lips. "For a man who has employed me to glean information, you are always so well informed, Mr. Frick. I cannot help but question whether or not you might be suffering from an overabundance of Pinkerton men."

"A man can never possess too much information. As I said, I am aware an incident transpired, but am not familiar with the details. Please share them."

Finnegan adjusted his shoulder holster. It occasionally rubbed on his knife wound and gave him trouble. "The esteemed Robert Pinkerton had come to use the warehouse as a hide, as you know. Some way or other, a small troop of anarchists became aware of his presence there. Anarchists, communists, socialists, and assorted other malcontents have formed a rather bitter dislike for the Pinkerton family over the years. The anarchists attempted to assassinate Mr. Pinkerton. As luck would have it, there were several rather well-practiced gunmen on hand to defend Robert. We dispatched our noticeably unwashed assailants and carried on about our business. Well, after moving Robert's luggage to a so-far-undisclosed warehouse."

Frick gave the story some consideration. "So, then, the men were in no way affiliated with the union?"

"As far as we were able to discern, they were acting on their own accord to settle a long-running score unrelated to your present difficulties."

Frick shrugged. "Well, then, the matter is of no interest." He ran one hand over his beard. "It is a strange predicament I am faced with, Finnegan."

The gunman shrugged in return. "As we are being informal, feel free to explain, Henry."

Frick grinned. "I have always imagined having a fellow such as yourself on hand would offer no end of opportunity and utility. Now I have you here and am already at a loss for chores."

Finnegan pulled a cigar from his pocket. "I am near certain another blackmailer will appear shortly."

"Ah..." Frick sat back in his chair. "The mention of such a corrupted character brings another minor matter to mind." He smoothed his beard again. "What do you know of Sheriffs, Finnegan?"

# Chapter 12

## *PITTSBURGH, PENNSYLVANIA*

### July 2nd, 1892

FINNEGAN PLACED HIMSELF ON THE WOODEN BENCH opposite the High Sheriff of Allegheny County. The man appeared decidedly nonplussed that morning, and Finnegan doubted whether the train ride or the duty to follow would cheer the man.

Sheriff William McCleary was a man of about forty with rapidly disappearing brown hair and a boney frame. His dress would have better suited a bank teller, and sweat stood out on his forehead, even though the heat of the day had not yet arrived. He removed a kerchief from a vest pocket and dabbed his brow. "I have never given that damn Frick one reason to torment me so." The sheriff cast a cold stare on Finnegan. "I have always given that imp a free hand in his damn right of way squabbles and coal claim schemes. There is no damned reason for him to involve me in this farse. I knew that man when he was lucky to get enough selling coke to pay for his dinner. For him to do this to me..." The sheriff mopped his brow again.

Finnegan rubbed one side of his face thoughtfully. "A

citizen of your county has been barred from his own property." Finnegan shrugged. "Frick wishes to have the gates of Homestead thrown open so that he may import more agreeable workers. Men who are not the rightful owners of the property act to violate his rights. You are the sheriff in this county; what more can there be to it?"

McCleary sneered. "A man should not be forced into such filthy business. I knew that damned Henry Clay when he put newspaper in his shoes. Now, he calls me like a dog and tells me he wants you Pinkerton scum to be deputized so that you might perpetrate your evil deeds under the banner of the law. Now, tell me, sir: if he has all you low thugs, where is the need to torture me so?"

Finnegan could have done without the man's complaining. It was early, and his arm was already paining him. "Sheriff, you seem to make an excellent point. Perhaps you should have simply deputized a batch of Pinkertons and left the duty to men more...enthusiastic to pursue it."

McCleary scowled. "Ah, that would be a fine damn thing for an elected man to do, would it not? A fine pickle I would be in when it came to be known I legitimized a gang of assassins to have at the town. Finding new employment would be the least of my worries. I would be blessed to escape this damned place without being strung up." He motioned behind him with one thumb. "So, what does a man do when he has been harried nearly to madness? He stoops to the same acts of madness the men around him have fallen to. I have three deputies with me that are decent young men from good families so that the madmen of Homestead will be less likely to murder them in cold blood." He leveled one finger at Finnegan. "You should not be here, sir. Your very presence could be the end of us all."

Finnegan slowly shook his head. "Sheriff McCleary, I

traveled to Homestead just the other day and had a lovely chat with both the Burgess and the fellow appointed to represent the working men. We had a most polite visit, and they did not once attempt to fit a rope around my neck."

McCleary mopped once more. "Do not attempt to gain any favor or credibility from your traveling with the sheriff or deputies. I will let it be known that you are not one of our number, even if you do not."

Finnegan waved one hand dismissively. "The luster of such petty baubles has been lost to me for some time. I currently carry the badge of United States Deputy Marshall. Naturally, my Pinkerton badge is well worn. For a brief time, I was no less than a captain in the Coal and Iron Police, though that appointment ended somewhat poorly." He rubbed his face again. "If you wish to disassociate yourself from me, I cannot say I mind a bit. It is always hard to say who you may wish to be lumped in with. I may fare better on my own. As you said, you fear lynching." Finnegan stood. "If it is of no care to you, I believe I will begin now." He moved several steps forward in the car and took a seat opposite a young, rather nervous-looking fellow. "Do you have any objection to my company?"

The fellow glanced around furtively before shaking his head. "No, sir."

Finnegan settled in. "You are one of the deputies, then?"

"Oliver Tedder, sir." The young man extended a hand. "Sheriff McCleary asked if I would care to become a deputy just yesterday."

Finnegan withdrew a cigar. "Bold of you to accept, young Oliver. I congratulate you. Not every man shows the courage to begin a new occupation when the opportunity is presented." Finnegan looked the young man over. "And why is it you were chosen, precisely?"

Tedder sat up a bit straighter, appearing as though he needed to defend his qualifications. "My family is in the flour business, sir. I often make deliveries to Homestead. The Sheriff wanted well-liked men."

Finnegan nodded. "You seem likable enough; I am certain you will prove yourself an intelligent choice during this assignment." He held out the cigar. "Would you care for a smoke?"

The young man shook his head. "It does not agree with me, sir." He glanced about again. "Sir, you are, in fact, Finnegan Gilhooley of the Pinkertons?"

"I am."

"I have read of your endeavors, sir, and there are a great many stories told about you in these parts."

Finnegan sneered and lit his cigar. "Pay no mind to newspapers or rumors, young man. In the end, they are always proved fiction, or horridly inaccurate, at best." He shook out the match. "What fairy tales have you been made privy to? Am I in league with Lucifer, or merely a pawn of the capitalists these days?"

"Um, well..." The young man glanced toward the Sheriff. "I was told that you shot several deputies in the vicinity of St. Clair."

Finnegan puffed out smoke and waved it away. "Purely conjured, I assure you. No, young Oliver, I shot the Sheriff, but I did not shoot deputies." Finnegan thought back on the matter. "As I recall, I can only lay claim to the shooting of the local Sheriff in that vicinity and a Captain from the Coal and Iron Police. Well, several sundry and assorted miscreants, as well, but that is only to be expected."

The streets of Homestead appeared so orderly that the town assumed a somewhat eerie atmosphere. The only citizens in motion were those with distinct purposes. No men loitered, no women paused to gossip, no children larked. This oddity of nature was the first thing Finnegan noticed when he disembarked from the train. The second thing he noticed was the broad frame of Hugh O'Donnell standing by the train platform. The union man wore a sort of welcoming smile on his weathered face and did not appear the least bit adversarial. He stepped forward to the recently arrived passengers with his hand out.

"Hello, Sheriff McCleary." O'Donnell fairly forced his hand into the Sheriff's. "What brings you to our lovely town today?" The union man smiled to all the deputies and settled on Finnegan. "Lovely to see you again, as well, Mr. Gilhooley. Have you taken up a new position with the county?"

Finnegan could not help but chuckle at the fellow. He was just so damned amiable. "No, Mr. O'Donnell, I have not felt the need to find fresh employment. I would also ask you to take careful note of the fact that I have not been deputized, and that the Sheriff has no intention of placing a badge on any man of my ilk. As you know, I place little importance on such matters, but the High Sheriff is near apoplexy just considering the notion."

O'Donnell's smile broadened. "So then, it is merely a coincidence that you find yourself in the company of these deputies?"

Finnegan held up one hand and shook his head. "Ah, yes, there is another fine point that must be made perfectly clear. I am not in the company of these men and am in no way affiliated with them. I am only a free man roaming the earth as he pleases and would greatly appreciate a firm distinction being made between myself and these assorted fellows. Some of them appear to be boys of good character, but it is impossible to say who one may wish to associate with until further acquaintance has transpired."

O'Donnell laughed. "In that case, I will hold none of the Sheriff's behavior against you. What is it that *does* bring you to quaint Homestead today?"

Finnegan scoffed. "Mr. O'Donnell, I do not bother you with questions as to why you loiter about train platforms at an hour when any honest man ought to find something productive to occupy his time. I would only ask the same courtesy of you."

The union man grinned and shook his head. "You are quite correct. As you say, you are a free man, and this is a country that treasures freedom. Please be about whatever business pleases you." O'Donnell turned to the sweaty Sheriff. "And is there any way in which I might be of assistance to you, sir?"

McCleary did his best to stand up straight and not let his voice crack. "Uh, yes, Mr. O'Donnell. Mr. Frick has asked... well, rather, Mr. Frick has lodged a complaint regarding the current status of the mills and has asked that I...as the Sheriff, of course, well, he has asked that I come here with a few deputies and secure the place. To assuage any doubts Mr. Frick might have regarding the safety of the property."

O'Donnell nodded somberly as he loomed over the much smaller Sheriff. "Ah, yes, I can readily understand how Mr. Frick might become anxious regarding the disposition of his property. When a large set of mills is not in use, there is always the worry that some miscreant or group of miscreants will use a moment such as this as an occasion to exercise their sticky fingers. Fortunately, for Mr. Frick, the notion occurred to the town council long before Mr. Frick's anxiety got the better of him." O'Donnell motioned toward the millworks. "As the men who built this place, we take a keen interest in protecting it. If you would care to have a look about the place, I would be honored to serve as your guide and answer any questions you might have, Sheriff."

McCleary passed his kerchief over his head once more. "Yes, that would be fine, sir."

"You will find that any honest man with honest intentions is warmly greeted in this town." O'Donnell turned to Finnegan. "Has that not been your experience, Mr. Gilhooley?"

"I could not say, Mr. O'Donnell; I have never been an honest man and could not begin to conceive of what an honest intention might resemble." The gunman motioned toward the town. "Please lead on, sir. I would be less than truthful if I said I have not been rather looking forward to this. It is not every day a chap gets to see the man who is accused of stealing something so massive as a millworks give the local Sheriff a tour of that same property."

O'Donnell shook his head ruefully. "Mr. Gilhooley, no man in his right mind would accuse me of stealing the millworks. Any fool can see it standing down there by the river, precisely where Mr. Frick's superintendent left it."

Finnegan laughed. "By God, I hope you are not shot or hanged due to this foolishness. It would be a pity if the one fellow with a sense of humor in the county were to perish."

"From your lips to God's ear, sir." O'Donnell turned and began leading the group toward the town. As they walked the streets, Finnegan noticed that the local saloons all remained closed. There were no visible signs of an insurrection. Nothing more than an exceptionally bland town holiday appeared in the offing.

Finnegan strolled next to O'Donnell. Neither man paid much attention to the Sheriff or his deputies as they made their way toward the millwork's main gate. "Mr. O'Donnell, I am told several other steel workers' unions have walked out in sympathy with your plight."

O'Donnell nodded. "One working man is a brother to another, I suppose. What improves the lot of one, improves the lot of many."

"I have also been told that donations from various anarchist groups abound."

O'Donnell stopped and turned to the gunman. "Mr. Gilhooley, I will make that matter very clear to you right now: we have no anarchists among us, and never will. We have no common cause with the anarchists or anyone who would make use of brute violence to gain their aspirations. We are not bomb throwers, sir. We are workingmen, asking only for what is fair." O'Donnell pointed back to the train depot. "Just yesterday, a collection of those unwashed vagabonds attempted to enter this town with the intention of distributing the same filthy and debilitating pamphlets they always drag along with them. They were told, in no uncertain terms, to either board the next train or ride a different type of rail from this place."

"My respect for you increases by the minute, Mr. O'Donnell." Finnegan resumed walking. "I have no great love of anarchists, although they do produce the most singular entertainment from time to time."

"I suppose you might look on the matter in that light." O'Donnell glanced over at his companion. "I am told you were instrumental in the hanging of the Haymarket bombers."

"They were a rare breed. Never have so many men labored so diligently to see themselves hanged. I can hardly take credit for the affair."

"I am also told you were instrumental in the hanging of the Molly Maguires."

Finnegan shook his head. "I rather liked the one and only Molly I ever had cause to speak with. If the choice had been left to me, I would have readily let the fellow walk free. You should not believe everything you are told, Mr. O'Donnell."

"I do not. That is why I broached the topic."

"I must say that you make for rather good company, Mr. O'Donnell. Perhaps when all this mischief is at an end, we should go on a bit of a junket together. I have been meaning to travel to merry old England so that I might see that large clock tower called Big Ben and possibly shoot Queen Vic and her Kraut concubine. While I am about my business, you could travel north to Scotland and have it out with Mr. Carnegie. You would likely not even break a sweat giving him what for. I am told he is of rather diminutive stature."

They came to the main gate. "It is a pity we find ourselves on opposite sides of this matter, Mr. Gilhooley. I rather enjoy your company, as well." O'Donnell turned to the sheriff, who had been ignored during the entirety of the trip. The union man waved a hand in reference to the thirty or forty of his fellow steel workers who stood at neat attention in front of the plank boards. "As you can see, Sheriff McCleary, Mr. Frick's property could not be better guarded. You will find sentries of this number and quality on watch at any and all possible points of entry to the mills. I can assure you, no man who was not employed at these mills when they were shut down could possibly gain access to the grounds in any way."

"Thank heavens we have gained that assurance," Finnegan grinned, and took a cigar from his vest. "Now this Sheriff will regain the ability to sleep through the night. Until now, he was all tossing and turning with worry that some damn blackleg might sneak through your pickets and make off with Mr. Potter's favorite inkwell."

O'Donnell placed his hands in his pockets and appeared quite at ease. "Mr. Potter need not worry over the disposition of his ink. As superintendent, he may come and go as freely as he wishes. As I said, any man who worked here ten days past may visit as they see fit." He shrugged. "Steel mills are dangerous places, Mr. Gilhooley; it is simply not safe for a man who is not a skilled steelman to linger about this place."

McCleary took in a deep breath. "I wish to inspect the interior of the works, along with my deputies."

O'Donnell looked to the collection of decent young men from decent families. "As I said, Sheriff McCleary, a steel mill can be a treacherous place for those who are not experienced. As a fellow with no small amount of experience, I am more than willing to give you a full tour of the works, but I will have to insist that these saplings remain outside the gate. For their own safety, of course."

Finnegan lit his cigar. "I, myself, am a man of no small experience, Mr. O'Donnell. Might I be privy to a tour, as well?"

"You have knowledge of steel mills, sir?"

"I have extensive knowledge of the uses for steel. I would go so far as to say the manipulation of steel has been the pursuit of my entire life."

O'Donnell shook his head again. "Very well, sir. You may accompany us."

The union man led the way past his fellow workers. Finnegan made sure to tip his hat as he passed. Inside the fence, O'Donnell made a great show of pointing out the several large smelting plants and various rail lines that crisscrossed the works. The Homestead mills were no small affair, and it took some time for them to circle all the way to the river where Finnegan could see the docks stretching out into the black water of the Monongahela. The lines of planks appeared quite exposed, a lonely place to find oneself. O'Donnell did not seem to find much interest in the river, so they passed over it quickly. After making a large circle, the three men came back to the main gate and emerged to find McCleary's deputies still nervously standing opposite the union picket.

Finnegan surveyed the deputies. "It is all right, men. Mr. O'Donnell has shown us the works and confirmed that no one has made off with them in the last fortnight. There will be no need to form a posse to track down any of the furnaces." The deputies stared back without the slightest sign of humor. "Mr. O'Donnell, there is not one man in this town who appears capable of appreciating a proper jest. If you have no objections, I would prefer to return to the train depot so that I might depart. I cannot tolerate such a dreary atmosphere."

O'Donnell, Finnegan, McCleary, and all the deputies reascended the hill to the train depot. O'Donnell seemed very pleased with himself. McCleary and the deputies seemed unspeakably relieved to be on their way. Finnegan only looked bored. As they approached the station, the most recently arrived train was just pulling in and belching smoke and steam as the engineer brought the great heap to a halt. The union man and the gunman stood next to each other on the platform.

"It is almost a pity I will not be able to take you up on your invitation to visit London, Mr. Gilhooley. I would very much like to see that great city, but I expect to be rather fast friends with Mr. Carnegie again soon, and I doubt my wife would authorize such a voyage unless I could show good cause."

"Well..." Finnegan gave an idle kick to a small rock on the wooden platform. "It might be best to wait and see how events transpire before we make any definite declarations." Finnegan's eyes narrowed and he formed a scowl as he stared at the disembarking passengers. "Oh, bloody hell. Mr. O'Donnell, I fear we are about to discover another matter in which we are in complete agreement." The gunman nodded toward three women who had just stepped from the train carriage. They wore very simple black dresses with black ribbons holding their hair back. Each carried a large bundle of what were obviously flyers to be distributed about town.

O'Donnell cocked his head to one side. "Are they some sort of church women?"

"Quite the opposite, sir. Those rather bland harpies are the advance guard of that which you have been hoping to avoid. They are no less than what might be called the informal ladies' auxiliary of the anarchist cause. They intend to plaster those damnable missives about this place and, if possible, incite a riot." He shook his head. "I assure you, they may prove far more dangerous to your cause than ten times their number in Pinkertons."

"Damn it to hell." O'Donnell ran a hand over his face. "What am I meant to do to chase off women? It is not as if I can manhandle them." He turned back to a sworn officer. "Sheriff McCleary, certainly you and your deputies could convince them to board the train once again without causing an unnecessary scene?"

The look on the Sheriff's face showed he was not in the mood for doing favors. "They are breaking no law I am aware of, Mr. O'Donnell."

"They intend to disrupt the public peace." O'Donnell raised his eyebrows. "Is that not enough for you to merely ask them to be on their way?"

"When they are seen to perform an act that is a disturbance to the public peace, I will make a fresh assessment." He shrugged. "As I am about to depart on the very train you see there, I doubt I will be having much of anything to do with that lot." He motioned to the deputies behind him. "Young men, we should find our seats. That engineer appears intent on a short visit here." The Sheriff and his less-than-merry men walked to the closest Pullman car.

"I cannot simply allow those rabblerousers to wander the town. We have done our best to keep any foolishness to a minimum, but there is no way I can be certain they will not accrue some followers. To allow anarchists into this town presently is to introduce madness into our midst."

Finnegan held up one hand. "Calm yourself, Mr. O'Donnell. Take comfort in the knowledge that the female of this particular species is, at least, less given to violent action than their male counterpart. They have also very likely been well-inculcated to expect men such as myself to herd them about." Finnegan sighed and shrugged toward the three women. "I will accompany you, and we will convince them to board the train once more. Keep your wits about you and do not allow them to unsettle you into a rash act. This kind dearly loves to martyr themselves a bit."

The two men crossed the platform to where the women lingered, fiddling with their frocks and preparing to enter the town. O'Donnell, small town gentleman that he was, stepped to the women first and then appeared to become rather befuddled as to what his opening statement might be. Eventually, he blurted what sounded more like an invitation than a warning. "Welcome to Homestead, ladies. Might I be of assistance?"

The woman in the middle, who was exceptionally thin and had a face as narrow as a hatchet blade, cast a deriding glance toward the union man. "We are in need of no assistance and are quite capable of finding our own way about this place, sir. Please, do not trouble yourself further." She turned to leave and only stopped when Finnegan stepped in front of her. "Sir, this is a public train station; I would ask you to clear the way."

Finnegan groaned and produced one of his many badges. "Madam, there is nothing public whatsoever about this station. This platform and building are owned by the railroad, and I am an agent of the railroad." The woman opened her mouth to offer a rebuke, but Finnegan cut her off. "There is no need to burden my ears with some sort of retort or rant, madam. I assure you, in my time, I have heard any given benediction regarding the rights of the masses you might be intent on offering, and I can also assure you that I am more than familiar with the drivel scribbled upon the pages of those bundles. There is no need for obfuscation between us. I know perfectly well what you and your associates are intent on attempting here, and you know perfectly well that I will not allow it. Now then, for the greater good of the town and for your own safety, I would ask you to please board the train that is making ready to depart so that you may return to Pittsburg." Finnegan licked his lips and waited for the lady's answer.

The woman stood to her full height and offered a somewhat worrisome stare. "And what do you propose to do if I will not board the train?"

"As a gentleman, I will assist you onto the train, madam." Finnegan placed one arm to the rear of the lady and motioned to the train with his other. The woman nodded and turned toward the end of the platform, seemingly acquiescing to the suggestion. Just as Finnegan was stepping forward to guide the lady, she turned and smashed the bundle of pamphlets into his shoulder, remarkably near where he had been stabbed. The weight of the bundle and the speed of the impact knocked the wind from the gunman, and he fell to the platform on his knees. "Oh, bloody hell." Before he knew what had occurred, the other two women leapt toward him and joined the fray by pummeling him about the head and back with their bundles. At some point, one of the bundles broke loose and the platform was covered in anarchist literature. O'Donnell stood still as a statue watching events unfold. The women screamed invective, and Finnegan was lowered to his hands and knees. Matters appeared bleak for the Pinkerton until he fought his Colt free from its shoulder holster and fired a round off into the platform. The women leapt back as quickly as they had attacked.

O'Donnell stared at the Pinkerton, who remained on his hands and knees. "Finnegan, are you all right?"

Very slowly, the gunman raised himself up from the rough-cut boards and smoothed his frock coat with one hand. That done, he looked to the three women and leveled the Colt on them. "If you damn witches do not get onto that damn train, I swear to the Lord our God, I will murder you three and cast your bullet-riddled bodies under the wheels." He cocked back the hammer on the revolver. "Be gone, damn you!"

The three anarchist ladies rapidly came to the conclusion that they had pushed the Pinkerton's goodwill too far. They dropped the two bundles that remained intact and fled to the relative safety of the nearest Pullman car. O'Donnell took a tentative step toward the gunman. "Finnegan, your nose is bleeding and your ear is turning a bit purple. We have a doctor in town, if you..."

Finnegan turned to the union man, his eyes ablaze. "Mr. O'Donnell, mustering the control to not dispatch those evil crones has taxed my last nerve." He closed his eyes and took a few deep breaths. "My apologies." He wiped some of the blood from his nose. "Being accosted without offering acknowledgment in kind has unsettled my disposition." He uncocked the Colt and returned it to its holster.

O'Donnell nervously moved his weight from one foot to the other. "For a brief instant, I truly wondered if you might not shoot them, Finnegan."

The gunman smoothed his coat once again. "I still may." He took one step toward the train and stopped. "Mr. O'Donnell, what time will the next train be arriving?"

"There will undoubtedly be one within the next two hours."

Finnegan removed a kerchief from his pocket and began dabbing his nose. "In that case, I believe I shall remain here until another conveyance presents itself. I would truly relish revenging myself this day, but it is likely not a wise notion to do so while the Sheriff and his deputies reside on the very same train."

# Chapter 13

## *PITTSBURG, PENNSYLVANIA*

### June 3rd, 1892

Frick wiped away the tears that had formed around the edge of his eyes as he laughed. Finnegan pursed his lips and waited for the man to regain his composure. All through the tale of the anarchist ladies' brigade, the industrialist had suffered from fits of mirth and even felt the need to pound one fist on the desk. Finnegan groaned and adjusted his shoulder holster so that the reinjured wound would not bother. "I am gladdened to see that I once again have provided you with entertainment, Mr. Frick."

The industrialist slowly caught his breath and looked up at the gunman. "You are not incorrect on that score, Finnegan. First a waiter and now a damned knitting circle. At this rate, I would fully expect a child or a small puppy to finally spell your doom." He began to guffaw again.

"Yes, well, it is always hard to say what may or may not pose a danger to a man. At all events, I did manage to persuade that wretched trio to depart, and their poisonous cargo was left on the platform and disposed of by Mr. O'Donnell. He will have his men keep an eye out for any of that insurrectionist type who might present themselves in the future."

Frick stared across the desk and wiped his eyes once again. "Oh, that is a damned fine tale, Finnegan. I do not believe I have ever quite heard the like of it." The industrialist assumed a look that the gunman did not quite care for. "It sounds as if you are becoming rather fast friends with Mr. O'Donnell."

"I do not know if I would frame it precisely as all that." Finnegan shrugged. "He makes for rather pleasant company compared to sheriffs or deputies. It is hard to credit how a man such as that can be doing something so unfathomably stupid."

Frick licked his lips. "Perhaps he could yet develop intelligence. He might yet see the light if a man he knew and respected was in the lead as the Pinkertons departed the barges."

Finnegan shook his head, obviously giving the suggestion no consideration, whatsoever. "We have already been over that ground, Henry. I am not a preventative and have no interest in assuming the duties of one." He smiled. "At best, Mr. O'Donnell might invite me into the mills. The other three hundred idiots would surely be asked to leave."

Frick tapped one finger on his chin. "Simply having Finnegan Gilhooley in the vanguard might be enough to make those spoiled brats scatter."

The gunman chuckled and shook his head. "If that is the case, I freely give my permission for another man to impersonate me. Only O'Donnell would recognize me."

Frick raised an eyebrow. "What would it take to put you on that boat?"

"More than you would offer."

The industrialist appeared to enjoy the dare. "Oh,

perhaps not. Let us consider a few minor items. You are recently married, and I have it on good account that you are in the process of building a firm foundation so that you and your blushing bride might live suitably. What number might convince a fellow in that situation that the prize was worth the risk?"

"As I said, more than you would offer."

"Hmm..." Frick rubbed his hands together. "Naturally, I must consider the added benefits this investment may gain me. All the while accounting for the glee I might gain by including a man like you in an action such as this. It is difficult to set a price on such a matter."

"Far simpler to ignore the subject, then."

"Oh, but a mercenary can always be had for a price. Even if that price is extravagant."

"I am not a mercenary."

"I will pay you ten thousand dollars to man one of the barges."

Finnegan swallowed and stared at the industrialist, trying to gauge if the man was serious in his offer. "Ten thousand?"

"I believe we can both agree that is a fine amount of money for nothing more than a boat ride."

Finnegan licked his lips. "You would pay that amount for me to do nothing more than...place myself on one of the barges?"

Frick held up his hands and appeared as though he had nothing to hide. "To receive that sum, all you need do is to ride one of the barges down the river and enter the mills at Homestead. I do not care what manner you conduct yourself in or what kind of fight you put up. It is worth that sum to me... well, on occasion, a man must spend some money on pure amusement. If not, what would be the purpose in having it?"

Finnegan rubbed his chin. "I will consider your offer."

"Oh, I am certain you will. I believe ten thousand would offer you and your betrothed ample security."

"It would." The gunman rubbed his chin a bit more. "Although my wife was quite specific in her requiring that I return to her."

"If you should perish it is not as if the woman could chide you."

FINNEGAN UNLOCKED the door to his hotel room and stepped inside. Swinging the door shut, he turned toward the bed where Sam Rooney reposed, appearing quite serene. The gunman rubbed his eyes. "Sam, I realize you have always possessed great facility with locks, but why on earth did you lock the door once again after entering?"

Rooney opened one eye. "I have many enemies. I cannot run the risk of one of them rushing in here unobstructed. How would I ever get any rest?"

"If no one saw you enter, how would your enemy know to strike here?"

Rooney shrugged in his supine position. "Very well, then: I locked the door to avoid ambush from your enemies. Between the current labor struggle and our mutually poor reputations, it is next to impossible to find a safe place to nap in this town."

"On that we are agreed." Finnegan took the room's one and only chair. He removed his hat and sighed deeply. "I have begun to consider whether or not returning to Pennsylvania was a mistake."

Rooney sneered at the very thought. "The last time we

were partnered in this strange land of coal and iron, the endeavor proved quite lucrative."

"And this time may prove out similarly." Finnegan removed two cigars from his pocket and tossed one onto Rooney's chest. "Frick has offered me ten thousand if I will ride along with the other Pinkertons on their doomed cruise up the river."

Rooney flung open his eyes and sat up on the bed, catching the rapidly falling cigar with one hand. "Finnegan, that is a damn fine offer."

"It is extravagant. It is tempting. I am not certain I would call it fine."

"Do not be daft." Rooney shook his head. "No man in his right mind could possibly pass up such a fortune. It must be by far the finest offer you have ever received. The man wishes to make you rich."

Finnegan sighed. "Frick does not wish to make me rich. He wishes to gain a bit of amusement from my hideous death. It may not be going too far to say that any Pinkerton traveling up that river will not return. What good is money if I am dead?"

Rooney sparked a match for his cigar. "Strange, I believe that is the first time I have ever heard you make mention of dying as a possibility."

"Age and matrimony change a man's perspective."

"Thank heaven I have not been thus affected." Rooney grinned around the cigar. "What are the specific terms Frick offered? Your trouble, Finnegan, is that you so often tend to play fair in matters concerning oaths and agreements. I assure you, Frick has never played a man fair in his life. Perhaps it is time you returned the favor."

Finnegan thought back on the offer. "Frick stated that I

must board one of the barges and enter the works by way of the river."

"I would suggest you discover a method for fulfilling those terms -- without the hoped-for maiming and death, of course."

Finnegan nodded. "You may be on to something there, Sam."

"Such matters are my specialty." He puffed his cigar, looking sly. "You were quite set on the fact that you could enter Homestead safely, but my presence would not go unnoticed. I take it you fared well?"

Finnegan squeezed the bridge of his nose. "I did well enough."

"I find interest in your classification methods." Rooney grinned around the cigar again. "I was told by one of those baby-faced deputies that you were fallen upon by a vicious knitting circle and barely escaped with your life."

"The lad exaggerates."

"And those bruises on your head and face?"

Finnegan lit his own cigar. "I trounced the whole of the striking workforce and herded them back to their stations. Commonly, I would never do such a thing without payment, but they disturbed my otherwise placid disposition."

"Fine work." Rooney reclined on the bed again. "It is odd to imagine that I once lost a fortune in a river, and you may now find one."

"It may be worth inquiring as to how Frick initially came into funds. The bugger may have a thrilling tale involving the netting of cash from the Hudson. It would be quite poetic to discover he only intends to transfer your money to me."

"Do not jest, Finnegan. The wound is still too fresh."

# Chapter 14

## *PITTSBURGH, PENNSYLVANIA*

### June 4th, 1892

FINNEGAN AWOKE TO THE SOUND OF KNOCKING ON HIS door. The gunman felt for his Remington with his right hand and picked up his watch with his left. It was nearly nine in the morning, and whoever was knocking might very well assume he should be awake by then. Sitting up on the mat he had made from spare linens and a spare quilt, he set his watch down and rubbed his eyes. "Yes, what is it?"

"Post, sir."

"Is that young Buckley?"

"It is, sir."

Finnegan made a habit of becoming chummy with bellboys in hotels. One never knows when he may require a coconspirator. "Thank you, Buckley. I am not quite roused yet. Be a good lad and slip it under the door and please make me mindful of your owed gratuity when next we meet."

"Very well, sir." There was a swishing sound from the letter being deposited. "Sir?"

"Yes?"

"The concierge has asked me to apologize once again for

a member of our staff attempting your murder. He wishes for you to know that he has thoroughly interviewed the entire staff and not a man among them wishes to see you dead, sir."

Finnegan hung his head. "That is good to know, Buckley. What of the chambermaids?"

"Oh, well...to my knowledge, the concierge questioned only the men, sir."

"I suppose that will have to suffice. Do not let me keep you from your duties, Buckley."

"Thank you, sir." The sound of the young man's feet could be heard bouncing from the door.

Finnegan slowly raised himself from the floor and made his way over to where the letter lay next to the door. He had taken to sleeping in his impromptu condition since being stabbed by the waiter. It was one matter to put up a brave front and not be run out of his hotel; it was another matter entirely to ignore common sense and not take precautions. From his position on the floor, he could easily get the first shots at anyone rushing into the room. He had considered rigging up a boobytrap of sorts utilizing a shotgun, but had thought better of it, considering the occasional presence of the aforementioned chambermaids.

Plucking the letter from the floor, Finnegan tossed himself down into his one and only chair before tearing the envelope open. He detested being awakened, but it was a small price to pay for news from his wife. He carefully unfolded the letter on one leg.

*Dearest Finnegan,*

*I am so very pleased to read that your*

journey has been both dull and profitable. I know there is nothing you abhor quite so much as boredom but, perhaps in this instance, it is for the best. Father tells me deposits have arrived from both Mr. Hauser and Mr. Roosevelt. He has also informed me that the first of what promises to be a steady pension has come in from one William Pinkerton of Chicago. I know that I have voiced some unkind phrases toward the Pinkerton family over the years, and can now see that I may have been unfair in that assessment. William, at least, must be a sentimental soul to offer such largesse.

I am still uncertain as to how long I will be in the Dakotas. The government agents here are proving to be rather intractable in their stance regarding the Sioux. You may find humor in knowing that, just the other day, a rather stiff Major asked if I was, in fact, Mrs. Finnegan Gilhooley. I informed him I was, in fact, Mrs. Gilhooley, and if the man did not become more amenable to our suggestions, thus allowing me to leave the Dakotas, I would be forced to invite my husband for a visit. The poor man turned white as a sheet. Of course, I instantly regretted the rebuke, but the fellow was being an awful bore and somewhat deserved the fright.

*I miss you terribly, dear Finnegan. Hopefully your terribly dull assignment with Mr. Frick will not keep you too long, and we will be together again soon. If nothing else, it would be jolly to see the look on that Major's face when you step off the train.*

*Love, always.*
*Molly*

Finnegan carefully folded the letter and placed it back in the envelope. While he had been quite studious in his correspondence to Molly, he had chosen to omit the more exciting occurrences he had experienced since hitching his star to Mr. Frick's wagon. In the past, he had frequently related an unedited version of events to Molly. Now that they were joined in holy matrimony, he had taken to leaving certain details out of his missives. He saw no reason to worry the poor woman. The gunman sighed and began to contemplate Frick's latest offer once again.

Finnegan returned to the small warehouse district of Bellevue. Looking the vicinity over, he took note of a familiar face. He approached the warehouse the anarchists had formerly occupied and presented himself to the large doorman, who now sported several bandages poking from his shirt and a sling around one arm.

Finnegan nodded to the fellow. "I must say, I find it impressive that you have remained at your post, but your position here seems no less obtrusive than the last time we spoke."

The doorman rubbed his chin with his good hand. "Finding myself shot by those damned Russian revolutionaries in no way relieves me of my need for funds, sir. Mr. Pinkerton is not likely to deliver my pay for lying about."

"I would think not, but would it not be wiser, given your previous experience, to station yourself within the building and peek out from the window to see if anyone approaches?"

The doorman raised his eyebrows. "That very well might prove more effective."

"It very well might." Finnegan opened the warehouse door and held it while the fellow moved inside. "I have always found it is best to live long enough to spend your pay. It is surely superior to the alternative, at any rate." He swung the door shut and left the man to his window. Inside the warehouse, he found a similar assemblage to the one he had discovered previously. The only noticeable difference being that a proper table had been located for the men to loiter around. Captain Heinde and his faithful second in command, Nordrum, appeared quite droopy and bored, while Robert Pinkerton sat with his chin down on his chest and was clearly asleep.

Heinde perked up at the sight of a visitor, eager for any distraction. "Finnegan, you have returned."

At the exclamation, Pinkerton startled and very nearly lost his seat. After catching himself, he peered blearily at the gunman. "Finnegan?" He wiped a bit of drool from his lip. "What brings you by?" His face darkened. "I trust nothing has befallen Frick?"

"Your patron is safe as houses." Finnegan shook his head.

"I left him in good hands. The man is not likely to get into trouble; he stays quite busy, unlike you lot. Can none of you find a useful occupation?"

Heinde shrugged. "Enough men have been procured. The barges are seen to. Now all that remains is to wait for tomorrow's nightfall so that the men may be assembled, the barges delivered, and all matters can be laid in motion." He shrugged again. "What is there to do on the eve of battle but to sit and stew and wait? I would indulge in drunkenness, but my employer sits right there."

Nordrum rubbed his eyes. "I can offer no better explanation."

Finnegan turned toward the man ostensibly in charge. "What of you, Robert? Can you not see that it would be fitting and proper for you to set an example by finding some productive pursuit for these layabouts? What would your father say?"

"He would likely join them in a debauch." Pinkerton sat forward. "Did you leave that shiftless Rooney in charge of watching over Frick?"

"Who better?" Finnegan took a seat on a nearby crate. "As you well know, the man is a marvel when it comes to offering protection. Frick could not be safer."

Pinkerton groaned, thinking back on the incident on the dock. "I know it is not charitable to speak ill of a man who has so recently rescued me from impending doom..." Pinkerton looked over the other men. "Still, it must be said, I am not particularly worried over Frick. It is the man's wife who is in need of protection."

Finnegan waved one hand dismissively. "Even Rooney is not capable of stealing a contented wife. Any man who is cuckolded by the likes of Rooney earns the afront." Finnegan smiled. "Although, it should also be said that I have never introduced the blackguard to my bride, and do not intend to. At any rate, Mrs. Frick is in the country with their ailing son, so there is little danger of romance developing."

Pinkerton shook his head disdainfully. "What is it that brings you here, Finnegan? I am forced to state the facts bluntly: we have nothing whatsoever to do, so I can hardly credit what we would require your assistance for."

Finnegan rubbed his chin and did his best to appear innocent or, at a minimum, a simple bystander. "Mr. Frick has requested that I accompany these fine gentlemen on their boat ride, Robert. He wishes to have a firsthand account of events available after the matter."

Heinde leaned forward, giving the gunman a suspicious look. "I would be more than amenable to giving Mr. Frick a report, in full, as soon as my presence is not required at the mills, Finnegan. Does the fellow enjoy your particular brand of storytelling so much that it is necessary for you to leave your other duties unattended?"

Finnegan pulled a cigar from his pocket. "I do not believe it is so much that the fellow fancies my storytelling, as much as he finds amusement in presenting me with difficulties. So far, he has found no end of mirth in my being stabbed by a waiter and pummeled by disgruntled anarchist hags."

Nordrum nodded sullenly. "I have heard the tale involving the waiter. Unfortunate business. I have never killed a waiter. Did you find it difficult?"

Finnegan offered a confused stare. "I found it necessary at the time and have not thought on the matter since. The bastard stabbed me. What in blue blazes does his being a waiter have to do with it?"

Nordrum stood to stretch his back. "I only imagine it might give one pause to gun down the man who brought you your coffee bare moments earlier. Perhaps I am mistaken in the matter."

"It has been my experience, dear Charles, that a man who pauses in such situations often lies on the ground by way of a conclusion." Finnegan lit his cigar. "Give one pause... honestly, Charles."

Robert Pinkerton began rapping one finger on the table. "Finnegan, we have known each other a bit too long for that explanation to not ring somewhat false."

The gunman raised one eyebrow. "I assure you, Robert, I have related events quite precisely. I was stabbed, the waiter was shot. Thus ends the tale."

"I am not in the least concerned with the circumstances of one of your various and sundry murders. The examination of that subject would stretch on until we both expired long before completion." Pinkerton leveled a finger toward his old friend. "What I wish to investigate is why a man such as yourself would engage in the slightest risk for the amusement of some overgrown boy such as Frick. There is more to this idiocy than you are letting on, sir."

Heinde raised one hand to get the floor. "Finnegan, if you wish to shoot poor Robert down for calling you a liar, I would ask you to wait awhile. Some of us have not been paid, as yet."

"Robert has called me far worse during our association, and I have always rather appreciated his honesty." The gunman turned toward his friend. "Even when it vexes me. What do you intimate, Robert?"

"Only that you have undoubtedly been offered compensation for this absurdity." Pinkerton smiled.

"Of course I have been offered compensation, Robert. Are you not being paid in kind for absurdity? Is that not the nature of mercenaries, great and small?"

Nordrum raised a hand. "Uh, Finnegan, would it be

impertinent to inquire as to the sum of Frick's added compensation?"

"Yes, it would." Finnegan puffed smoke. "How can any of you possibly to have the gall to feign shock at discovering I am greedy?"

Pinkerton chuckled. "Only you could keep a straight face while accusing others of gall. My brother has made me aware of the terms of your deal with him regarding Frick."

"William always was a chatty bugger." Finnegan rolled the cigar between his fingers. "Do you intend to be a pain, Robert?"

"I could not care less what you do or where you go." Pinkerton shook his head again. "I cannot claim that your presence will cause matters to play out more smoothly. I can assure Captain Heinde that it has proved to be impossible to kill you over the years, so there is the guarantee of at least one man surviving." Pinkerton waved one hand around. "If Frick should be killed while you are galivanting about, then you will be the one to answer to William, not I."

Finnegan appeared truly hurt. "Robert, are you saying that you are no longer willing to make excuses or suggest falsehoods to your brother in my interest? I credited you with more loyalty."

"You credited me with more energy. I grow weary in my old age, Finnegan. You may still take an interest in all this rot, but I do not." Pinkerton leaned forward and placed his head on the tabletop. "Inform Finnegan as to our set schedule and then be quiet. I was having a lovely dream before all this idiocy began."

# Chapter 15

## *PITTSBURG, PENNSYLVANIA*

### June 5th, 1892

Finnegan unfolded his napkin and placed it in his lap as the first course of the meal arrived. It appeared to be a fine bowl of soup, and the gunman was looking forward to it. He glanced across the table to see that his dining partner appeared pensive. "Something vexes you, Abel?"

The doctor shrugged and sat back as the food arrived. "Do you think it is wise to take your meals in the very restaurant that formerly employed your attempted assassin?"

"The bellboy assures me that the remainder of the staff has been thoroughly vetted." The gunman tried the soup and found it quite good. "At any rate, a man such as myself cannot spend all his time flitting about in an attempt to avoid danger. Better to simply accept that the occasional unfortunate incident will occur and get on with business."

"A valid theory, I suppose. Your existence is what you have made it. There can be little purpose to kicking against the prick, as they say." The doctor tried the soup. "Ah, that is fine." He dabbed his mouth with his napkin. "It would be a pity to never be able to frequent this restaurant again. Have you, by any chance, killed anyone since you shot the waiter?"

Finnegan shook his head. "Contrary to what has been said in a few periodicals, I do not kill two men every day before breakfast." He paused to contemplate the matter. "I do, from time to time, enjoy rather long periods of peace. Why do you ask?"

The doctor continued to taste his soup. "I find it interesting to somewhat trace the doings of former patients. If you save a man's life, it is always intriguing to see what he does with it. To a certain extent, a man in my profession can even claim his share of the glory if a man does good in the world; on the other side of the coin, I could be burdened with the responsibility of a fellow's bad behavior."

Finnegan cracked a bit of a smile. "I do not know if I would go so far as to say you saved my life, Abel."

The doctor took only a moment to look up from his soup. "No, neither would I. A more accurate assessment would be to say that I repaired your shoulder. The shoulder is attached to the arm. The arm to the hand you make use of to kill people. In that line of reasoning, I suppose what I am truly asking is: what you have been up to with your hand since you shot the waiter?"

"All that is a bit convoluted, is it not, Abel?"

"A man is responsible for what he sows in this world, Finnegan."

The gunman shook his head. "You were a surgeon for the Confederates, as I recall?" The doctor nodded. "And, as such, you saved the life of many a rebel scoundrel?" The doctor nodded again. "It is wholly possible that one of those scoundrels shot my father. So then, by your logic, you would be partially responsible for the death of a man you never met and bore no malice toward whatsoever."

"I suppose my guilt in the specific case of your father might be somewhat of a stretch." The doctor smiled and sat back from his soup. "Although, serving as a surgeon to any army is bound to leave a man feeling conflicted, no matter the cause."

"How so?"

"An army surgeon's sole purpose is to bandage and plaster men back together so that, God willing, they may someday return to the field and wreak additional havoc on their fellow man. The sole purpose of soldiers is to wreak havoc. Every side in a conflict is certain God is on their side, but it is men such as I who allow the stupidity to continue. I did not kill your father, Finnegan, but perhaps he would not have been killed if I had not rallied to the cause."

"If you had ignored your nation's call, you would not have been captured and imprisoned. If you had not been imprisoned, you would not currently reside in Pittsburg. Without your presence here, I might have very well bled to death. You may have played a small role in killing the father, but you were the key component in saving the son. Perhaps all things are simply as God wills them to be."

The doctor chuckled. "It is only that resigning oneself to fate seems such a lazy option."

"Oh, I would never go so far as to suggest that. There is a reason I never fail to strap on my guns before going out. It would be a strange thing, indeed, for a gunman to believe he is not the captain of his own destiny."

The physician sat back as the waiter took his soup bowl. "So then, we have come full circle. We are responsible for what we do and what we cause to be done. We reap what we sow, and the next generation of seed is ours to speak to, as well. Now might be a fine time to make the inquiry that initially brought this whole matter to my mind."

"It would be rude to invite a man to dinner and not speak with him. Inquire when ready, Abel."

"What do you Pinkertons intend to do at Homestead?"

Finnegan took a sip of his coffee and eyed his new friend. "I should begin by stating that matters at Homestead are not specifically within my purview. I have been dispatched here to serve as a protector to Mr. Frick and...indulge him in whatever larks he sees fit to embark on. Up to a point, of course. If you were hoping for the revealment of diabolical plans this evening, I am afraid I must disappoint you."

The doctor shook his head and tried his wine. "I do not require the exact time of your valiant charge. I am only interested in a broad view. What sort of horrid notion does Henry have in mind for those striking steel workers?"

Finnegan waved one hand about. "Nothing out of the ordinary. I have had the poor luck to be present in Chicago for several of the larger conflagrations between labor and capital. The story is an old and rather dull one, Abel." He paused to have more coffee. "The workers walk out of the mill, at which point their employer declares it is good riddance. The workers surround the mill in the hope of keeping out the blacklegs hired to take their place. The next portion of the tale is inevitable. Someone, be they Pinkertons or soldiers or coppers, will arrive and trounce the workers into flight. The blacklegs will enter the mill so that the whole wretched scene may be repeated in a month or two at the works down the road. There is little mystery as to what will occur at Homestead, Abel. There is only the question as to what scale of catastrophe it will be."

"Do you honestly feel a group of you Pinkertons can triumph over such a mass of steel mill hands? Those men are rather known for their tenacity."

Finnegan scowled and shook his head. "It is not a question of whether the Pinkertons or the workmen will triumph, Abel. Regardless of who still stands at the end of this strike, your friend Henry will be the victor. Frick is not the sort to play a game he is not certain of winning."

The doctor eyed the gunman. "Why participate in such doings if you are so cynical as to the outcome?"

"As I said, the situation at Homestead is not my particular commission. Mr. Frick and I play a different game, and I intend to come out the winner."

"As your physician, I feel dutybound to say only a fool or one endowed with far too much hubris would dare to play such a game with the likes of Henry. As a simple man living among men, I must say it borders on evil to play such a game with honest working men as pawns. Do you not care in the least what becomes of Homestead? The men can at least defend themselves, but what of the women and children? This idiocy condemns them to a long cold winter and empty bellies."

Finnegan shrugged and sat back as his steak was placed in front of him. "Any steel worker's wife worth her salt would happily butt heads with a rented mule. As for the children -- I spent many a cold and hungry night due solely to my own father's idiocy. As I have managed to make something of myself, so will the children of Homestead." The gunman sliced off a hunk of beef and popped it into his mouth. "They have many a fine cut of beef in this town." He dabbed his lips with a napkin. "I would also ask you to note the fact that I never once suggested the decent, God-fearing men of Homestead, Pennsylvania ought to either unionize or walk out of their mills in protest. Only scant weeks ago, I was blissfully unaware the damn town even existed."

The doctor shrugged. "Perhaps the entire argument is overly theoretical."

"The weight of Mr. Frick's money in my pocket will be tangible enough." Finnegan took another bite of his steak. "I have always found the tangible to be far more comforting than the theoretical."

# Chapter 16

## *BELLEVUE, PENNSYLVANIA*

### June 6th, 1892

It was just barely a new day. Finnegan used the light from the tip of his cigar to see the hands on his watch. Only a few minutes past midnight, and the men assembled on the docks could be heard laughing and joking as they awaited the order to load onto the barges. By and large, Finnegan did not like the look of them. In many cases, an army is decidedly more useful when its members are selected for their faltering morality, but Finnegan did not believe that would be the case with this particular brigade. Scum are only practical to employ when they outnumber their enemy or are far better armed. The assorted captains had assured Finnegan that the mercenaries would be well-armed, but there was no reason to think the well-off steel men would not be equally well equipped. It was also a certainty that the Pinkertons would be considerably outnumbered. The gunman puffed his cigar and hefted his empty lard can. He was glad to know his path would diverge from the rather loathsome mob before they made their final landing.

Heinde walked over and assessed the gunman. "You are worried we may run out of victuals?"

"It is quite empty, Captain. I intend to make use of it for my watch, pistols, and ammunition. I have detested moisture on my equipment since Fredericksburg."

Heinde smiled and looked the can over. "A pity such a scheme did not occur to me at Vicksburg. I could have been saved a great deal of embarrassment."

"Every fool is allowed to be young once." Finnegan dropped his cigar butt into the river and motioned toward the dimly silhouetted smokestacks of Pittsburgh. "I believe your tug is on the way, sir."

"Ah, good. Now we can finally see about getting this rabble onto the barges. It is not good to let such men as these linger much. It is a miracle there have been no fights on the docks, and only the good Lord's mercy will keep it from occurring on the boats."

"I would defer to you in matters of personnel, Captain." Finnegan hefted his lard can again. "I am only a lowly observer. Although, now that you mention the general condition of our fellow Pinkertons, I believe I will, with your permission, of course, situate myself on the tug. The view and the company will likely be preferable."

"I envy you, but cannot disagree." Heinde gave a small salute. "As you see fit, sir."

Finnegan offered a small salute in return and slowly made his way to the end of the more than fifty-yard-long dock that extended out into the Ohio River. He watched as the tugboat made a tight turn and came up to moor on the end of the dock, where it could be attached to the waiting barges by means of a large cable. A brawny man covered in all manner of coal dust and grime leapt from the boat and gave Finnegan a harsh glare. "You one of these here hired killers?"

"I am a hired killer, but not of the same class." Finnegan motioned to the boat. "Might I come aboard and speak with the captain?"

"He's up there in the wheelhouse." The man pointed with one thumb and then moved like a cat to the rear of the boat to begin joining the floating masses together.

As the hired thugs of the Pinkerton firm slowly began to shuffle onto the barges, Finnegan climbed up onto the deck of the tug, noticing the vessel had been dubbed the *Little Bill*. From the deck, he ascended to the wheelhouse, where a stout man of about fifty was lighting a pipe and investigating gauges. He looked up from one to see the approaching gunman. "You one of them Pinks?"

"I am, sir."

"Well, not to seem unfriendly or nothing, but I won't be needing no damn guide. I been hauling five loads a week down this river to the Homestead docks for the last ten years. I guess I can find the damn place all right, even in the dark." He puffed his pipe.

Finnegan shook his head. "I do not doubt your skill, Captain. I only wish to reside here for improved company and the ability to see to my own commission without interference from those behind us."

The captain cocked an eyebrow. It took only an instant for him to reach a decision. "I suppose I could do with a bit of company on a night such as this. Some conversation does help to keep a man's mind off dreary matters. I am William Rogers, and this is the *Little Bill*."

"I cannot claim to be well-versed in nautical matters, but it seems to be a fine vessel." He set his luggage to one side of the tug's wheel.

"If you don't mind me asking; why is it you have a big old lard can, friend?"

"My name is Finnegan Gilhooley, and I have found it is best for a man to be prepared for any eventuality."

"That is a damned solid philosophy, in my opinion. You are Irish?"

"I am."

"I got no problem with you bog trotters. You saw my man Hector, great Irish brute and a shoveler like no other. He can mind the boiler, toss coal, and dance a jig all at the same time, that one." The aforementioned Hector sprang to the door of the wheelhouse. "Are we rigged?"

Hector glanced to Finnegan and back to the captain. "They's coupled. You'll need to give it hell to get them both out in the channel."

"The *Little Bill* has a strong arm if you will keep him fed." Rogers grinned and began fiddling with valves.

"You want this Pink up here?" Hector posed the question simply and without bias one way or the other.

Rogers opened an impressive wheel valve and the entire boat shook. "He won't be no trouble. Are them mercenaries all loaded and tucked in proper?"

"They seem to be, but if you drown a few it won't be no great loss." Hector turned and left the wheelhouse.

"Don't mean to be rude." Rogers stood on tiptoe and surveyed the barges behind him. "I suppose you have heard all this before. Most don't hold Pinkertons in high regard, although this bunch is at least wise enough to toss off the lines on them barges." He pointed back. "You know that man?"

Heinde stood in the moonlight on what passed for the bow of the closest barge. He cupped his hands in front of his mouth. "We are ready, here!"

"That fellow is the ostensible general of this mob and he claims to be ready to depart." Finnegan waved to the other captain.

"I suppose this is as good a time as any to determine if those rotten old barges will float all the way down to Homestead. It is many a weary mile from here to there, and I offer no guarantees regarding any vessel other than the *Little Bill*."

Finnegan set down his lard can and began to make himself comfortable on one side of the wheelhouse. "If those hulks do sink, this would not be the first army lost to the waves. I assume a man in your vocation is familiar with the tale of the Spanish Armada."

Rogers nodded as smoke belched from the stacks of his beloved boat and the line between it and the barges became taut. The entire tug shook for an instant as it took up the weight of its cargo. "I have heard of those Spaniards who were lost to the sea. I have also witnessed how the Confederates were made gaunt by the blockade. Many an army has lost for want of a better boat."

Finnegan took in the wheelhouse and investigated how sturdy the structure was. "If we begin to take fire from the shore, these walls ought to be sufficient to offer us some safety."

Rogers groaned. "Do you truly believe that is likely? I considered the angst amongst them steel men to have been exaggerated. I considered this a lucrative venture so long as my boat is not shot to pieces."

Finnegan pulled a cigar from his vest as the boat and its dependents moved away from the dock and toward the middle of the river. "I do not know if there is cause to fret, beyond a few errant bullets fired from the shore. I doubt any of the union men in Homestead have taken it upon themselves to invest in cannon or mortars."

Rogers cranked on the boat's wheel to straighten it into the channel. "Huh, I never did pause to consider it until just now, but there's a cannon out in front of the Army of the Republic Hall there in Homestead."

Finnegan lit his cigar and flicked the match out one window. "What sort of a cannon?"

"Uh, well, it could not be more than a twenty-pounder."

"I am certain it is little more than a relic from a long-passed time, Captain Rogers. The accuracy of those pieces was suspect even when they were in good condition."

"In case you ain't noticed, them barges we are pulling ain't exactly small. Take a damned blind bat to miss one of them."

"The piece was likely spiked long ago, Captain Rogers." Finnegan puffed his cigar and considered the matter. "Although, I am once again confirmed in my decision to reside with you for the duration of this voyage."

As the tug laboriously dragged its oversized cargo up the river, the good captain expounded further on the value of the blockade in the last war. Finnegan was able to inform the gentleman as best he could regarding steamboat traffic on the rivers of the west. Rodgers had a particular interest in the boats of the Missouri. All things considered, the trip might have been any other where two newly met friends discussed varied matters as the miles slowly passed by. Nearly four hours passed before there was a lull in the conversation and Rogers grew bored enough to begin pointing out local geography to his visitor.

"As you can see, we're coming into the mouth of the Monongahela. The cross current will have poor Hector shoveling like dervish to keep the pressure up and the paddles flinging. We'll get through her soon enough, though. I've jerked heavier through this stretch. Them barges will follow whether they like it or not."

"I must say, this river is rather pleasant in the moonlight." Finnegan motioned forward. "What is that up there?"

"The Smithfield Bridge." Rogers spun the wheel a half turn and opened his main valve a bit fuller. "Damn decent of them to put it where they did. If it was a might nearer the mouth of the Monongahela, ventures such as those double barges behind us would not be possible. Likely as not, the first one to pass would get itself aground on one of the bridge buttresses and that'd be the end of bridge and barge both."

"Then it is a fine thing, truly, that it is placed as it is."

"It is placed thus due to the rivermen asking for it. For the most part, we get along pretty well here in this part of Pennsylvania. The bridge builders look out for the barge runners, and the steelmen don't bother nobody, and the coal miners don't complain. Terrible shame something like this here disagreement can come along and put everyone at one another's throats like this. Seems like one day I was hauling pig iron up this river, the next I got three hundred men with rifles. Damn shame."

"Take comfort in the knowledge it was not your doing, Captain Rogers." Finnegan pulled a cigar from his vest. "Would you care for a smoke, sir?"

"I would not mind that a bit." Rodgers reached out to take the cigar, when one of the small glass windows in the front of the wheelhouse exploded. The destruction of the window was rapidly followed by splinters and larger chunks of wood flying through the air. Instinctively, both men dove to the floor of the wheelhouse. "Hellfire and perdition!" Rogers cowered on the floor, but kept one hand on the wheel, nonetheless.

"It would appear this is no longer a secret army." Finnegan had pulled his Remington from his hip before flopping unceremoniously to the floor. He held his fire and soon realized the futility of firing back as the bridge grew smaller behind them. He replaced the revolver and rolled onto his back. "That is irksome."

"Damned irksome, if I do say so myself." Rogers held out his mangled cigar. "Landed right on it. Puts me in mind of the time we came up on a British frigate known to be running guns to the Confederates. She got out in front of us so we couldn't bring the big guns to bear on her, and this young lad by the name of Willy McGovern says to the captain that he'd like to take a shot at her with his musket, and the captain says that'd be fine. Willy took his shot at nothing in particular and the ball hit a fella up in the riggings who was smoking a cigar. The old gentleman fell out of the riggings and down into the hold, where he must have made contact with the magazine. The whole damn boat went straight down to Davy Jones from that one musket ball."

Finnegan slowly turned to look at his companion. "A thrilling tale, sir. If a man were to mount a fast horse on the Smithfield Bridge, might he outrun this vessel on the way to Homestead?"

Rogers held the wheel with one hand and rubbed his chin whiskers with the other. "Thinking on it, I would say that this boat will surely get to Homestead before a man on a horse would, what with the man on horseback being held up here and there and the river being the straighter route." He nodded back toward the bridge. "I am not certain we can outmaneuver that flashing lantern I see back there."

Finnegan looked back toward the bridge and could indeed see a flashing light. "Ah, yes, now that is more irksome, yet." He groaned and attempted to make himself comfortable for the moment. "Captain Rogers, I believe there will be something of a welcoming committee waiting for us when we attempt to make landfall at the works."

Rogers sneered and contemplated his broken cigar once again. "I do not know if I would wholly concur with you there, Mr. Gilhooley."

"I would say it is rather obvious the union men will be there to meet us."

"And I will assure you that if there are any shots fired at the *Little Bill*, we will not be making landfall where they originate. I am stubborn, not stupid, sir."

Finnegan grinned at the salty sailor. "What of your contractual obligations, Captain?"

"I guaranteed them barges would be brought up to Homestead. If that's where them fools behind us wish to part company, they are more that welcome to cut the tow line right there."

"A very reasonable assessment, Captain Rogers."

"I sure as hell consider it so."

Another thirty minutes had the Homestead works within sight. The morning had dawned clear and warm. No fog hung on the river. Finnegan and Captain Rogers had not experienced any more gunfire, but hung close to the large corner posts of the wheelhouse walls out of caution. Behind them, Finnegan could see the horde of Pinkertons had distributed out their rifles and pistols. Those that could took cover behind the barge's gunwales. Those closer to the center kept low and more or less trusted to luck for their safety.

Finnegan rubbed his tired eyes and the captain nudged him. "There, my friend, is something a fellow does not see any given day."

Finnegan had to agree, but did not voice his concurrence. In front of them lay the mighty Homestead Mills, but for once the outside of them was busier than the inside. A crowd numbering in the many thousands, obviously the majority of the townspeople, had dismembered one entire side of Mr.

Frick fine fence. Large pieces of the barrier now lay amongst the plant slag or had been pitched out into the green grass they had formerly separated the works from. Mobs were nothing new to Finnegan. He had seen the chaos of riots, but had not seen a collection of men, and women, quite so large since the war. This mob also seemed strangely restrained. Aside from removing what fence was required, it did not appear as though they had done any damage to the works.

As the tug grew closer, Finnegan could see those on shore held a mottled assortment of weaponry. Many of the men had rifles. Most of the women clutched tools, such as shovels, or even hoes. One especially active old lady was swinging about some sort of cudgel. In spite of the strong show of force, no one fired upon the approaching barges. Above the town of Homestead, a crowd of the curious, but so far uninvolved, had begun to gather. Men from the nearby turnpike, who were likely meant to be going to their jobs, lingered next to women who likely should have been on their way, as well. The spectacle was too good to miss. All seemed willing to trade a day's wages for the chance to witness a small war in their own backyard.

Finnegan rubbed his eyes before pulling the lid from his large lard can. He stripped off his frock coat and then removed his shoulder holster. He began packing the can with all the items he preferred to keep dry. His two pistols, holsters, spare ammunition and a goodly supply of cigars were placed inside. He kept one cigar back and proffered it to Rogers. "I believe we shall be parting ways presently, Captain. Might you trade a favor for an additional smoke?"

Rogers took the cigar and deposited it in his pocket. "What do you require?"

"When you bring this ship up to the shore to secure the

barges, I would greatly appreciate a goodly cloud of smoke produced from the stacks."

Rogers let out a chuckle at the gunman's audacity. "That is a damned bold plan, sir. Do you intend to slip off the river side and swim to the shore?"

"I do, indeed, Captain. A cloud of smoke to cower and paddle under would assist me greatly." The gunman nodded toward the ever-nearing mob. "I cannot say I would prefer to enter the clutches of those currently on shore. Under average circumstances, I am certain they are an affable lot. This fine morning, their disposition likely leans toward lynching, and I do not care to be the fellow to test the hypothesis."

"Test their what, now?"

"It is not of import, sir. Will you give me smoke for a smoke?" Finnegan fixed the lid to his lard can.

"Gifted cigar or not, you'll damn well have a billow of black to hide under, Gilhooley." Rogers reached down and tore open a hatch off to the side of the ship's wheel. Below, Hector stood with a blackened shovel in his hands. "Lad, there are enough of your fellow bastards from County Cork at the works to tear this hulk piece by piece with their bare damn hands. You had best get that boiler hot enough to start another hell. You lay down on me this day and we will both likely meet Saint Peter." Hector cocked his head to one side and then began to shovel like a man possessed. Rogers closed the hatch and looked to Finnegan. "I want that damn boiler fit to burst when we come up. I do not intend to linger about those mills, I assure you. *Little Bill* will be smoking like you've never seen."

"Very decent of you, Captain." Finnegan placed his hat and frock coat in one corner of the wheelhouse. "If the two of us and this vessel survive the day, I would appreciate the opportunity to reclaim these garments. The slouch hat was a gift from my wife."

Rogers shrugged. "As you say, if we survive the day. I will wait a few days before making them part of Hector's next payday."

Finnegan shook his head. "Entering into a donnybrook such as this, you ought to double the poor devil's compensation."

The captain disdainfully shook his head. "A fool's flight of fancy. Men always request additional pay when the specter of death looms over them. Tell me now, what dead man ever appreciated a handful of coins?"

Finnegan moved to the wheelhouse door. "Perhaps they request the additional funds so that it might be passed on to those that depend upon them."

Rogers nodded. "An excellent observation, sir. I swear now, in front of you and the Lord Almighty, should Hector perish this day, I will distribute no less than fifty dollars amongst the barmen and whores of Pittsburgh."

Finnegan grinned. "Well done, Captain. If Mr. Frick were so generous, we might not find ourselves in our present difficulties." He offered a small wave with the hand that did not hold the lard can. "I will see you after battle has ceased."

"Or in Hell."

"Either way, it has been a pleasure." Finnegan disappeared around the doorjamb and made his way to the port gunwale. He knelt beside it with the wheelhouse between him and the mob of union men on shore. Below the boiler rumbled. The steam engine groaned out in pain and the paddle wheel of the boat beat the water to a froth. Over all that, Finnegan could just barely make out the sound of what must have been Heinde barking orders to his small army and hollering down those who were clearly not in the mood to make a landing. Finnegan knew all too well how discipline was likely to erode in an army just before battle was joined. It was difficult enough to convince troops who had served together for years to make the first charge, let alone men hastily thrown together no more than a day or two previously. As the tug veered out of the channel and angled toward the muddy shore of the Monongahela, Finnegan could not help but wonder if good Captain Heinde would not find himself the victim of a mutiny before the landfall occurred.

Never one to dwell overly much on other men's concerns, Finnegan kept low and waited until the tug was very nearly upon the shoreline. Rogers yelled out from within the wheelhouse. "You'd best swim like Billy-Be-Damned if you intend to fight the current over to that spit of dock there." Finnegan could just barely see the structure the captain had referenced before a black cloud began to descend upon the waters of the Monongahela. He nodded thanks to the sailor at the helm and dove over the gunwale.

Swimming had never been Finnegan's strong suit. Over the course of his long and strange career, he had taken several dunks that required the fine art of swimming to extricate himself. The dunk in the Monongahela was the first time he had been submerged of his own volition and, as he thrashed in the less-than-pristine water, he began to doubt the wisdom of his actions. The current was stronger than he had credited, and the lard can did not offer as much buoyance as he had hoped. He fought forward, kicking and paddling with one arm as the smoke from the *Little Bill* began to dissipate in the small amount of wind that blew. He kicked and splashed until he felt as if he might have nothing left, but in spite of his age and a lack of practice, he made it to the muddy slop beneath the abandoned hunk of dock Rogers had referenced before the tug's smoke screen cleared.

The gunman hauled himself out of the water and into the mud, shoving his lard can in front of him until he was completely clear of the water and concealed from the mob by the boards that had been haphazardly spiked to the dock pilings. For a long moment, he lay on his back huffing and puffing like the old man he very nearly was. He stared up at the rotten boards above and might have been content to spend the remainder of the strike nestled in the slightly dank, but relatively comfortable, hideout, if a voice had not spoke out.

"Hey, what are you about there?"

Finnegan slowly rolled over in the mud to see a man in overalls wielding what looked to be a barrel stave. He was obviously one of the striking workers, but perhaps not a steel-man, as he did not appear fit enough. His belly protruded, and his chin had doubled. Finnegan slowly got to his feet and made a small attempt at cleaning mud from himself. "Only a fool on a fool's errand."

The man waggled the barrel stave menacingly. "You got to be one of them damn Pinks. Only thing lower than a Pink is a damned Pink deserter." He man lunged forward, swinging the barrel stave. Finnegan leisurely sidestepped the fellow and gave him a shove. As his attacker fought to regain his feet, Finnegan considered pulling the Cloverleaf Colt from his vest to see if it would fire when drenched, but a more playful notion occurred to him. "It is a savage black libel you attempt to place on my head, sir. I have never been a deserter, and I would rather serve in Hell's own army than join those Pinkerton scum. How can you speak so of a man who has come here to not only fight in kind with your cause, but has just now very nearly secured your salvation?"

The man finally regained his feet and stood still, holding

his barrel stave. "What are you on about? What were you attempting just now?"

Finnegan motioned to the lard can. "That, sir, is an explosive. A cleverly built load of blasting powder meant to knock a hole in the hull of that very tugboat you see in the river." The man stood on his tiptoes but could not see over the boards to view the tug. "I paddled out to secure it to either the tug or one of the barges, but I lost my way in the smoke and was forced to turn back for fear I would be swallowed by that damned brisk river."

The man stared at the lard can in wonderment. "Truly? A bomb?"

"Indeed, sir."

The man turned from the lard can to Finnegan. "Then you are one of them anarchists we been discussing in hushed tones ever since Frick cut our wages."

Finnegan assumed a very serious visage. "I have been sent here by your fellow revolutionaries."

"Fellow revolutionaries?" The man cocked his head to one side. "Mister, I ain't sure I got none of them. I only read about them in the *Police Gazette*."

Finnegan nodded. "You have more brothers in arms than you may well know, sir. As an avid reader of the *Gazette*, you are surely familiar with the Black Hand and the Clan na Gael."

The man stared, wide-eyed. "You are one of them disciples of that devil Professor Mezzeroff, ain't you?"

Finnegan took a step forward and placed one hand on the man's shoulder. "My dear fellow, who is it you believe built that charming device you see before you? Mezzeroff is no less than a blood brother to me, and we both intend to dance over Queen Vic's corpse, yet."

The man began shaking his head. "No, no, you got it all

wrong, friend. I mean, I sure appreciate what you might be trying to do here for us, but we just want more wages. We ain't no revolutionaries and we don't give a damn fig about Queen Vic. They been telling us at the meetings that we ain't to let your kind corrupt what we're trying to do here, even if you are acting with the best intentions."

Finnegan nodded intently and began turning the man toward the river. "I could not agree more, sir. As a matter of earnest fact, that very idea occurred to me as I was paddling about in your fine river. As I paddled, I thought to myself that some son of Pennsylvania should be about this errand, not I. An act of such importance as sending those Pinkerton bastards to the bottom of the river should be the deed of a working man who could proudly proclaim what he had done and enjoy the adulation and glory that comes with such a heroic act."

The man nodded slowly. "I suppose such a thing would be damned heroic, at that."

"It would be, sir." Finnegan walked the man to the last dock piling. "How strong of a swimmer are you, sir?"

"Oh, I can't say as I've put a toe in the water since I was a boy."

"Do you believe you could make it to the tug out there?"

The man leaned forward as best he could. "I can't quite see to the tug, mister."

"Here then, let me take that stave. Grip the piling with both hands and take a look out there." Finnegan took the man's weapon and let him lean out farther. When he was stretched out as far as he possibly could be, Finnegan broke the barrel stave over the back of the fellow's head. The man flopped down into the mud, face first. Finnegan turned to go, but paused, considered matters, and then rolled the poor sod over so that he did not expire in the mud. "Lord, please take note of how I have just spared one of your more simple-minded creatures."

Leaving the chunks of stave in the mud, Finnegan collected his lard can and moved up and out of the mud flat and toward the mills. Where the bare earth turned to grass, he pried the lid from the can and began reassembling his arsenal. Over his guns he placed the thin canvas coat that had formed the bottom layer of the lard can's contents. Feeling that he somewhat bore a resemblance to the average working fellow, albeit a bit wetter than most, he slowly walked uphill away from the dismembered dock and came out behind the majority of the mob, which had its attention firmly planted on the Pinkerton flotilla that had so recently docked.

Completely unnoticed by either the crowd or the Pinkertons, Finnegan climbed to the top of what had once been the mount for a massive block and tackle used for unloading boats on the dock. Above the fray, the gunman could look out to not only see, but also to hear what was occurring by the barges. The two barges had been brought to shore with the *Iron Mountain*, the barge Heinde resided on, closest while the *Monongahela* floated farther out in the river that bared the same moniker. A gangplank had been thrown down from the closest barge into the mud, but only one Pinkerton could be seen standing on it. Finnegan did not know the fellow, and thought he looked quite lonely until Heinde came up next to the man. Another gentleman Finnegan recognized, Hugh O'Donnell, emerged from the crowd and stepped to the area in front of the gangplank.

The oversized Irish steelman yelled out. "You men do not belong here! You have no right to enter these works. We have gathered here to resist you with all means at our disposal!"

Heinde held his rifle loosely in one hand. "We come here to assert the rights of the owner of this property. It is you men who are in the wrong here. Disperse from this property or you will be dispersed." He brought his other hand up to rest on the forearm of the Winchester.

O'Donnell shook one angry fist. "You will not enter these mills!"

"This is not your property." Heinde sounded calm, in spite of the situation. "If you interfere with our entering, we will mow you down and enter in spite of you. You may choose which." Heinde paused and his hands tightened on the rifle. "Which will it be, sir?"

O'Donnell dropped his head for a long moment before raising it again to address the Pinkerton. "I have no more to say. What you do here is at the risk of many lives. Before you enter these mills, you will trample over the dead bodies of three thousand honest working men."

"That is not what I..." unfortunately for all concerned, Heinde did not have the opportunity to finish his thought. Someone near the front of the crowd must have caught the eye of the man standing next to Heinde on the gangplank. The lowly hired hand brought up his rifle and the man in the crowd took the initiative by firing. The man next to Heinde fell to the gangplank and all hell broke loose. Fire erupted from both sides, and the smoke from the guns began to obscure the scene. When a bullet thunked into the wooden post next to Finnegan, he decided it was time to find a lower position from which to observe the fracas.

As he descended, he could see the body of the unknown Pinkerton laying on the gangplank. Heinde had nearly made it back into the barge he had so recently left. Gunfire was traded back and forth, with most of the Pinkertons firing at little more than the mill site and the mob firing into the much smaller target of the barges. Finnegan's brief inspection of the barges had led him to believe the gunwales could absorb a good amount of grapeshot before giving way, but it was always hard to say how well any given bit of cover would perform. Being amongst the rioters in a clandestine capacity was not particularly calming, but vastly preferable to being on the barges. Finnegan congratulated himself once again as he landed on the dock and decided to climb the hill somewhat farther into the mill grounds. He had a loose appointment in the neighborhood of the puddling works, and it appeared that the farther one could get from the river, the better off that fellow was apt to be.

The gunman was able to stroll up into the millworks unnoticed, only needing to duck or dive once or twice to avoid the fusillade from the other Pinkertons. When he paused to survey the scene a few hundred yards from the river, hunkered behind a castoff piece of plate steel, he noticed that the *Little Bill* still remained stationed by the barges. Captain Rodgers had not been able to make good his escape before the shooting had begun. Finnegan imagined the fellow now lay down on the floor of the wheelhouse, practicing the same sort of discretion that had served him well earlier.

"You must be near apoplexy worrying over your brothers in arms."

Finnegan turned to see Rooney kneeling beside him behind the plate. "I would congratulate you on your stealth, if I did not know such things are your specialty." Finnegan turned away from the scene by the river and sat behind the half-inch plate no bullet ever made could pierce. "Despite Heinde feeling the need to make it appear as though he was everywhere at all times during the war, I do not recall ever seeing the chap until he put on the coat of a Pinkerton." Finnegan held out a cigar. "I did see you from time to time as

I cowered in the mud. Thus, I consider you the one and only brother in arms I possess."

Rooney took the cigar and joined his friend in sitting well-sheltered from danger. "I rather assumed you might wish to do little more than linger and smoke after Frick had let slip the dogs of war." Rooney gave a small nod to the bag he had placed by his feet. "I took the liberty of packing extra cigars, along with that odd shotgun you requested."

Finnegan found a match and listened to a few errant bullets strike the plate steel. "I assume you found the cigars in the bureau next to the shotgun?"

"Naturally."

"In that case, I thank you, and am quite glad to have lived long enough to partake." Finnegan held the match over so that Rooney could light his cigar, as well. "If you had fallen, I would have partaken in your memory. How was the swim to shore?"

"A damn sight longer than I had anticipated and a might more grueling, to boot. It has been many a summer since I last swam." He puffed while more bullets thudded into the sand to their left. "I hear much gunfire, but very few screams. There was a time when better marksmanship was expected from the sort of mercenary thug that signs on as a Pinkerton."

Rooney shook his head. "I cannot be certain of that. You, for example, are undoubtedly one of the finest marksmen in the country, while I, to my knowledge, have never fired a ball that landed near the intended target. Taken together, that would mean the average between Pinkertons in only mediocre, at best."

"A very excellent point, Sam." Finnegan glanced around to see countless steel workers, tradesmen, and more than a few women, hiding behind whatever would offer cover or concealment. Although, most only made use of it while reloading their own firearms to give as good as they got. "I wonder if it is possible to sink a barge with several thousand well-placed bullets."

"Oh, sweet Lord, you do not think we will be forced to suffer here long enough for something like that to occur, do you?"

Finnegan arched an eyebrow toward his old friend. "Bored already, Sam?"

"I have not experienced the sporting morning you have, Finnegan. Roaming here on foot was little more than drudgery, and now I will be forced to sit and observe a sad battle with a predestined conclusion. The only item in question here is how many of those fools in the barges will perish before a larger body of men arrives to thump these workers into submission."

"By goodness, Sam; I fear age and tedium have made you cynical, my friend. How can you believe for a moment that the great cause these honest workers strive for will be ground to dust by the powers of filthy capitalism?"

"I believe it because I have not been drinking this fine morning." Rooney sighed and gazed over toward the massive buildings that comprised the mills. "It is a bit dreary, hunkering here in the mud and dirt. Might we not be more comfortable and gain a better vantage point amongst some of that scaffolding there?"

Finnegan looked to the mills. "It does sport more of this lovely plating. Those simpletons in the Navy ought to be quite pleased with this stuff; if every steel worker in Pennsylvania does not die here today, America's ships ought to be nearly unsinkable."

"I intend to never again cringe behind anything less than quality Carnegie steel." Rooney grinned around his cigar.

"A man must have standards if he is to hold himself in

any sort of esteem." Finnegan knocked some ash from his cigar and was about to resume puffing when the shooting inexplicably ceased. He looked over at his companion. "Well, now, that is a bit odd."

Rooney shrugged. "Not so awfully. Have you ever taken note of how men so readily fritter away coins for the purchase of a blunderbuss, but plead poverty when it comes to the purchase of ammunition? It is a strange state of affairs."

Finnegan considered the matter. "Heinde certainly did not lack for ammunition. There were many cases stacked in each barge. I suppose it is possible they have all paused to reload, but not likely."

Rooney chuckled. "No, not likely."

A voice that might have sounded authoritative, if it did not contain so much terror, could be heard from the river. "You there, O'Donnell, can you hear me out there?"

Finnegan moved to peek around the steel plate. "If I am not mistaken, that sounds to be Superintendent Potter. I was not aware he was among the men on the barges."

"One cannot be expected to know the whereabouts of every man who travels by barge." Rooney puffed his cigar. "Who the hell is Potter?"

"He issued orders hereabouts before the current mutiny."

O'Donnell's voice could be heard answering. "I can hear you, Mr. Potter. Surely, no man here bears you any ill will. If it suits you, you may pass freely. Are you injured?"

"I am not. How goes it with you, O'Donnell?"

There was a long pause before the union man answered. "My thumb has been shot away, Mr. Potter. I fear I will not be much use after this regardless of how matters stand."

"Many a man has done fine work with only one thumb, O'Donnell." The statement hung in the air for a moment, as though both sides were appreciating the absurdity of it.

"These men and I wish to speak with Sheriff McLeary. You know as well as I that the Sheriff should be brought here so that all men present can disperse to their respective and rightful places. You have strayed beyond the bounds of decency this day, O'Donnell. Get these people under control and bring the Sheriff."

"Mr. Potter, by introducing these assassins to this law-abiding community, you have abandoned decency. What happens here is your doing, not mine. I can no more ask these men to lay down arms now than you could ask your mercenaries to paddle home."

Rooney groaned and tossed his cigar butt down into the grass. "Good grief, these fools do prattle on."

Finnegan shrugged. "You preferred the shooting?"

"It was preferable to idiotic chatter."

Despite his opinion, Rooney quieted when Potter yelled again. "If you will not accept reasonable terms, you are still surely civilized enough to allow our wounded to be taken out of these boats so that they might receive aid?"

The muted tones of a rather heated debate emanated from where O'Donnell was concealed in the beam yard. "We are not savages. Load your wounded on the tug and take them across the river. No man among the workers of Homestead will lay hands on them. Get them up to the rail line so they can have aid. We have wounded and...dead, as well. Will you agree to cease fire while we attend to our necessities?"

"If you will honor it, we will."

"We will honor it, Mr. Potter."

Rooney shook his head, still behind the steel plate. "Well, this is a damned disappointing excuse for a battle. They have not been at it five minutes and already they are parlaying and trading terms. I dare say, General Meade would not stand for such behavior."

Finnegan chuckled and slipped back behind the plate after seeing the first of the Pinkertons being portaged to the tug. "What would you know of General Meade?"

"Ah, yes, well, I cannot claim to have known the man, but I did once spend a pleasant evening with his daughter." Rooney offered an innocent smile.

"Even as a youth you were foolhardy." Finnegan discarded his cigar butt. "Did you, by any chance, see whether or not Heinde was hit?"

Rooney took a quick peek over the plate and resumed sitting. I cannot hardly imagine how the jackass could have avoided it. He was standing there, not unlike a scarecrow, fairly taunting these fellows to kill him. I will never fathom what drives you damned heroes to such behavior."

"Do not lump me in with the likes of Heinde. I slunk ashore well wide of the fray as any proper coward should." Finnegan shook a finger at his friend. "I have engaged in many an act of madness over the years, dear Sam, but I do not believe I have ever sunk to heroics."

"My apologies, Finnegan. I did not mean to include you in Heinde's ilk." Rooney rubbed his face and glanced about. "Should we make use of this temporary truce to find a better vantage point, or should we depart the scene entirely?"

Finnegan gave Rooney a quizzical look. "If we depart, how am I to inform Frick of what occurred here?"

"In the same manner newspapermen inform a waiting public. You have witnessed the opening scene and now it would be perfectly acceptable for you to retreat and simply conjure the remainder of the narrative from whole cloth."

Finnegan sighed. "Another matter requires your attention this fine day?"

"Any matter that offers a reasonable assurance of not being killed would take precedence, in my opinion."

"A few dead and wounded men and you start to yap as though the rapture were upon us."

Rooney nodded toward the beam yard. "Do not forget poor O'Donnell's thumb."

"Ah, yes, that is unfortunate. Strange that a fellow should suffer an injury that fairly removes him from the profession that got him into trouble in the first place. The Good Lord does enjoy his small jests, does he not?"

"Just so long as he does not jest with me by manner of bullets." Rooney shoved the canvas bag that contained the cigars and armament toward Finnegan. "It is difficult enough to have witnessed a fine and ill-gotten fortune swallowed by a river. To be doubly punished by injury would be intolerable."

Finnegan took up the bag and made ready to be on their way. "Never having lost a fortune, I cannot speak to that particular pain. As for being shot or otherwise maimed, I *can* attest there is a great deal of variance in the matter depending on place, time, and the location of the injury on the body. Regardless, I should think the loss of a fortune would be more vexing. It is much more difficult to heal such a wound as that."

The creation of steel requires a great deal of coal and heat, but it also requires a great deal of water, for both cooling and fire control. For that reason, the pumphouse at the Homestead works was an impressive and imposing edifice. Concealed within its two stories were machines capable of enough horsepower to very nearly redirect the Monongahela. Although, since the mills were all uphill from the river, the redirection would only be fleeting.

Finnegan and Rooney had chosen the roof of the pumphouse, as it offered an excellent view of the surrounding area, and a degree of comfort other spots did not. A hip wall surrounded the roof and steel plate had been affixed to the steel beams that formed the pumphouse's internal structure. As the pumphouse was the key component in fighting fires in and around the mills, it simply would not do to have it burn down. As such, the building was steel, and quite impenetrable to rifle fire.

After climbing to the roof, the two ambivalent Pinkertons took up a position near the hip wall, facing the insurrection. Finnegan considered joining the two halves of his shotgun, but did not feel a pressing need. He left them in the bag and began taking in the scene below.

"It is good to see the *Little Bill* still floats. That Captain there is a stitch." Finnegan gazed at the small craft as it negotiated the river. "I wonder if he will return, or show some sense and get the hell out of here for good?"

"Hard to say. Madness seems rather commonplace in these parts." Rooney motioned to the edge of the town. "Now, there is a sight I never imagined to witness. How many women would you say there are in the group in front of that one-thumbed chap?"

Finnegan turned to the town limits. Where the mills ended and the town began, O'Donnell and a few other hardy souls had somehow or another convinced the women to leave the field of battle. Although, it appeared as though they were not quite trusted to leave of their own accord. O'Donnell and a few others were fairly herding them up the hill. "I would bet an honestly earned dollar that there are five hundred of them at least." The women began to disperse down several of the town streets, as they would not all fit on the main boulevard.

"You must feel strongly indeed about that estimate. I

cannot imagine you have more than one or two honestly earned dollars." Rooney sat down and opened the bag Finnegan had set by the hip wall. "It seems as though we have been here quite some time. I know I packed your watch in here someplace."

Finnegan shook his head. "How is it you do not own a watch? Is not promptness the cornerstone of proper blackmail? Bring this amount of money, to this place, at this time, and all that."

"Oh, the pawnbroker in...well, who can recall, is in possession of the last watch I possessed. I kept intending to invest in a new one with some of Frick's money, but the good citizens of Johnstown had already rebuilt the clock tower, so it seemed a needless expense." Rooney retrieved the watch and handed it to Finnegan.

As his vest was dried out, he affixed the watch chain to it and opened the timepiece. "Getting on eight in the morning, my friend. Things will likely not drag on much longer. Now that the women are gone, there will be no need for grandstanding."

Rooney nodded emphatically. "It is as though they do not comprehend that they are the cause of all this. Without women, all war would cease."

Finnegan nodded in turn. "And yet, they so consistently fix all the blame on us poor fools." He waved one hand toward the town. "As though any man present would ever consider striking for higher wages if his dearest wife had not first suggested he deserved a greater percentage."

"Without women, labor disputes would quickly become as common as unicorns. This mill could not find a willing man to sweat for pennies. We would all content ourselves with drunkenness and frivolities. I would go so far as to wager steel would never have been invented." Rooney appeared quite pleased with the observation.

Finnegan gave it some further consideration. "Yes, it would be a type of paradise. Although, it would be a bit dull to have nothing to fight and kill other fellows over. I am not certain what I would occupy the majority of my time with."

"You could learn the trade of carpentry, as our Lord and savior did."

Finnegan shook his head. "I loathe carpentry. Better the world should exist in perpetual chaos than lower myself to that." The door to the roof swung open and a spry young man began loping across the rooftop with a rifle in his hands. The young fellow seemed no more surprised to find Finnegan and Rooney on the rooftop than he would have been to see them on a city street. He settled in near them and began making arrangements to use the hip wall as a rest for his long, heavy-barreled rifle.

"Good morning, gentlemen." The young man smiled and placed a rolled-up coat on the hip wall. "I am John Morris, a puddler by trade. What line are you boys in?"

"Simple laborers, raising callouses and hell when the opportunity presents." Finnegan pointed to the rifle. "That is a fine arm."

"Oh, yes, I dare say it is. I traded many a hard day's labor in that damn mill to purchase it." He patted the large single-shot action of the weapon. "A genuine Ballard, none finer, the long-range model. I was taken for a pretty penny for the sight, as well."

Finnegan nodded and moved closer. "Yes, undoubtedly worth the expense. A globe front sight is just the thing for far flung targets. What is its chambering?"

"44-100 Everlasting." Morris grinned at the gunman's enthusiasm.

"Have you had opportunity to test the veracity of that claim? Does the brass take to multiple loadings?"

"Oh, indeed, and a lucky thing too. It is easier for a man to locate true love or a diamond mine than to locate this old Ballard brass." Morris chuckled at his newfound kindred spirit. "The lighter three hundred and sixty-five grain load offers less recoil, but the five hundred and thirty-five grain load carries like nothing else."

"Ah, yes, there is much to be said for additional weight, in terms of reach." Finnegan motioned to the barges. "You believe that piece will bridge the gap, so to speak?"

Morris nodded with vigor. "If you doubt the claim, you need only wait and witness, sir. Uh, what was your name, by the way?"

"Liam O'Brian." Finnegan motioned to Rooney. "That fellow is Fredrick Mezzeroff."

"Mezzeroff?" The steel worker offered a quizzical glance. "You wouldn't be that crazy Hun famous for playing with dynamite, would you?"

Rooney shook his head. "No relation, I am afraid."

Morris shrugged. "Pity, we could use a man who is familiar with blasting powder this day." He made an effort to set the rifle on the hip wall and to get it to balance. The marksman held the rifle and attempted kneeling and crouching. He shook his head, ruefully. "I simply cannot say if this will do, my friends. This is a fine piece, but it requires a firm rest."

Finnegan motioned above them. "Perhaps that water tower would offer the proper perch. Along the catwalk?"

"Ah, yes, it is best to lie prone, at any rate." Morris clapped the Pinkerton on the shoulder. "You are well met, sir."

"And you, Mr. Morris." Finnegan watched as the man

retreated to the water tower's base and began climbing its ladder with the long rifle slung over one shoulder.

Rooney cleared his throat and beckoned for Finnegan to lean nearer. "I may be straying out of my depth with this question, Finnegan, but should you not shoot that fellow?"

"Shoot John Morris?" Finnegan said the words as if they had known the man since childhood. "Whatever for?"

Rooney cocked one eyebrow. "Finnegan, I know you have always felt a kinship with your fellow -- I suppose murder enthusiasts might be a proper moniker -- but are you not forsworn in terms of loyalty here?"

"Finnegan rubbed his chin. "I do not follow, Sam."

Rooney squeezed the bridge of his nose. "Your new acquaintance makes ready to lay fire upon your old friends and employer. Are you not bound to act?"

Finnegan held up one stern finger. "Sam, I serve two masters, William Pinkerton and Henry Frick. Neither of those two men are present here today. If that fool Heinde did not believe he could be shot, he has already been disabused of the notion."

"Still..." Rooney shrugged. "Does it not seem rather a betrayal, so to speak?"

"A betrayal?" A grin spread across Finnegan's face. "Only a few days past, Robert Pinkerton himself," Finnegan motioned about, "who elected not to accompany us on this thrilling journey, suggested you were of too low a character to even stand among those miscreants on the barges. Now you question whether or not I should kill a poor puddler out of some obscure allegiance? Did you bring a flask here with you, Sam?"

Rooney waved one hand dismissively. "Oh, very well, then. Let the bugger shoot a few of the hirelings. You have convinced me that it is none of our affair."

"In all honesty, I am rather intrigued to see how he will make use of that bloody fine Ballard. I would wager the closest Pinkerton down there is a quarter mile off." Finnegan yelled up to the tower. "Morris, are you about in place up there?"

A voice drifted down. "I am. Will you attempt to spot my first shot for me so that I might adjust?"

"Gladly!" Finnegan yelled up. "Fire when ready." Finnegan turned to Rooney. "Now this should prove interesting."

Rooney shook his head and remained seated behind the hip wall. "Ah, yes. Once again, you revel in observing whether one jackass might somehow kill another. Why is it you could never show interest in what intrigues the majority of men? Would it be so awful to just once indulge in the pleasures of whiskey, cards, and lewd women? Why must you always play at death?"

"Death?" Finnegan shook his head. "That Morris is half mad to think he might hit someone from this range. I am no more playing at death than you are in danger of being struck by a bolt of lightning."

Rooney rubbed his face. "The fellow seems confident."

"We all are, previous to making fools of ourselves." Finnegan withdrew a small spyglass from the bag and turned to yell up at the tower. "Do you intend to fire during this particular labor dispute, or are you of a mind to wait until the next row, Mr. Morris?"

"This is not nearly as simple as it appears, sir!" There was a bit of a pause above. "Watch carefully, now!"

Finnegan laid the spyglass across the hip wall's top and gazed down at the Pinkertons. A shot rang out above and an instant later Finnegan pulled away from the glass. "I will be damned, Morris. I witnessed the impact. You were no more than a foot to the right and a few feet below that chap in the red coat!" Finnegan smiled over at Rooney. "The fellow does not disappoint." He looked back to the glass. "Oh, wait now... that appears to have somewhat riled them." Finnegan knelt below the hip wall. "I believe that shot marked the end of the tenuous treaty we enjoyed." What had to be dozens of bullets began clanging off the plate steel behind the two men, dozens more began to ricochet off the beams of the water tower as the far-off Pinkertons began to correct for distance.

Rooney had instinctively ducked his head down and covered up with his arms. Realizing the absurdity of the action, he looked up at Finnegan and assumed a more normal posture. He had to raise his voice to be heard over the clatter on the other side of the half-inch plates. "I suppose an occurrence such as this never fails to make one wince a bit, old friend."

"This steel is a far improvement over what we have previously hidden behind, but it is damned noisy." Finnegan craned his head up and noted that the bullets climbed ever higher on the water tower. A ricochet thudded into the heavily tarred roof near him. "If they keep this up much longer, a man will not be safe anywhere up here." He looked to the top of the tower. "I do not recall precisely, but it did not appear as though Mr. Morris would have much to cower behind on top of that structure." Bullets began to collide with the uppermost section of the tower.

A ricocheting round spattered lead across Rooney's right hand. "Ah, damn it to hell. Perhaps we ought to move off from here." The volume of fire increased yet again as the marksmen below began to zero in. "Nothing gets their blood up like a man sniping!"

The number of rounds impacting the tower increased to where the few small wooden adornments began to be knocked free. The chunks fell all around the two men below. "Bloody hell, they will not have a shell left among them!" Even Finnegan was finally forced to turn and cover up. Mercifully, it was only a moment before the firing died away and a thump could be heard as something heavy fell onto the upper scaffold of the water tower. A bare instant later, Morris's body landed on the rooftop some ten feet from Rooney and Finnegan. The gunman stared out at his fellow ballistician. "Where precision falls short, volume will make up the difference." Finnegan removed his hat. "He had great audacity. May the Good Lord take that into account in his reckoning." He replaced his hat.

Rooney rubbed his eyes. "I do truly long for the day when I cease to lose fortunes and can begin informing you that I do not require the funds afforded by endeavors such as this."

"Oh, Sam, it is not as bad as all that. Despite the momentary discomfort, I do not believe we were even in any real danger."

Rooney rubbed his hand where the flecks of lead had hit. "As time goes by, it is not so much the danger as the descent into madness that I dislike."

Finnegan nodded. "Yes, a descent into debauchery was always your preference. What is it you find so mad here? As I see it, events are unfolding in a rather predictable manner."

Rooney sighed. "It is the predictable nature of the madness that disturbs me most, I think. All this is so very unnecessary, so stupid, so wasteful. Any man here could see this approaching. Not a man here acted to stop it. The majority of these idiots relished the prospect. Make no mistake, Finnegan: this is madness, and any sane man can see it."

The gunman removed two cigars from the bag and

handed one to Rooney. "Speaking of disturbing observations, a fresh one has just flitted to mind."

Rooney took the cigar. "What might that be?"

"It occurs to me, that if you are the last sane man walking the earth, the human race as a whole is in dire trouble."

"The human race is perpetually in dire trouble, Finnegan. It matters little if I am sane or crazy." Rooney glanced over at Morris. "The poor devil was struck in the head. Thankfully, I have not seen such a thing since the war." Rooney pulled a flask from the bag and took a long draught. He looked to Finnegan when he was done. "Oh, you had to have known I would not place myself in a situation such as this without at least some forbearance for solace."

"Sobriety is hardly required to hide behind this wall. Drink all you like."

"In that case..." Rooney took another sip. "That thumbless fellow, O'Donnell, and his bunch, have asked all the steel workers across the country to walk from their posts in sympathy to these men here. Before I left to meet you, word had come over the telegraph that some workers as far east as Chicago had answered the call. This may become as large a conflagration as that mess in '77."

Finnegan shook his head and lit his cigar. "That foolishness in '77 was exacerbated by the railroad workers themselves. The idiots took to wrecking their own tracks and bridges. These steel workers had damaged nary a window shade in this place until all this stupidity began. If it continues on much longer, they will have no mill left to fight over."

"Perhaps that is what your man Frick wanted all along?"

Finnegan eyed his friend. "What do you suggest?"

"Homestead is not the world's only steel mill. Yet most steel mills are owned by Frick and Carnegie. Might it not be worth it to such men to sacrifice one puny mill so that all future steel mill workers would learn the value of obedience?" Rooney sipped again. "I have noticed that freighters need only beat one mule at a time to keep the rest behaving in harness. Mr. Frick has many mules."

"An intriguing notion."

"It does force a man to ponder his role in all this."

Finnegan arched one eyebrow. "We have no role in this, Sam. These men kill each other of their own accord, and we need not concern ourselves as to their motives."

"Perhaps that is the best course of action. I am so rarely given to fits of moral contemplation, and I am not well suited to it." Sporadic firing, slowly increasing, could be heard below. "Sweet Mary, what has them agitated now?" Both men turned and raised up to peek over their battlement. Below, they could see several of the Pinkertons had made an attempt to disembark from their vessels. A few had run down the gangplanks and a few more had tried to jump from the gunwales and traverse the muddy shore. Both attempts had proven futile. There was no cover between the union men and the barges. The quicker Pinkertons had retreated back up the gangplanks. Two, bogged down in the mud, had perished not far from where they had made landfall. "That fellow Heinde is no tactician."

Finnegan puffed his cigar and lowered himself behind the hip wall. "As fine as any who did ever plan a battle while I was in the ranks. Odd that he is just now paying the price. He is not a bad sort, all things considered. They ought to have loaded him on that tug. Perhaps they will bring out Frick's personal physician Abel to remove whatever limb is troubling him."

"I should never forget the sight of how they piled those poor wretches' arms and legs at Fredericksburg. I stumbled around the tent by mistake and..." Rooney took another long pull from the flask. "Ahh, but this is gloomy talk. Remind me again, what is to be my compensation for this laborious commission?"

Finnegan smirked. "As I reckon matters, one thousand dollars and the opportunity to be welcomed back into the Pinkerton fold is more than fair for sitting on a roof watching other men fight."

Rooney shrugged. "I suppose it is. Although I was forced to take the train here from Pittsburg and it is a dreary trip under the best of circumstances. That peril might require a gratuity, eh?"

Finnegan was about to retort, but the door to the rooftop was flung open once again. Two men stepped forth from the doorway as bullets were traded below. Unbelievingly, Finnegan stared at one of the men, unable to come to grips with recognizing the fellow. He was too stunned to do much of anything as they approached. As they neared, the chubbier of the two, a man covered in mud and quite disheveled grinned at the gunman. "Damn glad to see you are all right, my friend. I searched around all over beneath the docks to see if the same fate had befallen you." The man tossed himself down by the hip wall next to Finnegan and the stranger he had brought along took up a position one spot down.

Rooney sat forward so as to look around Finnegan at the newcomers. "You are familiar with these gentlemen?"

Finnegan rolled his cigar from one side of his mouth to the other. "I met this fellow when I came ashore under the docks." Finnegan cleared his throat. "I was forced to abandon the hide, sir. What became of you? I looked for you behind me, but saw nothing."

The chubby man massaged the back of his head. "I cannot say for certain. One moment I was considering swimming out to those barges as you suggested, and the next, the whole of creation went black. I can only assume I was struck by an errant bullet from them damned Pinks." He shook his head as if to clear it. "I found your lard can up by the end of the dock pilings. Some low mongrel had removed the dynamite from it."

Finnegan nodded slowly. "Yes, well...I was forced to abandon that, as well. A shame."

"Truly." The chubby man ceased rubbing his head and stuck his hand out for Finnegan to shake. "I am Clarence McGovern. I do not know if I had the chance to be introduced, formally."

Finnegan took his hand. "Call me O'Brien."

The chubby man motioned to his right. "This man here is Peter Fares. He doesn't savvy much English, but he seems all right. He heard we was having a tussle up here and came see what it was all about." Fares sat forward, smiled, and then sat back against the wall, where he began unwrapping a loaf of bread from some cheesecloth. McGovern stared over at Rooney. "Is he one of yours, O'Brien?"

Finnegan took a moment to decide whether it would be easier to continue spinning lies to the fellow or to simply fling him off the roof. Taking his role as a mere observer into account, he chose the less vigorous choice, although he opted to foist the brunt of the labor over onto Rooney. "Mr. McGovern, you are in luck this fine day. Not only will you inevitably witness the overthrow of the vile capitalist system that continually grinds us all down, but you will also be introduced to the man who will make it possible. Allow me to introduce the esteemed Professor Mezzeroff himself."

McGovern's mouth fell open. "You are Mezzeroff?"

Rooney cleared his throat to facilitate a Prussian accent.

"I am, indeed, sir." He extended a hand across Finnegan. "Pleased to make the acquaintance of a fellow traveler."

McGovern continued to stare, wide-eyed. "Did you truly build the bomb that killed the Tsar?"

"Sworn upon my soul, I was also the man that threw it." Rooney bowed his head. "My greatest success -- that is, until today."

"Ah, yes." Finnegan took over the narrative. "The Professor is deeply despaired by the loss of his most recent creation. We were just deliberating on a means to recover the item when you appeared along with this other fellow and provided the key to our eventual victory."

McGovern lurched back, shocked. "You truly mean *me*, sir?"

"I do, indeed." Finnegan patted the man's shoulder. "You must search out and discover the person or persons who have made off with the contents of the lard can. The salvation of our cause this day hinges on its being reclaimed. Use whatever means are necessary, but recover that item, sir."

McGovern chuckled and then nodded knowingly. "Mr. O'Brien, it would be my honor and privilege to assist you and the Professor. I am well equipped to aid you, too. As I made my way here, Peter and I passed one of our fallen friends and I collected a bully fine revolver. Let me show you." The man began to vigorously dig in one trouser pocket. He pulled and tussled to get the weapon free, but the hammer of the gun was snagged on the pocket lining. He gave a final jerk, and a muffled shot rang out. McGovern stared blankly at Finnegan. "O'Brien, I believe I am injured."

Finnegan looked down to see blood spreading across the fellow's upper thigh. He hung his head. "Hell and perdition."

Peter Fares leaned closer to inspect the damage. "Vat wrong wit him?"

Finnegan rubbed his eyes. "The damn fool has shot himself in the leg." He sighed. "I suppose I should be content he did not shoot one of us and cease to complain." Finnegan reached over and slowly withdrew the small bulldog revolver from McGovern's pocket. "A damn shame to perish from a wound inflicted by such a shoddy piece."

Rooney came around in a low crouch to view the scene. "Ah, Finnegan, I do not believe that is his life's blood draining away, but we had better get him to someone who is better versed in such matters."

Finnegan cocked his head to one side. "What's this now?"

"We must see about getting this bloated imbecile to a physician." Rooney pulled McGovern's belt free and began to fasten it around the wounded leg.

"A physician?" Finnegan watched in puzzlement. "I am not certain what amazes more: that you are compelled to assist this slug, or that you believe a physician is somewhere about these parts. The sheer size of this specimen renders your plan impossible."

Rooney shook his head and pulled the belt tight, much to McGovern's consternation. "Finnegan, as you well know, I generally only suffer fools until I am in possession of their money. In this case I must make an exception, and so must you. Given an alternative, I would leave this simpleton, but we cannot simply sit here and watch this man bleed until he can bleed no more."

Finnegan hung his head once more. "Very well, damn it." He moved to take one of McGovern's arms. "You have either had too much of that flask or not nearly enough. Old age is making you dull-witted, Sam."

McGovern groaned as they lifted him, each Samaritan on a side. He glanced back and forth between his saviors. "You said I was the key to our great victory."

"You were." Finnegan grinned at Rooney. "Sadly, you have now become the Irishman's burden."

WHERE THE LOWER DOOR OF the pumphouse let out onto the mill grounds, the Samaritans paused with their cargo. McGovern huffed and puffed between the two Pinkertons, while Peter Fares hung behind and observed. The strange Slav munched on his bread loaf and viewed the ongoing battle around him much in the same way a fellow might watch a play.

Gazing outside, Finnegan could see small puffs of black earth raised from errant bullets. He groaned. "I would have thought Robert Pinkerton to be too tightfisted for this to have gone on this long. If he were here, he would surely be sickened at the cost of so many cartridges killing nothing more than dirt and marring only steel plate."

"Damn, but this man is weighty..." Rooney used his free hand to wipe sweat from his brow. "Where should we deposit him?"

"Not two minutes previous you complained of my lack of compassion. Now, the fellow is far too heavy, and you know not what to do with him? You were a far sight more enjoyable to be around when you were consistently drunken and selfish." Finnegan adjusted his grip on McGovern. "How the hell should I know where to take him?"

"I apologize for the momentary lapse in judgement." He adjusted his grip, as well. "I assure you, it will not happen again." He motioned to a collection of small wooden buildings on the far side of the mill grounds. "I see them hauling another wounded fellow off over there."

"Ah, yes, naturally. I do not believe there is a point

farther from either cover or where we now stand. Quite perfect."

"Old age has made you irritable."

"Dragging this oaf is not likely to improve my disposition, either." Finnegan surveyed the ground in front of them. "Very well...I suppose it simply would not do to toss him out into the bullets after wasting so much time dragging him down here. Do you see those ties piled there?"

"Of course."

"That is our first destination." Finnegan adjusted his grip further. "At the next lull, we make for them. Fleetness of foot would be appreciated."

Rooney leaned to be seen around McGovern. "Switching sides so that you are the one exposed to the river would be appreciated."

"When you suggest stupidity, you are dutybound to accept the greater hazard." Finnegan lurched forward. "Now, damn it."

The three men lunged out into the open, resembling children ardently attempting to win the three-legged race at a church picnic. With each new lunge, the pile of railroad ties they sought grew nearer and nearer. Bullets could be heard whizzing past and dirt occasionally flew in their direction. In spite of all that, they kept a steady pace, and the pile of ties was no more than a few yards off when a wet thud was heard and McGovern's head lolled over. Blood sprayed across Finnegan's face and the three tumbled down to safety behind the ties. The gunman wiped his hands across his face and looked to Rooney. Seeing that his friend was uninjured, he looked to McGovern. The steelman had a gaping hole in his neck and was attempting to stop the flow of blood with his hands. Finnegan could plainly see it was a losing battle as the man turned pale.

Rooney winced and scowled. "Ah, that is a damn shame."

"Yes, the poor beggar very nearly..." He glanced back to where they had come and saw Peter Fares strolling across the bullet riddled space without a care in the world, quite merrily tearing chunks from his loaf of bread. "You daft bastard! Get out of there!" Fares stopped at the loud exclamation and stared at Finnegan for a brief moment before being struck in the head by a bullet. He fell and the loaf of bread tumbled away into the mud and dirt. "Bloody hell, this has become a madhouse."

Rooney stared out at the dead Slav. "I do not believe I saw the equal of that even during the war. That man was out of his damn head."

Finnegan rubbed his face, doing his best to remove McGovern's drying blood. "In truth, that fellow seemed a bit off from the beginning. I suppose an instance such as this is bound to attract those who have lost touch with their right mind."

"Ourselves included." Rooney looked around. "While I am not as inclined toward the appreciation of firearms as you are, Finnegan, I doubt those men on the barges possess a weapon that might shoot through one of these ties. Our duty to Mr. McGovern is seen to; I see no reason we should not reside here in safety."

Finnegan stepped a few feet from McGovern's body and sat down on one of the many ties strewn about. "We may linger here for a time. Eventually, we ought to reenter the pumphouse."

Rooney rubbed the back of his now-dirty neck. "Whatever for?"

"Our supplies still reside on the rooftop, along with my shotgun and your liquor."

Rooney scowled. "Yes, well, we can easily collect all that

when the firing has died down and these idiots come to their senses."

Finnegan shrugged. "I have several spare cigars and several pistols with which to pass the time. Did you, by any chance, leave your flask in the satchel?"

"Oh, you are a cold-hearted devil, Gilhooley. To point out a man's weaknesses so bluntly is quite rude, sir." Rooney gazed longingly toward the pumphouse. "Mayhap God will take mercy on me and the shooting will not last too much longer."

The two men began making the best of the situation, rearranging a few ties so that they would be more comfortable and gain better observation of the rather elongated battle. They frittered away the better part of two hours watching bullets fly about and discussing whether or not lulls in the action were, in fact, lulls, or only appeared to be. Several times, Rooney suggested that it might be opportune to rush toward the pumphouse, and several times bullets hit near him to disabuse him of the notion. Finnegan grew weary of watching his partner's attempts. In search of better amusement, he moved to the tallest portion of the tie pile, stretched out his back, and then wandered even farther down to see what he could observe. Peeking through various holes, he noted that the men on the barges showed no signs of ebbing off in their fire. He could also see several union partisans who were little better than boys running and dodging through the gunfire to deliver ammunition and what appeared to be sandwiches to the workers. When he saw one young fellow packing a basket and a metal can, Finnegan waved to the sport and the lad made a hard right turn toward the tie pile. Leaping like a thoroughbred, the boy fairly danced among the fusillade and reached the pile none the worse for wear and looking quite pleased with himself.

Finnegan laughed and clapped the boy on one shoulder. "That is a fine demonstration, young man."

The boy wiped sweat from his forehead. "I am getting better as the day goes on. When I first brought my father tobacco this morning, I was very nearly laid low. Now that I know what to watch for, I hardly even consider myself endangered, despite what mother says."

"Fairly incredible what a difference a day can make. What is it you carry there, lad?"

He grinned. "Pasties for any man brave enough to fight for the cause, sir." He held up the canister. "And coffee, as well."

Finnegan took two silver dollars from his vest pocket. "I always claim some cause, but would never go so far as to claim bravery. As such, take this in return for the food and coffee, young man."

The boy shook his head. "I do not know if it would be right to take money in payment from one of father's fellow working men."

Finnegan stuffed the coins in the lad's shirt pocket and then added another for good measure. "One for you, one for your father, and one for your sainted mother. A workman is worth his wage, and you impress, boy. Take that home knowing you have earned it." Finnegan opened the basket and removed the pasties wrapped in cheesecloth. He then took the canister. "Now, get home, boy, and do not return here. Your father has his tobacco and the rest will make do. You are fleet of foot, but no man's luck holds forever." Holding his booty in one arm, he spun the boy around with the other and gave him a shove toward the end of the tie pile. "And, for God's sake, be swift!" He watched as the boy spritely fled, dancing through the bullets once again. When the boy disappeared amongst the buildings of the mills,

Finnegan laughed and shook his head. "Ah, youth." He wandered back to Rooney.

The charlatan professor sat staring up the hill toward the town of Homestead with the occasional longing glance toward the pumphouse. He grinned when he saw Finnegan approaching. "Now, what is it you have procured there?"

"The supplemental items that are so readily required when you leave a drunken sot in charge of the packing." He sat down next to his friend. "Did it truly not occur to you to place even a bit of sausage or some cheese in that bag?"

"How was I to know this would devolve into a damned siege?" Rooney plucked a pasty from the cheesecloth. "Oh, well, now, this appears quite promising."

Finnegan held up the canister. "And there is even something to wash it down with."

"Oh, please Lord, let that be hard cider."

"It is coffee, you degenerate." Finnegan chewed his pasty and began working on the canister lid. "Perhaps if you spent less time deep in your cups and more time..." He looked up the hill where Rooney had been gazing previously. "Oh, bloody hell, just as Rogers foretold, these fools have stolen the cannon from their clubhouse."

Rooney nodded and munched his pasty. "Yes, I thought that a bit odd when first I saw them pushing the thing through the streets, but what good can it possibly do them? It is not as if they possess any cannonballs or shot canisters."

Finnegan hung his head. "As I recall, there was a decorative pyramid of cannon balls next to the old blunderbuss in front of the Grand Army of the Republic Lodge. It is an ancient brass twenty-pound beast."

Rooney shrugged. "Very well, then, they possess cannonballs. I doubt any of these working men owns a barrel of powder to stoke the thing."

"These steel men have shown great ingenuity, thus far. I would not put possessing powder past them."

Rooney finished his pasty. "I suppose, whether they possess sufficient powder or not, it is of little concern to us."

"I am not wholly certain of that, Sam. I seem to recall from the war that cannonballs rarely, if ever, travel the path they are meant to."

Rooney looked up the hill, with just a bit of worry showing on his face. "Perhaps it is time to retreat to that damn pumphouse whether we like it or not."

Finnegan got the lid off the coffee canister and took a sip. "I fail to see what is keeping you."

Rooney left his seat and stood, watching the unpredictable impact of rifle bullets out in the dirt between the ties and the pumphouse. "Finnegan, those fools could very easily send one of those balls bouncing right down here into us."

The gunman nodded. "And we could very easily be shot attempting to flee from this spot."

"Well, this is a damned conundrum." Rooney ran his hands through his hair.

Finnegan shook his head and sipped coffee. "There is no conundrum whatsoever." He laughed and sat back on the ties. "The chances of those men firing that ridiculous old cannon are nil. I was only jesting regarding the powder. In the unlikely event that they do coax a round out of the thing, the chances of the ball landing anywhere near us are very nearly equal to that of the Savior returning this afternoon."

Rooney groaned. "Damn it, Finnegan. I was the naysayer before you reminded me how those wretched artillery rounds bounced about during the war. Do you recall poor Monty Burgett?"

Finnegan cocked his head to one side. "The corporal who lost a leg?"

"Yes. That round no less than came back at us. It was fired from our own guns. It struck a rock wall and bounced back." Rooney shivered at the recollection.

Finnegan nodded with a confused look on his face. "Yes, I recall poor Monty lost a leg, but that is hardly the worst of it a man might have received."

"It is the worst I ever saw a man receive from his own artillery core."

Finnegan cocked his head the other way. "I would not say that. I saw no less than three men die that very day when a mortar exploded. The entire crew was shredded to bits; one fellow was little more than a pair of boots."

Rooney threw his hands in the air. "And poor Monty lost a leg. What I am attempting to explain is that cannon are not to be trusted."

Finnegan waggled one finger. "What you are attempting to obfuscate is your wish to return to your bottle."

"Be that as it may..." The boom of a cannon came from the town, followed by the all too familiar sound of a cannonball whistling overhead. "I will be damned." Both men clambered up the tie pile to witness the cannonball slamming into the gunwale of the closest barge before falling into the river. "I will be damned, Finnegan. Those daft buggers hit their mark."

"A respectable feat, even if it failed to cause any damage. Perhaps Rogers was justified in his concern regarding the field piece." Another boom was heard from the town. There was a whistling sound once again, but both men recognized the change in tone. "Hell and perdition!" Finnegan leapt from the tie pile as the cannonball crashed into it. As they had been trained to do in their youth, both men ran as hard as they could from where they guessed the ball had impacted. Ignoring the gunfire from the barges, they sprinted across the gap to the door of the pumphouse. Finnegan glanced back to see several ties tossed from the pile when the ball exploded. "By God, I would have bet against that."

Rooney huffed and puffed next to him in the doorway. "Yes, it would seem the art of prophecy is not with you today. I cannot believe the ball exploded. Did you not say they had been stored outside next to the cannon?"

Finnegan nodded. "In the weather, certainly. These steel men are far luckier than they are intelligent, for sure."

Rooney stood stooped and huffing. "Luck, hell. It was a genuine miracle."

Finnegan sneered. "If the ball had descended on the Pinkertons, I might give it credence."

Rooney threw his arms in the air. "The bloody thing did descend on Pinkertons, Finnegan. Only God is aware we are Pinkertons. How else should a sane man attribute it?"

"If God wishes to smite either of us, I doubt he would have waited this long." The gunman shook his head.

Rooney rubbed his eyes. "Enough of this rot. Let us get back to the roof so I might procure my flask and give this proper consideration."

"Ah, yes, I am certain that will clear your head." Finnegan motioned toward the stairs. "After you; I am more than willing to follow anywhere so long as we are surrounded by this fine plate steel. I daresay, that cannonball unnerved me a bit."

They began climbing the stairs with Rooney in the lead. "It seems a hundred years since we were last under fire from cannon. Do you recall that odd boy who was so desperate to be one of the artillery crews?"

Finnegan plodded and thought on it. "I believe I recall the boy. Red hair?"

"Yes. He so longed to tote a ramrod, and when they

finally put him on the line the mongrel forgot to block the wheel on his side. The gun recoiled and broke his arms." They reached the roof and Rooney stopped short in the doorway. "Ah, damn it. There is someone up here, Finnegan."

Finnegan craned his head around Rooney. He could see a stout lad of about twenty, sitting, lingering near the corpse of the sniper. "I suppose he has as much right to wander around the roof of a pumphouse as we do. What of it?"

"Just so he has not been making use of my cache." Rooney walked out from the doorway and raised his hand to the man. "Hello there, fellow."

The young man raised his head and offered a small wave in return before crouching a bit and moving toward the new arrivals. When he made it over to Rooney and Finnegan, he straightened and offered his hand to Rooney. "Silas Wain. I am a pipefitter and rivet man." He looked from one Pinkerton to the other and back again. "I apologize; if we have met before, I do not recall."

Finnegan stepped forward and took the man's hand. "O'Brien, and this is McCall. There are many workingmen here today; a fellow cannot know them all. What brings you up here, son?"

Silas raised both eyebrows. "I heard what I thought to be...well, at first, I could not have told you what it could be. I ran up here to get a better look and if I am not dreaming, and have not gone mad, I do truly believe some of the men have got that old cannon from the Republic House and are firing it."

Finnegan chuckled. "You are not mistaken. The first volley landed near to the intended mark. The next shot very nearly did for us, so we elected, as you did, to flee to this very stout structure."

The young steelworker appeared quite excited. "Do you believe they will fire the piece again?"

Finnegan shrugged. "They very well may, if they still possess sufficient powder."

"Oh, I truly hope they do!" Silas motioned toward the town. "I have never seen a cannon fire. Where is it located?"

"They have it back in one of the town streets, but I should warn you, young man: a cannon is nothing to play peek-a-boo with. Many an exuberant youth has briefly regretted that notion. Best to stay toward the center of this roof or well concealed behind the hip wall." Finnegan patted the lad on one shoulder.

"Oh, bosh." Rooney took the young man by one arm. "Come over this way. If your fortune holds, this will be the only time you see such a thing. I will even buy you a drink while we wait."

Finnegan held up a hand. "Sam, in light of what we have just recently experienced, can you claim this to be wise?"

Rooney shook his head. "In light of what we have recently experienced, I deem this to be perfectly safe." He grinned. "It is inconceivable, incredible, I daresay impossible, that two errant cannonballs could come close to hitting the same man on the same day. It would be tantamount to being struck twice by lightning. I am in no danger and neither is this chap."

Finnegan gave both men a small salute. "Your logic is undeniable, Sam. That being said, I believe I will sit over here and smoke a cigar until those fools run out of powder. I have seen enough of cannons for one day."

"The fewer men, the greater share of honor." Rooney led the young man over to the hip wall and found his flask within the satchel.

Finnegan sat puffing on a cigar in the shade of the small

cupola where the stairs met the roof. It really was a lovely day, and if a battle had not been raging down below the gunman might have nodded off and napped the rest of it away. He checked his watch and saw that it was nearing midday. In the distance, toward the far side of the river, a small spire of smoke was rising. Finnegan stood to get a better look. He grinned and turned toward Rooney and the cannon enthusiast. "The tugboat is returning, Sam."

Rooney leaned out over the hip wall. "Indeed. That captain has more guts than I might have credited him with." He turned and motioned toward the town. "I believe they are making ready, Silas."

The young man brought up the spyglass Rooney had provided him with. "Ah, now, this is exciting. I had thought I would have to join the damned army to witness such a thing."

Finnegan laughed. "As old as that piece is, you would likely have had to join Napoleon's army." He sat back down and resumed puffing his cigar. A boom was heard in the distance.

Silas leaned forward with the spyglass, an ear-to-ear grin covering his face. "I saw the smoke, sirs. By God, that is truly something."

An eerie whistling filled the air once again. Finnegan spit out his cigar. "Bloody hell!" He rolled to the side and flopped down the set of stairs behind him. Above, he heard a wet thud followed by the crash of a cannonball tearing part of the roof from the cupola. Dusty rubble and a few shingles came down onto the prostrate gunman, who lay on the first available landing of the stairs. He brought his head up to glance around. After making certain the cannonball was not lying near, he slowly got to his feet and reascended the stairs. When he reached the doorway at the top, he stopped and grimaced. Rooney stood by the hip wall, dumbfounded, while young Silas's headless body lay not five feet distant. Finnegan hung his head. "That is a damn shame." He peeked around the corner of the cupola. "Did that damn ball pass completely over the roof, Sam?" Rooney made no effort to answer; he only stared at the rooftop's most recently deposited corpse. "Sam! Ah, damn this." Finnegan rubbed his eyes and stalked across the roof to Rooney. When he reached his friend, he cuffed him across the face with a small backhand. "Sam!"

Rooney turned to Finnegan. "I would not have thought such a thing possible."

"Yes, you expounded on that point at some length." Finnegan hung his head. "It is damned unfortunate. He seemed like a fine lad."

"I just simply would not have imagined such a thing was possible."

"Yes, you made mention of that already." Finnegan knelt and picked up the spyglass Silas had been holding. He put his eye to the back and lowered the piece. "It is undamaged." Finnegan rubbed his chin. "This day overflows with odd occurrences, Sam."

"I cannot conceive of how such a thing could be possible."

The firing had ebbed off after the most recent cannon round was fired, but it began to pick up again in earnest. "Sam, I would not care to spend the rest of the day discussing a question, the answer to which is so very easily observed. Quite obviously, such a thing was possible, did occur, and caused that young fellow to lose his head. He lies not more than a few feet from the other dullard who ventured to wager his life on this foolishness." Finnegan used the spyglass to observe the approach of the *Little Bill*, which had precipitated the increase in gunfire. "Captain Rodgers may not be overly bright, but he is proving to be entertaining. They have shot out what small amount of glass remained to that boat."

Rooney remained quite still. "It is only that I would have thought the whole affair quite impossible."

"Good grief, man, do you intend to prattle on like that all day?" Finnegan pointed out toward the river and looked through the glass once again. "Ah, yes, there it is now." Finnegan chuckled. "Sufficient paint has been knocked from the tug to convince the captain that discretion is the better part of valor." The gunman watched as the tug made a slow turn and began to cross to the far side of the river once more.

"Damn it all to hell!" Rooney's fugue state appeared to have been broken. "This damn well should not stand, Finnegan."

The gunman sighed. "To what do you refer?"

"I say that we ought to go give the crew of that gun what for. They are no less than a damn menace and they have killed a good boy here for no reason."

Finnegan nodded. "Yes, a most excellent notion in my opinion." He grinned. "Come up behind them while they are busy at their work, just as we did in our youth?"

"And well deserving of it they are, too." Rooney knelt and collected their satchel.

Finnegan held up one hand. "Give me a moment. I wish to climb this tower and investigate the fate of that fine rifle that other fellow possessed. I notice it did not fall with him."

Rooney scowled. "Is it not a bit ghoulish to make off with a dead fellow's rifle? It is not as if you do not own a sufficient number already."

"There are not enough fine Ballard rifles still in the world to be so callous as to the fate of even one, Sam. If that poor devil were still alive, he would agree with me, I assure you."

The charlatan waved one hand, dismissively. "Very well,

then, go collect the damn thing. If it is still trustworthy, perhaps you can make use of it for one of that cannon crew."

Finnegan began carefully ascending the ladder. It had more than a few dents in it from errant bullets, and he hugged it closely so as not to be overt and draw fire from the barges. "If she is still in good condition, I will do my best to make that poor dead sniper proud. He seemed the type to not split too many hairs regarding allegiances."

THE TWO MEN descended the stairs to the ground floor of the pumphouse and peeked out the doorway once again to discover that the gunfire had largely ebbed. Only one bullet thudded into the dirt during the full minute they stood and gauged their chances.

Finnegan wiped a bit of dust from the action of the Ballard rifle he had retrieved from the water tower catwalk. "I am quite pleased to have saved this piece from an ignoble end."

"It is ridiculous for a man of your means to be dragging about such an item." Rooney shook his head.

"What on earth do my means have to do with it?" Finnegan swiped more dust.

"I assumed you took the rifle with the intention of selling it."

"I took possession of this fine gun so that I might shoot deer or whatever roams the slopes of the place I may settle with Molly. A Ballard also offers the added incentive of appearing quite fine above a fellow's mantle. I have never owned a mantle, or the claptrap that surrounds one, but I intend to, presently. I will sit in my rocking chair and gaze at my mantle, recalling the events of the great Battle of Homestead." He let a smile spread from one corner of his mouth. "Sadly, the last time I ever saw my dear friend, Sam Rooney."

The charlatan shook his head woefully. "Do not jest so, Finnegan. You may lay a hex on me."

"Poor, luckless, Sam. I never had reason to doubt the battle would end and he would resume his listless travels clouded with whiskey and chicanery, but then, no man can say when tragedy may descend upon you."

"This jest is in poor taste, Finnegan."

"Ah, I recall it well. The smoke had just cleared from the great conflagration and sad Sam found the town of Homestead overpopulated with wailing widows. He, of course, had no choice, and was dutybound to comfort the one who seemed most well-off. He spent the rest of his days with brats underfoot and an inherited grocery store to tend to."

"By God, you are a cruel one, Finnegan. I would rather you had suggested my death."

Finnegan motioned to the doorway. "It would appear that the brave men of the Pinkerton Agency have begun to conserve ammunition. Of course, that does not mean we ought to dawdle."

Rooney nodded. "Yes, I would hate to be the chap who gave a poor marksman greater confidence."

Finnegan checked his guns and various gear to make sure everything was in place. "Very well, then. To our old stomping grounds by the railroad ties, and then on from there to find the cannon?"

"As usual, on the verge of heroics, I begin to question the necessity." Rooney pulled his hat down.

"I would not call it necessity. I will say that I am damned bored with sitting around watching these idiots die in strange ways. Some activity may take my mind off such gloomy matters." Finnegan ran from the doorway with his newly acquired rifle in one hand. Rooney followed closely with their satchel. Nary a bullet fell near them during the trip to the railroad tie stack. Once there, they paused to pick a path toward the town proper. "That was by no means as sporting the second time."

Rooney stopped to peek through a hole in the ties toward the barges. "Whoever commands may have realized their ammunition supply will not last forever."

Finnegan shrugged. "Many a man begins the day rich in some commodity and is forced to sell it dear before the sunset."

Rooney wiped sweat from his face. The day was growing warm. "Do you believe the tug will attempt to return for them?"

"I do not."

Rooney looked to the barges again. "I would not care to charge up this hill. It is not steep, but the men above have fine cover and there are so very many of these steel men."

Finnegan nodded. "Heinde will have little choice in the matter, soon." Finnegan scowled and looked at the barges for himself. "The daft bugger ought to have attempted a charge the moment he saw the tug turning. To wait now is folly. He has but one option; he should accept it and run the hazard."

Rooney took a quick sip from his flask. "Perhaps Heinde no longer commands? He was surely hit, though I cannot say how thoroughly."

"Nordrum is no fool, or at least he never seemed to be. He should order those men over the gunwales and be done with it. Many would fall, but it would be preferable to lingering in one of those damn boats waiting for these steel men to conceive of a plan to murder them all in totality. It is, at best, silly and, at worst, madness to put off the inevitable."

Rooney carefully returned his flask to the satchel and

took up the bag again in preparation for another run. "Perhaps they see little difference between dying in a rush up this hill or dying on the boats."

"I would prefer the hill." The gunman shrugged again. "But then, that has always been my way."

The charlatan smiled at his old friend. "If you were in their place, what would you attempt?"

Finnegan had the answer ready. "I would go over the gunwale with as many fellows at I could muster. Up the hill in short rushes, until I reached the town, where a horse might be procured hurriedly." He motioned to the east. "I would make for Pittsburg and pray to God that I could retain my anonymity once there."

"Somehow, I believe you could truly bring about such a miracle. The Good Lord has always doted on you as though He finds you to be a special amusement." Rooney motioned to the river. "I doubt those men in the barges are so fortunate."

Finnegan looked away from the river and back up the hill toward the town. "If a man does not believe himself to be blessed with fortune, he should cease to gamble." He pointed toward one of the town's brick buildings. "If I am not mistaken, it appeared as though they set up their field artillery somewhere in that vicinity. We ought to move to the opposite side of the building and then attempt to come up behind them."

Rooney nodded. "I have not heard the cannon roar since that last errant shot."

"Perhaps they have frightened themselves into some sense."

"Perhaps." Rooney rubbed his eyes and glanced about the millworks. "Finnegan, you do understand that I will not be of much assistance when we move to take the cannon."

Finnegan patted his old friend on the back. "You frequently provide distraction at the opportune time."

"Even so, I have often wondered why you request my presence for such matters."

The gunman paused to consider the question. "I suppose I simply enjoy your company."

"Ah, well, that explains the matter rather well." Rooney clutched the satchel. "Shall we be about our business, then?"

"Indeed." The two men began to move up the hill. There were few shots ringing out, but the day's events had made them both cautious. When they reached the brick building at the end of the street, they slunk around the far side and made it to the rear of the structure, seemingly unobserved. They paused at the back door of the building and Rooney set the satchel down next to Finnegan, where he crouched. "What would you say are the chances of our being able to disable that damn cannon without these steel men becoming aware of our allegiances?" He leaned the Ballard against the wall and opened the bag.

"Even though they have hitherto only done injury to their own men, I would say we are likely to become ostracized."

Finnegan withdrew the two sections of shotgun from the satchel and linked them together. He slid four shells into the gun's tubular magazine and worked the action to load a shell into the chamber. One additional round was added to the tube. "Very well. I see no particular reason to murder the fools. If you concur, I will order them away from the cannon. If they will not comply, I will shoot them. We had best disable the piece by spiking the touchhole with something. There must be a nail somewhere hereabouts. At any rate, we had best be on our way quickly when our work is concluded."

Rooney cleared his throat. "Finnegan, I have had the opportunity for reflection during our journey here. Do you not believe it might be best to simply inform the fellows that they are killing their own people rather consistently with each shot, and it would be in their own best interest to cease fire?"

Finnegan bit on his lower lip, shotgun in hand. "Yes, that might be preferable."

"I was somewhat agitated initially, as well."

Finnegan nodded. "As you can plainly see, it is oftentimes useful to have a fellow such as yourself around, Sam. This sort of matter is why I request your presence."

"Always proud to serve." He motioned toward the street. "Although, in the event they refuse to cease fire, I must insist you shoot the jackasses." Rooney picked up the Ballard. "I may even make an attempt on them myself."

"You could not have chosen a finer rifle to begin your career with, Sam." The two men slunk up to the corner of the building, then quickly came around to the street with Finnegan in the lead. He could see a group of men standing no more than fifty yards distant. He held the shotgun low, but ready, as he approached. He was just about to call out to the men, when two of them parted and provided a clear view of the cannon. Finnegan stopped in his tracks and stared at the artillery piece. "If I am not mistaken, we are witness to the eventual fate of all cannons, Sam."

Rooney came up next to Finnegan, the Ballard clutched firmly in one hand. The brass barrel of the cannon had been split down one side, and the right wheel had come off the weapon's carriage when the frame beneath the barrel had splintered. "Now that you mention it, I do not believe I ever saw a cannon that did not eventually meet that fate." Rooney put the butt of the Ballard on one boot and stood at ease. "I suppose now they will be forced to find a new amusement."

"Us, as well." Finnegan leaned his shotgun against the

brick of the nearby building and lit a cigar. He stood puffing as one of the men gathered around the cannon took notice of the two observers and ventured back toward them. Finnegan watched the broad, old fellow approach. When he was within earshot, Finnegan waved. "Today I have seen a navy and an artillery core come up short; would you care to form a cavalry regiment?"

The old man grinned and pulled his rather tattered felt hat down over his bald head. The man was clearly aged, but did not move as though he were. "A fine notion, but me and the boys have discussed the matter and believe it is time to get after that damned attacking navy with their own kind. I could use two strapping fellows like you two to assist me."

Rooney looked from the old man to Finnegan and back again. "You wish our assistance?"

The old man slowly nodded. "I do, indeed. I would not imagine the prospect of work to be all that distasteful to men such as yourselves. If you were morally opposed to honest labor, you would reside down in those barges with the scum of the earth."

Finnegan slowly removed his cigar from his lips. "Yes, well, that would surely be a shame. How might we be of aid, sir?"

The old man leaned in conspiratorially. "You boys ever heard of a Conestoga Charger?" Both men shook their heads. "Well, let me be the one to tell you, it is a hell of an item, and just the thing to bring this here battle to a quick conclusion. You take notice of how close that one freight track comes to the back end of that one barge?"

Finnegan rubbed his chin. "I would say there is not more than thirty feet between them."

The old man grinned with what remained of his teeth. "If that, my friend. Them damn Pinks are moored up right where we generally bring down the big Conestogas on the track, fill 'em with whatever it is the tug brought us, and then we haul them back up here with the steam engine doing all the work." Finnegan and Rooney both nodded, but the old man could see they were not gleaning an understanding of the upcoming plan. "Damn it, boys, can't neither of you understand what's being discussed here?"

Rooney rubbed one side of his face. "You wish to ride down to the river in a wagon?"

"Hell no, I don't want to ride down to the damn river." The old man gave Rooney a look that said he suspected the charlatan of being simpleminded. "I don't want to go nowhere near them Pinks; that's the whole purpose of the wagon."

Finnegan snapped his fingers and grinned. "Ah, yes, I see. You wish to build a whirligig." He smiled at Rooney, clearly proud to have finally keened the old man's strategy. "This fellow wishes to fill one of those freightwagons with lumber, or some such, light it aflame, and then roll it down these tracks so that it crashes into the barges and sends all the Pinkerton men to varied levels of perdition." Finnegan turned back to the old man. "Is that the essence of your plan, sir?"

The old steelman nodded slowly. "That is the essence of my plan, young fella, and I hope you boys are a damn sight quicker about stacking lumber than you are at getting a man's drift. If you ain't, we're bound to be here all damn day." The old man began stalking off toward the freightwagons and lumber piles near the tracks leading down toward the river.

Finnegan and Rooney remained back for a moment. Rooney leaned toward Finnegan. "He is a dedicated old bastard, I will give him that. It would be a pity to kill him when nature may choose to at any moment. Perhaps we ought simply tie him and stash him somewhere until this conflagration is at an end."

Finnegan waved one hand. "There will be no need for such antics. The old lunatic's plan will come to nothing."

"It seems a reasonable notion for burning a barge, Finnegan."

"It seems a reasonable notion every time men the world over conceive of it, and every time it fails in effect. I do not know why, perhaps no man knowns why, but rolling flaming wagons down hills comes to naught. At any rate, I have witnessed many a fine disaster in my time and have yet to see a Conestoga wagon leap thirty feet."

Rooney rubbed his eyes. "And if you are incorrect in your thinking and we are a party to the immolation of those men down there?"

Finnegan shrugged. "I quite flatly informed both Heinde and Nordrum as to the foolishness of barges. If they become the first men in history to be defeated by a flaming wagon, then I would say they deserve their fate, as they have clearly lost God's favor."

Neither Finnegan nor Rooney much cared for physical labor, but they found the stacking of lumber somewhat of a welcome alternative that particular June day. The old man had selected a pile of much-abused planks and timbers previously used for stacking and cooling bar stock. Both men had done their best to put their backs into their labor so as not to be discovered as the shameless lay-abouts they truly were. With sweat pouring from him, Rooney helped Finnegan to cast the last timber up and onto the pile they had built in the rear of the Conestoga.

The old man climbed to the wagon's seat holding a bucket which slopped oil, hunks of grease, and kerosene as he ascended. "I'll say this for you boys: you stack lumber faster than you see the light." He sloshed the bucket's contents around on the pile. The black ooze made a popping sound as it seeped into the grey wood. The old man tossed the bucket into the wagon bed for good measure and slowly climbed back down to the ground. "Now, you boys will be able to tell your grandkiddies how you was there the day Abner Fickle brought about an end to the great Battle of Homestead."

Finnegan raised an eyebrow. "Abner Fickle?"

"Something wrong with the name my daddy and the Good Lord leveled on me, son?"

The gunman shrugged, simply glad to no longer be laboring. "I would not say there is any one aspect of it I find objectionable, it is only that it does not particularly strike my ear as the name of a man who would end a battle."

Rooney shook his head. "That is no way to regard the matter. For all we can say, Lord Nelson's original moniker was none other than Abner Fickle."

Finnegan shrugged again. "For all I can say, Lord Nelson stands before us."

Fickle struck a match and tossed it into the wagon bed. In an instant, flames began to lick up amongst the timbers. "Who in hell is Lord Nelson?" He sneered and took hold of the wagon's brake lever. "Educate me later on, boys. Currently, I only wish to see Pinkertons burn." He gave the lever a stout pull, and the wagon began to roll forward.

Finnegan withdrew a cigar from his vest pocket and watched the wagon depart. The conveyance had the better part of a half mile to descend before nearing the barges, and the rig began to pick up speed at a rather impressive rate. The hill had not appeared to be all that steep, but the wagon fairly rocketed along. For a brief moment, Finnegan began to imagine the jittering old pile of wood really might clear thirty feet of distance and make it to the intended target. Such wild notions were instantly dispelled when the wagon flopped off the tracks and crashed into an old boiler roughly halfway to the river. Flaming wood and debris scattered about in the black earth and slag that littered the millworks. Finnegan recognized the area where the wagon had met its demise. "Ah, yes, well, it would appear that cannon ball exploding tossed one or two of the ties onto the tracks down there. Pity, I should have been proud to aid in immortalizing you, Mr. Fickle."

The old man stood, clenching and unclenching his weathered fists. "Hell and perdition, why didn't neither of you two get the idea to check the damn tracks to make sure there wasn't obstructions?"

Rooney took a seat on a nearby bucket. "In truth, sir, the thought did cross my mind. However, I have spent some time near those ties recently and did not care to offer my services for fear of being shot. Had I known it would all be in the name of the legendary Abner Fickle, I would have obliged." He motioned to Finnegan to provide a cigar. "Not every flight of fancy leads to greatness, sir. We should congratulate ourselves on the attempt and leave the remainder of the war to other men, in my humble opinion."

"I would heartily second that." Finnegan puffed out smoke and handed Rooney his cigar.

"This ain't over. Not by a damn stretch." Fickle turned to the two undisclosed Pinkertons. "Trouble here is we been putting too damn much stock in piddly claptrap like wagons and tracks. We got to see to it that there ain't no damn way to fail."

Rooney lit his cigar and held it high. "Here, here. The power of prayer will determine the outcome, brothers."

"Prayer, hell. I still want to burn 'em. You lazy bastards follow me. You can damn well smoke and walk at the same time, I should hope." The old man began trudging toward the river. The failure of the whirligig appeared to have taken some of the strut out of him.

Rooney looked to Finnegan. "Do you think it wise to continue associating with this fellow? If he continues to plot and we continue to aid him, he may yet arrive at a functional scheme."

Finnegan spit out a piece of errant tobacco and puffed his cigar. "The old bastard does seem to possess a great amount of dedication. I would suggest a cautious approach. We shall accompany him and assess what it is he has planned next. If the next stratagem bodes ill for the Pinkertons, we need only find a convenient place to hide his body." Sporadic shots rang out from both the barges and the steel works. "His demise will not be difficult to comprehend. We need only distance ourselves from it."

Rooney sighed and began walking in the direction the old man had gone. "By God, Finnegan, you have a gloomy sort of occupation."

The shadows inside the massive millworks were only interrupted by the occasional slash of sunlight that poured in from the filthy windows above. Finnegan and Rooney had followed the old man nearly down to the river's edge before turning to enter one of the gigantic mill buildings. The three men marched along, following a set of railroad tracks that entered the building. At one end of the building a steel colossus of girders and vats loomed. The rest of the building was taken up by the long set of tracks and what appeared to be somewhat standard railcars.

"What is the purpose of this place, old timer?" Rooney asked, marveling.

"This is where we make track for the railroad. One red hot piece at a time. Made enough in here to stretch all the way to the Pacific." The old man stopped and eyeballed Rooney. "How is it you don't know what a track mill looks like?"

Finnegan fielded the question. "We are not steel workers, only humble masons. We have come here to assist our fellow workmen as best we can in their time of need."

"Awful damn lazy for Samaritans." The old man stopped and pointed toward a collection of twenty-gallon barrels. "But we can remedy that." He stepped to the closest barrel. "They build these damn stout. I reckon we ought to have no trouble rolling them down to the river without them giving way."

Finnegan stepped next to another barrel and gave it a small shove. The barrel did not budge. "What is inside these, sir?"

"Lubricating oil." The old man waved a hand around. "Everything in the whole damn place needs lubricating oil. The heat, the rust, the wear. Oil's the only thing keeps the whole damn mill from locking up tighter than a nun's corset."

Finnegan raised an eyebrow. "What, pray tell, do you intend to make use of this for?" The gunman noticed that there were more than a few cozy corners nearby into which he might deposit the inventive old fellow.

"Well, in case you ain't noticed, we are just now upriver from them damn Pinks. What I am intending on is to roll these here barrels down to the river. Once we get 'em down there, we'll knock the bungs out of them flood the river with this here oil and then light the stuff aflame. Them barges will burn right where they're floatin'."

Rooney shook his head and grinned. "Sir, I am hesitant to expound on another man's chances of success, but I must say, I believe rolling these barrels anywhere to be a waste of labor."

The old man squared up in front of Rooney. "Now, just what in the hell are you trying to tell me about lubricating oil, Mr. Mason?"

Rooney cleared his throat. "I will tell you this, quite plainly, sir. I have ventured to the environs where that oil is brought up from the earth, and I can assure you that it does not float on top of water, as it is heavier than water. If we pour that filth into the river, it will simply sink to the bottom where there is no chance of igniting it." Rooney crossed his arms and appeared rather satisfied with himself.

"Well, if that don't beat all the damnedest, dumb nonsense I ever did hear." The old man spit down into the slag at his feet. "You don't know a damn thing about oil. Any fool knows it floats on water."

"Impossible." Rooney smiled to Finnegan. "If oil could float on top of water, what would it be doing beneath the ground? If it were not more dense than water, it would be puddling out on top of lakes and rivers the world over, and we would be constantly surrounded by an endless fire storm. Oil sinks in water, sir. It is plain common sense, and we do not need to pour several barrels of the stuff into a river to prove the point."

"No, no, no." The old man shook his head. "Son, you are assessing this thing plumb backwards. Now, it's plain to see that you don't know a damn thing about oil but, from the look of you, I'd say you've stumbled into your fair share of saloons?" Rooney nodded. "Good, then you've witnessed many a barkeep pouring mineral oil on top of whiskey to keep the spirits from escaping around the cork."

Rooney sighed. "Mr. Fickle, surely a man of your years must know that whiskey is a far cry from water."

"You damned pup, I ought to..." Fickle cocked back his arm, but Finnegan held the limb back.

"Sam, Mr. Fickle, I cannot say as I know to a certainty whether or not oil from the earth or mineral oil will float on water, but there is a chance these barrels may contain whale oil. In that case, I would surely predict it would float."

"Ha! There, you pup." Fickle waggled a finger at Rooney. "What the hell you got to say to that?"

Rooney sighed again. "My dear chap, if whale oil were capable of floating, how could those great beasts reside beneath the water?"

Finnegan rubbed his chin. "If the oil within a whale does not float, why does the beast not sink to the bottom like a stone?"

Rooney scowled. "That I cannot say."

"What I cannot say is how two such daft bastards as you have lived to see your hair begin to grey." The old man threw his hands in the air. "I do not have the slightest inclining as to what allows a whale to lark about as they do. What I can say for certain is that those damned Pinks ain't gonna come walking out of them barges to get their dinner, so some such as us will damn well have to push them out. Now, if you two won't help an old wheelwright roll these barrels, you could at least do me the favor of closing your damn mouths." The old man turned from the younger men and began to slowly rotate one of the barrels.

Finnegan turned to Rooney and shrugged. "I suppose it would appear cowardly not to at least allow the old fellow the opportunity to prove you wrong. By this time, I have become genuinely interested."

Rooney sighed one last time and moved to the nearest barrel. "As nothing else requires my time presently, I suppose I must agree."

The three men made two trips to the river with one barrel each. When all six barrels stood with their bungs facing the river, positioned so that the fluid within would spill into the Monongahela, the old man declared he was ready to begin the experiment. Fickle moved from one barrel to the next, bashing out the bung plugs with a ball peen hammer. As he went, the black goo within the barrels began to spill out into the otherwise clear water. As it spilled, Fickle was beside himself with joy to take note of how the slick floated atop the river.

"Now, then, I suppose that puts an end to that particular bit of idiocy." Fickle sneered at Rooney.

The charlatan stared in amazement. "Wonders never cease; I would not have believed it was possible."

Finnegan shook his head. "Why? It is not as if you know anything regarding oil."

"Still, common sense would dictate..." He threw his hands in the air. "Such is my punishment for attempting to make use of common sense once in my life." The occasional shot could still be heard from the millworks or the barges, but the volume had fallen off considerably. Rooney watched as the slick glinted in the midday sun and slowly made its way toward the barges some quarter mile down the river. He turned to Fickle. "How do you intend to ignite that awful stuff, sir?"

Fickle folded his arms in triumph. "Damn nice to see you have finally arrived at the conclusion that I am well versed in matters pertaining to oil. As a pup and a mason, you would not be privy to the fact that nothing on this green earth burns like that slimy grease yonder. The rotten goo bursts aflame almost all by itself in the mills just by getting hot. Any spark is liable to set it off, be it in a gear box or on the water like that there." He nodded, approving of the extending slick. "Yes, boys, just give it a few minutes and them damn Pinks will feel hell licking at 'em before they even have a chance to meet the devil." He sighed and watched the slick expand. "I reckon you boys had best scamper up the hill and grab a few more of them barrels. Don't want it to give out before them boats are good and lit."

Finnegan turned and began walking up the hill. "As you think best, sir."

Rooney sidled next to him as they walked back up to the millworks. "Finnegan, I do not mean to intrude into your half of the business, but I am more than a bit surprised you have not laid that old fool low yet. I cannot say as I would care to see the old man dead, but should we not haul him off and bind him up somewhere before he lights that oil?"

"Sam, those men cannot stay on those barges indefinitely. The tug is quite obviously not returning, if it did, I doubt it would be allowed to collect the barges. If they are not driven out by that old man lighting the river on fire, they will be forced out by some other means." Finnegan strolled through the millworks and grabbed hold of another barrel. "We have rendered those fools all the aid we can. From this point forward, as I see it, only God can save them." He looked down the hill toward Fickle. "I must say, I would prefer to let that old bastard bring about the end of this siege. He takes such pride in his flights of fancy."

"I am certain Heinde will appreciate the sentiment as he burns." Rooney grabbed a barrel of his own.

"Men such as Heinde ought to know they are bound to

burn. There is no reason for them to expect it any less in this world than the next." The two men rolled their respective barrels down the hill to the place on the riverbank where Fickle waited. When they got there, the old man knocked the bungs out of them and more oil sputtered into the Monongahela.

"You got another one of them cigars, young fella?" Finnegan nodded and handed the old man a cigar. "Damn decent of you, son." Fickle reached into his pocket and withdrew a match. "Here's to you, boys." He struck the match on one of the metal barrel bands, lit his cigar, and then tossed the still flaming match into the river. A dull sizzle came from the water. "What in hell?"

Finnegan rubbed his face. "Perhaps you ought to begin at the source there, sir." He motioned to the oil still flowing from one barrel.

"Uh, yup, I guess I ought to have thought of that." The old man produced another match and knelt by the barrel. "Now, you pups keep back. I seen many a fella lose his hair when this stuff gets to blazing." Holding his face back from the barrel as best he could, Fickle struck another match on a band and flipped it into the oil as it oozed out. The match issued a sizzling sound once again before drowning. "Damn it all, anyway."

Finnegan held up one finger. "It occurs to me that the overall temperature inside a steel mill must be very high."

Fickle nodded. "I seen a demon ask for a break in there. What of it?"

"You may require a hotter flame to ignite the oil, sir." Finnegan shrugged.

"First thing either of you pups said that makes any sense." Fickle turned to Rooney and wrenched down on the sleeve of his coat.

Rooney pulled his sleeve free and took a step back from the old man. "Just what the hell are you about?"

"We got to make us a torch. I need some cloth and a stick." Fickle puffed his cigar.

"Well, I do not have a stick in my possession, and you are daft if you believe I will donate my clothing." Rooney motioned to a pile of lumber upriver. "I will bring you some of that tarpaulin and an old stave if you will promise to remain here and not attempt to disrobe my associate while I am gone."

Fickle waggled an arm toward the lumber pile. "Just so's you're getting to it." As Rooney departed to fetch torch materials, Fickle turned to Finnegan. "Your friend is damn high strung for this sort of work."

Finnegan surveyed the barrels as the last of the oil emptied into the river. "All this is new to him. At the next insurrection, he will be better practiced."

Fickle puffed smoke into the air. "I suppose some folks is just slow learners." When Rooney returned, Fickle took the hunks of tarpaulin and wrapped them around one end of the gnarled stick Rooney had located. With the cloth wrapped tight, Fickle dipped the torch head into the last dribble of oil and touched his cigar cherry to it. In an instant, sparks sputtered from the cloth and the torch was ablaze. "Now we got us a going concern." Fickle stood on the riverbank and brought the torch down into the slick on the water. Sadly, one half of the torch uttered a mournful sizzle, and the slick failed to ignite. "I will be damned!" Fickle glanced up at the nearest barrel, sneered, and plunged the still burning torch into the barrel's bung hole. Sparks flew and the barrel exploded, casting Fickle and what remained of his torch into the river.

Finnegan and Rooney ducked away as the barrel went up. As they turned back, they could see Fickle, with his extinguished torch, standing knee deep in the river. Apparently inert oil clung to his pants and shirt. The old man had a rather inscrutable look, so Finnegan called out to him. "Are you all right, Mr. Fickle? Do you still have your hair?"

The old man cast the useless torch down into the river and trudged to the shore, where he slipped several times trying to ascend the muddy, oily bank. After a few attempts, Finnegan and Rooney came forward and lifted him back to the safety of the grass, some of which still smoldered. Fickle wiped a smear of oil and a small amount of mud from his face. "I cannot say why the Good Lord should see fit to put me through such trials." He spit the mangled cigar from his lips. "I cannot say why the Good Lord chooses to so very often test the men who attempt His good work." He squeezed water from his shirt sleeves. "But he surely does." He pulled his hat from his head and squeezed the water from it. "Might I inquire, have either of you gentlemen ever been of note?"

Both men stared back quizzically, but Rooney fielded the question "In what regard, sir?"

Fickle threw his hat down onto the oily earth. "In any damn regard. Do either of you two have the slightest reason for believing that ten damn minutes after you pass on a single soul will recall your name or remember that you lived? They'll be talking about that damned Carnegie and his lap dog Frick a hundred years hence but, I ask you, will one man recall the name Abner Fickle?"

Finnegan chuckled. "I can assure you, after seeing you cast into the river, I will not forget you."

"I was hoping for just a bit more than that, son." The old man hung his head for a brief moment before raising it. A smile played across his lips. "Oh, I got a notion just now. I do believe I have it, boys." Fickle began walking off toward the millworks. "I reckon a man's only worth remembering if he does a great deed, and history never recalls how many attempts a fella made, anyhow."

Fickle led the way into the foundry. On any other day the interior of the massive chamber would have been lit by the glow of molten steel. On this day, it felt remarkably like entering a tomb. While Finnegan and Rooney gazed awestruck at the sheer size of the machinery, Fickle passed by it with nary a glance. He left the main area and led them off into a small building built inside the larger, near the rear of the foundry. Fickle tried the knob on the shack's door, then kicked it in without ceremony.

"Can't hardly believe they locked this up. As if some of them fools truly believe they got a share in this outfit." He felt around on the wall and found a kerosene lantern, which he lit to illuminate the interior of the small space. He pointed to a large red box in the back. "That, there, is what we're after."

"Ah, bloody hell." Rooney stared at the chest. It bore the words *GIANT POWDER DANGEROUS HANDLE WITH CARE*. "Mr. Fickle, let me say that I have some experience in the application of that awful stuff, and no good ever comes of it."

Fickle shook his head. "Ain't the worst stuff. We get good use from it, blasting the slag out of furnaces. 'Course, we set it off using a box with one of them wires running out of it, and that ain't what we need today." He grinned in the lantern light. "Unless one of you pups wants to go running over by them barges to spool the wire out?"

Finnegan shook his head. "No, sir, I would not care to."

"Can't say as I would, either." Fickle glanced around the shack and located a rather large pry bar. He inserted the tip of the bar into the large lock that hung from the front of the chest. A quick thrust broke the lock free, and it clattered to the floor. "Yes, boys, somebody was sure concerned about Mr. Frick losing his dynamite. If the fella has to replace this, he'll likely be living in a hovel due to expense." Fickle moved to open the lid of the chest.

Rooney stepped forward and stopped the old man. "Mr. Fickle, do you have any experience with blasting powder or dynamite?"

"Just watching other fellas blow slag, but it don't appear a complicated endeavor, young fella." He moved to open the chest again.

Rooney held the chest lid down and turned to Finnegan. "What is your appraisal of this?"

Finnegan groaned and rubbed his face. "If Mr. Fickle has conceived of this notion, surely another man will, presently. There is little purpose to putting off the inevitable." He winced and looked to the chest. "Can you, in truth, handle that safely?"

Rooney appeared almost offended. "I should think you, of all men, would recall my history and competency with blasting implements."

"I recall you making a long series of claims and explaining that the extent of your training was composed of reading the pamphlet included therein."

Rooney grinned. "Yes, and I rather hope there is another somewhere in that box. A fellow does so often forget minor details that prove key to success." Rooney motioned around. "Is there another candidate you would wish to put forward for this particular duty?"

"Sam, if you blow us to Kingdom Come, I shall never forgive you."

Rooney lifted the chest lid. "Then we both wager much."

He rifled through the chest's contents a bit while Finnegan backed away to the far side of the shack. "Ah, yes, here we have something." Rooney held a pamphlet up. "Bring the lantern a bit closer, Mr. Fickle. I should be able to bundle you up an explosive for a proper anarchist in short order."

"What in hell is an anarchist?" Fickle leaned forward with the lantern.

"In truth, I could not say. I do not believe I have ever had the opportunity to chat with one." Rooney noticed that Finnegan had edged his way out of the shack and was nowhere to be seen. "I suppose every man is bedeviled by some terror." He pushed the lantern closer. "Let us see what can be done to aid in your bedevilment, Mr. Fickle."

In the span of half an hour, Rooney managed to package together some dozen small cloth bags with fuses sticking out from them. He whistled while he worked, with Fickle standing by, holding the lantern and sweating bullets. When Rooney declared the arsenal complete, Fickle went to locate a cart to haul his loot. Rooney left the shack and located Finnegan, who lingered on the opposite side of the foundry. He poked his head around one side of a massive press when he heard Rooney approach. "Are you quite done fiddling with that damn brimstone?"

Rooney shook his head. "Honestly, Finnegan, how did you settle on dynamite as the one item in all creation to be afeared of?"

Finnegan stepped out from behind the press. "I do not fear dynamite, only the fools who juggle it." He glanced over to Fickle, who had only just located a handcart. "And what sort of horrid brew have you provided that particular fool with?"

Rooney chuckled. "Mr. Fickle strikes me as a fellow showman, so I have taken the liberty of providing him with a few stage props. Flashes and smoke; nothing more, I assure you."

Finnegan arched an eyebrow. "You have devised a method to tame dynamite?"

"No, and I cannot say as I would wish to, but it was not an option, at any rate. The only blasting caps in that chest are the new electrical variety and, as you told Fickle, we do not care to aid in unrolling the wire. Mr. Fickle requires more... portable equipment, so I have provided it. He has some dozen or so bags of blasting powder, complete with fuses."

"Sam, I have seen blasting powder bring down half a mountain. I would hardly call its effect nothing more than smoke and flashes."

The charlatan shook his head again. "Packed tightly into a hole, powder has great force. What do you imagine propels the bullets you fling so callously?"

"My rapier's wit. What are you on about?"

Rooney patted Finnegan's shoulder. "Dear fellow, if powder is not packed tightly into a crevice or drill hole, it is little more than a bright light and some annoyance. When Fickle makes to fling those tawdry bombs into the barges, they will explode with no more force than a good sneeze." Rooney appeared quite pleased with himself. "If my calculations are correct, and they should be, as I know more than a little regarding both explosives and falsifications, our Pinkerton cousins will be properly bamboozled by the magic trick and surrender, believing they are near defeat."

"Puffs of smoke and no more?" Finnegan could not keep from appearing impressed. "That is a fine bit of bamboozling, Sam. If he lives, Heinde should thank you for creating the excuse he should have spawned hours ago."

"I rarely receive the credit due me." Rooney watched as Fickle loaded the arsenal into his cart. "I informed dear Mr.

Fickle that the honor of ending the engagement ought to fall to steel men, and no others."

"As a fellow would have to wander quite close to the barges to fling one of those bags over the gunwale, I cannot help but agree with your sentiment."

Fickle wheeled his cart out of the foundry and into the bright midday sun. "Ought we to find a spot to observe the fracas?"

Finnegan groaned. "I grow weary of elevated positions, Sam. We consistently suffer sour luck upon climbing."

"What might you suggest, then?"

"My preference would be to keep Mr. Fickle in sight, while remaining far enough afield from him to avoid dismemberment. Regardless of what you claim regarding smoke and flashes, I believe that man will find a way to kill himself or someone else before this day ends."

Rooney nodded. "If we remain far off, it should prove entertaining, if nothing else."

It appeared as though the urge to unionize ran deep among the steel men of Homestead. They could certainly work well together when the occasion called for it. A few dozen men had thrown in their lot with Fickle and hurriedly constructed two mobile battlements from railroad ties, timbers, and any other material they felt might be sturdy enough to stop bullets. With their war engines seen to, one particularly bright fellow realized that simple cloth bags of powder would do little beyond gagging the Pinkertons with smoke. Almost magically, clay pots with tight fitting lids were located. One man stuffed the bags inside, while another augured a hole in the pot lids to accommodate the fuses. A third man packed nails, slag, and pebbles around the bags inside the jars.

Finnegan and Rooney had taken up a position some hundred yards from the impromptu bomb factory. "Well, Sam, they have taken your harmless prank and transmogrified it into the makings for a massacre."

Rooney sipped his flask. "Transmogrified? Where do you run across these things?"

"I am married to a schoolteacher." Finnegan motioned to the work in progress. "Will their scheming produce authentic bombs?"

Rooney rubbed his chin. "I would think not. They still must fling the bloody things. When they land amongst the Pinkertons, the jars ought to break on the deck of the barge. The jar breaking will cause the whole bundle to be a flash in the pan, as they say." Rooney looked away from the bomb makers up the hill. "Oh, bloody hell." A troop of women were approaching, carrying what appeared to be pillowcases and pillows. "These damned tradesmen are more inventive than I might have imagined."

Finnegan scratched his head, looking at the women. "I am afraid I do not follow."

"They intend to pad the jars to aid in their flinging. When the bombs land, the jars will not shatter. The constriction of the jar will cause the nails and such to be flung about. It should make for quite a vile scene given how those men are stacked in those barges."

Finnegan shook his head. "Well, as I said, something must force them out. Better this than starvation five days hence."

The assorted steelworkers assembled a ragged, but impressive, collection of down-guarded bundles, which were divided between the two movable walls. Once they had their equipment in place, a dozen men each grabbed hold of the handles that had been added to the inside of the battlements. The mills produced the strongest men in Pennsylvania, and they made use of their strength, walking the walls forward into the rapidly increasing fire from the barges. The Pinkertons imprisoned on the river shore knew nothing good could come of the approaching war machines, and they spent bullets accordingly. One steel man fell when a ball found its way through a crack, but he was quickly replaced by another disciple. Slowly, the walls made their way forward until they were a scant fifty feet from the river and the barges. Having gained the desired position, the steel men dropped their burdens and reassembled toward the center of the battlements. Each side produced planks some fifteen feet long. Six men held the foot-wide planks, while others placed the bombs on the far end away from the wall.

"Ah, now that is inspired." Rooney could not help but smile. "A catapult, with men taking the place of the counterweight."

Finnegan groaned. "If they had shown half as much intelligence in the past year, this entire debacle would not be occurring."

The first bundle was set on the end of one of the planks. A man lit the bomb's fuse and leapt back as the forward men lifted the plank like a lever and flung the silly looking explosive over the mobile wall and out toward the barges. Just after the bundle made its apex, the bomb exploded, raining nails and whatever else was contained in the load down onto the Pinkertons. Invective and bullets were offered in answer.

The steelworkers cheered and instantly made another attempt. The second bomb soared through the air and made it into the nearest barge. Some quick-thinking Pinkerton grabbed the deadly delivery and cast it into the river. That time, a cheer went up from the Pinkertons and curses were leveled by the steelworkers. Not to be deterred, two more bombs were made ready behind both walls. One was flung and fell into the nearest barge, where it was not removed in time. A blast could be felt, and the smoke billowing out of the boat could be seen. Moans and screams followed.

The detonation of the first wall's bomb somewhat distracted the men behind the second wall. One of the plank holders turned and upset the bomb after it had been placed and lit. The bundle fell to the ground and the steelworkers appeared at a loss as to what they should do.

"Bloody hell, that does not bode well." Finnegan cringed as the bomb exploded. When the smoke cleared, one steelworker lay on the ground and several others were clearly maimed. "By God, these fools pay a high price for their folly."

Rooney pointed toward the barges. "Finnegan, is that what it appears to be?"

The last of the smoke cleared so that the barges were fully visible. "I believe that to be a white flag, my friend." Behind one gunwale of the nearest barge, a stick with a bit of white cloth had been raised and was waving. An errant bullet struck the stick, causing the flag to fall, but it was raised again soon enough and left to wave. "Heinde, if he lives, has picked a fine time to come to his senses."

A large figure appeared behind the walls. His mop of red hair and damaged hand wound up with a cloth made him recognizable as O'Donnell. The union man yelled to cease fire and then stepped pensively in between the two battlements. "You Pinkerton men wish to surrender?"

"We do." The voice came from within the barge. It was neither angry nor powerful, only broken.

"Under what terms?" O'Donnell yelled, relief resounding in his voice.

"We require safe passage to the railroad depot. We will board the train and be gone."

The men behind the wall with O'Donnell did not appear to be satisfied with the offer. A small scuffle broke out, but O'Donnell knocked one man to the ground and browbeat another. He yelled back to the barge. "Leave your weapons on the boat and you will be allowed to pass into town to the..." There was a short debate between O'Donnell and another man. "We will allow you to enter the theatre."

"We keep our arms."

O'Donnell hung his head for a moment. "Leave them. They are no longer the implement of your salvation. Only good sense can save you now. Leave your guns, go to the theatre. You may await the train there, but it must be a special. No one here will allow you to simply meander up the road and return to cause trouble tomorrow. When you go, you must leave Pennsylvania."

"There is nothing I would damn well rather do, sir." There was the sound of some scuffling inside the barge, but it ceased quickly. "Very well, we agree to those terms."

"Excellent." O'Donnell cupped one hand around his forehead. "Come out one by one and show your hands plainly so that we will know you are not armed."

"You will not fire?"

"I give you my word." O'Donnell turned and yelled to the several hundred steelworkers who surrounded the barges and mobile walls. "Do not fire on these men! These men are surrendering! We have won the day; show that we are civilized working men!" He turned back to the barges. "Come now!"

A young man wearing a blood-stained suit jacket slowly emerged from the nearest barge on shaky legs. He made palsied steps down the bullet-riddled gangplank with his eyes flashing from side to side. The fellow reminded Finnegan of the well-born boys from nice families that had been recruited to accompany the sheriff days earlier. He staggered as his boots left the plank and made it to the grass of the riverbank. For nearly a full minute the young man stood, stock still, except for his flitting eyes. He awaited the end, but it did not come. His first indication that he still resided among the living came when the plank behind him creaked and he turned to see that another Pinkerton hireling had found the courage to descend. The second joined the first on the banks and a third soon appeared. All three stood, appearing as ghosts with only the blood streaks on their clothing serving as proof of their being men. None seemed to know what to do or how to proceed. After what must have felt like an eternity, a fourth man Finnegan recognized as Captain Charles Nordrum emerged from the barge using his left hand to hold his right, crimson, arm. The captain came down the plank with halting steps.

Above the four men, slightly uphill, the workers were beginning to form into two masses, one on each side of the Pinkerton refugees. With a foreboding calm, the union men surged together, but left a clear path toward the town. Angered faces and blazing eyes marked the edges of the path presented. Nordrum let go of his right arm and left it to dangle. He used his good left hand to grab another fellow by the shoulder and urge the man forward. "Come now, boys. They have given us safe passage." Nordrum took two or three steps uphill. "Come now, boys. They have pledged not to harm us."

A hulking steel man with a beard nearly to his belt lunged forward out of the crowd on one side. "We pledged not to kill you." The brute raised one massive arm. "But I will be damned if you will pass without harm." He brought his fist down onto Nordrum's injured shoulder and smiled as the Pinkerton captain screamed and fell to the ground. Nordrum's three compatriots pulled him to his feet once more and began staggering up the hill as the crowds surged forward, cursing and hitting the men as they traveled. The brute back at the riverbank turned toward the barges. "Come out, you damn hell spawn, and get what you have earned this day!"

Above the melee, Finnegan and Rooney sat on a pile of ties, observing their fellow Pinkertons. Rooney hung his head. "Ought we do something to assist them, Finnegan? They are hardly saints, but no man deserves such treatment."

Finnegan motioned to the Ballard, which Rooney had been diligently dragging along with him through the ordeal with Fickle. "The rifle you carry there fires a single round before requiring to be reloaded." He motioned to the crowd of enraged union men. "Which one would you choose to shoot?"

"Yes, I suppose there is not much that can be done for them." Rooney motioned to the barges. "Look there, they are carrying a fellow out. Is that Heinde?"

Finnegan squinted in the sunlight. "I believe it might be. If he still draws breath, perhaps he will see the sunrise tomorrow. Pity, if he has been out of his wits since the morning. It is a shame that so many of the men who brew battles never witness them." Finnegan's face showed no emotion as the men with the stretcher entered the gauntlet formed by the steelworkers. As the line of Pinkertons increased in size, so did the roar from the crowd of union men. The first few Pinkertons managed to pass with only a few insults, as blows rained down on them. As the line grew longer and began to stretch halfway up the hill, the union men became more vicious. It seemed as though the first opportunity to vent their anger had only sharpened their thirst for blood. Soon enough, the Pinkertons were crawling on their hands and knees toward Homestead.

It took a full half hour for the last of the Pinkertons to find the will to stumble out of the barge and face the mob. Three men emerged after the crowd had gathered to light the barges aflame. Only imminent death by burning could force them to run the gauntlet. They yelled something Finnegan could not quite make out as they entered the crowd. The union men had no mercy left for the last few cowards in line. Two of the men were knocked to the ground and stomped until they ceased to move. The third ran almost to the top of the first rise before he was struck with a shovel and disappeared into the writhing mass of enraged workmen.

Finnegan sighed as he watched the barges burn. "Well, I suppose that is, as they say, that." He pulled a cigar from his coat and found a match.

Rooney looked up the hill toward the town. "Do you believe they will give those poor devils safe harbor in that theatre?"

"If they will not, there is not much we can do to change it, now is there?"

Rooney took a long sip from his flask. "No, I suppose there is not." Rooney glanced around at the various disheveled parts of the millworks and the flaming barges. "Goodness, they did make a terrible wreck of this place."

Finnegan nodded. "A surprising portion of it is the result of the one mad genius, dear Mr. Fickle. Did you notice if he was killed when they fumbled that last bomb?"

"Well, I should certainly hope so, for his sake." Rooney took another long draught. "The only proper position for a man of his sort is as a martyr. It simply would not do for such a fellow to survive his finest hour. What could remain for him after a day such as this?"

Finnegan shrugged. "He struck me as the sort who might enjoy a round in the saloon celebrating his greatness."

"Oh, no. Not saintly Mr. Fickle. Best he found his reward when he did. To linger on would have only diminished his reputation." Rooney tipped back his flask but, nary a drop fell. "Good God, how long have we been about this foolishness?"

"It is nearing sundown, or I dearly pray it is, at any rate."

FINNEGAN RUBBED his eyes and groaned. The citizens of Homestead had been very accommodating to anyone they perceived as a friend. Coffee and tea had flowed freely. Stew and whole loaves of bread were also available to those devoted to the cause. Finnegan and Rooney had their fill, then stepped back into the shadows. They had been watching the goings-on at the theatre and the railroad depot since night had fallen. Inside the Homestead Theatre, built as a gift to the town by the benevolent Mr. Carnegie, were some three hundred Pinkerton hired guns, who no longer possessed their guns. At the telegraph station, attached to the train depot, the diligent Mr. O'Donnell had been at work since the last Pinkerton had passed through the gauntlet and into the assumed safety of the theatre. Finnegan had moved close enough to the union leader several times to listen to the man expound without being seen. O'Donnell had been burning up the telegraph line to contact the railroad begging for a special train to be dispatched to collect the Pinkertons. O'Donnell opined that every moment the Pinkerton army resided in Homestead was one more moment the mob might break down the theatre doors and begin hauling men out to hang from the furnace braces.

Finnegan leaned against the back wall of the telegraph station and gazed up at the perfect summer stars above. "Mr. O'Donnell may regret the mercy he won for those men before the night is over." The gunman reclaimed his coffee cup from Rooney and took a sip. "His burden would have been significantly lessened if the Pinkertons had burned with the barges. As things stand, he must now improvise a method to remove his new pets from the town."

Rooney took a sip of his own coffee and appeared despondent. O'Donnell had been far too diligent, in Rooney's opinion, in removing liquor from the town. "There are grumblings among the steel men about burning the theatre. Those silly buggers may have simply traded one tomb for another."

Finnegan turned suddenly and concealed his face as O'Donnell came around the corner of the building, fairly dragging Burgess McLuckie by one arm. O'Donnell looked to the two men he perceived as strangers. "Could you give us a moment of privacy, gentlemen?"

Finnegan nodded, never showing his face, and drew Rooney around the corner. Once out of sight, Finnegan moved back to the corner so that he might eavesdrop. McLuckie's gravel-filled voice began the discourse. "Hugh, the charity you have shown today will surely prove your undoing. If you do not give the men leave to have at those devils they will soon enough do as they damn well please. You might well perish with them."

"John, we cannot afford passion. Do you not realize that Frick would like nothing better than for a massacre to come to pass here? The sight of three hundred Pinkerton heads on stakes would warm his heart until his dying day." O'Donnell was breathing hard from the excursion of a long day's reasoning. "Frick longs for us to kill those men. We have won a battle here today, John. We have struck a blow for working men all over this great nation. To let it degenerate now into barbarism would be a loss I do not believe my poor soul could tolerate. All this blood cannot have been for nothing."

McLuckie sounded near panic. "Hugh, if you allow one of those pinks to leave this town, I fear they will run us both up a scaffold."

"If those damn mercenaries are killed while they lay unarmed and bleeding, we will surely both swing." O'Donnell did not seem much calmer. "Can you not understand that we have yet to seize victory? We have won nothing yet. When these men are gone, Frick will see to it they are replaced. That ill-kept rabble is not an army. A real army is coming, John. When it arrives with cannon and cavalry, all we will have to defend ourselves with is the reputation we earn this night. If we act as though we are animals, they will exterminate us like animals. If we behave as civilized men, we may well be offered civilized respect. Putting those men on a train is our only hope, John."

McLuckie groaned. "Hugh, I am not certain how much longer it will matter whether I am with you on this thing or not. These men have been through hell today. I do not know how much longer they will take my counsel."

"When these men cease to take our counsel, John, we had both best begin running. Whether they make use of our advice or not, we will surely be blamed for their actions." A train whistle sounded at a station somewhere far down the line to announce that an express was about to move through without stopping. Both men grew silent for a long moment. "John, did you hear?"

"I truly believe I did, sir."

"That is God's own grace coming down this rail line, John. This night we shall witness a miracle."

"I will surely agree, but the miracle will be to get those pinks on the train without a lynching. Your hard labor may all be for naught when you open the theatre doors."

O'Donnell let a note of desperation sneak into his voice. "We shall manage, John. We must. We have come too damn far to let it all become a shambles now. You talk to the puddlers and the furnace men. I will see if the bohunks can be made to understand. The train is on the way. We are almost free of this damned day."

Finnegan moved away from the corner and joined Rooney near the front of the depot. "We are soon to witness the sort of oddity a man is not likely to see more than once in a lifetime."

"That could be said of almost anything I have seen since sunrise. What is apt to befall us next?"

"We are about to observe a victorious army aiding their vanquished opponents retreat, so as to gain favor with the next army in the line. A war on three sides makes for strange behavior."

Rooney leaned close to Finnegan. "Are we to board the approaching train or do we remain hidden as we are?"

Finnegan raised his eyebrows. "Sam, it remains to be seen if anyone will board that train. The burgess himself has begun to fear the rope."

"As he damn well should. His leadership has not improved the general aesthetic here." Rooney looked to the theatre. "It is unfortunate. I imagine most of those imbeciles had no notion of what they were being recruited for; the majority are likely little more than farm boys who craved adventure."

"Better recruited than conscripted as we were, eh, Sam?"

"The end result is no less saddening."

Finnegan sighed. "Perhaps I will never truly know your inclinations, Sam." He sighed again. "What would you have us do?"

"I believe I might sleep better when next I lay down if we somehow assisted those dumb caged beasts onto the train."

"You show surprising loyalty to the men who have cast you aside so frequently."

"Robert and William Pinkerton are not in that theatre, Finnegan. Sons and heirs such as them are never within sight of unpleasantness such as this."

"Oh, very well, then. No need to force my hand by appealing to what little better nature I possess." Finnegan surveyed the space between the theatre and the depot. It was not much more than one hundred yards, but even that distance could pose a tremendous difficulty with the whole town up in arms against them. The boardwalks of every nearby street were full of seething men staring toward the theatre with murder in their eyes. "This will require...a more deft touch than either of us or O'Donnell is quite capable of." Finnegan turned back toward the rear of the depot. "Remain here and await the train." He reached into his vest pocket and withdrew the small Cloverleaf Colt he kept there. Concealing the tiny gun in one hand, he passed it to Rooney. "Take this. If the engineer or crew make an attempt to depart without the dreaded Pinkertons onboard, do not allow it."

Rooney hung his head. "In such a short span I have gone from a noble blackmailer to the low sort who takes hostages. It is sad what rot such as mercy and loyalty will drive a man to."

"I am certain the madness will be forgotten as soon as we return to a town with liquor. Do not allow the train to depart. I go to collude with O'Donnell."

"The man knows you by sight. He may raise the alarm and have you tossed in the theatre."

"By this juncture, I imagine the fellow requires any friend he can muster." Finnegan made his way to the rear of the depot, where O'Donnell stood arguing with a few eastern Europeans who presumably were the spokesmen for their various nationalities. Finnegan walked up next to O'Donnell as though they were old acquaintances and smiled at the man who had begun his own war not more than twelve hours earlier. "Might I have a word with you, Hugh? It will only take a moment."

O'Donnell stood and stared with his mouth hanging open. Eventually he snapped the orifice shut and nodded. "Um, certainly...sir."

Finnegan led the way to the alley between the depot and a hostelry that he had done so very much eavesdropping in. "O'Donnell, what you attempt is very nearly as ill-planned as the rest of this damned insurrection. If you trust your life to the temperament of steel men and bohunks, you had best go and hang yourself right now."

The union man only stared for a long moment. "Gilhooley, what in Hell's bells are you...How did you come to leave the barges? How have you not been discovered?"

"O'Donnell, this place is not nearly as well defended as you fancy, and I am not nearly as famous as you give me credit for. Now, listen while I explain how you may still avoid the rope. You and I are in agreement that your only hope is to transfer those men to a train. If you cast them away from this place, still breathing, you may yet live out your days without climbing the scaffold."

O'Donnell appeared almost gripped by mania. "I have made every attempt to explain, but...most of the foreigners do not understand and the rest will not listen. They are past reason, Gilhooley."

Finnegan grabbed the oversized ombudsman. "Then make use of the ones they will listen to. The women are all gathered at the church as we speak. Go there and explain to them that their men's necks will surely stretch if a massacre happens this night. Have the wives form a new gauntlet, this one to guide the Pinkertons to the station. Even these crazed devils would not murder unarmed men in front of their wives, or at least I should hope not."

O'Donnell nodded slowly. "By God, Gilhooley, that might just be the palliative."

Finnegan motioned toward the church. "Then be about your damned business."

"Thank you, Gilhooley."

"Go now, damn it. I will remain here and...I suppose I will see how many men I can shoot down before the theatre is overrun. I would counsel speed, sir."

The Catholic women led the way, bearing candles from their church. Just behind them were various protestant faiths. The only sound that could be heard in the entire town was that of the locomotive clanging and creaking into the station. The women slowly, but surely, formed a line from the theatre to the depot without a word falling from their lips. O'Donnell, Finnegan, and Rooney all watched in amazement as the town's mothers and daughters accomplished with silence what thousands of screaming men had failed at.

Without being told, Finnegan made his way to the large double doors in front of the theatre and pounded on them with one fist. "You there, inside! A train is here to remove you from this place. I would council rapidity if you wish to make use of it."

"I got to check with the captain..." was the only reply.

It took what felt like an eternity, but eventually a new voice came to the door. "You say a train is here to remove us."

Finnegan cupped his forehead in one hand. "Yes, damn it."

"What assurances do you offer that this is not a ruse to draw us out?"

"Assurances? Sir, you are unarmed and trapped in a wooden building amongst an enemy horde that cries out for your blood. A ruse is not required to end your life, only a match..." Finnegan assessed the voice. "Is that you, Nordrum?"

"I am Charles Nordrum. Who are you?"

"Finnegan Gilhooley, you silly prat. Open these doors and get your men to safety. I cannot stand here all night discussing the matter. If you wish to spend the remainder of your life cowering in this theatre, say so and be done with it."

The door opened a small crack to reveal a sliver of Nordrum's face on the other side. "It truly is you, Finnegan. How could you have possibly..."

Finnegan hung his head. "Charles, I am certain that after a proper amount of time spent reflecting on the enormity of your folly, you will come to understand that where I stand currently was an easily attainable position, while your position required a near-herculean effort of imbecility. However, we do not have time to discuss the matter, just now." He motioned over his shoulder. "The town's women have come together so that you might not be torn to pieces attempting to board the train. Announce to those who are able that they must assist the wounded and leave the dead. Speed is of the essence, sir. These women will not wait on you all night."

Nordrum chuckled. "As I limped here with blows raining down on me, I never once imagined you would be the one to come to my rescue, Finnegan."

"Yes, well, you never did have much in the way of imagination. Collect your damn foundlings and be gone!" He wrenched the door open and took the initiative once again. Inside the theatre, he found most of the able-bodied men lying about with their backs to various walls, while the wounded lay on the theatre's red carpet, adding to the coloration. "You men! Get on your feet and make ready to depart this instant. Any man who is able is to assist those who are not. If a single one of you is seen to be shirking his duty this night, I will shoot the blackguard down and let those steel men string up what is left." Hundreds of frightened eyes blinked at him. "Move, damn you!"

Almost in one mass, all the beaten Pinkertons began springing to life. Under the supervision of Finnegan and Nordrum, they collected their wounded, moved those who had expired to one side of the theatre aisle, and lined up to make good their escape. "Good, men. Excellent." Nordrum opened the door once more, but declined to peer outside. "Oliver, go out first, assisting Mr. Brown. We have nothing to fear, young man. The unpleasantness has come to an end."

Finnegan gave the boy and the wounded man a small shove. "Enough of that rot. Make for the depot as though your feet were aflame and the rest of you were catching." He gave them another shove and they stumbled out the door. More men began to follow at a speedy trot.

"You ought not to panic them once again, Finnegan. They have been through much, already." Nordrum watched as two men carried Heinde past on a stretcher.

"I would not suggest panic, but a bit of rapidity would not miss the mark. You have many men to goose onto that train and little time to do it in. The situation is tenuous, at best." Finnegan scowled. "And why are you still here annoying me, at any rate? Get to the damn train and see to the organization of your men."

"I command. I ought to be the last man to leave the field."

"Vex me further and you will remain on the field. The wanton waste you officers indulge in has always turned my stomach. Go see to your duty and forget whatever stodgy foolishness the idiot who believed he was your father imparted." Nordrum only stared for a long moment, holding his bum arm. "Be on your way. You may challenge me to a duel when your arm heals." The Pinkerton captain walked out the doors amongst the stream of his men. As the line slowly progressed, Finnegan watched the theatre clear out and did not hear the sounds of a melee commencing outside, though he waited for it every moment.

As the line came to an end, only two men remained. One was a giant ogre with a drizzling bullet wound in his leg, the other was a boy of only fifteen or so. The young man could hardly keep the ogre on his one good leg to hop. The lad looked to Finnegan. "Is it far to the depot, sir?"

"Ah, bloody hell. How is it that such a pathetic pair as you are always presented just as I intend to flee?" He sighed and slipped under the giant's arm. "Run to the damn depot boy. We will be along, I assure you."

The boy was pensive in the doorway, but the ogre soothed him. "Be on your way, Timothy. This nice gentlemen will assist me. You have done your duty and more." The man winced and he attempted a step forward. "We will be just fine."

The boy glanced furtively out the doors. "Very well, sir. I will see you on the train."

"You surely will, son." They watched as the boy departed.

"Noble little sprat."

"He is a fine lad of exceeding character." The two Pinkertons began moving through the doorway in a hopping sort of walk. "Are you not Finnegan Gilhooley?"

They were nearing the passage formed by the women. "Whether I am or not, I would thank you to defer from using that name. This is hardly the place to bandy around such talk."

The man groaned and continued to hop. "By God, I have heard some terrible things regarding your character over the years, but you seem an alright sort aiding a wounded man like this."

"If it would get you out of this town one moment sooner, I would happily throw you onto the train. Do not mistake a man's practicality for comradeship."

"Ah, well, still..." The wounded Pinkerton eyed the crowd of angry steelworkers who lingered just outside the protective circle of the town's women. "Still, it was decent of you to let the boy make a run for it. This arrangement seems most tenuous."

"You cannot imagine how correct you are. By the by, might you find the gumption to bounce a bit faster? I do not particularly care for the way these fellows are moving closer to the ladies' auxiliary."

"I cannot say as I do, either." The wounded man quickened his pace as the steam whistle of the train sounded. Captain Nordrum had been damn quick about heeding Finnegan's advice regarding the loading of the train. As they made it to the doors of the stationhouse, the wounded man chuckled. "It occurs to me that you may have been the perfect choice for a chaperone. This train would be halfway to Pittsburg before anyone took notice that a man such as myself had gone missing, but it will surely not depart without a personage such as yourself aboard. It would not do for the Pinkertons to lose the Battle of Homestead and Fearsome Finnegan Gilhooley all in one day."

They clambered out onto the train platform and began hopping toward a passenger carriage. "You might be surprised by how few minutes thirty years good service buys a man on days such as this." They reached the passenger car and a fellow with blood caking the front of his vest reached down to assist the wounded man up the few stairs.

"Many thanks, Gilhooley."

"Yes, perhaps we will have a lovely chat in reminiscence someday when we are both in the penitentiary." Finnegan looked down the line several cars to where the engine belched smoke. Rooney suddenly stuck his head out the rudimentary window in the cabin of the metal behemoth. "Sam, lovely to see you."

"Finnegan!" Rooney had to yell to be heard over the locomotive. "This has been a wonderfully relaxing outing, but might we depart with the rest of our ilk! I Doubt there can be much more to observe!"

"Do you still have that Ballard!"

Rooney hung his head. "I have placed your damn rifle in this very locomotive! Now get on the damn train before we all hang for our trouble!"

Finnegan waggled a finger at his old friend. "Show caution in the handling of that weapon! They are no longer produced!" Finnegan climbed aboard the train and found a seat somewhat removed from the moans of the nearest wounded man. He quickly felt the lurch of the train cars being brought into motion and heard the steady huff and puff of the locomotive laboring up to speed. Outside the carriage window, he could see the few lights in the houses of Homestead and the many candles of the women's brigade fading out of sight. Soon enough, the car began to slowly swing from side to side, signaling a normal pace for a normal journey.

Finnegan sighed deeply and found what appeared to be his last cigar in his vest pocket. He lit the slightly bent J.C. Newman and puffed out a plume of smoke before cracking the carriage window. When he settled back into his seat, Nordrum had sat down beside him.

"Might you have another of those, Finnegan?"

The gunman puffed again. "As it happens, I do not, but even if I did, I doubt I would provide it to you. As an officer, you should well know that every man is in charge of providing his own small comforts, and ought to plan ahead for proper provisions for the duration of the campaign."

"You are quite correct." Nordrum gripped his wounded arm, which someone had been kind enough to place in a sling for him. "Improper planning appears to be the only consistency in this particular campaign."

Finnegan shrugged. "As Napoleon said, no scheme survives contact with the enemy. We all plot and predict. If luck is on our side, we are hoisted on shoulders and made an example of genius. If our luck fails, we are pilloried as fools. Today you are a fool, perhaps next month you will be a genius." Finnegan tapped ash out the cracked window. "What is the condition of Captain Heinde?"

Nordrum rubbed his eyes. "He has lost much blood and is quite pale. The wound in his arm may require it to be removed. It is difficult to say if the wound in his chest will undo him. Such matters are impossible to predict. I have seen men with worse wounds never leave the saddle and inexplicably knit. I have seen others fall and never rise again. As you say, such matters largely hinge on luck."

# Chapter 17

## *PITTSBURG, PENNSYLVANIA*

### July 9th, 1892

Finnegan stood in front of the desk once again, and once again Frick appeared perplexed by the news he had to deliver. "What I fail to understand is just where the hell you have been, Mr. Gilhooley. I have been reading about the great Battle of Homestead in the newspaper instead of hearing the news from the lips of my very own informant."

Finnegan set his feet a bit farther apart and put his hands behind his back. "Mr. Frick, my commission was to accompany the men aboard the barges, make landfall, and return with a report of what I had witnessed. Now then, as any man among the Pinkertons who is still living will readily attest, I fulfilled my commission. I think it best that I obtain a declaration from you on that point and the matter of my pay is settled before continuing."

Frick sneered and sat back in his chair. "You are more business-minded than I might have given you credit for, Mr. Gilhooley. What was the amount to be leveled upon completion of the task?"

"You stated it to be ten thousand."

"Yes, so I did." Frick withdrew a large folio from one desk drawer and unceremoniously flopped it open to reveal bank checks. He took up his pen, but then paused. "Just to satisfy a bit of morbid curiosity, Mr. Gilhooley, what might you do if I chose to not render payment?"

"It is always difficult to say how a man might react to such an unexpected turn of events. Especially given the fact that Henry Clay Frick has always been particularly well-known to honor all obligations."

"I have never before known a man who can chill the blood while issuing a compliment." Frick dashed off the check and tore it from the folio. "Given your high opinion of me, I can only assume you will accept a note in lieu of cash?"

"Certainty, Mr. Frick." Finnegan took the note, carefully folded it, and placed it inside his vest pocket. "Now, then, what might you wish to know, sir?"

"Where the hell you have been, to start things off?"

Finnegan shrugged. "New Jersey."

"New Jersey?" Frick slowly shook his head. "Did you enjoy the peace and solitude of the Pine Barrens?"

"I cannot say as I was there long. Myself and an associate felt compelled to assist the Pinkertons in boarding the train at Homestead as the debacle ended. Once on the train, we could hardly skip back into the town unobserved, so we remained on the train until it disembarked the Pinkertons. I suppose the engineer did not wish to have anyone accuse him of leaving the Pinkertons in the general area of Homestead, so the train stayed in motion until crossing into the State of New Jersey. Once there, my associate and myself began the rather meandering endeavor of finding our way back to Pittsburg. It is not so easy to cover the distance when one does not have an express at their disposal."

"You faced a difficult journey by train and have now

returned triumphant? That is what ten thousand dollars buys me?" Frick cocked his head to one side.

"Naturally, I will tell you whatever it is you might wish to hear, Mr. Frick. You have only to ask. Although, I might point out that the bulk of my payment was surely meant as an incentive to run the hazard with the Pinkertons, not to play at being an informant."

"Yes, I suppose you are correct on that score." Frick shrugged. "As I said, on occasion I manifest a morbid curiosity." He folded his hands on his chest. "The newspapers have been quite thorough in describing what occurred. At what juncture would you say it went awry?"

Finnegan arched an eyebrow. "From the very beginning, sir. The workers had posted lookouts so that the presence of the barges was well known long before they approached the millworks. In point of fact, we were fired upon before we neared the millworks. Without the element of surprise, the barges were easily surrounded and cut off before a single man could depart."

"Any man other than you, that is?"

"I was fortunate to have a different objective in mind from the rest of the men." Finnegan thought on it for a moment. "And, I suppose I have never been accused of being indecisive. Captain Heinde paused when he should have joined the fray. I cannot say as matters would have ended better, but audacity is sometimes the only realistic option."

"So, then, your brave Pinkerton brethren became bogged down and were surround by the rabble?"

"A rather well-armed rabble, sir. You have been paying those men well enough for them to secure a considerable arsenal."

Frick put his hands in the air. "Precisely what I have stipulated to on several occasions. They are paid at an impressive rate, to be certain." He shook his head. "The newspaper claims they gained access to a cannon?"

"An old twenty-pounder from the Army of the Republic Lodge, sir."

"Ah, now that is audacity." Frick drummed his fingers on the desk. "How is it you are unharmed? I would think that, of all the Pinkertons in the world, you are the one they might most like to float down the Monongahela."

"I swam ashore when the boats first arrived, dressed in a manner in keeping with a working man, and secreted myself among the workers during the conflagration."

Frick chuckled. "Truly? You were among them the entire time?"

"I was. Yes, sir."

"Perhaps such an act of boldness is worth ten thousand dollars." He rubbed his chin. "No one discovered you?"

"Hugh O'Donnell became aware of my presence just before the train arrived."

"Hugh O'Donnell? Who is that?"

Finnegan stared at his employer for a long moment. "The man elected by the union members to speak for them."

Frick snorted. "Do you, by any chance, know the best method for negotiating with a labor representative, Mr. Gilhooley?"

"I do not."

"Declare that you will no longer have negotiations with labor representatives. Once his fellow insurrectionists have ground the man down into the dirt for ineffective bargaining, he is much easier to deal with, and generally signs a personal contract for less than he was receiving previous to the unpleasantness." Frick glanced to the calendar that hung on his wall. "I would predict that in four weeks' time Mr.…what was his name again?"

"Hugh O'Donnell."

"Mr. O'Donnell will be standing in your place, hat in hand, begging to be employed once again at the new wage level."

"I have known many a man who steadily worsens his situation and then abandons pride at the end of a downward slide. I do not know if I would make that accusation toward Mr. O'Donnell. My prediction would be that if he does not hang, he will likely move on."

"Hang?" Frick rubbed his chin. "You do not truly suppose we might find a method by which to hang the ringleaders?"

Finnegan rubbed his eyes. "It has been my experience that an ample amount of money can purchase most anything from judges, juries, and hangmen. I would caution you, however: the purchase of such ignominious acts rarely benefits the purchaser in the way they had hoped and often sullies a man's reputation in ways that cannot be repaired."

"Reputation." Frick sneered. "Another item readily purchased. You need only inquire of my absentee partner Mr. Carnegie. He is busily repairing a lifetime of greed, rapacity, and a few other sins that might even curdle my blood, but never mind. The liberal application of money has propelled him just within reach of sainthood, or had before this most recent unpleasantness. The old coot is fairly well burning up telegraph wires to learn what any fool can read in the papers." Frick smiled. "I suppose I take some pleasure enfeebling Mr. Carnegie's attempt at redemption. He likely believes this unfortunate labor dispute has caused the loss of all gains from the last ten million he has thrown away." Frick flipped his folio shut and placed it back in the desk. "What was our topic before I was distracted?"

"The hanging of Hugh O'Donnell."

"Ah, yes." Frick drummed his fingers on the desk. "Well, never mind that, for now. You say you made the acquaintance of the man while he was busy stealing my millworks?"

"I met the man previous to the battle and again during."

"You are on reasonably friendly terms with the scoundrel?"

Finnegan hooked his thumbs into his gun belt. "As well as two men on opposing sides can be friendly, I suppose. For a short period of time, we shared the goal of removing the Pinkertons from Homestead without further incident."

"Excellent. If the fellow will tolerate your presence, go and keep an eye on him. If he seeks your counsel, suggest action in our favor. If, by some bizarre twist of fate, the simpleton conjures some method to elongate this donnybrook, shoot the silly bugger." Frick held up a finger. "In a manner that does not betray our affiliation, of course."

Finnegan hung his head. "Mr. Frick, I will not shoot Hugh O'Donnell -- or any other man -- down without cause."

Frick waved his hand about. "Lure the fool into attack, then. Whatever suits the code of conduct you men bend to."

The gunman sighed. "You wish for me to observe Mr. O'Donnell?"

"Yes, observe him, report on his movements. If he will take counsel from you, counsel him in our favor. Obviously, if he threatens your person, or...well, threatens anything you may hold dear, such as the ideal of liberty, or a toothsome pork roast, please, shoot him down presently."

Finnegan took a cigar from his vest. "Mr. Frick, I shudder to think what the newspapers might say if the leader of the rebellion was murdered by a well-known Pinkerton detective."

"Detective?" Frick raised his eyebrows. "You are referred

to by several titles, Mr. Gilhooley, but I was unaware detective was among them."

"As most men do, I make use of titles when they benefit me. You would have me return to Homestead and look in on Mr. O'Donnell?"

"With all due haste. Let the silly fellow know that there is no need for all this raucousness. Those madmen need only come to understand what constitutes their property and what does not. There is no need for this to become exacerbated further."

"I have already offered that very advise to the man." Finnegan thought on it for a moment. "Although, much has transpired since then." Finnegan nodded. "My service to you may yet prove productive."

"Oh, I would no more expect that than I would expect the second coming, but it will be entertaining, to be sure." Frick leaned back in his chair. "You have no reservations returning the quaint hamlet of Homestead? I would think you might very well have poor associations with the place."

"There is little purpose to bemoaning the wreckage after the storm has passed. The men of Homestead await your next move, Mr. Frick. They would profit nothing from hanging me off a furnace brace."

Frick smiled at the gunman. "You assume Homestead is solely populated with union men intent on their ongoing struggle. Might you not come into contact with another anarchist, or merely an old enemy?"

"As recent experience has shown, such unpleasantness can just as easily occur in Pittsburgh as in Homestead." Finnegan motioned around the office. "While your fearless, Pinkerton-assigned defender is away, someone might very well storm in here and shoot you, sir. All men run the hazard every day, whether they feel they have earned opprobrium or not."

# Chapter 18

## *HOMESTEAD, PENNSYLVANIA*

### July 10th, 1892

Finnegan stepped off the local onto the Homestead station platform as though it were any other small town in the world. All signs of the former riot had disappeared. The streets had been cleared of rubble. The fence around the millworks had been set back in place, along with a fresh coat of whitewash. Even the brass cannon had been spirited back to its place in front of the Grand Army Hall. Only a truly close observer could ascertain the fact that the pile of cannon balls had been rearranged so that the few missing specimens would go unnoticed. The taverns were still closed, and the people appeared to be going about their business. For a town at the center of an insurrection, the entire hamlet was quite pacific.

Finnegan strolled from the station to the Amalgamated Union Hall. A few random townspeople took notice of him, but not enough to raise his hackles. He found the hall's large door unlocked, so he made his way inside. The expansive structure was empty as a tomb, and equally silent. Finnegan looked over the central area of the building with its lines of crookedly assembled chairs. He was about to leave when he heard two rather panicked voices. The gunman walked across the meeting hall to what appeared to be a back office. Through the door, Finnegan spied O'Donnell's hulking form and the only slightly smaller form of Burgess McLuckie. From Finnegan's perspective, the two men seemed to be joined at the hip. Seeing that the room was empty with the exception of the two town fathers, Finnegan knocked on the doorjamb to get their attention.

"If the two of you are deeply engrossed in official business, I can remove myself until you have concluded matters," the gunman smiled.

McLuckie held up a badly wrinkled telegram. "Ah, so this news arrives at the same moment as a damned assassin. Well, do your worst, bushwhacker. We are not armed."

Finnegan leaned against the doorjamb. "Mr. McLuckie, the more acquaintance we gain, the lower your opinion of me sinks. Truly, I cannot imagine who has been whispering in your ear to make you imagine I came capable of such awful behavior."

He shook the telegram again. "If you are not responsible for this, and you are not here to bedevil us, why the hell are you here?"

Finnegan sighed. "Sir, I have not the foggiest notion of what news that telegram might contain. As for my purpose here, I will be completely forthright: I have been dispatched here by Mr. Frick so that I might attempt reasoning with you gentlemen."

"Reason! What the hell do killers know of reason!" McLuckie balled up the telegram and threw it in the general direction of Finnegan.

O'Donnell stepped forward, holding out one hand. "John, please, as I told you, Mr. Gilhooley was essential in getting the Pinkertons out of town without further loss of life, and..." O'Donnell hung his head. "And, as I have been trying to explain, we have nothing to fear from the militia. They are the sons of Pennsylvania, just as we are. No man among them would...invade our town."

Finnegan could not help but chuckle. "Mr. O'Donnell, you have such incredible notions rattling about in your head." He motioned to the telegram on the floor. "Although, exploration of the depths of your naiveté is likely best left for another time. How is it you have been made aware the militia is coming?"

"Two days past, Burgess McLuckie and I traveled to Harrisburg to meet with the Governor and plead our case." O'Donnell made the statement as though such things happened on a regular basis.

Finnegan stooped to pick up the telegram. "What, pray tell, was your case, gentlemen? Were you seeking pardons?"

McLuckie squared up in front of the gunman. "That is a damn black accusation, sir. What would we be requiring pardoning for? We have committed no crime."

Finnegan unrumpled the telegram. "After we examine Mr. O'Donnell's notions, we must take some time to examine your understanding of the law, sir." Finnegan flattened the brief document out on the door. "Ah, I see the good Sheriff McCleary is as helpful as ever." Finnegan turned to the two men. "I take it you left a confederate in the capital to keep watch?"

O'Donnell shook his head. "The Governor's personal secretary is a second cousin to a puddler."

"And we are all brothers in the eyes of God." Finnegan finished reading the telegram. "So, then, McCleary has announced he no longer has the ability to enforce order in this place. There is an announcement somewhat late in coming." Finnegan sighed. "As such, the good Sheriff has requested the militia be sent here to seize control and keep you rabble at bay." The gunman chuckled. "I do not believe it is quite dignified for the two of you to appear shocked at this news. I seem to recall telling you of this very circumstance; I can only assume others had brought the possibility to your attention, as well. After all, when a small army has been thwarted, it is common practice to assemble a larger one and try again. Have neither of you gentlemen read the Bible?"

O'Donnell hung his head. "Mr. Gilhooley, we have nothing to fear from the militia, and we have no need of pardons. We have done nothing more than defend our jobs from a horde of immigrants and the hired thugs bought to murder us. The governor himself said as much."

"Oh, tsk, tsk, Hugh, you may believe all manner of fairy tales and hokum, but even you would not sink so low as to believe the word of a politician. Could you see both his hands when he gave you his word? Chances are, he was busily scribbling out your death warrant while he smiled your way."

McLuckie ran one calloused hand over his face. "Gilhooley, were you truly dispatched here by Frick to offer terms?"

"No, not particularly." Finnegan slowly shook his head. "It is more as if I were dispatched here to make one last attempt at convincing you to surrender without terms and cast yourself on the mercy of... well the multitude of enemies you face. Sadly, it would appear I have arrived too late, by far."

O'Donnell waved one hand. "Early or late has nothing to do with the matter. We would never surrender to the likes of Frick under any circumstances."

Finnegan groaned and returned the telegram to the floor. "Good grief, O'Donnell, do you not see? I should think nothing could be more clear by now. You have lost, sir. You are done. Vanquished. Victory has been snatched from you. You are the defeated. I do not know how else to put the matter before you."

"You would term the imminent arrival of our fellow working men, our fellow citizens, a defeat?" O'Donnell shook his head ruefully. "Mr. Gilhooley, have you no faith in your fellow man?"

"I had great faith in the chap before becoming acquainted with him. More to the point, I would not call it faith, but I have found both soldiers and generals to be wonderfully consistent. The men who are coming here are not your fellow citizens; far from it. The men who approach are the dregs swept together after failing at all other labors. The average Jack in the service of the flag resides in that position to obtain three square meals a day and a roof over his head. The buggers would happily burn this town to ashes if they were offered as little as bonus pay or a week's leave. They will light the place aflame without even those incentives, the only difference being a noticeable lethargy in the second instance." Finnegan hooked his thumbs into his gun belt.

McLuckie did not appear overly confident, but he took umbrage, just the same. "No American general would order such an act."

Finnegan laughed and removed his hat. "Ah, yes, that most noble breed, the general. While I am not normally a gambling man, I would not hesitate for a moment to wager this last year's earnings on the character of the man who commands the soon-to-arrive troops. He will assuredly be a fellow who climbed to the vicinity of the rank he currently holds in the past war and has been steadily stewing over his inability to climb higher since Appomattox." The gunman reseated his hat. "Now, what might you imagine a gentleman such as that might consider to be the proper reaction to a rebellion or insurrection?"

O'Donnell stared, stone-faced. "American militias do not burn towns."

"I am certain that was formerly the option of the good citizens of Atlanta." Finnegan assumed a less jocular visage. "If you give those soldiers or, more particularly, their general, cause, they will surround this place and pound it to smithereens with artillery. I am told several of these eastern militias have been well-equipped with the new one- and two-inch Gatlin rotary guns. As a matter of course, every private will be well-armed with the new forty-five caliber breechloader, and most will also be equipped with sidearms. They will first take the heights overlooking this place, reduce the buildings to the extent they find it entertaining, and then promptly shoot the survivors down like mad dogs."

O'Donnell appeared somewhat angered by the graphic announcement. "Are you attempting to frighten us, Mr. Gilhooley?"

"I am attempting to impress upon you the desperate necessity of right action."

"And what would that be, sir?" McLuckie attempted to sound snide, but the question came off as genuine.

"Call a town meeting with every man who has reached his majority in attendance. Explain to them that, under no circumstances, should any man in this town show the slightest aggression toward the soldiers."

O'Donnell shook his head once more. "No man among us would take action against a soldier wearing this nation's uniform."

"And you can be assured of it when you lock all the rifles in this union hall and throw the key into the river." Finnegan pulled a cigar from his vest. "It is a volatile situation you gentlemen find yourselves in. Best to avoid even the possibility of a spark." He chuckled as he searched for a match. "Although, in truth, if I were either of you gentlemen, I believe I would use the town meeting as an opportunity to run unobserved." He located a match and struck it on the doorjamb. "If either of you are interested in assuming a new identity, I would be more than happy to put you in contact with an acquaintance of mine who is well-practiced in the art. He has been so many different fellows over the years, I imagine it takes a moment for him to recall which name he is currently using when he rises from bed. It is likely both a blessing and a curse to go through life without the stain of yesteryear."

O'Donnell dragged a chair over to him and took a seat. "Mr. Gilhooley, how is it you have come to believe Burgess McLuckie and I are bound to hang? It is an absurdity, but yet you persist."

"I bring the matter up solely because several others have brought it to my attention. Some of the men who have made mention of it might even be able to make it a reality." Finnegan shrugged and puffed his cigar.

McLuckie pursed his lips. "They did not hang Lee or Davis, and those men rent the whole damn country asunder."

Finnegan blew a smoke ring. "You are correct, although I would point out that, when it comes to insurrection, size is the defining characteristic. Lee and Davis could hardly be held accountable for actions half the nation felt were justified. On the other hand, John Brown and his sons swung from a scaffold with nary a man questioning the wisdom of the sentence. It would appear the line between madness and patriotism is merely a question of numbers."

O'Donnell hung his head in his chair. "You are a difficult man to befriend, Gilhooley." He spit down onto the floor. "Very well, we will call the meeting and confiscate the guns."

Finnegan knocked ash down to the union hall floor. "And what of my other suggestion?"

"I have not come this far only to be labeled a coward at the end." O'Donnell stuck his chin out to emphasize the point.

"And you, Burgess McLuckie?"

The politician glanced between the gunman and the steelworker. "I suppose we shall have to see how events unfold. I have never known dead men to show much care for other's opinions."

"Ah, now there is that practical kind of thinking I have been attempting to instill in you gentlemen." Finnegan grinned. "There may be hope for you yet, sir."

# Chapter 19

## *HOMESTEAD, PENNSYLVANIA*

### July 11th, 1892

The varied civil servants of Homestead were, in Finnegan's opinion, a very diligent group. Since the building had been used as a depository for wounded and dying Pinkertons, the Homestead Opera Theatre had been cleaned and primped to the point that an observer would never guess it had done duty as a triage hospital scant days previous. Even the few rugs that had been befouled with blood had received scrubbing and were now the slightly lighter shade of mauve they had originally been.

Finnegan stood in the rear of the building watching the town's democratic processes at work. The gunman always took a keen interest in the attitudes and actions of men trapped in various maelstroms. It was endlessly intriguing to see what reactions were conjured. Naturally, O'Donnell and McLuckie occupied prominent places on the theatre stage. Other municipal potentates flanked them. Finnegan had no idea what their official titles might be -- likely the dog catcher and a Vice-Burgess for good measure.

O'Donnell had held the stage for more than fifteen

minutes, preaching a gospel of tolerance, if only toward one's brother soldier. "What we must all come together to appreciate is that we do not want Pinkertons here, but we do want the militia." He made only limited movements with the hand that was minus a thumb. It was rare to see the big man wince from the injury, as he wanted to set an example for others to follow. "The men of the Pennsylvania Militia are our brothers. Those men come from the same class as us. Many of them likely have fathers or brothers in the mines or working furnaces in other mills." O'Donnell let a wide grin play over his face. "And let us not forget that every man in that militia, from the lowest buck private to their general, is paid by virtue of the steel tariff!" The remark brought about a small round of applause and a few whoops. "Yes, folks, let us not forget that every day Mr. Frick's mill sits idle, the militia's coffer grows a bit fuller." Laughs could be heard. "The simple fact of the matter is that the militia is not coming here to occupy the town, the militia is coming to our aid. Now, then, does anyone here have a comment they would like to make regarding the plans laid out this evening by myself and Burgess McLuckie?" O'Donnell motioned about the auditorium. "Any one at all...yes Arthur Tutty, stand up and speak, sir."

A tall, thin man toward the center of the audience stood and smoothed the sleeves of what was likely his best shirt. "Uh, I suppose you all know me, and them that don't are likely better for it." A few more laughs could be heard. "At any rate, like a lot of the men here, I done my bit and served it out, maybe not in the state militia, but in the ranks, and I reckon one sergeant hollering at you is the same as the next. What I want to say here is that I guess, no matter what outfit comes to town here presently, we ought to give them the respect soldiers deserve. With that in mind, I move that any man who insults the troops get ducked in the Monongahela."

Several cries of "*Yeah, duck 'em!*" were heard from the crowd.

"Excellent, excellent." O'Donnell waved his good hand. "I am certain we can all get behind Mr. Tutty's suggestion. All right, then, would anyone else care to comment?" He did not wait long for takers. "Fine, then, we are in agreement. At first light we will bring all the rifles over and place them in the union hall as a show of good faith toward the boys in blue." McLuckie had been the one to suggest the idea be framed as a show of support for the militia. After all, what law-abiding town could have a need for guns when it was surrounded by a protecting army. "Very good. Now, Mrs. Clifton and Mrs. Ross will see to the selection of a proper number of members and instruments to form two marching bands to welcome the troops, and the rest of us will do our level best to spruce the place up. It is not every day we have a general by for inspection." A chorus of laughs and small jokes were sent the big man's way. "Yes, well, just don't ask me to sing. Thank you all for coming, we had better all get home and get a decent night's sleep." He moved over to the seated members of the town council while the population of Homestead slowly made their way toward the exits.

In Finnegan's opinion, the man's speech had shown a great deal of audacity. When a town is about to face an invading army, the traditional reaction was for the townspeople to dig in, build defenses, and make ready for a siege. O'Donnell was suggesting nothing less than opening the town gates, or the mill gates, rather, and inviting the army in for tea and biscuits. Finnegan did not doubt for a moment that the policy was the only one which would ensure the continued existence of the town. What he could not say was whether or not it would buy most of the union men mercy.

# Chapter 20

## *HOMESTEAD, PENNSYLVANIA*

### July 12th, 1892

To the east of Homestead stood the Munhall Station. The building was actually larger than the Homestead Station and it needed to be. Munhall was the point where most of the incoming freight for the mills was unloaded and shipped downhill on a separate track. The arrangement kept the hubbub of large shipments out of the town proper. On a beautiful July day, the large station house could be clearly seen from the town, but Finnegan was only paying attention to the smoke from the steam engine even further off.

"Ah, how the Army does love to flit about by rail. I was offered the opportunity to travel by rail on more than one occasion during the war, but I always demurred. As a youth, I was too fearful of the rebels blowing up a bridge during the transit or some such nonsense. Thankfully, the capacity I served in offered much autonomy."

O'Donnell lowered the spyglass he had borrowed from the fellow who had formerly been a sea captain. "Gilhooley, I can never quite say if you are mocking me or attempting to be friendly, and perhaps you do not quite understand what the term *friendly* implies." He sighed. "Either way, I do not comprehend why you are still lingering here."

Finnegan shrugged and peered at the approaching train through his binoculars. "I remain partially because I have been asked to do so by the fellow I am meant to be serving at this time. Another portion of my motivation stems from the simple want of entertainment. It is an urge all men must indulge from time to time. I must also admit that I have come to take something of a personal interest in you, Mr. O'Donnell. Never before has such a tragic figure conspired to fill my coffers quite so much. You are a great windfall, sir, and, as such, I feel obliged to watch over you a bit."

O'Donnell appeared dubious. "You will fight off the soldiers when they come to hang me?"

"No, but I will see to it the body is returned to your wife. I give you my word of honor."

"As I said before, it is difficult to know if you are a genuine bastard or only putting on airs." O'Donnell took up the spyglass again, but rapidly found what he saw disagreeable. "How much money have you profited from this town's misery, Gilhooley?"

"Thus far, an amount more ample than I had any right to hope for when this journey began. You may find this difficult to credit, but two months past I had no intention of coming to this place, much less rejoining the ranks of the Pinkertons. My only intention was to collect some funds owed me and avoid joining my darling wife in the barrens of the Dakotas for a time. Have you ever traveled to the Dakotas?"

"I cannot say as I have." O'Donnell looked from the town to the approaching train, and then back again. "I must admit to one regret: on this day I greatly regret ordering the saloon closed."

"I can offer you a cigar, nothing more."

O'Donnell stretched. "You never drink?"

"Never have and never will. I have seen it produce far too much stupidity and death."

O'Donnell shrugged. "As I feel the imminent approach of both stupidity and death, I cannot imagine one good reason to face it all sober."

"You may have a solid argument there, sir." Finnegan watched as the first of two trains pulled into the Munhall station. A plume of steam came from the engine and partially obscured people could be seen disembarking. "I believe I see the good Sherriff McCleary among them."

"That man has been a damned disappointment. I cannot count the times he sat at my table and ate dinner." O'Donnell rubbed his tired eyes with his good hand. "Many a man I thought could be trusted has turned tail and run this month. Many a man I thought to be a coward has stood his ground. It is strange what trying times will bring about."

"McCleary finds himself discomfited on all sides, sir. Best not to judge the man too harshly." Finnegan chuckled. "As I have been so diligently attempting to explain to you men, you are, in fact, breaking the law by denying access to these mills. One can hardly blame the Sheriff for taking the side of the wronged party in a legal dispute."

"It is wrong for Frick and Carnegie to use men like us and then callously cast them aside when a cheaper alternative presents itself. We are men, not cattle."

Finnegan hung his head. "My entire life I have been assailed by you damned idealists and your ridiculous notions of what is right or wrong, or who is in the right or who is wrong. Right and wrong never put bread on my table, sir. There is simply the way matters are and what must be done to survive. Idealism only leads to an empty stomach and a broken heart." The gunman shook his head. "I have never met a one of you rebels who does not end worse off than when he started, and for what? Was Frick attempting to cast you into poverty or starvation? If you had forced the fellow to take terms, what terms would you have offered? Did you truly believe men such as Carnegie or Frick would allow you to take possession of such a massive outlay as the mills of Homestead? Frick would surely rather see the place razed to the ground than allow you to have it, but what if he did? What was your inspired plan for the town of Homestead?"

O'Donnell rubbed his temples. "Yes, well, in retrospect it may not have been the best laid plan." He motioned down the tracks. "Is that a second train approaching?"

Finnegan made use of his binoculars. "It is, indeed. From the muzzles projecting from the side of the cars, I would venture to guess it contains the troops."

"I had rather been hoping the general might forget to bring those." O'Donnell tried a smile.

"It always saddens me to see a dream denied." Finnegan deposited the binoculars in the pocket of his frock coat. "Well, I suppose it is time to collect your dear Burgess McLuckie so that you may speak with whatever conquering hero the governor has sent to protect the rights of robber barons everywhere."

"You would be referencing the robber baron who employs you, I suppose?"

Finnegan began walking toward Homestead. "If you knew what the fellow was paying me, you might begin to question who is robbing whom."

Seven regiments in all began to take possession of the heights on Shanty Hill above the town of Homestead. First the infantry marched in to secure the ground. After that, the artillery was unlimbered and positioned to cover the town below. The Gatlin guns Finnegan had predicted were placed at key points so that their fields of fire might overlap. In no more than thirty minutes, some four thousand men surrounded the sleepy hamlet of Homestead.

Finnegan, O'Donnell, and McLuckie watched the occupation take shape from the shade of the railroad depot. Finnegan puffed a cigar and took in a sight he had not witnessed the like of in many years. "They say no less a personage than Tecumseh Sherman himself is responsible for those crackerjack troops. I have been told he was bitterly disappointed in their performance during the labor riots of '77 and has since seen to an improvement in their training."

"They do appear to know their work." McLuckie stared up the hill as a man stares at his gallows being constructed. "I do not know if I find their professionalism more or less comforting."

Finnegan looked into the glass of a nearby window and straightened his collar. "At any rate, I suppose we had best climb the hill, gentlemen, and have a chat with the general up there. I have found that, whether a fellow has good or bad intentions, it is best to learn what they are well in advance of any rash action."

McLuckie sneered and turned to O'Donnell. "Why not let this damn Pinkerton go up there and have tea with the enemy? I am in no particular rush to be thrown in a stockade."

Finnegan arched an eyebrow. "You expect those men to build a stockade just to hold you, Burgess? Goodness, you have developed an oversized sense of your own importance."

The gunman smiled. "All jesting aside, if you do not climb that hill, I will not climb that hill. I am here to observe you gentlemen, not to act as an errand boy to generals. Come now, sir, is it not rather late in the game to allow your courage to fail you now?"

McLuckie stood to his fullest height and smoothed his coat. "Very well, there are surely worse fates than a firing squad." He glared at Finnegan. "I am certain you will meet a worse one."

"Come now, John." O'Donnell did his best to put himself together and disguise the wound on his hand. "It is not so terrible having a fellow such as Mr. Gilhooley to accompany us. If the worst should happen, at least there will be someone to return home and explain what occurred."

"Oh, lovely." McLuckie began the slow walk uphill toward the soldiers. "I am so very proud to know the likes of Finnegan Gilhooley shall deliver my epitaph."

The three men slowly ventured up the hill toward the first line of pickets. Once there, O'Donnell explained that they were a committee sent to welcome the general and the troops to Homestead. A corporal who appeared to be near twelve years of age escorted the three men up to the Carnegie School House where they had been told the esteemed Major General George R. Snowden had made his headquarters. The general had taken up a position toward the rear of the one room building at a table formerly occupied by the schoolmarm. He had one frightened looking aid with him when the three visitors entered. O'Donnell took the lead, looking a great deal like a man who wished to get a desperate chore over and done with. The massive steel man stepped in front of the table.

"Uh, yes, uh, General, sir. We come representing the citizens of Homestead and the Amalgamated strikers."

General Snowden, a compact man with a weathered face, languidly looked up from the letter he had been composing. He capped his pen and slowly set it beside the letter. "I am always glad to meet the citizens, the good citizens, of any community."

O'Donnell cleared his throat. "We have been peaceful and law-abiding citizens."

The general slowly stood and leaned across the table, wielding one finger. "No, you have not. You have not been peaceful and law-abiding citizens. That is why I am here."

O'Donnell cleared his choked throat once more. "General, we have got four brass bands we had hoped to parade for the benefit of the troops, sir."

"I will not be having any of that damned brass band business while I am here. That sort of thing is not wanted."

O'Donnell took a step back from the table. "General, sir, could you please inform us as to what it is you *do* want?"

Snowden's eyes narrowed. "I want you...gentlemen, to distinctly understand that I am master of this situation."

"I believe the Gatlin guns do a fine job of illustrating that point, sir." Finnegan offered a smile to the grumpy general.

Snowden slowly brought his eyes to bear on the gunman. "And just who the hell are you, sir? The mayor of this town, perhaps? Come to explain that the past week has been nothing more than a picnic gone awry?"

"A humble representative of the Pinkerton Agency, sir. Finnegan Xavier Gilhooley, by name."

Snowden stared for a moment. "Good God, I have heard some terrible things about you, sir." He surveyed the union men for a moment. "How is it you find yourself accompanying these two? I should think recent events would have made your kinds mutually exclusive."

"Catastrophe makes for strange bedfellows, sir."

Finnegan grinned at the union men and the general. "It does not matter if the catastrophe is natural or of man's own making. At some point, all survivors find common cause."

Snowden began to chuckle. "Yes, well, if I had more time and a different commission, I would enjoy hearing the tale of how you three came to be bedfellows. As it stands, I do not possess either the time or the inclination for tales." Snowden ceased chuckling. "You gentlemen representing the town should return to your homes. Mr. Gilhooley, you ought to return to...well, whatever place it is men such as yourself emerge from. That is all. Good day."

McLuckie assumed a rather angry scowl. "Do you truly intend to dismiss us without so much as explaining what it is you expect of us or what your intentions are? You may be a general, sir, but we are citizens, and we have our rights."

Snowden pursed his lips and then shook his finger at the union men once again. "No, sir, none of that! Not today, not ever. You will not stand here and obfuscate your behavior like a boy caught raiding the cookie jar. No, sir. I will not allow that. You men were citizens with a full complement of rights. You were that very thing, until you deemed it necessary to violate the laws of this nation. You are having these matters explained to you by myself instead of a constable or sheriff only because of your sheer numbers. Normally, scofflaws such as yourselves are merely clouted over the head and put about your business. You men are only unique in that you have convinced so very many of your fellow fools to follow your example." Snowden paused for a moment to collect himself. "You ask what is expected of you, and I have told you. You are expected -- nay, ordered -- to return to your homes. Myself and my men are in control of this place now. Any attempt by you or the townspeople to challenge our authority will be met by whatever level of force the commanding officer present deems necessary."

O'Donnell swallowed with an audible click. "You wish for us to go home."

"Yes, Mister...whatever your name is. Go back to your home and await whatever fate you have earned for yourself. By your presence here, I can only assume you to be some sort of rabblerouser who fancied himself a leader of men earlier in the month. I am ordering you to return to your home and await the arrival of the aforementioned sheriff so that you may be brought to heel." Snowden slowly lowered himself into his chair. "If you wish for a quicker adjudication, you need only make trouble with my soldiers." The general took up his pen once more. "On a personal note, I would not care to be in your particular predicament, gentlemen. My men have orders not to detain anyone coming or going from this town. If I were you, I believe I would make use of that small mercy and be gone. Somewhere, a hangman is likely opening a can of resin in expectation of meeting you."

"Does that admonishment apply to myself as well, sir?" Finnegan smiled at the small spitfire.

"I shudder to imagine what fate awaits you, Mr. Gilhooley." The general snapped his fingers, and his frightened aid snapped to attention. "Captain Becker, see to it that these men leave the camp. I do not much care where they go from there, but they are to leave the camp."

"Yes, sir." The aid fairly leapt in front of the table and motioned toward the blatantly obvious door. "This way, gentlemen."

Finnegan leaned to be seen around the aid and tipped his hat. "Always a pleasure to meet a general, sir."

Snowden only shook his head and went back to his letter composition. The three visitors were shown the way out, and

Captain Becker was nice enough to lead them to a convenient point in the picket line so that they might leave the camp. Once out of earshot of the soldiers, McLuckie shoved his hands into the pockets of his coat and began to mumble. "Damned sawed-off little bastard. What in the hell gives him the right to speak to citizens in that manner?"

"Roughly four thousand Springfield rifles give him the right to speak to you as he did, Burgess McLuckie. I might also point out that his advice was strikingly similar to the advice issued by myself before we climbed this hill. The two of you really ought to flee before Mr. Frick determines a proper method for hanging you." Finnegan could not help but marvel at the stubbornness of the two men he ambled with. "Truly, what purpose can there be in continuing this foolishness? Pride is a fine thing, gentlemen, and I applaud determination wherever I find it, but this has surely crossed over into the ridiculous. Why not do as that grim little man suggested and be gone?"

O'Donnell shook his head. "We cannot leave when the people of this town need us most."

Finnegan stopped walking and stared at the large steel man. "Need you most? Dear Hugh, so far your leadership has resulted in every grown man in this place being flung from his occupation. The mills you once labored in have become a battleground and you are now surrounded by your very own state militia. I am not certain this town can survive much more leadership from you and the good Burgess McLuckie."

The Burgess gave the gunman a very cold stare. "I cannot say as I much enjoy your company, Mr. Gilhooley." The politician sighed. "I assume you have traveled a great deal. Might you suggest an acceptable place to flee to?"

# Chapter 21

## *HOMESTEAD, PENNSYLVANIA*

### July 15th, 1892

FINNEGAN PASSED THE SALT ACROSS THE TABLE IN THE small café. The last few days had been particularly disappointing for Mr. O'Donnell and, eventually, even Finnegan had begun to feel a certain amount of pity for the man. In light of that, the Pinkerton had offered to buy the labor leader lunch.

O'Donnell's injured thumb had been supplemented with several insults in recent times. First, the esteemed tug, the *Little Bill,* had been contracted to deliver supplies to the occupying army. The sight of the same boat the strikers had formerly done battle with steaming up with impunity was a great blow to the morale of the union men. Second, roughly a third of the troops had moved down off the heights and garrisoned around Mr. Frick's fence. Once the soldiers had officially surrounded the works, other tugs brought what the union men had dreaded all along: strikebreakers. The imported workers disembarked from the tugs over the same ground where the Pinkertons had been undone days earlier. The morning of the fifteenth, smoke had begun to roll from the chimneys of the millworks. The defeated look on O'Donnell's face was more than even Finnegan could bear, so he had offered to buy the defeated hero a plate of steak and potatoes.

O'Donnell sliced off a piece of steak and held it up on his fork. "Very nearly a last meal, Finnegan."

"Oh, there does not appear to be need for the dramatic, Hugh. I know you can hardly be expected to take heart from recent events, but it is important to view matters in the proper perspective. You are an intelligent man; some part of you must have expected just such a conclusion."

"Still, it is difficult to witness." He chewed his piece of free steak. "There is word that notice will be posted tomorrow offering employment to any former laborer who did not take part in what the company is referring to as a disturbance." He tried a free potato. "I would assume most men will show the sense to count themselves in that group and move on with their lives." He sipped his coffee. "The good Burgess McLuckie and I can certainly not be counted amongst them, regardless of what line of morality we decide to follow."

Finnegan nodded. "As I well know, there is a fine line between fame and infamy. By the by, once possessed, both of those commodities are very difficult to pass off or bury."

"Yes, I suppose so." O'Donnell held up his injured hand. "For myself, it does not much matter one way or the other. A man cannot do much in a plate mill with only one thumb." He chuckled. "Now that I have so amply demonstrated by abilities in the area of organization, do you think Mr. Frick or Mr. Carnegie might consider offering me a position in management?"

"In my opinion, you would make a fine choice, Hugh.

The people in this town certainly appear apt to follow your lead."

"Yes, I suppose the success of the venture is not so important as the proper execution according to plan, when it comes to management positions. I would make for a fine fit. That is, if they do not fit me for a rope." He popped another potato into his mouth. "Although, if I were truly an intelligent fellow, I ought to have already purchased a train ticket and been off from this place so that I might find a new position sweeping a floor or some such."

"You are far too glum regarding your prospects, Hugh." Finnegan began dismembering his own steak. "This patch of smoky dirt is hardly paradise, and a man such as you, thumbless or not, will never want for work. It is unfortunate that so many men tend to hold such narrow visions. I have always suspected that is what leads to just the sort of..." he smiled, "*disturbance* we have recently witnessed. Mr. Frick could not see beyond a meager increase in profit, and you could not see the availability of train tickets. Now, you have both lost in some respect."

"Well, no man could accuse you of having too narrow a vision, Finnegan Gilhooley. Perhaps I ought to enter into your profession after this, as I still possess one good thumb to draw back a hammer with. I might make a crackerjack assassin."

Finnegan grinned and shook his head. "I am not an assassin, Hugh."

"How many men have you killed?"

"Oh, by now there would be no method for coming to a specific number."

"If that is the case, I would speculate that you are, in fact, an assassin, whether you prefer the term or not."

"I am so rarely given my preference; I see no reason why

this matter should be any different." Finnegan ate more steak. "Have you given any serious thought as to your next profession? As you say, you still possess one thumb. A number of options are open to you."

O'Donnell rubbed his chin. "I have often mused that mining might strike my fancy. Certainly not one of those awful coal mines, mind you, but there is still plenty of opportunity in the west for gold and silver, or so I am told." He gobbled a potato, somewhat brightening. "Do you have any knowledge of such things?"

"I know of at least one very determined young man who left the employ of the Pinkerton Agency to pursue a gold mine in the southern desert."

"How did he fare?"

"As far as I know he turned a commendable profit off the hole by selling it, lock stock and barrel, to some rather naïve New York speculators. After that, he returned to the Agency and has plugged on ever since."

O'Donnell contemplated the matter. "Perhaps, then, it would be less labor to simply go to the great city of New York and search about for suckers."

"Also, a commendable profession." Finnegan sipped his coffee. "A man such as you will have no trouble locating honest labor that suits your character. The only time a man like you is truly defeated is when he refuses to abandon the past and admit he has not won. It is important that you realize the very tangible difference between not winning and being defeated."

"I suppose you are correct, Finnegan." O'Donnell forked his last potato into his mouth. "I must say, when we met, I did not foresee you ever purchasing me a meal. I ought to figure some method to mummify this steak and hold it as a keepsake."

"Best to eat it now. Food provided gratis always tastes better."

The union man took the suggestion and began to dismember what remained. "Where do you go from here, Finnegan? Another strike? Another piece of dirty business seen to for your masters?"

"Oh, nothing so theatrical as all this. My masters have precious little use for men such as myself in these times. After the conflagration you brought about here, I might pause to wonder if the Pinkerton Agency will last much longer at all. When a donnybrook such as this occurs, surely someone must take notice." He sipped more coffee. "From here, I intend to sidle into a gentlemanly retirement. I have recently married, and I believe the dear lass deserves a more pastoral existence. Perhaps we shall purchase a farm, and I will try my hand at that ancient endeavor."

O'Donnell stared across the table for a long moment. "I believe I might prefer having my thumb shot off every day to farming."

Finnegan sneered. "What would a steel mill man know of farming?"

"Likely a great deal more than an assassin." O'Donnell shrugged. "But, then, I suppose every man must find his own way and disregard what wisdom he dislikes. That is precisely what has brought us to this table. If it brings you to a farm, you will be better off."

The two men finished their meal largely in silence. When they were finished, Finnegan paid the bill and the two stepped out into the dazzlingly bright June sunshine. Birds flitted through the nearby trees as the two aging men stretched out their backs from having sat for too long. O'Donnell turned to Finnegan and appeared to be about to speak when a voice sounded over his shoulder.

"Hugh O'Donnell, you are under arrest. Surrender yourself. Do not attempt to flee."

Finnegan leaned to one side to look around the steelworker. "Ah, hellfire and perdition, it is that damned sheriff of yours again, Hugh." Finnegan straightened up. "It would appear he only requires some four thousand or so deputies to find his courage."

O'Donnell slowly turned to face the sheriff and his two deputies. "McCleary, what the hell is the meaning of this, now?"

The Sheriff approached with his two rather grizzled deputies in tow. They appeared to have been recruited from a less-than-reputable saloon. "You, sir, are under arrest for the murder of Edward Connor."

O'Donnell straightened to tower over the Sheriff. "Who the hell is Edward Connor?"

The Sheriff stopped and allowed his deputies to move next to him. "Edward Connor was a Pinkerton agent. Presently, he is a corpse."

"I did not fire a round during the entire incident, you sniveling cur. How in blazes can you charge me, of all people, with murder?" O'Donnell looked from the Sheriff to Finnegan and back again.

The Sheriff valiantly dug in his pocket and produced a warrant. "You, sir, are charged, along with Burgess McLuckie, as the two of you are responsible for inciting others to riot and, as a result, murder. You cannot stand there in front of a sworn law officer and God almighty and claim you had nothing to do with the men who died here." The Sheriff turned to Finnegan as though he were seeking confirmation.

The gunman shook his head. "Oh, do not inquire of me for the answers to such heady matters. I am only experienced in the traditional sort of murder. I know nothing of the art by proxy." He scowled at the reluctant lawman. "Are we not all of an age where we have ceased to appreciate such blather. There is no need to attempt an explanation to Mr. O'Donnell. He has known full well for some time now that you or some other lap dog would appear with documents purchased from whatever curative salesman has reshaped himself into a judge in this county. When papers have been bought and paid for, it matters little what is written on them." Finnegan rubbed the bridge of his nose. "Do you intend to jail O'Donnell and McLuckie while they await their trial?"

"Ah, um, well, I suppose that may depend..." Sheriff McCleary rubbed his face.

Finnegan groaned. "Are you truly realizing just now that you likely do not have the funds in the county coffers to feed these two men during the several months that are required for the preparation of a murder trial?"

"Well...as an officer of the peace, I understand that money should be no object in the pursuit of justice, and yet..." The Sheriff leaned toward Finnegan. "Even the cost of these hired deputies strains things a bit."

Finnegan glanced over the two rather shabby specimens. "Such fellows cannot be pulled away from their other endeavors cheaply." The gunman licked his lips. "I would propose a compromise. Mr. O'Donnell and Mr. McLuckie will accompany you to Pittsburgh so that they may be formally indicted. After that, they will be released on their own recognizance pending their trial. Does that suit you?"

McCleary seemed pensive. "What assurances do I have they will appear for the trial?"

"I will give you my personal assurance," Finnegan smiled at the Sheriff. "Is the word of a Pinkerton Agent in regard to the murder suspects of another Pinkerton Agent not sufficient for bond?"

McCleary's eyes narrowed. "You will personally guarantee the appearance of O'Donnell and McLuckie?"

"Not as such. I have no damned intention of lingering in this place for as long as it takes for assorted attorneys to get their fill of sensationalism and extortion. What I will offer you is a convenient excuse to allow the defendants out on bond." Finnegan smiled. "If they should flee justice, I give you leave to blame the whole sad affair on me and get on with your next election campaign. A small matter such as a few absconded criminals will not tarnish my reputation a lick."

McCleary considered the matter and could find no fault with the notion. "Very well, then. I will take your word as bond." He looked to O'Donnell. "You will come peaceably?"

"I will." The union organizer extended his hand to Finnegan. "Thank you."

Finnegan shook the man's hand. "As I just finished explaining, it is less than nothing, Hugh. I wish you well."

# Chapter 22

## *PITTSBURGH, PENNSYLVANIA*

### July 23rd, 1892

After the arrest and prompt release of the "ringleaders" of the Battle of Homestead, little of note had occurred in the small hamlet worth reporting. Finnegan had traveled to the town on a daily or semi-daily basis, but the information he was able to pass on to Mr. Frick became progressively more boring as the days passed. Frick's imported workers had been spirited in without incident, and the majority of the town's citizens had found discretion to be the better part of valor as they applied for their former positions with the company. Tugs, such as the *Little Bill*, plied their trade up and down the river while smoke rolled from the stacks of the millworks. If an observer had not been present for the riot, one would never suspect such an ugly incident had ever occurred.

As the atmosphere calmed, Finnegan's purpose became more and more ambiguous to define. Finnegan had heard rumors that anarchists were once more planning to invade Homestead to attempt to foment another strike, but the notion was difficult to believe from the appearance of the place. Finally, a few days late of when Finnegan would have preferred, Henry Clay Frick announced that, for all intents and purposes, and, more importantly, as far as he was concerned, the labor dispute at the town of Homestead had come to a close, and Finnegan had officially fulfilled his commission. To show his appreciation, Frick had invited the dreaded Finnegan Gilhooley to dine with him for lunch at the quite swanky Duquesne Club. While it was not Finnegan's natural environment, he had long ago decided that a wise man never misses out on a free meal.

The gunman and the industrialist sat in a booth that looked out over the majority of the restaurant. All around them, the elite of Pittsburgh were picking at their lunch and stealing glances at the unfamiliar man Mr. Frick had invited into their midst.

Frick smiled over his duck. "I cannot say for certain, as I have not been a member of this club all that long, but you may be the first Irishman to dine here."

Finnegan tried his lamb. "Surely, Mr. Carnegie is a member here. If they will admit Scots, they will likely admit anyone."

"Perhaps so." Frick glanced about, enjoying the attention they were receiving. "Although, if you are not the first Irishman to dine here, you are certainly the only assassin. I believe those old crones in the corner there are attempting to discern whether they recognize you from the engravings in the *Police Gazette*, without, of course, admitting to reading such a rag."

"I am more than a bit shocked to hear you admit to such a vice."

"Oh, we all have our vices. I suppose there are worse habits than indulging in torrid literature. Have you ever taken the time to review what is written regarding men such as yourself?"

"I try to avoid any knowledge of it."

"Yes, well, I cannot say as I much enjoy reading about myself in respectable periodicals. I would imagine you feel the same regarding the tawdry ones." Frick pulled the wing from his duck. "What sense of the mood did you discern in Homestead?"

"It would appear you will be without labor difficulties for some time. The local shopkeepers have even begun to sell goods to the blacklegs you have been bringing in. They move about the town as any other citizen might."

"Do you believe that will change once the soldiers are sent away? Even I do not have enough sway with the governor to keep them there indefinitely."

Finnegan shook his head. "It was quite a stroke allowing those men who would not claim affiliation with the union to return to work. To single out any of the newly imported fellows would be an admission of former union involvement. I do not believe you will have difficulties." Finnegan chewed his lamb. "A proper descent into madness often buys a great deal of peace for some time."

"I am pleased to hear that." Frick sipped coffee. "I have enjoyed our acquaintance, Mr. Gilhooley. It is not every day that a man of my station is allowed to affiliate with a man in yours. I imagine we both must exercise great caution in our affiliations."

"Always a wise practice." Finnegan tried his vegetables. "Would you mind terribly if I made a personal inquiry? There is something I have always wished to ask a man such as you."

Frick shrugged. "Feel free."

"It is my understanding that you come from fairly modest beginnings."

"I do, somewhat. We were certainly not denizens of the gutter, but we were not wealthy." Frick took a moment to review the gunman. "You have an interest in my origins?"

"Only as it pertains to a question that has been nagging at me. I would like to know why it is that you continue as you do?"

Frick raised an eyebrow. "As I do?" He chuckled. "How is it precisely that I do?"

"I have read a fair amount about you, Mr. Frick."

"For research purposes?"

"Pure, unadulterated boredom. I have had much time on my hands recently." Finnegan cut a slice of lamb. "It would seem that you began in the position of a coke seller and then climbed to control the entire market here in Pennsylvania. So much so that Mr. Carnegie came to depend on you for the continued production of his steel. When Mr. Carnegie attempted to purchase your holdings, the two of you came to a compromise and joined the two concerns together. Now, between the two of you, you chaps have a hand in nearly every dollar exchanged in the state."

Frick nodded, as though such matters were quite common. "Your information is correct, Mr. Gilhooley. Although, I must observe that I still have not noticed a question being put forth."

"My question is simply this: why is it you arrived at the office this morning?"

"I arrive at the office at the same time every morning, with the exception of Sunday. Where else would I get off to?"

"Well, that is rather my point. If it so pleased you, I would assume you have more than ample resources to travel most anywhere in any style that you might prefer."

"I intend to visit Mr. Carnegie in Scotland when circumstances allow." Frick finished his potatoes. "I am not certain what you are alluding to. I have a great responsibility in the form of this company. I cannot simply run off when the urge comes on me."

"But do you truly have no interest in examining all the varied and splendorous portions of this world that do not pertain to business? Can you not shuffle matters off onto another, as Mr. Carnegie appears to have done to you? Is your sack not yet full enough to suit you, so that you might move on to other endeavors?"

Frick chuckled again. "And what might you consider to be an endeavor equal to the operation of the nation's largest steel concern?"

Finnegan did not have to give the question much consideration. "I have taken great enjoyment in hunting the large deer species known as elk." He sipped his coffee. "The hunting is done at high elevation and is quite the vigorous endeavor."

The industrialist sat, blinking, for a long moment. "Mr. Gilhooley, are you suggesting that I ought to abandon the leadership of one of the world's largest concerns to traipse about shooting some animals of which I have no knowledge?"

Finnegan shrugged. "I am merely suggesting that you have no notion of whether or not you might enjoy such an endeavor. You are still a relatively young man. Does nothing perk your interest beyond the collecting of money and petty victories such as this recent debacle?"

"You would label setting a precedent that will be made use of by every corporation a petty victory?"

Finnegan smiled. "As I have never heard you speak kindly of your fellow industrialists, I see no reason you would go to the trouble of picking fights to preserve their rights. Is there truly nothing that gives you passion?"

"I enjoy collecting art, but I have never found it overly satisfying." He thought on it for a long moment and leaned across the table. "I suppose there can be no harm in sharing a small bit of otherwise uninteresting information with you. After all, if you were to pass it along, I doubt even the *Gazette* would believe you."

"They have a stern policy against printing truth. Please, continue."

"In the city of New York, Mr. Carnegie has built a sprawling, gawdy, monstrosity of a home." Frick glanced from side to side to see if anyone might be within earshot. "I have recently made the purchase of two whole blocks just to the south of Mr. Carnegie's monstrosity. I intend to fill those two blocks, in their entirety, with a towering, dignified, awe-inspiring home that will make Mr. Carnegie's wreck look like an old miner's shack. How is that for passion?"

Now it was Finnegan's turn to sit and blink. "You wish to build a home larger than your partner?"

"Yes. Is that not the sort of endeavor you inquired about?"

"No, Mr. Frick. I will be completely honest with you, I would say you have once again strayed into pettiness."

Frick sneered and attacked his duck once more. "Perhaps so...but all men do in one way or another. It is the inevitable result of ambition." He pointed across the table with his fork. "Take you, for example, sir. You are a man who likely came to this country in the hull of some stinking vessel I shudder to even consider. What did your father do to earn his living?"

"Farmed a small plot and murdered tax collectors."

"Two damn fine occupations. Does the man still live?"

"He does not. He died in the war between your states."

"Ah, yes." Frick sipped his coffee, regaining his enthusiasm for the conversation. "Just as you may well have, but you did not. Not only did you survive a conflagration that was none of your affair, you became affiliated with one of this country's great visionaries. You fled British rule to come here and make yourself something of a king, in your own professional circle, at least. You are recently married and well compensated from your latest adventure. Now, obviously, is the time for you to, as they say, take your leisure. Become a gentleman of the library, write your memoirs. Naturally, you will wish to pursue those elk you mentioned. Nary a reason to ever engage in perilous activities again. The truly probing question is whether or not you will proceed in that manner."

"I likely will."

Frick slowly shook his head and tried the duck once more. "I would bet against it, sir. Men such as us live the way we live because, in some form, we gain enjoyment from the petty triumphs we achieve. You are correct in thinking the second million is not nearly as sweet as the first. Truth be told, they grow progressively less satisfying as they accumulate, but I continue to accumulate them. Did you glean any sense of satisfaction from gunning down that waiter in the street?"

Finnegan calmly sipped his coffee. "Mr. Frick, I believe you may be confused in regard to the base motives of my work. I shot the waiter so that he might cease stabbing me. Without his attacking me, I would go so far as to say I surely would have let him pass by and go about his business."

Frick chuckled. "I did not mean to insinuate that you travel about indiscriminately killing people, Mr. Gilhooley. It would be foolish of you. A talented man should never give away that which he can charge a fee for. What I was alluding to was whether or not you felt a fresh...sense of accomplishment. Somewhat paltry antagonist he might have been, but the waiter did very nearly succeed. You courted death once more, which is rather your stock in trade. Did the incident give you no sense of pride?"

"Perhaps a small amount." Finnegan thought on it. "A man often gains a sense of satisfaction from running the hazard and surviving, although you are quite correct regarding the diminishment."

Frick shrugged. "Perhaps we ought to switch professions for a time. You could relish that first million for what it is and...well, if I were ever attacked with deadly intent, even by someone as unassuming as a waiter, I imagine I would simply find myself palsied and quite incapable. I cannot conceive of how you live as you do, Mr. Gilhooley. Perhaps men such as us are not meant to understand each other's obsessions or delusions."

"Perhaps not." Finnegan took a sip of coffee and cleaned his lips with his napkin. "Speaking of murder, do you intend to hang O'Donnell and McLuckie?"

"O'Donnell? Have you not brought him up before?"

"He is the man the strikers elected to speak on their behest. McLuckie is the town Burgess. They linger in abeyance as we speak with some undoubtedly conniving judge attempting to decide if their deaths will curry your favor. Will it meet with your approval?"

"My approval? Mr. Gilhooley, do you by any chance recall the events that transpired in a small hamlet not far from here known as St. Clair? The sad affair of the Molly Maguires?"

The gunman nodded. "All too well."

"I have heard many a tale of it during my time in the coke fields. Those men did not cause nearly the trouble that damn puddler and politician caused my works, and yet your very own employer saw to it their necks were stretched. Why should I not have the same rights asserted?"

"I suppose you are entitled to such things. Although, I would point out that the murder of the Molly Maguires did not lower the cost of digging coal. Killing O'Donnell and McLuckie will not save you one thin dime on your steel."

Frick waved one hand about dismissively. The issue was hardly worth the discussion. "I do not intend to have anyone hanged. Much has changed since the Mollies swung. At any rate, nothing is more pusillanimous to me than a judge or a prosecutor who believes I am in his debt for some reason. As though it were not the mills that created every penny of his damned salary." Frick cleared his throat. "No, the puddler and the politician may do as they please. I would not even much care if they sat about attempting to foment another strike. At the very least, it gives a fellow something to cogitate on." Frick appeared somewhat sullen.

"How do matters stand with your child, Mr. Frick?"

"Ah, yes. He was rather poorly this morning, but all children go through stages of illness and wellness. It is to be expected. He has a fine physician. Likely the sprat will live to be a hundred."

"I have no doubt of it." Finnegan offered his most comforting smile. "So, then, it is back to the office for you, and I am off to make a show of farming and stalking elk before I inevitably fall back into old habits."

Frick balled up his napkin and set it next to his empty plate. "For two men the world at large would term successful, it would seem we are a sorry pair in some respects. It has been said that even the most comfortable prison is still a prison."

Now it was Finnegan's turn to chuckle. "I assure you,

however you term our current state, we find ourselves in circumstances far superior to any prison. Such fine lamb is not to be had in the tombs."

THE GUNMAN and the industrialist walked from the club to Frick's office, enjoying the fine summer day. They stopped at the front steps to the office building and Frick extended his hand to the Pinkerton. "It has been an interesting experience having you about. Good luck to you, Finnegan Xavier Gilhooley."

"And to you, Henry Clay Frick." Finnegan shook his hand and the two parted. Frick disappeared inside the building and Finnegan crossed the street to where he had noticed Rooney lingering so as to avoid notice. The gunman sidled up next to his old friend and passed the charlatan a cigar. "Well, I have officially been released from service."

Rooney took the cigar and leaned against the side wall of a stoop. "I suppose that rather marks the end of my service, as well."

Finnegan patted Rooney on one shoulder. "Will you be returning to the waiting arms of our old employer? I would imagine saving the life of a genuine Pinkerton heir must earn a man a substantial increase in pay."

"Now that you mention it, it likely would." Rooney shrugged and searched for a match. "In all earnestness, I was giving consideration to returning to blackmailing Frick until you brought that up."

"I believe we determined that blackmail was a dangerous business, dear Sam."

"The danger will be greatly reduced once you board a train to go find your wife. The lesser grade of assassin does not much worry a fellow after he has locked horns with a champion."

"You always were a fine one for compliments."

Rooney found a match and lit his free cigar before proffering the flame to Finnegan. "Of course, what with blackmail being, by and large, a profession of letter writing, I see no reason I should not be able to find the time to serve the Pinkerton brothers while bleeding Frick white. If a man is not willing to work, he should never complain of lacking funds."

"You are a fine example for every young man in the nation to follow, Sam." Finnegan puffed his cigar and slipped his thumbs over his gun belt. "Would you care for me to accompany you to Chicago? I would relish the sight of William Pinkerton welcoming you back to the fold and cringing as your salary was quoted."

"Are you not far too busy a fellow for such digressions? Does not the comely schoolmarm beckon?" Rooney grinned around his cigar.

"All wives beckon their husbands; such is the continuous state of matrimony. Any man who enters into marriage had best come to terms with it. In my current case, it is only that I am fully aware of my darling wife's ability to see to her own concerns, and while she sees to them there will likely be little to keep me amused." Finnegan tapped ash to the street. "Have you ever had cause to visit an Indian reservation, Sam?"

"I cannot say as I have. It is my understanding that they are generally located quite far from the bright lights of the large metropolises I prefer."

"They are, indeed, which ought to make them the sort of spot I favor, but it has never been the case in my experience. Reservations tend to be filled with half-starved waifs, chicken thieves, and any other assorted scum which has reason to choose a location simply because it lacks the trappings of civilization, such as justice. As we speak, Molly is attempting to negotiate a fragile peace between what remains of a band of Sioux and the Army in the northern Dakotas. I have been told there is a breed of rather large horned sheep that were formerly populous there, but other than shooting one of those beasts, I cannot say what a man would do with himself there."

"Yes, I can readily appreciate how boredom would quickly overtake a fellow in such an instance." Rooney shrugged. "You find yourself with time on your hands, and I am certainly not bound by any sort of due date with the Pinkerton heirs. Perhaps we ought to plot another train robbery? The last one proved so very lucrative."

Finnegan laughed. "Sam, you have obviously colored that particular memory to suit your vanity. We were no great shakes as train robbers. If you recall, the train was robbed by other men previous to our even making the attempt."

Rooney shook his head disdainfully. "Always the curmudgeon. Do you recall that we ended the day with the very payroll we initially sought?"

"Only by the slimiest of luck, Sam. That sort of biased assessment of events is what will someday prove to be your undoing."

"Yes, but until then it is far preferable to frowning my life away. You are too sullen for such a lucky man, Finnegan. I was only half jesting when I said..."

A series of soft popping sounds could faintly be heard emanating from the office building across the street. Finnegan squinted toward the building. "Sam, if I did not know better, I would say that was gunfire."

Rooney guffawed. "Who the hell would be shooting in there?"

Finnegan nodded. "Yes, it is rather absurd to..." The glass

shattered out of the window Finnegan knew belonged to Frick's inner office. "Bloody hell." He drew his Remington and ran across the street with Rooney on his heels. The two men ran past the doctor's office on the first landing and charged to the second floor.

The scene they found upon entering the office somewhat defied belief. As they passed the anteroom, they could see four men flopping around on the floor of the great industrialist's office. One man was clearly Frick, the next clearly Ridgeway, the oversized attendant. The other two men appeared to be a small fellow in a cheap suit and a carpenter, judging from the fellow's sawdust-covered clothes. Finnegan swept his pistol over the assemblage. Exempting Frick, he could not say who among them might require shooting. All the gunman could say for certain was that quick action was required; Frick was flinging blood all over the furniture from what appeared to be either gunshot or stab wounds. Not knowing what else to do, Finnegan reached down and grabbed the small man in the suit by the scruff of his coat collar and began bashing him with the butt of the Remington.

"For the love of Saint Michael, clout the other one!" Finnegan gave the suited fellow another good hit while Rooney produced a lead sap and began moving toward the carpenter.

Relieved of his fight with the suited fellow, the carpenter snatched a hammer from the floor and staggered to his feet to face Rooney. "Damn you, I am not the villain here!" He waved the hammer defensively in front of him.

Frick motioned toward the suited fellow while he held his other hand to his bleeding neck. "That one." He croaked before fully collapsing to the floor.

Finnegan brought the Remington down on the back of the small man's head and he ceased to fight. The gunman let the man drop to the floor and turned to the butler. "Ridgeway, what in hell's bells is about here?"

The attendant lurched up off his knees and went directly to Frick's aid. "Man claimed to be in from New York supplying workers. He come in here and started shooting."

Finnegan glanced down to see a bulldog revolver lying on the carpet. "Sweet mercy, Sam, fetch the doctor from the first floor."

Rooney replaced his sap in his pocket and left the carpenter to his own devices. "I'll see to it." He ran from the office and his boots could be heard clunking down the steps.

Finnegan heard the man beneath him groan and make an attempt at rising. Finnegan placed a boot on his back and held him down. "Make no attempt, you daft bastard." Finnegan stared down at the fellow's back. "I see no reason you should not be of some use before being sent to your rewards. You may hang, sir, after you inform me of your history a bit." Finnegan looked to the butler. "Ridgeway, give me your tie." The attendant used his left hand to undo his tie while pressing a cloth to Frick's neck with the right. "Many thanks." Finnegan knelt and bound the suited man's wrists. "That ought to keep you from further trouble." Finnegan turned to see Rooney dragging the doctor into the office.

Frick scowled and leveled one angry finger toward the attacker on the floor. He grunted out words as best he could. "Do not kill him, Finnegan; better to let him live and know he failed."

The doctor knelt and began investigating Frick's neck. "Shut your yap, Henry, and for God's sake stop moving your head. I do not know what you may dislodge." The physician turned to the gunman. "Get that jackass out of here; he can only serve to agitate."

"Quite right." Finnegan hoisted the man up to his feet.

"Come along now, chap." The attacker's head lolled about and his eyes were glassy. "Come now, walk properly. A man ought to have some pride in his gait after sealing his fate." The attacker stood to his full height and began chewing on something. "None of that, damn you." Finnegan cuffed the man on the jaw and a gnarled blasting cap went bouncing down onto the carpet. "Ah, now that is the mark of a true anarchist."

FINNEGAN SAT in a rather creaky wooden chair on the far side of the police station from where the suited attacker was manacled to a chair by one wrist and a desk by one ankle. The small man had been quiet for the most part, exuding a calmness that made Finnegan rather uncomfortable. He preferred his crazed murderers to be a bit more...well, crazed. When Finnegan had first arrived at the station, the building had appeared empty. The Pinkerton had led his stumbling suspect around the place in search of some sort of law. In the rearmost office, he had run across a single sergeant. The officer had his blue jacket rolled up for use as a pillow on the bench he napped on. Some stomping and kicking had roused the fellow, and soon enough the proud defender of Pittsburg had seen to what he obviously considered routine. He unceremoniously shoved the suspect into a chair, chained him, and produced a pencil and paper to glean the man's vital statistics. While that occurred, Finnegan retired to the far side of the station to observe and consider the day's strange events. He watched until the sergeant set down his pencil and crossed the room.

The rather stocky crusher of about fifty took a seat on the writing desk near Finnegan. "You are a Pinkerton, sir?"

Finnegan nodded. "I am."

"Were you charged with watching over Mr. Frick during the recent unpleasantness, then?"

Finnegan smiled. "Discharged from service this very day, all of about ten minutes before that fool made his attempt."

"Now there is a bit of poetry, eh? I always had a wonder as to whether or not men such as Mr. Frick kept a bodyguard." The sergeant folded his arms. "That one over there is rather something to ponder, as well."

Finnegan leaned back, reviewing the small would-be assassin. "Will he speak to you?"

"Aye, and quite the polite scamp, at that. Gives his name as Sasha Berkman, and was quite pointed about mentioning how he got it into his head to kill Mr. Frick all of his own accord. Mentioned that several times. He has also requested an attorney. He's brought that up twice now. Seems in an awful hurry to get to a trial."

"He is young." Finnegan rubbed his chin.

"That he is, sir."

"Did the lad mention what sort of profession he follows?"

"He did not, sir, but you are more than welcome to inquire. For what it is worth, I would not care to converse with the man that split my head open with a revolver butt. Who can say how another might look on the matter?"

Finnegan slowly raised himself from the chair and crossed the room. He stood, looming over Berkman. The gunman waited for the prisoner to look up at him. "You are Sasha Berkman?" The prisoner nodded. "Where do you come from?"

"I lived in New York for quite some time." The small man spoke softly, without a hint of malice.

"Yes, you very well may have, but you were not born there. Where did you get your accent, Sasha?"

"Latvia."

"Yes, I might have guessed as much. You are an anarchist?"

"I am proud to call myself an anarchist, yes."

Finnegan looked the young man over. "That is a fine suit, Sasha. How did you come by it?" The prisoner did not answer. "Yes, and to have such a fine revolver to conceal within along with a lovely dagger." Finnegan leaned over and began rifling through the coat pockets of the young Teuton. Berkman made a move to stop him, but Finnegan only gave the boy a firm glance. "Now is not the time to gain my ire, young fellow. You will enjoy your stay here in the jailhouse much more if your arm is not broken." Berkman set his arm on the rest of the chair. "Very good." Finnegan continued searching and came up with a small piece of paper from the inside pocket of Berkman's coat. The gunman held it up for the sergeant to see. "A broker's ticket."

The policeman approached. "So it is. One of Patrick Geary's, if I am not mistaken."

Finnegan turned to the sergeant. "You are charged with inspecting the pawnbrokers' goods?"

"No, I place my uniform overcoat in the man's keeping every summer." The policeman shrugged. "I have no need of it and the item is easily redeemed when the leaves change."

"I see."

"There was a time when a blue bottle could very well get a pretty penny for his revolver at Geary's place, which I preferred to hocking my coat, as I have need of the garment in chilled weather, but never have found cause to use the revolver." Finnegan only stared in answer to the policeman's declaration. "Sadly, that particular source of income has been taken from us since a fellow purchased one of the beat men's guns and used it to rob the First National. Now Captain McClintock flatly states we are not to pawn our weapons."

"That is a fascinating tale, sir." Finnegan pulled his watch from his pocket. "Where is this Geary's shop located?"

"He is down in the tenderloin, where a man is apt to require funds on short notice." The police sergeant winked.

Finnegan groaned and looked to Berkman. "Will this man be safe in your custody?"

The sergeant scratched his grizzled cheek. "I suppose he's as likely to be called home by the Lord here as any place."

The gunman rubbed the bridge of his nose. "Sergeant, what I inquire, is whether or not you will keep this man in custody or hand him over to the mob, should one materialize at your door?"

Both the sergeant and Berkman seemed a bit surprised by the question. The sergeant glanced to the station's large front doors. "What would a mob want with this ne'er-do-well?"

"This simpleminded homunculus has attempted to kill, or has killed, one of the wealthiest citizens of this state. What is more, his victim is currently engaged in a labor dispute with the nation's largest millworks. On the chance that Frick lives, nearly any man in the state may wish to kill Mr. Berkman to curry favor with Frick. On the chance that Frick dies, well, any given union man may be apt to hang Mr. Berkman from a lamppost to illustrate that their particular group does not condone Frick's murder. Are you quite understanding the position you currently occupy, Sergeant?"

The sergeant appeared a bit panicked. "What in heaven's name am I meant to do if a mob presents itself?" The sergeant stared at the large double doors. "I do not have so much as a revolver to defend myself."

Finnegan hung his head. "You saw fit to pawn the item at a shop other than Mr. Geary's?"

"No, it is home in the bureau drawer, but that makes it no more useful to me."

The sergeant jumped when one of the doors swung open and Rooney came trotting in. "He is one of my fellow Pinkertons; do not be afraid, Sergeant." The gunman was losing hope of being able to slough the amateur assassin off onto some other form of authority. "Sergeant, are all your confinement cells grouped together?"

"We have four in the cellar; they hold various ruffians from earlier in the day." He motioned to a small door on the end of the main floor. "We keep that for them that are especially truculent. The door is double thick and, as you can see, no man born of woman will be beating that latch off."

"Very good. Toss Mr. Berkman in there and then go to check on the other men below. Can they overhear what is said on this floor?"

The sergeant pondered for a moment. "I cannot say, sir. I have never been locked in one of them cells."

Finnegan sighed. "Please see to your work, Sergeant." While the policeman took care of Mr. Berkman, Finnegan moved to side of the room opposite the small holding cell with Rooney. The gunman leaned close to the charlatan. "Does Frick live?"

"I was not aware the two of you had become so close that you would become agitated over his well-being."

"My agitation stems from the proximity between him discharging me and his mauling. I cannot say if the Pinkerton heirs would honor their contract at such close quarters."

Rooney nodded, glad to see his friend had not become overly softened. "Well, take comfort in the knowledge the neighboring doctor assures everyone Mr. Frick will live many more years. As he stated the matter, Mr. Frick's injuries appear severe but are, in fact, quite minor. That damn pencil sharpener has more sand than I might have credited him with, though. I watched as the physician pried a bullet from his neck and the bugger barely made a sound. I cannot say as I might have conducted myself with as much dignity. He also inquired several times as to what had become of his assailant."

"That bugger is still in good form and the clouting does not appear to have affected his memory." Finnegan glanced to the doors. "Has word of this spread?"

Rooney nodded. "There was no method to contain the news. Although, I have learned over many a weary year that word being disseminated does not necessarily pose harm, assuming the word is of one's own making." Rooney grinned. "Between Frick's office and here I have spoken with no fewer than three journalists from esteemed periodicals. I informed all of them that I was present at the attack, where Mr. Frick received a minor blemish, and the attacker escaped quite skillfully despite our best efforts."

"You are a gem, Sam." Finnegan patted the man's shoulder. "Any man who cannot appreciate your gift for connivance is not worth keeping about."

Rooney smiled, "Well, for what it is worth. We two were not the only men present at the incident. Many a tale is likely flitting about as we speak."

"You saw nothing in the street on your way here to indicate a mob may be put together for Mr. Berkman?"

Rooney raised an eyebrow. "Berkman?"

"Yes, the fellow claims his name is Sasha Berkman."

"Hmm, I will have to adjust that when I sit down to write my memoirs. Berkman is a wholly unacceptable name for an assassin. It holds no tone of malice whatsoever."

The gunman rubbed his chin. "It truly does not have much of a ring to it, but what do you imagine would be a proper name for an assassin?"

"As Finnegan Gilhooley is already taken, I might suggest Cain Malafoe."

"By God, Sam, that is a fine one. Is it a real name or did you conjure it?"

"It is the name of a humble baker who labors not two blocks from here."

"It does seem rather wasted on a baker. Does it appear the man may have any other ambitions you are aware of?"

Rooney shrugged. "No, but that is the nature of the secreted assassin. Perhaps the man merely lies in wait. With such a wonderous moniker, one should certainly hope so."

"Indeed." Finnegan glanced about the police station, slowly returning to his initial train of thought. "Yes, well, the disappointing Mr. Berkman had a pawn ticket in his possession that was likely used to produce the necessary funds for outfitting a murder plot. I believe we ought to visit the shop in question at our earliest convenience."

Rooney nodded. "But you are hesitant to leave your hard-earned lawbreaker in the hands of that specimen I saw when entering?"

"Indeed I am. The good sergeant has apparently left his revolver at home amongst his spare socks."

Rooney looked past Finnegan to the cellar door the sergeant had disappeared into. "I cannot say as I blame the fellow overly much. In truth, I am hesitant to even carry this cudgel for fear it will be turned against me. I cannot say how the incident with the carpenter earlier may have gone if not for swift intervention."

Finnegan sighed. "We all have our role to play in this life, dear Sam. At any rate, I am certain that a few of the sergeant's fellow officers are certain to appear when the next shift comes on duty." Finnegan looked around again. "It may be too optimistic to assume one of them may soon drag in a reprobate. I have been here quite some time without witnessing such an act." He turned back to Rooney. "Would you care to investigate the disposition of the pawnshop owner while I remain here guarding the attempted murderer from fellow enthusiasts?"

Rooney waved one hand. "Certainly. It is not as though I have anything better to amuse myself with, presently."

Finnegan appeared a bit perplexed. "Well, Sam, it is only that you were surely relieved of duty at the same moment I was. By my watch, that is several hours past. I intend to follow up on matters only out of stubbornness. You need not continue. As far as I am concerned, you have fulfilled your commission. You have more than earned your pay."

Rooney rather ruefully shook his head. "It does truly pain me to make this admission, Finnegan, but it would appear I have a tendency to somewhat veer into misanthropic behavior without some project to keep me occupied. If you have need of assistance, I stand ready." The charlatan shrugged. "Between the two of us, I suppose it could be argued that I owe Mr. Frick somewhat more than you do. It was rather gentlemanly of the fellow to spill out so much blackmail money when he had an imperfect notion of what I was holding over him."

"It is fascinating to see what qualities you value in a man." Finnegan pulled a chair over to him. "As you find yourself amenable to continued assistance, would you mind terribly getting off to the shop of one Patrick Geary?" Finnegan handed Rooney the pawn ticket. "To inquire as to what the fellow may know regarding his customer in the solitary cell."

Rooney regarded the pawn ticket for a moment before placing it in his pocket. “Why not. A man often finds the most interesting items in the den of a pawnbroker.”

Finnegan surveyed the room and began dragging his chair across it toward the holding cell. “I shall remain here to make certain Mr. Berkman lives long enough to meet his end with a proper hangman.”

# Chapter 23

## *PITTSBURGH, PENNSYLVANIA*

### July 24th, 1892

FINNEGAN WAS STARTLED AWAKE IN HIS CHAIR BY Rooney shaking his shoulder. The gunman lurched and nearly fell to the floor before catching himself. His head swiveled about the dark police station. "What is the hour, Sam?"

"Well past midnight."

Finnegan surveyed the station once more. "Pity's sake, is there no crime in this town? What on earth could they require such a large police station for if they never take the time to arrest anyone?"

"It has been said that a large force of crushers, seen frequently in the streets, acts as a deterrent to lawlessness." Rooney shrugged.

"That may very well be the case. It certainly appears to be at work in this place." Finnegan stretched and slowly got to his feet. "I take it you have been to see about Frick?"

"Indeed. The hour was too late for much else after my visit to the pawnbroker."

"Frick lives?"

"He does. If Mr. Berkman swings, it will not be for murder, but only for a mundane attempt."

"One of many that doubtless comprises the poor fool's biography." Finnegan turned to look toward the back room of the station where loud snores crackled from the half-closed door. "Uh, damn the luck of falling into this place. Would you excuse me for a moment?" Finnegan limped to the rear of the station, stiff from sleeping in a chair. In the back room he found the sergeant, asleep on a cot that appeared considerably more comfortable than the position Finnegan had spent the night in. After reviewing the scene, Finnegan kicked one leg off the cot and sent the sergeant tumbling to the floor.

The aged policeman picked his head up off the wood and slowly looked around. "What is afoot here?" He rolled to inspect the cot. "What is this about?"

"Your pallet has betrayed you." Finnegan grabbed the man by one arm and tugged him up to his feet. "Are you quite awake?"

"I damn well am. I cannot imagine what occurred. That particular perch has always been so good to me." The Sergeant knelt to look over the cot once more, but Finnegan stopped him.

"Look here, this is surely not the time for that." He dragged the man out of the back room and into the main area of the station. "Is there a stove and coffeepot in this place?"

The sergeant rubbed his face. "Most certainly."

"Good. Get a pot brewing. It is time for you to take over the watch of our prisoner and you had best stay alert while you are about it."

The sergeant groaned. "Yes, sir. I see now." He made his way over to a flight of stairs and began climbing to the station's second story. "I will see to the coffee."

Finnegan returned to Rooney. The charlatan motioned to

the lone holding cell. "Has Mr. Berkman been cloistered in there all this time?"

"He has." Finnegan finished stretching his limbs.

"Might it not be wise to let the fellow out for a short while so that he might answer the call of nature?"

"If he wished for an easy existence, he should not have adopted such a stupid hobby. Besides, what do I care if he befouls a Pittsburgh police station? It is not as if we intend to live here. What did you learn from the pawnbroker?"

"More than we very well should have hoped for." Rooney pulled a chair out and took a seat. He had not been napping the evening away as the other men had. "Mr. Geary is that fine breed of Irish entrepreneur practical enough to always be on the lookout for the next source of profit. For a meager sum, which I intend to be reimbursed for by William Pinkerton when next I see him, the fellow was more than willing to inform me as to the history of the pawn ticket you discovered."

"Somehow, I knew you would have many interests in common with a pawnbroker. What did you learn?"

"The pawnbroker recalled the ticket and showed me the rather impressive harmonica and comb set a gentleman placed in keeping as collateral. The same gentleman took partial payment by way of a foreshortened revolver. Does that bring anything to mind?"

Finnegan nodded. "It does, indeed."

"I rather assumed it might. Now then, this fellow with the comb set has hocked and redeemed his items several times in the past when he has found himself lacking funds. The pawnbroker has gotten to know the fellow well and explained that the man is known to operate a laundry just slightly upriver of Homestead, of all places."

Finnegan rubbed his tired eyes. "That is an intriguing bit of information." He withdrew his pocket watch and checked the time. "By my reckoning, we should be able to be at the fellow's door by first light, or near to, assuming we can rouse a stable keeper and convince the fellow to conduct business at this late hour."

"A stable keeper? Finnegan, there are trains departing nearly every hour on the hour. We would be far better served making use of the rails."

The gunman shook his head. "I have grown damn weary of trains these last few weeks. It seems all I do is board trains and disembark."

Rooney stared quizzically. "And shoot waiters and watch union men cannonade your fellow detectives."

"I wish to go for a ride, as we did in our youth, Sam. Why not? It is not as though we have any great reason to rush."

Rooney shrugged. "You grow stranger as you age, my friend. Very well, we shall have some of that lazy sergeant's coffee and go find a livery keeper to awaken."

Finnegan tied his horse off to a scrub oak tree that was growing just off the muddy trail that led to the laundry. Beyond the collection of shacks and one small house was the river. The Monongahela languidly made its journey in the background as Finnegan watched steam roll from the shacks. The wind shifted, blowing the steam toward the two men.

Rooney turned his nose up. "Ugh, the pawnbroker did not mention the stench."

Finnegan inspected his rented saddle and shrugged. "A proper laundry must have soap. If you wish for soap, you must occasionally make soap. Though, I agree, I could do without the smell." He checked over his various revolvers. "Are you perfectly certain you do not wish to have one of my guns?"

Rooney rubbed his tired eyes. "Finnegan, perhaps you have not been getting a proper amount of rest. You appear oddly anxious regarding what will undoubtedly be discovered a bore. We will likely walk down this muddy strip, speak with the proprietor of this smelly spot, and learn he is in the habit of pawning combs before making poor investments."

Finnegan arched an eyebrow. "The fellow pawned an heirloom to purchase a pistol for an assassin. I would wager the last thing the man had in mind was boredom."

"Dear Finnegan, as you well know, I have infinite respect for your abilities. However, perhaps in this one instance, it might behoove us if I made the inquiry to the laundry man. As you may recall, I spoke to the pawnbroker without incident. I see no reason this visit to the laundry should end any differently."

Finnegan straightened and put his thumbs in his gun belt. "You can foresee no reason this visit should transpire differently?"

"Not every morning must feature gunplay and bloodshed, Finnegan. Your methods are all well and good when no other option presents itself. My methods, comparatively, are much better suited to gleaning information without conflagration."

Finnegan rubbed his face. "You believe your methods will elicit the information we desire, the identities of Berkman's confederates, without undue hardship for ourselves or bloodshed for the enemy?" Finnegan offered a challenging smile. "If that is the case, and you are willing to warranty performance, I would be more than pleased to allow you to converse with anyone we may encounter. I will merely observe, my old friend. Who can say? Perhaps you will endeavor to teach me a more civilized way of conduct."

"You will truly put your trust in my methods?"

"I will."

Rooney nodded. "You are growing wise in your dotage, Finnegan."

The gunman adjusted his revolvers. "So wise that I will also carry my armament. On the small chance your methods prove unequal to the task."

They both began strolling down the muddy path toward the laundry. "The trouble with you, dear Finnegan, is that you have spent far too much of your life in the wild places and amongst men of violent disposition. You can no longer understand that sensible men are governed by an overreaching ambition to go through life in ease and comfort. If an opportunity to choose comfort or peace is offered to most men, they will inevitably select it."

"I will not argue the matter with you, Sam. All I will do is to point out that Mr. Berkman appeared to be of a somewhat violent disposition, and I doubt his comrades differ from him greatly."

"It is a terrible thing to go through life so deprecating of your fellow man, Finnegan. I prefer to view them as an endless font of opportunity."

"As any good sneak thief would."

The two men approached the collection of lean-tos and shacks, glancing about for inhabitants. One of the buildings was better built than the others. The structure's long shape put Finnegan in mind of a calving shed. The door on the end of the long shed opened and a woman in a plain black dress made her way outside with what appeared to be a basket full of unclean laundry. After pulling the door shut behind her, she looked up at Finnegan and Rooney and gave a start.

She looked around, seeming to search for the rest of the troop that must surely accompany the two men, but found nothing. "Oh, I am sorry, sirs. Are you here from Homestead?" Both men slowly shook their heads. "We are expecting a large load from the new workers. You are not here to deliver a load from Homestead?"

Rooney flashed his most trustworthy smile. "Madam, we come with unfortunate news regarding the pawnbroker, Mr. Geary. The man has suffered an accident and the items he holds must be either settled for or sold. As per the gentlemen's notes, we are here about a set of combs and a fine harmonica belonging to a Mr. Fritz. We wish to inquire as to whether or not the gentleman would like to redeem his belongings."

The lady appeared grim for a moment, then brightened. "I believe Mr. Fritz would be most interested to meet with you. He always misses his harmonica when it is in use as collateral." She set the basket on the ground and motioned to the door behind her. "Please, come in."

Finnegan thought the invitation sounded slightly ominous, but it may have only been the woman's thick Russian accent or her rather homely appearance. She led the way inside the structure. Finnegan followed Rooney and had to duck to get through the doorway. As he stood up inside, he saw a long room with a table running down the middle. Lead half-spheres and coils of fuse were scattered across the top of the table. No less than six men were gathered in the tight space, diligently working on an assembly line of sorts. The men slowly turned to face the visitors.

Rooney cleared his throat. "Well now, it does my heart good to see such an industrious group of fellows as you all.

Those are a lovely collection of soup bowls you have manufactured. Very stout. I am certain they will fetch a fine price."

The men only stared while the woman, who had slunk behind the visitors, spoke. "Comrades, these men tell me they have come about a pawned set of combs. Have times become so difficult that you are now collecting for pawnbrokers, Mr. Gilhooley?"

Finnegan slowly turned to look at the woman. "You have me at a disadvantage, madam."

"Emma Goldman. I can see no harm in us being introduced, as you will likely never have the chance to report back to your masters."

Finnegan slowly nodded. "A pleasure to make your acquaintance, madam. I have, on occasion, read a few of your contributions to the *Alarm*. The English version, of course; I never have developed the ability to keen the slightest bit of German." Finnegan turned to Rooney. "Ms. Goldman pens the most fantastic letters to the editor suggesting propaganda by deed. They never fail to put me in mind of the rantings of good old Professor Mezzeroff."

Rooney managed a small smile. "Imagine that."

Goldman took a step closer to look through the gloom. "I do not know your name, sir, but you are so very familiar to me."

"I have been blessed with a face that resembles many famous men." Rooney motioned to the door, which had been rather briskly swung shut after they entered. "If it would be of assistance to you, I would be more than happy to step back outside so that you might examine me in the daylight."

"Indeed." Finnegan smiled at the assembled men who wore looks somewhere between amazed and horrified. "It would likely be best if both of us stepped outside and merely left you gentlemen to your work. You appear quite busy and certainly do not need the likes of us bothering you while you are otherwise engaged."

A small, aged man in his undershirt threw down the bomb casing he had been laboring at and turned toward the visitors. "You are Finnegan Gilhooley, the devil that hanged the Haymarket martyrs. You ought to burn in hell for the evil you have done." Spit flew from the man's toothless mouth.

Finnegan shrugged. "You anarchists so consistently curse me for making your martyrs without ever pausing to consider that if it were not for men such as myself you would have no martyrs at all. If that were the case, I have no notion of what you might rant on about all day long."

The men stood angrily blinking at the visitors. Rooney licked his lips and leaned toward Finnegan. "Perhaps this is not the most opportune time to jest with these gentlemen."

"I see no reason to avoid levity. It is true that it sometimes aggravates men, but there is little these fellows can do beside flinging invective." Finnegan smiled at the men. "They have pawned mother's hairbrush to obtain a cheap pistol. I doubt the remainder of their arsenal is all that impressive."

Rooney let out a small chuckle. "That is true. However, there are six of them."

"There will be fewer presently if they decide to act stupidly."

"You burn in hell, Pinkerton!" The angry old man snatched up an axe just as Emma Goldman took the liberty of leaping toward Finnegan. Rooney caught the 'Queen of the Anarchists' halfway in her leap, but their joined momentum brought them crashing into Finnegan, anyway. The gunman went sprawling as the old man with the axe attacked. From the corner of his eye, Finnegan saw a man near the rear of the building produce a rotten old muzzleloader and take aim. Finnegan tangled one boot in the old man's feet as he lunged, and the prospective axe murder tumbled into line with the man wielding the muzzleloader. The report of the weapon was a dull thud in the half-buried room. The old man coughed up a bit of blood and fell to the dirt floor. Finnegan rolled over and fired his Remington toward the man in the back. Smoke began to fill the confined space as he fired, but he could still see the man fall back toward the rear wall, dropping the rifle as he tumbled.

While Rooney did his best to subdue Goldman, one of the remaining men tore a shotgun from beneath the worktable. Finnegan snapped off the remaining shot in his Remington and hit the man in the shoulder. The force of the impact swung the man, and he fired off both barrels of the shotgun into his two remaining confederates. One of the men died instantly, while the other slowly lowered himself to the floor, holding one hand against his neck while blood spurted from between his fingers. "Fritz, why you do this?"

"I did not, I did not intend to." Fritz, the former owner of a very fine comb set, watched as his friend's eyes slowly shut.

Rooney had Goldman face down on the dirt floor by then, and glanced up to see only one man remained standing. "Good God, Almighty."

Finnegan slowly sat up on the floor. In front of him, Fritz continued to bleed from his shoulder, but the man did not appear to mind much. His attention was focused on his dead friends. Finnegan shook his head in disappointment. "Drop that damned blunderbuss and we will get you to a doctor. I know of one in Pittsburgh who is so low as to offer treatment to anarchists." Fritz languidly looked at the gunman, then opened the action on the shotgun and pulled two empty shells free of the breech. "Damn you, do not be doing that." Finnegan dropped his Remington and tore his Colt Lightning from its shoulder holster. "Do not be doing that!" Fritz reached under the table and came up with a shotgun shell. Finnegan shot the man twice in the chest. "Bloody damn fanatics." He stood and collected his Remington from the dirt where it lay. "A true pity. I had such high hopes for your methods, Sam."

Rooney pulled Goldman to her feet, flung open the door, and forced the woman out into the sunlight. Finnegan gladly followed. Outside, Goldman continued to stare at the doorway. "You capitalist swine. You killed them all, damn you."

Finnegan holstered his guns and began dusting himself off. "In point of fact, madam, I barely had the opportunity to raise my hand in anger toward them. For the most part, they killed each other." He finished cleaning his frock coat and glanced to the building. "A damned odd fight, to be certain."

Goldman attempted spitting at Finnegan. Rooney twisted her wrists in his grip. "None of that now, you debauched banshee." Rooney pushed her down to the ground, where she turned and stared up at him from the dirt.

"No, no, it cannot be..." She stared at Rooney's face. A face all too familiar to those who had attended rallies preaching revolution. "It cannot be you." She turned to Finnegan. "Kill me, then, you bastard."

Finnegan chuckled and began reloading his Remington out of habit. "Kill you, dear lass? Even if the killing of unarmed women were a regular practice, I should not even think of it in your case." He finished with the Remington and replaced it in the holster before beginning the same operation with the Colt. "Far better for you to leave this place knowing it is by the mercy of the man you call devil." He nodded toward Rooney. "That knowledge, coupled with the discovery that your idols are made of clay, or drunken Irishmen, as the case may be, should give you much to consider for the remainder of your life." He replaced the Colt. "Go now.

Flee back to wherever it is you came from. Be certain to spell my name correctly in your next damn article."

Goldman slowly lurched to her feet. She stared daggers at Rooney. "You are not Mezzeroff."

Rooney offered a small bow. "In that matter you could not be more correct, madam. I am not Professor Mezzeroff. Though, technically, neither is anyone else."

# Chapter 24

## *CLAYTON, PENNSYLVANIA*

### August 1st, 1892

Ridgeway showed Finnegan from the front doors, down a long hallway and up to a gilded bedroom door. The attendant cleared his throat and smoothed his frock coat. "You are to be on your way home, sir?"

The question had a friendly tone to it the gunman had not expected. "Ah, well, now that you broach the topic, I suppose I would say that I travel from here to my wife in the Dakotas." He smiled, considering the odd nature of his existence. "My wife and I have always been given to roaming. As such, I rather consider the location of my wife to be home. At least until we find the time to set up proper housekeeping."

The towering attendant grinned. "It is good to be married."

Finnegan nodded. "It is, indeed."

Ridgeway swung the bedroom door open. "Mr. Frick is expecting you. Please inform him that I will be bringing his midday soup in an hour."

"I will be sure to inform him." Finnegan walked into the room and found Frick sitting up in bed on a pile of pillows.

The industrialist was fairly swaddled in bandages. Finnegan took a seat at the chair obviously set by the bed for visitors. "Mr. Ridgeway will be along with your soup in one hour. I gleaned that the time of arrival was beyond negotiation."

Frick cracked a smile. "He is unique, is he not?"

"Very much so." Finnegan sat back in his chair. "The esteemed Dr. Hastings tells me you will surely live. Do you feel any different, having braved the hazard and survived?"

"I am in a great deal of pain. Is that the usual result?"

"Yes, without exception, in my experience."

The industrialist drew a deep breath. "They tell me I shall survive. They also inform me that my son will not." Frick gazed out with wet eyes. "You have seen much death, Finnegan?"

"A great deal, yes."

"Do you ever understand it? I am told Berkman, the man who rendered me as I am, still lives? You allowed him to live. I am told you shot several of his confederates outside of Homestead. How was the choice made? Was the matter in your hands, or was it simply fated? Why is it that I should live and my boy, a damn fine boy, should die?"

Finnegan let the questions hang for a long moment. "Berkman lives because killing him was not a necessity. The men at the laundry died because they chose it." He shook his head. "I know nothing of fate or why good boys need die." He shrugged. "I can tell you that doctors are often mistaken. Your boy may yet live to old age."

"Yes, well, I suppose it is important to continue with that attitude until matters are settled." He wiped his eyes.

"I should inform you that my associate and I have made a thorough investigation of Mr. Berkman's activities in the days leading up to the attack. I believe the men outside of Homestead were Mr. Berkman's sole form of support. He does not appear to have been affiliated with a larger group. At any rate, it would appear as though you need not worry over further reprisals. At least, not from that quarter."

Frick nodded as best he could with his bundled neck. "Has anyone ever attempted your murder...for the things you have done?"

Finnegan adjusted his gun belt from habit. "On several occasions in the past, and undoubtedly on occasions to come."

"Have you ever felt as though the rebuke was deserved?"

The gunman stood and straightened his coat. "In almost every instance, yes." He adjusted his guns once more. "Good-bye, Mr. Frick. I must say, you are somewhat unique yourself."

# A Look at: Neither Victory Nor Defeat (Finnegan Gilhooley 6)

He's finally found peace. But some men aren't built to stay home.

Finnegan Gilhooley thought he'd earned his quiet life. After years of hard roads and harder choices, he and Molly have settled into the rhythms of a Montana ranch — cattle, clean air, and no one asking anything of them. It's everything they fought for.

Then the Navy comes calling.

A spy ring is working to sabotage the country's march toward war with Spain, and the men in uniform think a couple of seasoned ranch hands might be exactly the unconventional help they need. Finnegan knows better than to say yes. He says yes anyway.

Now he and Molly are tangled in a world of foreign agents, government secrets, and enemies who don't fight fair—and all either of them can think about is why they ever left Montana.

***AVAILABLE MAY 2026***

# Thank You

Thank you for taking the time to read *Trample Over the Dead*. If you enjoyed it, please consider telling your friends or posting a short review. Word of mouth is an author's best friend and much appreciated.

Thank you.
*R.F. Ryan*

# About the Author

R.F. Ryan lives in Montana with his beautiful wife and comparatively ugly gun collection. When he is not writing, he can usually be found out in the woods hunting. He's currently retired from a variety of odd jobs that have interfered with his free time, including (but not limited to): ranch hand, green chain operator, bounty hunter, private investigator, and process server. Robert has written over twenty books in multiple genres, both fiction and non-fiction, and has penned hundreds of outdoors-focused articles for websites and print magazines.

www.ingramcontent.com/pod-product-compliance
Lightning Source LLC
LaVergne TN
LVHW040214110826
845146LV00005B/1290

* 9 7 9 8 8 9 5 6 7 5 8 8 5 *